THE MANY SELVES OF KATHERINE NORTH

EMMA GEEN

BLOOMSBURY

LONDON · OXFORD · NEW YORK · NEW DELHI · SYDNEY

Bloomsbury Paperbacks
An imprint of Bloomsbury Publishing Plc

50 Bedford Square   1385 Broadway
London   New York
WC1B 3DP   NY 10018
UK   USA

www.bloomsbury.com

BLOOMSBURY and the Diana logo are trademarks of Bloomsbury Publishing Plc

First published in Great Britain 2016
This paperback edition first published in 2017

British Library Cataloguing-in-Publication Data
A catalogue record for this book is available from the British Library.

ISBN: HB: 978-1-4088-5843-1
        TPB: 978-1-4088-5844-8
        PB: 978-1-4088-5845-5
        ePub: 978-1-4088-5846-2

2 4 6 8 10 9 7 5 3 1

Typeset by Integra Software Services Pvt. Ltd.

To find out more about our authors and books visit
www.bloomsbury.com. Here you will find extracts, author interviews, details
of forthcoming events and the option to sign up for our newsletters.

For Mum

My love, always.

Come Home

It's still watching; eyes like bullet holes, leaking inner light.

That look feels so familiar. We're far from our old territory, I can't let myself think of it as her, but why else would a fox have come to my rescue?

'Tomoko?' I ask.

The stare doesn't flicker, but what did I expect?

I huddle over myself to try and stop the shivering. My hands are turning leaden, my cheeks burning with cold. Why does the night seem more miserable when I'm human? It's not just the lack of fur, but something psychological, I'm sure of it.

Giving up, I wriggle deeper into the pile of black bags until my back comes up against the wall. Entrenching myself like this is possibly stupid. If they find me I'll have to run, and fast. But surely they won't look for me here, in some abandoned alleyway, wherever this is. I'm still hazy about how I've ended up here myself.

My thoughts are a flurry of pages, I'm left clutching fragments – Tomoko tiptoeing atop a fence; the yellow-toothed leer of

Grandma Wolf; Mr Hughes, his face a furnace; and Buckley ... Buckley, silent.

The disorientation has lodged in my stomach, almost a physical force. Like on teacup rides as a child, when I'd throw the full weight of my body against the wheel until speed turned the world soluble and its streak found new axis around Mum's face; her blue eyes, across from mine, squeezed almost shut in sickened laughter.

And still the fox stares.

An unbroken look would have been a challenge from Tomoko but this feels more desperate than threatening. Could it be frightened of them too? It saved me after all. Though just the thought seems insane, let alone any answer to 'why'.

A lump pushes inside my throat as if with the force of questions. Questions, regrets, pleas. Where did this need to speak come from? I've always had an uneasy relationship with such human quirks.

'Did you come back for me?'

The eyes disappear, reappear – a blink. I lick my raw lips.

'Blink twice if you understand.'

... Nothing.

'I didn't want to leave you. You do remember?'

No. Of course not. But I do. That night is seared into me, as indelibly as if I'd tried staring down the sun.

Uncanny Shift

I wake to eyes.

Evening light falls between the floorboards, painting strips of a yellow hide and alert ears. Tomoko. Her musk mixes with earth and cardboard, grease and old blood – the smells of home.

I nuzzle my snout into my paws but, seeing me stir, Tomoko's tail beats a greeting from the ground. I take one of her ears between my teeth and nibble until her panting slows. Her blood sugar smells low but the light is still strong; if we leave now we'll get the best pickings.

I stand and stretch, tail pulling the line of my spine. Tomoko catches the hint and snatches up her doll, shaking it with a kill-ing blow. She found it in a garden when she was still mostly cub; now its hemp hair is all chewed off, the face a haze of stuffing.

As she plays, I consider our options. It's a Friday evening and good weather balloons inside my ears, perfect for scavenging at the park – burger remains, dropped chips, onion rings secreted in screwed balls of paper. But going to the park means visiting the humans later and the risk of losing an easy meal.

Thud.

Sawdust drifts down from the floorboards; from where Tomoko tossed her doll against the ceiling. At my look, she snatches it back up to chuck over my head. Tomoko would prefer the park – burgers are a favourite of hers – but the gardens are more reliable.

Mind made up, I make towards the exit. Tomoko reaches it ahead of me, squeezing between the bricks in a scrabble of hind legs; she's growing fast. I hunker flat and worm through after her.

Outside is a swamp of senses; raw nostrils and static, eyes wincing at the light. Then sound separates: the squeal of tyres, chattering children, birds screaming territory. Smells sing of mellow grass, crisp air, the syrupy rot of wood.

'Evening. All good?'

Buckley. The slow sound of his breath has been inside my head since I woke. I scratch the swelling of a flea bite on my stomach.

'Eh?' he adds at my silence.

'Yeah, fine.' But greetings are hardly needed, it's his absences that need announcing, the nights I wake to static on the intercom and the trapped loops of my own thoughts. 'You?'

'Good.' He sips something, the sound pinching in distaste. 'Though the coffee machine is broken again. This is like drinking burnt toast.'

I've used the machine in question a hundred times but right now I can't even visualise it. Though only a mile from here, our Centre could be another universe.

Crickets trill over the creak of cooling soil, evening peace only disturbed by the meaty sounds of Tomoko chewing on a worm. The lingering of musk tells me that the tom next door trespassed in the day, so I pad across to the crab apple tree and rub my bum against the trunk to renew the scent.

Above, the brown sun sinks in a yellow sky. Tomoko snaps up the last of the worm and follows my look with her ears; she can comprehend this world better than I can – she was born to it, after all.

As I watch, she freezes, ears strained forward in pinpoint, then launches into the thicket. I plunge after. The gossip of grass, *ping* of skyward grasshopper, then the fence rears and I leap.

Here, concrete; burnt rubber; spilt lemonade, sticky sweet. I lick the residue and patter to the edge of the road. Pause. Sniff. Look left, look right. The tarmac is choked with fumes but a look shows it to be clear. Tomoko tilts her head as I double-check. She knows the ritual but does she understand? I won't be able to look after her forever.

In the garden opposite we creep into the tall grass to observe the patio. Voices pip through the wall, melody without words, but outside looks clear. I leave Tomoko hidden and cross the paving slabs to where burnt sky pools in glass.

A creature slinks out at my approach. It's a lean beast, slender snout and pricked ears. The whiskers twitch as I consider it; strange, even now, to think it's really me.

Glass squeals beneath my paw as I swipe down, once, twice, three times; whip into the safety of undergrowth.

Muffled voices. A chair scraped back over tiles.

'*Mummy! Mummy!*'

They were waiting.

The door rumbles open on to tart tomato, grinding steps. *Clink*, china on concrete; the creak of straightening knees.

'Mummy—'

'Ssh, you'll frighten the foxes.'

5

Door *snap*. An inward breath. I bite Tomoko's scruff to hold her.

One. Mustn't trust humans too much.

Two. I know what they can be like.

Three. I was one once—

She breaks away with a bound and the garden fills with the sloppy sounds of her eating. Pasta. We couldn't have carried this away to cache anyway.

I stand guard as she finishes, peering up at those high moon faces. The smallest condenses as it reaches out; misty haloes spread from the hands flattened to the glass.

The clattering of the dish tells me that Tomoko has finished. I whip onto the fence and into the next garden.

MINE MINE MINE

Cat. Piss graffiti up every surface, a fist to my nose.

I twist my ears – there, the slurp of tongue on fur at the far end of the garden. My hackles rise but I resist the impulse to look; it will be attending to us as intently as we are to it.

Our ears turn to keep it in focus as we cross the garden; the licking doesn't stop but I nose Tomoko under the fence first, just in case.

On the other side, the stench of urine is blanketed by a greasy fog – our meal has already been tossed on the lawn. We're lucky the cat didn't get to it first.

In the blinding smell, Tomoko pounces before I've even located the meat. Chicken bones; these would be perfect for caching but as Tomoko's already started I allow myself one too – fatty gristle, melting on tongue, stomach loosening in relief. When human, I forget how quickly hunger becomes the norm.

'I'll fill you in as you eat,' Buckley says. 'Lauren's messaged a couple of tasks she'd like wrapped up by the end of the night.'

'Listening,' I say, nearly choking on the chicken.

'All right?'

I grunt and continue gnawing. Even though sub-vocalising doesn't use the mouth, it's easy to get confused when eating.

'OK. Well, most important job for tonight is finding a missing male. His tracker malfunctioned so we need you to sniff out which earth he's denning at. Crystal is standing by with a new chip.'

At the mention of Crystal, I find myself thinking of the rubber and squeak of her Converse, their black fabric stitched with gold dragons that fly past my head with every step. I've met her as a human, but when I try to summon a face, all I come up with is the smirk of dragons.

'One of our males?' I say.

'Territory along.'

His pained tone confirms he knows what he asks. Yes, I'll be able to find the male more easily than the other researchers but humans aren't attacked for entering another territory.

'Sorry. But Lauren says it's a priority. We'll find a way of distracting Tomoko while you're working.'

I snort around my mouthful.

'OK, there's that. The second task we need to look at is' – comms stutters as he flicks a pen against his chin, a habit that long ago moved past irritating into comforting – 'the cub data. Ideally they'll want to start data analysis of the diet by the end of the week, so it'd be great if we could wrap that up tonight.'

I mumble something that could be taken as agreement and spit out a splinter of bone. In practice he's just described a night of skulking through enemy territory and sniffing faeces, but it's all straightforward procedure. As long as I'm careful and Tomoko is safe, everything will be fine.

With my bone finished, I wait for Tomoko to be done with hers. The garden is already thickening with shadows and the composted tang of exhaling vegetation. The slurp of the cat's grooming has stopped, replaced by the grate of claws on wood. I lift my snout to the flight of a passing moth, listen to its muslin wing-beats blend into sky.

'It's hard to imagine sometimes.'

'Hmm?' Buckley says.

'This job. When I'm out here, it can feel like it's not, well, real.'

'Sounds like you're going native.'

I flinch, despite his teasing tone.

'The other night, curled in the den, listening to the rain, I thought ...'

'You thought?'

'I thought, that maybe this is all there is.'

Silence, my hackles rise. Then his voice returns, touched with warmth.

'That's not true. I can promise you that.'

I pull my lips into a grin. 'But maybe I'm imagining you too. Everything I think I know – sub-vocalising, transducers to the auditory cortex – it could be pure fantasy. You could be a crazy voice in my head.'

'I prefer the term neuroengineer.'

Tomoko's ears flick at my barked laugh but she doesn't pause in her crunching; she's used to my oddities by now. I crouch next to her and feel the warmth of her sharp ribs. It seems impossible that only four months ago she was a stranger, a tiny bundle of fur nestled to her mother's stomach. My nostrils twitch with the memory of the den's oily stench, the hot ghost of pigeon on my tongue as I stared at the squirm of cubs. But no vixen likes adults in her birthing den; she flashed teeth and I dropped my offering and ran.

A bone lands in the flower bed, and I look up to see Tomoko gape a toothsome yawn. Time to move on. I lead the way to the

8

allotment carrying the leftovers. Tomoko scampers in widening circles, tossing a bulb she's found, but as I dig the cache she pauses to watch. Bones deposited, I paddle the earth into a loose mound and dribble pee on the spot. Despite the smell of food, this should trick the rest of the family into thinking that the cache has already been emptied. Buckley's too kind to comment on the poor scientific practice, he knows how I feel. Whatever the ethics, Tomoko's still small for her age; I can't let her starve.

Turning to go, I stop. My hide tingles with the bristling of hair – we're being watched.

I sniff and listen. Nothing out there I can sense and yet I'm sure of the feeling; it's been coming over me increasingly often of late. Another fox perhaps? I flare my nostrils again, but having a good nose doesn't automatically mean I can understand scents. If it is a fox, it's not one of our family.

Perhaps I'm just imagining things, or perhaps I'm not the only one bent on interloping tonight; although the smell isn't recognisable from neighbouring scent markers either. It could be homeless; in which case it would be cruel to grudge it our cache. Life without a territory is harsh, not to mention short.

Tomoko squeals as she miscalculates a catch and the bulb hits her on the nose – she's obviously not noticed anything amiss. I snatch it up so that she follows, nipping my flank, as I make our retreat.

Back on the pavement we trot past towering dustbins, breathing in their maggoty ambrosia, though the stench is too dim for any of the lids to be open. Tomoko finds a plastic bag and guts in to the stench of vinegar. The wrapper brings salted fireworks to my tongue. I work the paper to stodge then snap for more but Tomoko dances out of the way. At my second lunge, she leaps to meet me. A scrabble, then we're leaping round the flash of each other's tails, miming bites and batting with paws. A wop on the nose leaves me reeling and she bounds over the fence. By the time I shake my head clear she's at the other side of the garden, tossing the paper teasingly.

'Buckley?'

There's a pause – back at the Centre he will be eyeing the time – he could say no, but instead he laughs.

'Go on then.'

I jump down, grass liquid beneath my paws. It's thrilling to just run, to run and run and run.

I was a girl once. Went to school. Did homework on the Tudors and differential equations. Wore stifling grey tights. Grew into a teenager. Left school for a job.

Tomoko blunders through a flowerbed, perfume weighed with manure, the pip of a fleeing mouse.

I was a mouse once. Nibbled the juicy bubbles of berries. Let it go. Let it go.

Next garden, the hard reek of dog. Tomoko dodges within range of its leash, weaving from the snapping jaws, but I can do better.

'No!' Buckley says but I'm already thrusting out hind legs—

I was a bird once. Flew over cities, saw the secret patterns of land.

Teeth snap but I'm over the fence and away. Its thinning barks chase us between the houses.

'One of these days you're going to get mauled.'

Buckley's rebuke would be more sincere if he wasn't laughing. Tomoko whines and sprints down the embankment, across the tarmac, gold beneath the street lights. I race after; grass, pavement, road—

My tail prickles. I turn.

There. Back in the hedge – a shadow, the glint of fur, two staring eyes.

A roar, light erupts, wheels squeal

I leap

———

Wrong

I am wrong.

Pain. A world of hard angles, so bright it burns. My ears are clogged with quiet, I claw at them, feel soft flesh. And my paws – furless, beige, spotted with blood. I've been hit. Fuck!

I wrestle against my snares but hands seize me; the loom of a pale face – human. Oh fuck!

'Kit . . . Kit!'

Buckley's voice breaks through my panic and I stop struggling. Just our cubicle. Just Come Home.

'You're OK. You're OK.' I can feel the jog of his heart through his chest. 'It was just the fox Ressy. You're OK.'

'I was—' My voice breaks, this throat hasn't been used in a week.

'It was a car,' he explains. 'The Ressy died almost instantly.'

The car. The crunch of my body hitting the bonnet; a sound that isn't meant to be heard – not that loud, not that close. And agony – so intense it negated itself, screaming into silence . . . into here.

It all happened so fast that I wonder. Wonder whether these memories can be real. Like standing beside a window as it bursts, fragments dispersed with such speed that it feels that the irruption must not have been of it . . . but me.

'Look at me, Kit. Look at me.' Buckley's hand is on my cheek, the conviction in his eyes willing me back into the moment, here, with him, and my mind is so claggy, this body so removed, that it takes me a long moment before I shirk the touch, look away, down at the hands in my lap. My hands. Human hands.

I try to stand but Buckley gently pushes me back.

'Tomoko,' I say. 'Tomoko!'

'Is fine. She was safely across the road.'

'She's alone,' I say.

His face is pained but he isn't cruel enough to voice what I already know. There's nothing I can do for her. Not like this.

'She'll be fine,' he says. 'Come on, let's get you cleaned up.'

He busies himself with removing my CP cap. My scalp tingles as the probes retreat, followed by the kiss of air. I watch, unmoving, as he untangles me from the snarl of tubes and wires. The JumpPyjamas are spotted with blood – the skin of my left elbow is torn where the fluid drip came out in my panic.

Buckley cringes as he notices, his look darting to the door. The window of our cubicle is a hard square of black.

'The night nurse will be along soon,' he says. 'Let's get you up.'

With his help, I stumble off the JumpPallet and into his chair. The screens above flash red. 'Trauma threshold.' 'Signal failure.' 'Death.' The visual feed, a snowstorm of static.

'Buckley . . .'

At his gesture, the screens black out.

'You're fine.' The weight of his look wills me to believe. 'Listen to me. You're going to be fine.'

I nod.

'Here. Put pressure on this while I get the First Aid.' He presses my hand against the tissue and ducks beneath his desk. I watch him rummage, trying to blink the fireflies from my eyes. In my ears, the sound of distant sea.

'The other fox?' I say.

'Tomoko is fine. I promise.'

'No. The other fox.'

'What other fox?'

'The one following us.'

His frown deepens.

'I saw—' I begin. But what *did* I see?

He squeezes my foot and ducks back to his search.

I saw . . . a watchful shadow. The flicker of flame. A fox, and yet it almost reminded me of – of what? The thought has already slipped from me.

Buckley emerges with the First Aid, pulls out plaster-tape. When I rub this face I find the touch numbed. He says something, but I can't find any words in it.

I let the hand on the tissue slip, watch blood trickle free. Red snake over pale skin, coiling in the creases of a palm.

Come Home

Should I have known, even then?

The question is chasing its own tail as I wake, with a force that suggests it's been circulating even in my dreams.

Remembering, I startle and look across at the dustbin. In the sluggish pre-dawn light, a darker patch is visible amongst the shadows – the fox hasn't left, it's just sleeping. The extent of my relief is almost embarrassing. I still can't quite believe that it's here. Could it really be Tomoko? I know it's crazy to think that way, but suppressing the hope is beyond me.

Only now do I realise I'm shivering. The cold is a deep ache inside my muscles, my tongue cardboard inside a dry mouth; all familiar sensations but not in my Original Body. I roll my stiff shoulders, arms stinging as the black bags, tacky with cold, unstick from my skin.

There's no sign of anyone through the alley opening, at least by sight; the reek of rubbish has overpowered all sense of smell, not that I would have been able to tell much with this nose anyway.

Still, the management at our Centre are as human as you can get. I'm willing to bet that they'll have called off the search until morning. Best to move whilst I still have darkness on my side.

I stand to find feeling has left my feet entirely. As I stumble, a small sound comes from beneath the bin.

'Tomoko?'

I crouch to see the glint of amber eyes. I had been going to ask if it was coming, but that seems stupid now.

Sensation returns to my feet in stabs, their slap against concrete unnervingly loud in the thin dawn air. It takes me a while to catch the patter of paws beneath but the fox is definitely following.

The street I break out on to is one I don't recognise; so I take a right, for no real reason, just to keep moving, that's the most important thing right now. Go fast, keep low, stay close to cover. Buckley always used to tease that I was born half-feral. *Feral* – it's just common sense.

Even in my Original Body, even after everything, it's hard not to feel Buckley's with me, watching; hard not to mistake the wind in the wires for his agitated breath. His presence has always been so . . . ubiquitous.

A chill runs up the loose legs of my JumpPyjamas; designed to be composted after every jump, they aren't made for heavy wear. I should have changed before my escape but it was hardly a priority at the time. Before I even begin to think about what I'm going to do to avoid capture, I need to find clothes. This was never an issue I had to deal with inRessy. And buying is out of the question, they'd be able to trace the purchase; besides, my Specs are back at the Centre. So what? Steal?

The yellow blink of a traffic light strobes the street; something about the pulse making me feel as if it's my consciousness that's fading in and out. In the absence of sun, the nearby solar orbs have turned to it, hanging above the street like giant eyeballs, the photo-voltaic panels, constricted pupils.

Despite the dark, birds are already starting to stir, small lungs emptied into the sharp air. Infield, birds are my guardian angels; their calls regularly alert me to predators even before my nose. Right now though, their calls are song, not alarm; yearning stirs within each glass note. After last night, I'd almost forgotten it's technically summer.

The houses around me are starting to give way to shops; the dirty husk of a garage replaced by the blinking lights of a super-market; now a charity shop; now the empty baskets of a bakery, cleared out for the night. A sign tells me this is Redland – I can't have run as far as I thought last night.

On an impulse, I stop and back pace; catch sight of a tail tip disappearing behind a dustbin as I turn – the fox is obviously still nervous of me.

And, yes, there's a white bag on the doorstep of the charity shop. Inside is a bundle of babygros and a dark green coat, still perfectly usable. I shrug it on to find that it comes down beyond my knees, but after last night, the warmer the better.

See, things are working out OK. You can handle this.

Some of the babygros go into the pockets as an afterthought – they'll be better than nothing at keeping my feet from freezing when I've stopped running. For now, though, the most important thing is to stay agile. If they find me, that, and my wits, is all I'll have.

Dawn is bleeding through the clouds as I set out again, the horizon is already shaken with the rumble of distant traffic. Across the street, red bursts from grey as a light bulb wakens the colour of curtains. If humans are stirring, it's best to stay off the main roads.

I take the next left and find myself back in residential, hewn brick and Georgian sandstone, well-kept gardens, fences in white gloss. I vault over a gate and snatch a milk bottle from a step. Its weight sloshes reassuringly against my chest as I hurry on.

The garden a couple of walls down is so thick with weeds that I'm sure no one comes here often; it'll be as good a place as any to wait out the day. The old shed is locked but there's a snug gap between it and the wall – safe enough if I stay crouched.

The milk is so cold it's more texture than taste. Still, I finish the bottle in one go, only to regret the decision as the chill wave hits my stomach. Easy to forget my Original Body isn't as hardy as a lot of Ressies'.

Two eyes watch from the gate. The fox is still with me, even if it's keeping its distance. Wise. Trusting humans is always a risk. And yet it's accompanied me this far. I don't know what to make of that, unless it *is* her. Although how she'd have recognised me in my Original Body, I don't know. Now it's lighter, I'm sure it's a young female. If only I had a better sense of smell; I knew her more by scent than sight.

'Tomoko?' I whisper.

But why do I keep quizzing her with that name? Even if it was her, she'd never have heard it – I couldn't speak when I was a fox, not to her.

I try gekkering instead – like we would when we played – but even to my own ears I'm making a pitiful job. Of course, foxes also gekker when they fight, so perhaps it's for the best.

Even with my knees inside the coat, the shuddering is beyond my control. I wish the fox would come closer. I wish I could snuggle up to her like I would with Tomoko. But my stench is human, my face naked like a fox with mange.

'Hey.'

I lick my lips and hunker forwards.

'It's still me.'

But at that I start giggling, from tiredness or the stupidity of talking to a fox, I don't know. That look is so intelligent it's hard to believe that she doesn't understand *something*. Because even if English is useless, that doesn't mean communication is impossible – if I believed that, I'd never have become a phenomenaut. Sometimes a body is all the language you need.

I duck and bring my chin to my knees in what I'm hoping looks submissive, but without ears flexible enough to flatten she might not get it. In fact, her attention doesn't seem to be on me at all.

'Breakfast, huh?'

One of her ears twitches towards me, then returns to examining the road. But it doesn't matter if she can't understand, doesn't even matter if she isn't listening, just telling my story helps. And fox or not, she's a better audience than thin air.

4

Uncanny Shift

It's thirteen days before they let me return to work after my 'incident'. How does Mr Hughes do it – speak in quotation marks even over the phone? Something about the vapidity of that voice brings an image of him startlingly to mind – morose jowls, the 'V' of two fingers curling in quotation. 'Your unfortunate incident.'

How about 'V' for *fuck you* and your constant glibness. But I'm so glad to be called back that I just thank him, my eyes squeezed shut in the hope that this will prevent him from hearing the tears.

Later, I lie in bed quivering, deaf even to Mum's shouts, because it's only hours until I'm out of here. *Here* – not just a room but skin. How can other people call *this* their totality?

There is so much more.

The bus the next morning takes forever. The drumming of my foot annoys even me.

Stop it, Kit, stop it.

I put my forehead against the window instead, feel its tremble against my temple. With my eyes shut, I can almost imagine myself back in the hive – the dark brought to life by the hum of a hundred bees. Within that earthquake my whole body seemed ablaze, until boundaries melted and I felt myself leaking into something larger. We. Us.

I straighten and chew on the back of a hand, the skin there is loose, as if my skeleton could slip its guise any moment. My face, however, feels as taut as snake skin on the verge of being shed.

Thank god the joke of 'sick leave' is finally over. It's not like my Original Body got pulped by the car. Though it's bad enough that Tomoko is out there on her own; bad enough that the cub study had to be cancelled. Whilst they could technically print off another copy of the fox Ressy, Lauren made it clear that their grant will never stretch to cover the cost. In some ways I should be glad that ShenCorp are treating me with kid gloves; Mr Hughes must have been tempted to use the boxing variety.

My fellow passengers sit with the blank expressions of those still inwardly entangled in duvets. Beside them, holographic people dance across the windows, advertising tooth-sprays and insurance policies with such vivacity that it's almost tempting to think that we're the counterfeit. For a second my pale reflection overlays a flawless, beaming face; sharp eyes to her heavy lashes, bald head to her blonde mane and, as if to explain the difference, she lifts a pot of beauty cream, two hands pressed around it in the shape of a heart.

Across the aisle, a baby watches me over its mother's shoulder, chewing mechanically on a plastic duck and, ridiculously, my mouth starts to salivate too. I blink at it and look away, only remembering after that this is friendly for cats, not babies. Its smell of sweetly sour milk mixes with the bus's usual smellscape of disinfectant, coffee, sweat. Hell, I smell of rancid dairy too. Ever since I started projecting, and realised what it was not to always have the scent in my nostrils, its pungency finds me in odd moments.

And at last – Park Street.

My Specs beep to remind me this is my stop but I'm already hefting my bag over my head and swinging out of the door. I almost reel back as the city condenses in rush and noise. The bus hisses as it pulls away, dull eyes at the window following without seeing. Now up the hill, keeping close to the shop fronts as I weave through the morning commute. The humans here always strike me as improbably perpendicular, every chin thrust out with the confidence of a silverback. What is it that gives them such assurance? As if they're all alphas. A suited man jostles past and I bare my teeth at his glare. This is what the city reduces you to – meat, meat that's in the way.

Reaching University Road, grey gives way to green. A blackbird shouts its territory from a hedge and I whistle back, smiling at his furious reply. One more street, then here I am. ShenCorp.

Our Centre is taller than its neighbours, but something about it still seems to squat, its concrete almost brutal against the surrounding sandstone. The ShenCorp clam logo sits high on the wall, as stark as the scent of fresh urine. The building might be a monstrosity but it's *my* monstrosity, and right now, it's a welcome sight.

I jog up the steps and Dave glances up from his booth to wave me on with the flap of a hand. I sort of feel sorry for him – most days his job seems to consist of staring into the far distance, only broken every few months by tussling with some crazy pro-lifer, though it's never been clear to me what they'd do if they ever did manage to 'liberate' a Ressy.

I flash my card at the scanner and enter the lobby, or 'Isaac Hall' as we're supposed to call it. Not that anyone does. My soles whisper against the marble floor, something almost reverent about the sound, and right on cue the screen on the far wall flickers into life.

'ShenCorp is the world's leading Consciousness Projection Provider giving insights into fields as diverse as animal science, oenology, and astronomy' – one day I will walk stealthily enough for it not to register, I promise myself this every morning – 'launched by Phenomenautism's inventor, Professor Shen. ShenCorp was the first Projection Provider to enter the global market—'

I ignore the rest of the self-congratulatory reel and follow the edge of the room, running a hand along the fish tank so that tiny damsels cluster to the warmth of my finger in blue sparks.

Hello, fish.

At our corridor I put a shoulder out to stop the swinging doors from hitting me in the face and continue into the white space. No marble floors or fish tanks here. The animal photos on the walls are static, that's how old this place is. Buckley says that before ShenCorp took it over, he used to have his Biotech seminars in these rooms. If a client ever asks to see a projection, there's an especially fancy room just for the purpose next to Mr Hughes's office, but the real work is done here.

Jo waves as I pass but the other cubicles are shut; even though most of their lights are green, it's too early in the week for people to have started projecting. The younger children will be in seminars, those over seventeen going over the notes for their next project. Shouting comes from Hanna's door, so I don't stop to say hello. It's a mistake to get mixed up in the arguments with her neuro.

At the last door, I push it wide with a foot and exhale into the familiar space. Our territory. Home.

It seems larger in here today; whilst I was away, Buckley's pushed the JumpPallet against the wall and stowed my blue wash bags underneath – a reminder that while most of my time in this room is spent consciously elsewhere, the mess is nearly always mine. The BodySupport equipment hasn't been put out yet, though the curve of screens over his desk show some sort of pre-fig fMRI. It doesn't look quite right for my brain patterns, even though, as a phenomenaut, your scans can become as familiar as your reflection.

The normality here feels almost wrong. I died – my Ressy died – yet life carries on as ever. Admittedly, even on a normal Come Home, there's always the sense that the world I return to should have somehow shifted, a corner of the curtain pulled back. But perhaps it's not the world that changes.

I rummage in the drawer where Buckley keeps his cache of biscuits. There's a primal satisfaction to sneaking food in cubby-holes like this, security against the capriciousness of nature. I gnaw on the Bourbon and glance over his origami papers. He's already completed one piece today, killing time waiting for me to arrive. Something folded out of red wrapping paper. I right it. A fox.

Still no Buckley, though. I head back out to the kitchenette. But it's empty too.

Second floor. I put my head round the door of the common room. Si is on the sofa, well-loved stuffed toy tiger under one arm as he types in his SpecSpace. I'm sure he's at least fourteen, but a lot of phenomenauts are like that, at once younger and older than their age.

'Seen Buckley?' I say.

He shakes his head, then stops short with a frown. I follow his look to the tables and see one of the new phenomenauts looming over Julie, aggression clear in her stance. Daisy, I think her name is:

23

specialism entomology; there's always something a bit odd about phenomenauts who exclusively handle invertebrates.

Easily taller than me, she can't be older than sixteen – old for a phenomenaut just starting out. The newness shows in the vanity of her black wig; Julie and Si are only wearing beanies over their baldness and I tend to find myself not even bothering with that these days.

As I watch, Daisy snatches up Julie's dolphin plush bag and starts twirling it. Buckley mentioned something like this might be going on. The constant changeover of phenomenauts means that the pecking order is always in flux. I walk over, pulling my lips back to reveal teeth.

It takes Daisy a good couple of seconds before she notices me, a couple more for the dolphin bag to stop its flight.

'Hey. Kit, isn't it?'

I stare back. Actual height doesn't matter when it comes to threat displays. I know how to make myself *look* large.

A muscle slips in her face. 'What is it?'

1. 2. 3. And . . . She glances away, eyes sweeping the common room for support that isn't there.

'Why are you smiling?'

I pull my smile wider, if 'smile' is what she wants to call it. My eyes are starting to go a little dry from not blinking but I can keep this up for a while.

Her expression collapses. 'I don't understand.'

Except she does. Only a human would pretend that they didn't.

'We were just talking,' she says. 'Not that anyone around here seems to know what that is.'

My hands, hidden in my pockets, curl into claws. If she notices, she doesn't show it; she can't have learnt many transferable combat skills in her work as insects.

The bag drops to the floor.

'Weirdos.'

I wait until she's out of the door to stop my staring but she won't be back. You almost have to feel sorry for her. She was probably an alpha at school but ShenCorp is a world away from the playground. I massage the strain of my cheeks and turn to Julie.

'OK?'

She nods, only meeting my eyes for a second.

'I'm looking for Buckley,' I say.

Her shoulders twitch, lacking even the confidence to be a real shrug, and I give up. Even her neuro jokes that she should work with clams, not cetaceans.

Still, on the way out, I rub my hand against the door frame. It's not that sweaty but if anyone here had a halfway decent nose they'd know whose territory this is.

Back on the stairs, I make a detour past Mr Hughes's office in the faint hope that Buckley's been called into a meeting, but Mr Hughes is just entertaining some important-looking suits. Mr Hughes has been having a lot of these meetings of late. They must be some new contractor; no doubt he'll start with the boasting once it's confirmed. He frowns to see me looking in and I hurry on. Only one more possibility.

Another two flights and the stairs end in a metal door. 'No Entry' the peeling sticker says. 'This door is alarmed'. They don't let phenomenauts onto the roof, not since Isaac Wallace, even though that was before ShenCorp had officially separated from the university.

The door is slightly open, enough in itself to tell me that Buckley is here – no one else has the inclination or the permission. It opens grudgingly, wind snapping in my face, then there he is – a tall, forlorn figure, standing at the fencing staring into nothing.

I huddle against the wind. *Forlorn.* What a word to use for Buckley. He's always moving, doing, saying something. If it's not gesturing or chatter, it's his fingers, fidgeting, folding, giving the flatness of paper shape. But now he's still; arms lifted slightly from his sides, as if waiting for the wind to take him.

I've never liked it here, not even with the illicit thrill of when, long ago, Susie and I would sneak up to spy. Seeing Buckley transformed like this, the rumours, exciting when whispered at the back of tutorials, fleshed themselves in ominous weight.

I glance back at the stairs.

'Kit!'

But now Buckley is striding over, reaching in for what for a moment I think is going to end in a hug, but ends in steering me inside.

'How long have you been standing there?'

'Just a second,' I say, peering over a shoulder, almost cheated as the door clunks shut behind us.

'I didn't think you were coming back today.'

'I said I would.'

'I know. But on the phone you sounded . . .'

'Sounded?'

He shrugs. I shiver with the last of the cold and lead the way back towards the stairs.

'But you're feeling OK?'

'Sure.' I glance back to reply and he seizes the hesitation to bound forward and block the way, one eyebrow raised, but he can't stop the corner of his mouth from twitching and neither can I.

'I guess things are still a little – dunno. But, honestly, mostly I'm OK.'

We walk the next flight side by side.

'When's your next session with Niti?'

'They've moved it forwards, worried about my "incident", as Mr Hughes is calling it.'

'No harm in playing it safe.'

'Prodding and poking isn't going to help.'

I know what his look means but at least he has the sense not to voice it. Back when he used to jump, phenomenauts were only ever given the occasional psychometric profiling. These days I lose track of the name badges I'm paraded in front of – when it's not Niti's check-ups, it's the GP, psychologist, orthopaedist, neurologist. Too many '-ists', all 'playing it safe'. Everyone knows their main remit is to stop Shen from being sued and, as the average age of phenomenauts is now under thirteen, that may make a certain amount of sense. Yet, at nineteen, I would have hoped the sessions could have stopped for me. No such luck. Some days the red tape is looped so tight I feel like a present topped off with a bow. Or rather, a growth in a Petri dish, an anomaly – the girl who stayed jump-ready. The girl who didn't give up.

Buckley is a worrier, though, he can't help it, and as he pushes our cubicle door open, he looks down at me with the expression that says 'We must be sensible' or 'I was very upset when you were toying with that lion, you know hyenas aren't as strong' or 'Don't you *dare* pretend to lose control of your wings again. I'm too young to have a heart attack'.

But today he doesn't say anything. The cheer has already slunk from his expression, only exhaustion in its place. Mr Hughes can't have been easy on him for his role in my death.

Are you OK? I think to say, but the image of him standing, alone, on the rooftop returns to me and I lose courage and nod at his screens instead.

'What are these?'

He darts over to swipe them offscreen. 'Just Mr Hughes keeping me busy whilst you were away. There's a report to be handed in by tomorrow. Want to help?'

'Buckley, I'm ready.'

He scoops up my bag from the floor and puts it onto the JumpPallet.

'*Buckley.*'

His shoulders slump. 'This one isn't going to be easy.'

'Is it ever?'

'Perhaps you're right.' His face brightens and he mimes crawling with fingers. 'How do you fancy eight legs?'

By early afternoon we're ready to go, or as near as. I sit on the pallet in my JumpPyjamas and skim the manual one last time. In training they always said to spend at least a morning studying the documents before projection, but no number of words can prepare you for the raw experience. Besides, there's only so much you can learn from a document written by bioengineers who've never projected in their lives.

I shove the manual out of my lenses and take another look at the brief instead. Most of the funding comes from RIBA so, instead of the usual population, behavioural, social surveys, the focus is on the mechanics of weaving. There's a memorandum at the end noting that some of the money came from an arachnological charity. A quick Internet search reveals that they're campaigning to stop the use of a pesticide that's causing spiders to weave irregular webs, which explains why Mr Hughes assigned this project to me rather than Olenna or Daisy.

Seeing me take my Specs off, Buckley raises his hand and I toss them to him. Now for BodySupport. First things first: the oxygen tubes. I slip them up my nose to the smell of plastic and stale air. Next, catheter bag; I double check it's properly clicked in, give the skin around the cannula a swab just to be safe, and turn to the Vitals patch – check. MuscleStim – check.

I pat the fluids drip but decide to leave it; same for the colostomy bag. There's an eight-hour jump limit on invertebrates so I'll probably just wake up peckish and a bit constipated. And if I do shit myself, no one round here is going to judge me for it – you can't work in consciousness projection for long without gaining an appreciation of the inevitability of certain bodily functions. At least I'm not a bloke. Original Bodies often experience erections whilst their minds are elsewhere. And though most female phenomenauts have to wear cups for their periods, I'm lucky enough to have not had one in years.

Buckley watches me double-check my setup, his expression dark. BodySupport gives him the creeps, which is a bit unfortunate if you're a neuro. It's not like I *like* it but it keeps my body ticking over whilst my conscious mind is away.

All sorted, I lie down. My toes rise gradually to my eyeline, then sink back as the pressure-relief mattress starts doing its thing. The leather is cold against my bare arms and I have to wriggle to try and find a comfortable position.

It doesn't take long for Buckley to reappear with the CP and at my nod he slips it on my head. My scalp tickles as the nodes wriggle to ensure they've good contact with skin, reminding me of nothing more than ape fingers combing through my fur. I can almost hear the snap of flea carapaces between teeth and have to swallow the saliva rising to my mouth.

Buckley steps back from making his adjustments and swivels a thumb. *Good or no?* I dip my head and he returns to his screens.

Meditation is always sensible before a jump but I can tell that right now it'd be a wasted attempt – I'm actually shaking with the anticipation. Buckley hums tunelessly over the click of switches.

A clunk announces the electromagnets going live. The projection can only be moments away. I try to pre-empt it. Now? Now? Now? Sliders whir, the supercomputer thrums. Any second. Any

5

Uncanny Shift

'Houston, we have consciousness.'

A voice.

I yearn towards it. Try looking but can't. Can't move either. No sight, no taste, no touch – no anything. I panic, but without a body the fear is just texture, electricity.

'Rise and shine, Kit.'

Buckley.

'It's a beautiful morning here in Greater Bristol. Temperature is 18 degrees, sunny with low cloud. King William is on the throne and you're currently embodied as an orb-weaving spider.'

A jump. Of course. A spider. The job for RIBA. No wonder I can't feel anything. Everything is as it should be. I let myself slip into the calmness of his voice and wait for the world to unfurl.

'Exits are to the rear, or rather, should I say, the anus. But, seriously, in the event of an emergency please psych the exit-potential.'

Oh, Buckley. This is part procedure, part parody, but I've worked with him so long I'm not sure I'd be able to tell the two apart. Mainly he's using humour to keep me sane.

'If you're ready, let's get those beautiful bug eyes patched in.'

A pause, followed by a click, then nothingness disgorges greys and whites, primitive shapes multiplied in diamonds. I throw my thoughts at them with little success – there doesn't seem any understanding to be made.

'Remember orb spiders have terrible visual acuity,' Buckley says; between his scans and our history, his guesses can be uncanny.

'But continuing protocol, if you're firmly buckled in, we're about ready to get going on the proprioceptive signals.' The soft patter of his fingers comes over comms.

'OK, and in, 3 ... 2 ... 1—'

Wrong

Warping

Unravelling

Dying

'Easy. Eeeeeasy. Just breathe.'

I cling to the warm drawl of his voice. Sometimes it's the vowels that make all the difference, that pure breath flowing from his lungs to mine – just breeeeathe.

Not that I technically have lungs.

The temptation in these moments is to lash out, to run, but fight–flight is useless here. I can't fight my embodiment, can't escape it. Right now, I can't even scream. All I can do is wait for it to pass. My abdomen gulps greedily at air.

'You're good in there,' Buckley says. 'Everything's good.'

And if Buckley says that, then it is.

As the unease fades, I lie, just wallowing in the release. Seven years of jumping, more than any other phenomenaut to date, and still Sperlman's Shock screws with my head. It's the rupture that does it, the headfuck of waking to find myself something else. I've known kids who've dreamed of jumping for years only to throw it all in at their first taste, and I don't blame them.

As the quiet settles, I reach inward for a sense of this body. My head is a protruding nub. What I once called my belly is swollen into something bulbous – an abdomen? And legs – if they can be called that – slender, insubstantial, too many to get a clear sense of. A better understanding will come with movement but even so I feel numb – a spider has a tiny number of nerve endings compared to most of the bodies I've inhabited.

'All right?'

Buckley is never happy until I've given verbal confirmation so I attempt a reply, only to find blankness has replaced lips. Yet working actual muscles isn't the trick to sub-vocalisation, the larynx simulation should handle all that.

'OK – I'm OK,' I manage.

'Everything feeling about right?'

'Think so. Give me a sec.'

I psych at what twenty minutes ago would have been human limbs. Something twitches, but I don't seem to move. My proprioception is completely skewed. This body is too simple for a direct mapping, but running off the Ressy's own motor plans as I am it shouldn't take long for everything to come naturally. So I experiment, stimulating whatever I can – like reaching for my own hand in the dark, only to find it gripped by someone else. Adaption to a spider was never going to be easy.

After a while I begin to sense some kind of repetition, stimulus and response tracing the outline of something. Of me. A ripple of legs follows, tiptoes of touch. I'm walking. Part of me yells that I shouldn't be able to do this, that I shouldn't be such a frenzy of legs, but the action is as easy as breathing. I don't know how a spider moves, not conceptually, but this body does and so, somehow, do I.

The world is a charcoal smudge. Nameless tastes lick my legs, skin prickles in flurries. Uncanny Shift is swiftly overtaking Sperlman's – the foreignness of this new world replacing the initial shock of becoming *other*. Right now I'm a stranger, even to myself – it's an almost physical hurt. But still I scamper. Only the drive to move.

At last a strip of darkness towers above. Whispered impulse beckons and legs reach out. Claws hook in cracks and the light falls to greet me.

At the top I stop. Consider. About me, white breathes through a slew of grey; everything is nonsensical, bizarre. With Ressies like a fox, the mind will shift into its sphere of meaning with time, but there's no point even trying with most invertebrates. Such Ressies are pure impulse: they tug, you go, more like riding than becoming. Yet thinking too much will get me nowhere; I give in to instinct.

For a while that seems to be waiting. My abdomen fidgets; in my mind's eye, images blink a random procession. Tomoko. Buckley. A flame . . . jumping from one idea to the next, anything to distract me from the emptiness. Then I feel the dribble. Juices are oozing from my rear and hardening into weight – my spinnerets are producing silk. The realisation takes me by surprise. Of course, I've read about this but the actual experiences of a body are rarely as I'd expect.

The silk pulls a line of tension through my core followed by a sharp tug as the breeze catches it. A tremor follows and instinctively I clinch the thread taut, then tether the end with needling of my feet. Only as I step out, do I realise that it's a tightrope. It bounces and dips beneath me, my belly oozing another thread behind. Now back again, nimble claws hooking and tugging, then fasten once more, lower into the dimness.

Where did this dance come from? Such steps have never spoken to me before but now they come to me as easily as breathing. The knowledge feels right, a part of me, and yet when I'm human once more it will blink out; anything left behind, nonsense.

My mind is performing somersaults too – trying to understand what exactly it is I'm doing. Best guess, I'm creating a Y junction for the frame of the web, but this is mainly based on previous knowledge of spiders. With invertebrates I have to wonder if I'm actually gaining any understanding or if I'm just distorting the incomprehensible to fit human constructs. Of course, there's that possibility with every Ressy but it rarely feels such a farce as this.

But these thoughts are distracting me from the Ressy impulses. Keep this up and I'm going to make a mistake. No more philosophising.

I climb back into the light trailing more thread. Clamber, point to point, back legs teasing flow; circle, tighter, tighter. A rhythm of squirt, pin, step. Sink into the symmetry. Just let myself go . . .

By the time it's finished, I'm ravenous. Or perhaps empty, silk used up, my innards are a gulf. Either way, all there is left to do is wait.

And wait.

It's hardest in bodies like this; without sensible external sensation to distract me, it's easy to spiral into rumination. Instead, I turn my mind to the past. The life – the *I* – before being a spider already feels foreign but I've a store of memories for times like this, stars to cling to in the dark. Such as the day I was accepted into ShenCorp. The rush of that email, my disbelief turning into excitement – I was going to be a phenomenaut. The printout we took to show

Gran Gran, its texture silky smooth, like her hands around mine; Mum's on my shoulders, shaking.

The web ripples. My legs fizzle in the breeze.

Then, the trips to our Centre. Those first few bus rides were so exciting, watching Bristol stream beyond the window. I hadn't even taken buses on my own before; I'd only just turned twelve.

These memories have been handled so many times their edges are worn soft but what else do I have? I reach for the next.

First meeting Buckley, a lanky figure, not quite boy, not quite man, eyes never quite meeting mine. Did he really used to hunch, or did I make it up? He doesn't now.

As time trickles on, I feel as if I am dissolving into the web. The wind stirs quakes inside me, pauses in its breath like white noise. This silk is more than my home, it's become an extension of my skin; I tense as each shudder passes up my feet – prey? No, I'll know it when it comes. So sit tight; thoughts above, like boaters on water.

What next? My first projection. No, I never have clear memories of that. Just the excited dread before, afterwards watching my breakfast swirling down the toilet bowl.

A face leers, its eye sockets hollow.

I slip and thrash. But the face is already gone.

'All right?' Buckley asks.

I haul myself back to my perch, abdomen gasping.

'I'm OK. I'm OK. Just a hallucination.'

'What was it?'

'Eyes. A face. Something watching.'

His tongue clucks against his teeth, an ominous noise. Hallucinations always happen in Ressies with poor stimulation; to a human mind the inputs from an insect embodiment are so basic as to count as sensory deprivation. But Buckley's right: I normally experience colours and flashing lights before anything complex.

'It's only been two hours. Can you stick it out a little longer?'

Only two hours! Paranoia skitters round my thoughts.

'I'll read to you. Give you something to focus on,' he says.

This jump is quickly becoming unpleasant, but it's my job.

The quiet is tar as I wait for his words, then his voice returns.

'Britain called on to "do its part". EU Commissioner Julian Rylands today called on the Prime Minister for Britain to "do its part" in shouldering environmental refugees. The European Commission has been under increasing pressure since the start of this year's southern droughts—'

The news. It's one of Buckley's favourite diversionary tactics. All the manuals recommend it. 'Keep the phenomenaut intellectually and emotionally engaged in the human world.' 'Retaining an attachment to the trappings of culture is the surest way of staving off nativism.' Behind the fancy words, the main idea is simple – no phenomenaut must ever relinquish their humanity.

As Buckley's precise words patter through the article I try to focus, but such stories lack meaning here; the world has already shrunk to the expanse of my web. I fixate on his voice instead, sensing the shape of the sounds as if I were a finger pressed to his lips. It's slower than usual, slightly slurred; perhaps he was up late last night. But the sentences are starting to unravel.

'– hurricanes – president said – without support – and—'

A luminescence drips through the ether; cobalt, now star-burst red. But no, this body can't even sense colour. I feel the brush of nettles over skin.

Come on, Kit. Don't trip out only two hours in.

Words begin to crumble, revealing innards of brute breath.

'Buckley,' I try to say.

Sourness washes up my legs. Someone, somewhere, laughs.

'Buckley!'

Am I even sub-vocalising?

Buckley!

Please.

Help

An impact to the web startles me back to myself.

Prey.

I leap, thread to thread, meaty taste loud up my legs, hunger like a second heartbeat. Its wings buffet me but the struggle is hopeless.

My abdomen moistens and I rear, spewing nets of iron, as my legs stitch it into a writhing tomb.

———————

Pins and needles, so much. So heavy. Much many.

No, not many. Why did I think that? More like large – lots.

The many is me. I *am* the lots.

I start to laugh, then gasp at the raw sensation of having a throat. *My* throat.

'All right?' Buckley asks.

I open my eyes, stunned for a second by the force of colour and detail, then am overawed all over again as I realise all this is just inside the whiteness of the strip light. Amazing how quickly you can forget.

My eyes are pulled to the pink blob rising from the bottom of my vision – my nose. I reach up to touch the point of flesh and some of the tingling arranges into its shape. My cheeks are wet but I don't think I'm sad.

'All right?' Buckley repeats.

I hum, not feeling ready to face this ornate construction of lips, tongue and throat, but am forced to anyway as I start to cough on the dryness of the oxygen.

A rumbling approaches, yet only as his head appears does it occur to me that the sound means that sensations are becoming interpretable again and that it was the wheels of his chair. He grabs the JumpPallet to pull himself the rest of the way.

'Prefer to lie there for a bit?'

'Um.' I blink up at him, readjusting to the idea that I should be relying on more than instinct. This body is quite happy to lie here, but what do I want? I reach out to the hollow feeling in my stomach, a stark contrast with the fullness of the spider Ressy after I had sucked the innards from the fly. It turns out what I want is what this body wants anyway.

'I think I'd like . . .' I say, picking over the words with a frown. 'I think I'd like a sandwich.'

He grins. 'I'll see what I can rustle up.'

I'm thankful for the silence he leaves behind, it makes the noise of this world, hell, this body, more bearable. There's a pulse behind my eyes that suggests an imminent headache but after being a spider that's no surprise. Now I've readjusted to the notion of colour, the ceiling is cool snow into which the ache of sensation can nestle.

The pins and needles have spread into a general fuzziness but it isn't necessarily uncomfortable. My face feels hot, lips and tongue seemingly swollen. I poke them to check – but no, they're fine, though the movement reminds me that I'm still plugged into BodySupport.

Sitting, I pat the pallet to reassure myself, not of it, but of the singular solidarity of my arms. Moving as a spider was like syllables that never join in meaningful expression but the business of a human body is one voice.

My fingers wriggle under my inspection. '*Worms*,' I whisper and put them to work pulling off the Velcro of the MuscleStims.

Buckley arrives back in time to help me tidy it away.

'Feeling more human?'

I smile at the old joke and reach for the sandwich but the movement puts pressure on my bowels.

Buckley steps back surprised as I scuttle past.

'Loo!' I shout back. And race along the corridor as fast as I can.

6

Come Home

Something is crawling over my face. A spider? Earwig? I twitch my nose to try to budge it, then let it be.

My gummy eyes open on to a slate sky. It doesn't feel as if I've been sleeping so much as hovering between hallucination and unmoored thought.

Now it's daylight ShenCorp must be searching in full force; no way I'm moving from here before dark. One false move and that'll be it; no way they'd ever let me go free after what I've seen.

I crane my neck up but there's no sign of the fox and I let my head drop back. She'll be back once she's had her breakfast; somehow I'm sure of it.

With my head comfortable in the crook of my arm, I try to return to sleep but the image of a spider itches against my eyelids – a tiny dot suspended in front of the blur of a face. Mum used to pick money spiders out of my hair when I'd been romping about the wood as a child.

It's lucky to find a spider in your hair.

Because they bring you money?

No, you're lucky to make a friend.

Did I make that exchange up? It feels almost trite. If I'm honest with myself, I don't really remember what Mum said in those moments; these days I can't even remember how her voice sounded. But the crux of the memory is clear: there wasn't a creature that she didn't love.

For the longest time that's what I thought zoologists did – loved. It was a shock when I started at ShenCorp and realised that some people were more interested in animals in the abstract. That the environment was The Environment, a creature the authority of its Latin name, sightings to collect like butterflies pinned to blotting paper, collecting a second fur of dust. Mum loved creatures in their individuality.

In the family pictures she is always feeding something – a sensuous trunk curls around the offered branch; a flurry of ducks fight over thrown seed; the chubby toddler that was once me smiles, face smeared with chocolate.

In the faded shots of her voluntary work at the chimpanzee reserve she appears to the camera as a moon-faced girl, clung to by contemplative feet as if she were a tree.

Sometimes I find it strange to think that I'm the same age as the girl in those pictures. At others, I wonder what was left her once all the giving was over.

7

Uncanny Shift

'You do know that you didn't die?' Niti's eyes are hidden by the screen glare of her Specs. Their inversed text is too small for me to read.

But that's always how phenomenautical check-ups have been, expecting complete openness from us even as the therapists retreat. They remind me of nothing more than whelks, safe inside their shells as they slowly bore through those of their prey.

I look away to escape the Specs' glare. On the street below a stream of students bow beneath umbrellas, now and then overtaken by the sprint of someone less prepared. Imagine that being your largest concern – to not get damp? To sufficiently absorb a string of facts to regurgitate, gannet-like, on to end-of-term exams? How simple that life must be. And if it weren't for a twist of fate, I could have been one of them.

'Katherine? You do know that, don't you?'

I release the hand I've been chewing and make myself stare into the blankness of her Specs. And after a few seconds, it works – Niti glances away, brushing a loose strand of hair behind an ear. Grooming to break the tension – a lot of animals do this.

'I got hit by a car,' I say. 'My internal organs were reduced to paste. What do you call that if not death?'

'Shock is understandable. But that was the ResExtenda body, not yours.'

'It was mine at the time.'

'Temporarily.'

'I died in it.'

One finger fidgets against another in her lap, the cut-glass rings as brutal as knuckle-dusters. I let my eyes unfocus on the tiny hole in the side of her nose that must contain a piercing when she's not at work.

'Let me get this clear,' she says finally. 'You're saying that you're dead?'

'No. Not anything crazy. But being alive doesn't change the fact that I died.'

'The technical term is hurt. Would it help to think of it that way?'

It's hard not to roll my eyes. 'Don't you think that's a bit of an understatement?'

'*ERT* . . . Experienced ResExtenda Termination.'

'Right.' I force my lips into a smile. ShenCorp and their insatiable fetish for acronyms.

But now it's my turn to look away. Can she see through my face to the thoughts skittering beneath? Because I did die. At least, the fox me. My fox life. Give it whatever euphemism you like but it doesn't change what happened.

Of course, it always feels like a part of you has died when you leave a long-term Ressy forever. It's less traumatic than being hit by a car, yes, but the loss – that creeping feeling that I've left something behind, that's there with every Come Home. These innumerable incremental deaths.

'If this makes you uncomfortable we don't have to talk about it now.'

Her inflection makes it seem like a question but really it's a statement – we *should* be talking about this. Niti always wants to talk about everything. To help me 'self-narrate'. According to her, this will allow us to 'encompass the experiences from each ResExtenda body under one story' – one *me*. I wouldn't mind that much if it weren't the case that only her version of events is ever deemed correct, deemed *healthy*. If only we hadn't somehow become a royal *we*.

'So. How have we been doing otherwise? Settling back into work OK?'

'Fine.'

'Some more detail would be good.'

The tiredness starts to push behind my eyes.

'Well,' I say, 'I've been thinking about eating my own shit.'

To do her credit, she doesn't even raise an eyebrow.

'Just the cecals. Good nutrition, you know. Or maybe a worm or two. Protein.'

But now her Specs are coming off, a pinch of fingers massaging the bridge of her nose. She looks more human without their glare; the brown of her skin is touched with grey.

'I get it. I really do,' she says eventually. 'I don't take any more pleasure in asking the same questions every session than you do in answering them. But I don't think you understand the gravity of the situation. You were involved in a very serious incident and it's my responsibility to ensure that you're fit to work.'

Perhaps I'm not looking 'understanding enough' because after a pregnant look she continues.

'You do know that I could send you home if I'm not fully satisfied, maybe even permanently.'

'Sorry.' Seeing her own exhaustion has left me embarrassed. It's not Niti that's the problem, she's just trying to do her job too. 'I was being stupid.'

'So you haven't been thinking about consuming faeces?'

'No. Of course not.'

She puts her Specs back on with a shake of the head.

I squeeze my hands between my knees. 'But you wouldn't stop me working. Would you?'

'If it was necessary for your health. Have you been having any nightmares? Flashbacks?'

'No.'

Again, that look.

'Sleeping like a baby,' I say.

Of course, many babies sleep terribly. And everyone gets nightmares now and then.

My smile struggles under her scrutiny but, with a shake of the head, she moves us on to the IAT. I settle myself in front of the old monitor and position my fingers on the left and right keys.

The IAT has been the most ridiculous part of this whole exercise of bloated bureaucracy ever since they started employing it a couple of years back. Talking things through is one thing but the IAT is designed to 'access the subject's subconscious associations', things I might not be aware of myself. Yet if there are such thoughts, I'm damned if I'd want ShenCorp to know about them.

Now that the eye tracker is satisfied that I've 'read' the questions, two words flash to the top of the screen: 'Me' to the left, 'Not-me' to the right. I flex my fingers, take a breath ... and hit the spacebar. A picture of a fox appears on screen. I start to count in my head. 1. 2. 3. Hit the right key for 'Not-me'.

In theory, the program processes the millisecond differences it takes the subject to respond at one end and spits their 'implicit associations' out the other. Well, fuck that. I make sure to take three seconds to reply every time. Not that I can be sure that a difference of milliseconds doesn't come through. Perhaps it's all nonsense but resistance, however ineffective, is the only thing that makes it bearable. Some days ShenCorp feels like a bottomless stomach that will consume anything of myself I give it. It's not wrong to want to keep something back.

The picture of the fox disappears, replaced by the sharp face of a girl, little mouth pursed, frown pleated into the dome of her bald head – '*Got a problem?*' I glare at the black pinpoint of the screen's camera. Want grumpy pictures of me, well, here's a grumpy picture. . . . and 3. Hit the right key.

The program walks me through more pictures of foxes and random fauna, more unflattering photos of my face, frown deepening with every snap. Then we're on to other rounds – pictures of unblemished skin, followed by those with cuts, then cascades of random words. *Good. Bad. Self. Theirs. Excellent. I. Happy. Depressed. Other.*

As I hit the right button a red cross appears on the screen. Crap. The keys swapped round in the last batch, didn't they? Right is 'Me'. Left is 'Not-me'. Right 'Me', left 'Not'.

This test is enough to melt anyone's mind. I'd bet good money it screws up people more than it helps. But of course I'm going to fuck up if I'm not concentrating. So, easy breaths. Now. 1. 2. 3 . . .

When the screen finally blacks out, I push my chair back and Niti comes over to touch her Specs to the port. As she puts them back on she shakes her head at the time.

'You do know the idea is to answer as quickly as you can?'

She really is taking this seriously today.

I shrug and smile. For a second I think she's going to make me do it again but we're on a schedule and there's still the plasticity tests to go.

Plasticity. Now this is where I really do start to sweat.

I perch on the edge of the seat under the Spinner. Today there's the potter's wheel drawn up in front of it. Most sessions it's just tests with coloured blocks but Niti likes to mix it up – anything that requires somatospatial learning does the trick. I think she's trying to make the test fun, ignorant of the fact that no phenomenaut will ever be able to enjoy this.

Still, as the dome of the helmet descends, I try to tell myself it's just a hairdressing machine, which kind of works . . . until it pinches into my scalp and the magnets start to thrum. Fuck.

'All ready to go,' Niti says.

I slap a slab of clay onto the wheel. Even if I'd known it'd be this today, practising outside of work would do me no good. It's not skill they're looking for – pottery has sod all to do with Phenomenautism – the only thing they're interested in is how efficiently my neurology adapts and there's no practising for that, not to mention that it only gets worse with age. At nineteen I'm lucky to still be here. Freakishly so, considering how long most people last.

As the clay collapses into a pat-like mess for the second time, Niti touches my shoulder.

'Try and relax.'

I'd prefer it if she told me how to throw a goddam pot.

When the test is finally finished the helmet releases me. My forehead feels tight from where it was clamped; I explore the dip with my fingertips. Niti notices me hovering.

'You know it takes time to process. But I'm sure it will all be fine.'

'Uhuh.'

She shoos with her fingers. 'Go on. Go wash your hands.'

I scrub off the worst of the clay and retrieve my bag. Niti frowns as she steps ahead to open the door, probably still pissed off at me for saying I ate cecals, but as I make to leave, she takes my elbow.

'I know this can't be easy. On top of everything with your mother.'

Her grip remains firm as if awaiting a response but what can she possibly expect me to say to that?

'If you ever want to talk, you know where to find me. You do know that?'

I nod, unable to meet her eyes as she finally steps aside and I can escape into the corridor.

The tests must have lasted longer than I thought, it's already lunchtime when I reach the common room. A whole morning lost to the inane exercise.

Buckley is already eating with Si. There are a couple of the other tween phenomenauts flinging grapes at one another but their names escape me. I'd swear the phenomenauts here get younger every day.

Buckley smiles as he sees me, pushes out the bench opposite with a foot. 'All OK?'

I dump my cheese pasty on the table. Out of the packet it looks greasy and unappetising.

'Great.'

The flicker of his eyes says that he knows I'm bullshitting but he must gather that I don't want to talk because he lets Si draw him back into whatever it is they've got going in their shared SpecSpace. From my perspective it comprises waving madly at the empty tabletop and making barricades out of cutlery.

I work the stodgy pasty through my teeth; the taste is as unpleas-ant as it looks. At least it's pretty bland under my human nose – not like the scream of scent you get in a lot of Ressies. I had thought that I liked this flavour but perhaps they changed the recipe. Or my tastes have changed. Well, little matter. I'm used to eating foul things and it's important that my Original Body gets enough fuel, so I distract myself from the flavour by watching Buckley and Si play.

Buckley and I haven't messed about in SpecSpace for ages. We used to do it all the time when I was young. I mean, we still do occasionally, but it's no use pretending that things haven't changed. Of course, I'm not a kid any more, and it's not like we're not as close these days, if anything it's the opposite, but sometimes I can't help yearning for the simplicity of that earlier time.

Noticing me watch, Buckley looks up. He doesn't say anything, or even smile, just holds my gaze until I excuse myself by taking another bite of pasty. From anyone else it'd be a classic form of dominance play but why would Buckley feel the need for that? It's this that unnerves me, that sometimes I just don't understand him.

Si tugs on Buckley's arm, pointing to an invisible something in the Spec game. It's odd that Si's own neuro doesn't spend much time with him. I always found Anisha friendly but maybe she doesn't want to invest in a relationship that will likely be cut off in the not too distant future. Neuros were certainly closer to phenomenauts when I first started. They've probably learnt to hold back.

Tiring of their senseless flapping, I wave myself into their game and watch Si shoo multicoloured cows towards the line of cutlery with wriggling fingers. From the other direction, Buckley drives a milling mass of yowling cats by creating a wall with his hands. The resultant collision is beyond my understanding. Some of the cats swamp the cows in a whirlwind of claws, other cows stomp with sparkling hooves, but I'm not even sure that obliterating the enemy is the aim of the game; in a quieter part of the battlefield, one of Buckley's cats naps on a cow's back.

I wait for what looks like a suitable lull in the chaos. 'Can I play?'

'You can take over from me,' Buckley says, but at that Si looks up like a startled deer.

'Never mind.' I return to picking apart my pasty, though I can't pretend not to be bothered by Si's dislike. Of course, Buckley sees it with his usual optimistic slant.

'He's in awe of you,' he'd said when I raised it with him last.

'In awe?' But my laughter had choked off as I saw that he wasn't joking.

'You haven't noticed? All the young phenomenauts are. You've been jumping for longer than anyone, almost certainly longer than most of them will.'

'That doesn't mean anything. I was just blessed with an amazing brain – in terms of plasticity.'

His mouth had cringed into a smile. 'So, nothing to do with bloody-mindedness?'

He'd accepted my punch without complaint.

The pasty sticks in my throat as I'm reminded again of my results being crunched through the supercomputers down in the basement, but it'll be a few hours until I get the all-clear – or its opposite. Niti's threats are one thing but if my plasticity isn't good enough I'll be out of the front door in a day. Regardless of the fact that I've been jumping for longer than anyone, they're merciless when it comes to the results. And that's the worst thing of all – despite Buckley's jokes, the factor that matters the most in this job is out of my control.

As if sensing my train of thought, Buckley brushes my sleeve with the back of a hand. *It'll be OK.*

I pull a face and bury it in my pasty but when the orange light blinks in my Specs, I almost poke myself in the face in my haste to open the email. Buckley flinches too. It's not the results, but if Buckley's worried, then being laid off must be a real possibility. God, why did I have to say that cecal nonsense to Niti? Today was not the day to get on her bad side.

At my silence, Buckley makes to stand.

'Just a message from my dad,' I say, still feeling weak.

'Right. It'd be unlikely they finish processing before the end of the day.'

I stare at the remnants of my pasty, unable to face any more.

'The write-up can wait until tomorrow,' he says. 'There's somewhere I think we ought to go.'

8

Uncanny Shift

'This isn't it.'

The drum of rain on the bonnet highlights our sudden quiet. Only a minute ago Buckley was singing along to the music, my accompaniment beating on the dashboard with a packet of mints; now, though, we're just sitting, staring out at the grey day.

'This isn't it.'

He glances up from returning the keycard to his wallet. 'It's the right road.'

I wipe away the condensation and peer out at the sandstone houses with their air of quiet respectability. There are lots of streets like this in north Bristol but I'm certain I've never been to this one.

'No. It's not.'

'It's the right coordinates.'

I shake my head.

'Check yourself if you like,' he says, gesturing to his Specs.

I accept the packet in my own and a messy topography of roads and housing overlays the windscreen. The car icon sits directly on top of our plotted destination but this tangle of roads is a world away from the sounds and smells of the territory I know and love. I push the hologram from my lenses and glare out at the hanging baskets of petunias on the closest fence.

'See?' Buckley says.

'Maybe you entered the wrong coordinates. We can check with Lauren.'

He leans over and pokes the Specs back up my forehead before I can bring up her number. 'Tomoko'll be here, or nearby with the other cubs. I promise.'

But my disbelief isn't anxiety – though I've admittedly plenty of that. It's this place that gets me. *Nothing* about it is familiar.

He cracks his door with a grin. 'Come on, at least allow me the pleasure of proving you wrong.'

It's true that I'm not going to prove anything by sulking in the car so I step out to face the house. A house that I'd swear I've never seen before in my life, let alone one I lived outside only weeks ago.

The trim lawn leads to a patio guarded by tiny ceramic men, coned hats painted warning red. *Territory markers.*

'It'll be fine, trust me.'

I shrug Buckley's hand off. 'Yeah.'

He opens the gate and I duck after. Closer, I can see that the paint on the men is peeling. They must have been here for some time, but there was never anything like them at my old home – that I noticed. Could it really be that they just never entered my awareness as a fox? It's not like humans often notice the markings of other animals.

But Buckley is already on the porch, reaching for the bell.

'No. No. No,' I sub-vocalise.

You don't mess around on someone else's territory, not ever, not without very good reason. But without comms, Buckley can't hear me.

There's no cover here but before I can retreat, Buckley throws back a smile. There's two of us. We're humans. This is suburbia. The worst that can realistically happen is that we get chased away.

A figure wells behind the frosted glass.

'Yes?'

An elderly lady stands in the doorway, squinting up at Buckley through small gold specs that aren't really Specs at all but old analogue glasses. To my relief, she seems even more nervous than I am. It's hard to defend your territory when you're old.

If Buckley has processed any of this he doesn't show it. Spreading his palms in greeting, he starts to lay out our case.

I'm Buckley Maurice and this is my colleague Katherine North. We're calling on behalf of ShenCorp and the Fox Research Centre at the University of Bristol. Perhaps you aren't aware but a family of foxes has been living in your back garden, and we'd be very grateful if we could make some quick observations.

The way he puts it makes it all sound so simple. Even more impressive, technically every word of it is true, although he's left out the part about my being one of those foxes. Trust Buckley. Now she's gathered that we aren't a threat she actually seems excited about the company. Still, as she grabs an umbrella and they start round the side of the house, I keep a step back – just in case.

We edge past dustbins and a rusting fridge to emerge in an over-grown back garden and my stomach contracts. Ahead of us is my shed. Though, of course, it looks different to *my* shed – what was once a fortress is a tenth of the size, and yet . . .

I overtake the others and push through the long grass. The planks are soft where the paint has flaked away and the windows are feathered with lichen. I never knew our home was in such a bad state but, of course, our real home was underneath. I kick my way round the perimeter until I spy a dislodged brick in the foundation.

Kneeling by the opening, I breathe in a slight sourness but that's all I can be certain of. There *is* something that could be the residue of fox but it could equally be my imagination. Human noses are useless and human ears aren't much better. I'm going to have to rely on vision.

Face to the hole, the rancid air immediately sets me coughing; I clamp my lips and plug the gap around my cheeks with my hands. Complete dark.

A couple of seconds and greys separate from black. The shape closest to me could be an old pizza box – Tomoko and I used to bring them back to suck on the grease. Those ghostly white patches along the far wall – bones? Maybe. The only thing I can be certain of is that the den is abandoned.

I pull back and scrabble amongst the trampled weeds. My back tingles under the old lady's eyes but I keep searching, working round the perimeter of the shed, turning up a couple of feathers and the stiff body of a vole. It's been dead for some time. Tomoko would have eaten it if she were still living here. I shut my eyes and listen to the drip of rain from the crab apple tree; its trunk is stunted, perfume faded to a murmur.

Can this really be my territory? The landmarks of our old haunts have sunk into mud. So hard to believe that I could squeeze into that hole and sleep in that cold, dank space. Yet this has to be my old home. It's not it that's changed.

Contextual spatiality.

Dr Vince's precise voice rises through my memory. In training there was a whole lecture on how the appearance of place changes with each body, another on how to orientate yourself in such scenarios. Academically, I understood the concept, even thought I'd experienced it several times, but faced with it in a place I once called home, it turns out to have depths I hadn't even imagined.

At the swish of grass I look up, somehow expecting Tomoko, but, of course, it's only Buckley. He crouches next to me.

'No?'

I shake my head.

'OK?'

'Yeah.' I cough to cover the croak of my voice.

'Is there a problem?' The woman calls from the path.

'Nothing to worry about. We just think this den has been abandoned.' He lowers his voice and turns back to me. 'She'll have moved on to another earth. There'd be nothing here for her with you gone.'

'What if she got hit?'

'She was over the road. I checked on the recordings. Come on. She'll be with the other cubs, I'm sure of it.'

It's true that Tomoko wouldn't want to den here on her own. I uncurl my hand to reveal the vole — dewdrop eyes misted — and return it to its rest.

Back on the patio, the woman hugs the umbrella, her eyes wide on my muddy hands. I wipe them on my trousers, glad that Buckley distracts her with small talk as he leads the way back round the front. How does he do it? I feel completely empty.

As he sees the woman safely inside the house, I take one last look around. My first impression was right — this is the home of a stranger.

The uncanniness doesn't get any better as we return to the road.

'We can always do this another day,' Buckley says.

I stare up the street, as if recollection were a late bus that might turn the corner any moment.

'No. I want to. It's just—'

'She'll be fine. I promise.'

'It's not that – I just realised that I don't know the way to the allotment. I lived here nearly four months and I don't even know where I am.'

He removes his Specs and shakes off the droplets that have gathered in the scratches of the hydrophobic coating.

'There's no going back, is there?'

Buckley talks about his jumping days so little, it's easy to forget that he's been through nearly everything I have. I scuff the remains of a cigarette butt on the kerb.

'We've got the map,' he says eventually. 'Finding the allotment won't be a problem.'

I'm feeling a little better by the time we reach the allotments. We'll find Tomoko. She'll be settled in with the other cubs. Everything will be fine. I'm still shaking a little but this could equally just be the cold.

Our immediate problem is getting in. As a fox I slipped in and out of here so easily it hadn't even occurred to me that the access might be restricted for humans. Buckley gives the padlock an optimistic shake, but no such luck.

'If we can get someone with a key.'

He gestures at his Specs and starts to type against the back of his free hand, but finding someone willing to come and let us in when it's pissing it down seems unlikely. I start along the link fence, searching for somewhere to squeeze through. There's an old walnut growing just outside not too far along. I place my foot on a knot and swing up for the nearest branch.

'Kit?'

The third branch is a short hop. I crouch there for a second, casting around for my next footing. Claws are a hard luxury to lose.

'I'm not sure this is a good idea.'

I block his voice out to concentrate on edging myself out away from the trunk. Why even have a locked gate when there's this tree here? Hands in contact with the branch, I shuffle forwards until it groans under my weight, and leap—

'Kit!'

By the time I've straightened, Buckley is scrabbling onto the first branch. Seated there he pauses, chest heaving visibly beneath his waterproofs.

I press my face to the fencing. 'Buckley?'

Seeing me he unfreezes, long arms reaching for the second branch.

Buckley, afraid of heights? He was an ornithological phenomenaut in his time.

He looks from his perch to the drop, finally to me. I nod and he jumps, slams into the ground, huddles over his right leg.

'Are you OK?'

For a horrid second he's silent, then he curses. 'You're a fucking monkey.'

I laugh. Only now realising how hard my heart is beating. 'You're a monkey too, just one that spends too much time sat in front of screens.'

'Keeping you out of fucking trouble.'

'Sorry.'

But he's gone quiet again, head bent beneath the patter of raindrops. I can feel that my face is screwed up too. Buckley is in *pain*. Occasionally he'll curse over comms when he spills his coffee in his lap or stubs a toe. There was even one time when he leant too far back in his chair and crashed onto the floor – I never let him forget that – but this is different. Somehow, I almost thought it was impossible for him to get hurt.

I crouch a step away, caught between crawling closer and giving him space. Should I be doing something? If it was Tomoko I'd nibble her ear but I get the impression that would only anger Buckley. Instead I hug my own knee.

'Buckley?

'Buckley?

'Is it . . .

'Can I . . . ?'

The question takes me several starts.

'Should I get someone?'

He shakes his head.

'Is it OK?'

'Fine. Just no more stunts today. Please.' There's flattened anger in his voice and I don't risk saying anything else as I follow him across the allotment. His back is taut, muscles standing out through his raincoat. We know how to be silent together, that's one of the things I like about our friendship, but this feels different. Perhaps it's just the rain; though it's been years since he was a bird, he still hates it.

When we reach the main den it holds no better news. I kneel in the wet grass and pull back my hood to try to listen . . . but there's nothing. If only I had fox senses; a single sniff, a twitch of an ear, would tell me everything I needed to know. But I don't.

I lean in to the hole, ears straining to the point where I can hear the pump of blood inside my own head, but not a murmur of fox. The whole family could be inside right now and I'd never be able to tell.

My hands knuckle against the soft earth. Human hands. Skin their horrifying pallor, thick with their stench. If Tomoko were here she'd only run. My eyes itch with the threat of tears and I laugh. It's so ridiculous. Buckley, huddled inside his raincoat, gives me a strange look.

My smile feels like a leer. Only one more stop to go.

The rain has eased off by the time we reach the road. A tentative spark of sun peers between the clouds. This place is almost peaceful. Nothing is how I remember it today.

I'm aware of Buckley's watchful silence as I pace the small stretch of tarmac. This road is even less familiar than the garden.

There isn't one drop of blood, not a single orange hair. The body must have been disposed of, or dragged off to be eaten, but still, it's almost as if it never even happened.

And, of course, that's when the email arrives.

'Kit?'

From the change in Buckley's tone the disaster must show on my face but strangely I don't really feel it.

'We've been summoned to see Mr Hughes,' I say. There's no need to add what that means, coming right after a meeting with Niti.

I can't meet Buckley's expression, look to the embankment instead. My heart starts to squeeze.

The rustle of grass. Musk, the scent of growth and rot.

A shadow. Eyes of coal.

It steps out into the street light. Fur licked to flame.

An engine roars. Light erupts, wheels squeal.

I leap—

There's an image of a face painted across my eyes. I blink, but the image won't budge. Panic clamps around my chest. The mouth moves but it isn't real. There *shouldn't* be a face there.

I struggle to sit but can't. Then reality flushes into the image and I realise that the face *is* real, that it's Buckley's, somehow leaning over me though he was on the pavement only a second ago. His lips move again but my ears are too full of static to understand. I paw at my forehead, half expecting blood, but only find smooth skin.

Just the fox body. Over now. Over.

Buckley's lips mime.

Kit

It occurs to me that I'm sitting in the middle of the road, that there's a car behind us, a curious face peering over the wheel. Buckley has placed himself between me and it. He helps me up and I stumble over to the pavement.

'Are you OK?'

'The other fox.'

'Tomoko's here?' He glances around.

'No. The other fox.'

His expression is strained.

'That night,' I explain. 'Right before I was hit.'

'There was no other fox. I checked the recordings.'

'It was right there. In the gap in the hedge.' I point but he shakes his head. 'It was dark. It would have been hard to see on your screens.'

He gives up on keeping his trousers dry and sits next to me. 'I suppose.'

Suppose. My fingertips trace the hard grit of the pavement for the certainty of the sensation.

'Buckley.'

'Yes?'

'That night . . .'

'That night?'

Another car rumbles past; I stare through the blur of wheels at dark tarmac.

That night, something died here, there's no doubting that. What I can't work out is whether it was me.

9

Come Home

It all comes back to that fox. It should have been my first sign. So why did I put it to the back of my mind so easily? Because Buckley said he hadn't seen it? Its *wrongness* had been almost visceral, stayed with me for months, though I didn't recognise it for what it was until the next watcher. And by then backing out was impossible.

I glance through the evening dimness towards the fox – *my* fox – curled up amongst the weeds.

'What do you think?' I whisper. 'It couldn't have been anything natural.'

It doesn't stir.

'Not that you're particularly natural yourself ... But I can trust you, can't I?'

The only answer, the drone of rain on leaves.

When it's finally dark, I prepare to leave my hiding place. I can't help hobbling as I set out, last night's run raised blisters on my heels. InRessy I would never let the pain get to me like this; I've been too soft on this body by far.

Right now I need to work out my next move. Seeking the help of another phenomenaut would seem the obvious answer but they're too close to ShenCorp to trust. Even if I could, would it be fair? If Mr Hughes found out he'd only try to silence them too.

Old school friends? We haven't spoken in years.

And Dad?

I slow. Is he worried about my absence? He should still be in Chad, photographing his precious hippos, but he could have been sent a message. It's unlikely though, the polar bear jump was sched-uled to run until the end of the week and if Buckley were to tell him it's been extended he wouldn't think anything of it. As for Mum ...

I perch on a garden wall, eyes watering at the release of pressure from my feet. The fox hunkers down a few steps away and starts to hunt for fleas.

No point pretending, I'm on my own with this. If I want anyone to believe me over ShenCorp, I need proof. And to get proof, I *have* to return to the Centre. Which really would be insanity.

My mind feels a night sky, emptied of all thought; or overcome by one terrible one, too large to see.

'I have to do this, don't I?' I say. 'Go back?'

The fox just nibbles fur showing no sign of even hearing.

The shop windows are still lit on Park Street, mannequins with a hand on a hip or running through hair, but at this hour it seems less of a catwalk and more like teenagers experimenting in front of their bedroom mirrors. Looking feels voyeuristic so I drop my gaze to the pavement where the alchemy of street lights turns the puddles to gold.

At the turning to the Centre, the fox won't go any further.

You're on your own in this, Kit.

I creep on but as soon as I'm close enough to see the gleam of light on the clam logo, feeling flees my legs. The space between me and the entrance could be as substantial as the tarmac itself for all it's in me to walk it.

Coming back here was all very well, but ShenCorp has twenty-four-hour security; if anyone sees me that will be it. I back into the hedge and crouch.

How many times have I walked this road? Hundreds? Thousands? It's become so familiar that I'd stopped even noticing it. Broken now. That old life, so close I could touch, beyond me forever; like finding a frequented bridge collapsed. For a moment of startling vertigo, it could have been years, not a day, since my escape.

A lone car moves through the night, placated to a purr by distance. The back of my neck tingles.

Someone else is here.

I lift my head to find myself staring into two eyes, so white and round they could be moons in orbit of my face. The shadows around them gather to reveal the leer of wonky teeth.

Grandma Wolf.

I burst out of the hedge, stumbling in panic, not caring about staying hidden.

Only the echo of my own footsteps follow but the force of terror carries me. Just keep running, running, running – until I trip.

My hands ring from where they slapped the concrete and for a time all I can do is breathe.

Easy, Kit. Just breeeeathe.

When the static withdraws from my ears, I sit. There's a tear in a trouser leg; these things aren't made to last. I'm lucky it's not that big.

Stupid. So fucking stupid.

Why did I run? Grandma Wolf would be no match for me if it came to a fight – she's even smaller than I am, not to mention old. And it seems unlikely ShenCorp sent her after me. She has enough problems with them of her own.

Last I saw her, it had been a neuroengineer training day and, with Buckley away, I took my lunch in the courtyard. Somewhere nearby, a raven croaked at the greying sky, grumpy with the promise of rain. The twinge of turning weather fretted at my mood too. Still, it wasn't raining yet and walls quickly become oppressive, so I projected the latest draft of the bonobo report onto the bench top and chewed on an apple as I proofread.

Buckley and I would put so much effort into these papers; all those carefully built observations, arguments, 'facts'. Even on the bus home, I'd keep working; for lack of another surface, mapping the document onto the back of a hand where words flexed with skin as if tattooed.

But sometimes I'd wonder, for what? Such marks could never match the experience itself. However much Buckley and Mr Hughes praised me, I'd squirm at their fundamental insufficiency. Because how do you cram the lived experience onto a page? The words available to me were never enough. Something would always slip the sentences. Human language developed around human bodies, it never quite fits other ways of being.

At the time I thought it'd get easier with practice, that I'd find some clever system of staying true to the experience *and* the science, but in retrospect, the opposite was closer. The more I came to understand, the more difficult it was to disseminate. Knowledge that seemed perfectly self-evident inRessy became confused, even insane, back in my Original Body. Truths just wouldn't translate.

But sometimes, between consciousness and sleep, comprehension seemed an itch just beyond the reach of my fingers. Was it understanding, or simply learning to give more of myself over?

Distracted by the report, it took me a while to notice that the raven's cough had quickened into the shrill used for trespassers. I turned and jolted to see an old woman crouched in the flowerbed. White wisps of hair puffed from the gaunt mask of her face, those eyes so dark they were almost black. Yet what was most alarming, what took me longest to believe, was that that croaking came from her throat.

Grandma Wolf.

At least, that's the name she'd been given around the Centre. Though she might look like she could be your crazy grandma, beneath the skin there's nothing human. If Kyle can be believed, he laughed at her once and she chased him up a tree.

This wasn't the first time I'd seen her. She breaks into the Centre every couple of months, making a total joke of the security. But I'd never been caught alone with her like this.

No one knows how she keeps getting in, let alone why she'd want to. I've heard too many rumours about her to count – she was a professor who used to lecture in the building, back when it was part of the university; or a high-class call girl who lost her marbles along with her looks; or even an Asian princess, run away from her responsibilities from across the sea. Although admittedly only Si actually believed that one.

Making sure not to alert her, I opened the message tab in my Specs and dropped Mr Hughes a line. But Grandma Wolf was edging closer. Perhaps there really was something to Kyle's tree story.

She pounced and I leapt from my seat, only to realise that she was already running away. She stopped in a corner of the courtyard and huddled in on herself to stuff her cheeks with what I now realised was my sandwich.

Perhaps salvaging the rest of my lunch and retreating inside would have been the best response, but she was between me and the door, so I sat back down and hugged my coffee in case she decided to go for that as well.

She threw little glares at me as she ate, as if to say 'Don't try it'. But it's not like I wanted the sandwich back now.

With the last bite swallowed, she dropped the remains and sucked on her fingers.

'Hey!' I said. 'You didn't eat the crusts.'

She studied me, fingers still stuck in her gob. And call *me* crazy, but there was something piercingly sane in that look.

I put a hand against the bench, ready to push myself up, but to do what I didn't know.

'How could you steal my lunch and not eat the crusts?' I said, ashamed of the whine in my voice.

The fingers popped out, damp with earth and saliva, but when her lips parted all that emerged was a purple tongue that licked a spot of chutney on her chin.

When she'd first snatched the sandwich I'd thought it the kind of desperate hunger I'm used to inRessy, but now I was wondering if it had been more calculated than that. She had played me for a fool.

Either way, Grandma Wolf couldn't care less, she'd already headed over to the dustbin and stuck her head right inside. I obviously wasn't considered a threat, but despite my annoyance, she was right, I stayed sitting like a stupid lump.

When she emerged, it was with an armful of rubbish. She crouched to sort it – crisp packet on one side, half an apple on the other; a drinks can joined the crisp packet, an umbrella the apple. *Useless and not.*

'Any buried treasure?' I said.

She glanced up long enough to expose a row of yellowed teeth and returned to her sorting. Impossible to tell if it was a smile or a threat. Or both.

'Miu!'

Mr Hughes had appeared in the doorway; yet now he was here, I found myself more annoyed than relieved.

'A while since we've seen you. How about we go for a little walk, eh? Take a turn.'

Grandma Wolf bristled, a snarl curling down her mouth. Condescension was not the tone I would have struck if I'd been Mr Hughes. But he didn't even flinch. Inwardly, I cheered her on to lunge.

When the arm he offered was rejected Mr Hughes looped his hands into the waistband of his trousers and stuck out his gut.

'I was talking to our friends the other day, Miu. They asked after you. Wanted to know if you're being a good girl.'

I couldn't understand it – at those words Grandma Wolf *deflated* as if there had been a pin taken to the pouch of a toad. My teeth bit right through the cardboard of my cup, though I hadn't even noticed I'd been chewing on it. With the savagery emptied from her face, she looked a tired old woman.

'Good girl.' Mr Hughes held out the arm once more. 'Now, how about that walk?'

This time, she took it.

Yet before the door shut behind them, she stabbed a look back at me.

'I'll remember you,' it said.

I had run into Mr Hughes coming out of the lift later that afternoon. Though his weight is more fat than muscle, he carries it like a silverback, and the courage almost left me.

'Mr Hughes?'

'North?' His tone was almost expectant.

'Grandm—' I caught myself. 'That woman in the courtyard. Miu? What you said to her?'

'Yes?'

'You said something about friends? Her friends?'

He tapped his temple. 'Ah yes, Miu's a cunning one, you have to give her that. As she keeps escaping the home, I had to ask her psychiatrist how to deal with her. She hears voices, apparently; "her friends", she calls them. Lord knows what she's thinking. Fairies probably!'

Under that crescent of teeth I felt forced to nod.

'But best keep it to yourself. Patient confidentiality and all that.' He continued down the corridor, a limp hand raised in farewell. 'Don't hesitate to contact me next time you see her.'

Only once the lift doors had shut did I release my breath. Either I was turning into an old cynic early, or that was a steaming pile of bullshit.

'You're as bad as Kyle,' said Buckley when he was back from his training. 'She's mentally disturbed. She deserves our kindness but otherwise you should stay away.'

Then later, when he noticed how quiet I was being: 'Seriously, Kit, put her from your mind.'

And as it was Buckley, I did.

Come Home

A steady drip patters onto my forehead. I poke out my tongue and swill the drops around my mouth but it's more of a tease than anything. Remembering my milk bottle, I grab it from outside the hedge and gulp down the inch of water.

It's day time, human time – this body is human, even if I don't consider myself fully such, and it's hard to overrule instincts like the sleep cycle. It's different inRessy, of course, where inbuilt brainstems give me a different pattern of wakefulness, but I don't have that luxury now.

In the light, I can finally make out the interior of the hedge I found after running from Grandma Wolf. The ground is clotted with crisp packets and the sad worm of a condom. I push the rubbish into a corner with my heel, then try to find a position to avoid the dripping. With enough contortion, I succeed, but within a second it's clear that sleep is beyond my reach. My stomach is screaming hunger and my bowels for a shit. At least I think that's what the sensations mean – sometimes it can be hard to distinguish the two.

Venturing out right now would be foolish; it's broad daylight and this isn't far from ShenCorp. I shut my eyes but it feels like my abdomen is in a vice. The fox is asleep but it would be bound to take offence if I shat here; it's not going to help our relationship if it thinks I'm marking territory. Not to mention that it would be unpleasant to wait out the rest of the day with the smell.

Pain knifes my side again. No choice. I poke my head from the shrub and give a cursory sniff – the iron scent of rain and car fumes. There doesn't seem to be anyone around, though traffic zips past the mouth of the street. No way to avoid being seen but so long as I'm not recognised it'll be fine. Being a phenomenaut is all about calculated risk.

The light is cruel in my eyes as I slip out, my muscles uncoiled and impotent, like when I'm cold-blooded and the sun has yet to blush life into me. My tongue runs over the blunt instrument of my teeth; this body has none of the weaponry I'm used to relying on for hunting. Still, I scour the pavement as I walk – you never know what someone might have dropped.

It's bizarre to stand alongside other humans again, to walk in step as they make their way to work or the shops. I keep expecting someone to call out – 'impostor', 'not human', 'not one of us'. Can't they see through the thinness of skin? I feel I must wear my otherness on my sleeve, but for the most part people don't even look. The rain helps, people are too busy hurrying to reach the dry to take much note, and yet it seems there really *is* nothing to mark me out. So I'm almost glad when a suited lady lifts her umbrella to flash my bare feet a frown. Sinking seamlessly into the morass of humanity would feel like a lie.

And yet it makes me queasy to wonder who could be watching. A casual remark passed to the wrong person could end in disaster. At least ShenCorp won't go to the police. They'll want to keep this quiet. For a second I ponder going to the station myself but dismiss the thought quickly. Who in their sane mind would believe my story over Mr Hughes?

It must be a recycling day because a green tub sits outside every house and after a bit of rummaging, I find some shoes held together with a rubber band. But they just squeeze against my blisters, so I toss them back.

A small bush overhangs the street, heavy with red berries; even without the ultra-violet allure seen through a bird's eyes they look tasty, yet eating them wouldn't be a good idea. I'm going to have to be careful not to confuse foods that are safe inRessy with those the human body can handle. No Buckley to remind me what's poisonous now.

Finding somewhere to go to the toilet isn't any easier. I hesitate outside a pub for a good five minutes, not because I don't believe that I could sneak in without being seen, but the idea of being trapped inside four walls fills me with panic.

In the end I find a patch of scrub in a derelict garden and scrape out a small hole to squat over. The shit is loose and smells worse than it should but this isn't exactly a surprise, not after my stomach has had nothing but milk and nutrient drip for over a week. I bury it with the earth and stamp it down. Leaving my scent around like this feels risky but Mr Hughes thinks like such a human he can be relied on not to track me by smell.

Back via the pub, the greasy waft of cooking rises from vents below the street. It's almost too much. On the other side of the building some industrial rubbish bins sit in the side alley. I lift a lid and rummage. Admittedly the human digestive system is more fickle than others but opposable thumbs have their uses — if Tomoko and I had been able to open these we never would have gone hungry.

Sniffing the bags doesn't reveal much; all I can identify with this nose is the stench of refuse. The only human sense one can ever really rely on is sight, so I pull out a bag at random and gut it. Slimy gunk slides out, wriggling with maggots. Their squirming transfixes me. Those sightless, tender bodies. The stark scent of rot.

My feet stumble back before my thoughts catch up and the lid slams shut. No. Maggots may be a tasty protein snack as a fox but not a good idea in this body.

'Hey!'

A man stands in the alley entrance. I don't recognise him from ShenCorp, but that means nothing. I leap up onto the bin and launch myself at the top of the wall. One foot is seized, but then the other connects with flesh and I'm free. I land hard on the other side and launch into a hobbling run.

His shouts thin to nothing at the end of the street – he's not following, didn't even try. Not ShenCorp then, surely? Maybe just one of the pub employees. The relief surges into my head and I sink to the pavement.

A woman across the street looks back at me as she pushes on a door, face twisted with pity and fear. What must I look like to her? Some homeless teenager? And yet, isn't that what I am now?

Animals without territories never last long.

I shrug my chin inside the coat. Until I work out a way to get inside the Centre, I need to figure out how to survive. That means I need shelter, water, food – the three essentials I'd scout out at the beginning of any jump, so why does the thought seem so daunting now?

I grind the ball of a palm into my forehead. Hunger has thinned my thoughts to a thin gruel. InRessy it was never like this; even when my body was starved, it never affected my thinking to this extreme – my brain, back at the Centre, always had enough substance from the nutrient drip.

When it's clear that pummelling my brow isn't going to work, I let my head fall back. Black clouds distend the sky, their weight reaching down to settle into my bones. I'm trapped – the past unreachable, the future a gaping chasm; my only option slipping sideways along the numb infinity of nows. If ShenCorp finds me they will lock me up, four tight walls, the stranglehold of their truth, accept it or rot.

I should have seen it coming. People can never stand the challenge of another point of view. It was there when I told people about my job; clear in the curling of lips, or widening of eyes. Once or twice people simply turned away. Animals are just animals, they would proclaim, for eating, for servitude, for entertainment, not for *understanding*. Buckley would call them idiots, yet it never seemed to me as simple as that. They were more scared than stupid. Sometimes I can almost see it myself: if the sun can't revolve around the earth and men must be born of monkeys, shouldn't at least our version of reality go unchallenged? For the alternative is, what? Uncertainty as far as the eye can see. It's much easier to call any challenge mad, stupid, *animal*, much easier to silence the alternatives. I curl my fists against the crumbling concrete.

But I'm being watched.

The woman from earlier is at the window, frowning. Though I don't recognise her, that doesn't mean anything when it comes to ShenCorp. I rush back to my hedge.

Back inside, I curl up shaking. Sleep still seems an impossibility; the leap from the wall burst my blisters and now my feet throb with the kind of dull hurt that spreads throughout your entire body. It's just a matter of focus but right now I can't seem to push the pain away.

During jumps I'm a master of waiting – the long sleepless nights crouched in the roots of a tree or the slow stalk of a hunt, these are the kinds of infinite spaces that will drive you mad if you try to fill them, so instead I learnt to let them fill me. But something more than pain is keeping me from that space right now. Can't think straight, but can't not think either. I wrap the babygros around my feet and tug on the knots until the new ache is almost worse than that of the blisters.

At a huff, I look up and see the shadow of the fox stir. It freezes at the sudden movement.

'Hey, it's just me.'

But the turn of phrase leaves me cold. 'Just me.' I'm not sure who that is any more.

Uncanny Shift

'We don't know that the meeting is to lay you off.'

Although Buckley is only trying to help, I don't want to have this conversation yet again. More than anything, I'd like to eat my clam in peace.

My beak parts crunch through the shell and I use what I can only think of as my tongue to push a remaining fleck out of my mouth.

'I know you're worried but Mr Hughes would be a fool to get rid of you. You're our best phenomenaut,' Buckley says. So much for the quiet meal.

'But I got the fox Ressy killed,' I say, swallowing the flesh. 'The whole study wrecked.'

His hesitation speaks volumes. A wave rumbles above, tugging the bulb of my head into a wobble.

'We secured plenty of usable data. Just because we can't think of a benign reason for the meeting doesn't mean there isn't one.'

I don't grace that with an answer.

There's a chalky taste up one of my tentacles and I look to see that it's clutching a rock. It drops it under my scrutiny, almost guiltily. Another glance tells me that the other tentacles are milling along the sand, probing as if with bored nonchalance.

'Dammit.'

'It'll be fine.'

'No, not that,' I say. 'These tentacles are driving me nuts.'

Without looking, it's impossible to tell where my limbs are at any moment, though the influx of information would fry my mind if I could. Eight tentacles make the inbuilt Ressy neural matter necessary, but it also means that each limb comes worryingly close to autonomy.

'How can they move by themselves and yet their taste and touch be mine?'

'If you were born an octopus I suppose it would seem completely natural.'

'I can't imagine this ever being natural.'

Another tentacle unfurls towards the rock and I curl it under my body. It almost feels like being possessed.

But I'm wasting time. Sperlman's crippled me for nearly an hour and as an invertebrate I'll have to pull out at the end of the day. This isn't a long study; we'll need to have the population profiling well under way ready to make observations tomorrow.

So move.

All it takes is the intention and the tentacles get to work pulling me along the seabed. It's amusing to watch their swaying tiptoe, like that of a drunk, lanky gentleman. Silt sifts around my tentacles, the touch ripe with the taste of grit and brine, but I have no real sense of how the movement is taking place. Although the minutiae of locomotion are always carried out by the Ressy ganglia, never before have I experienced this distance, as if this body were more *it* than *me*.

Even in the gentle current, my flesh feels flaccid; inside is only flexibility, as if I could simply stretch out of myself, on and on until cells break into molecules, indistinguishable from the water I breathe. That was the worst of Sperlman's this morning, the sense that this Ressy has no concrete form at all.

Sand undulates about me in every direction; here and there outcrops of coral jut up like many-fingered hands reaching for the glass ceiling. The gentle push of water. Unbroken quiet.

Until it isn't.

The roar is more force than sound. Water torn. I tumble, vertigo like pain, my innards smashed jelly.

Only for the roar to stop. As abruptly as it began.

I fall to the seabed, stark taste of sand across my head, guts a beaten drum. For a while all I can do is lie, watching the silt resettle into a silence so pure it's hard to believe that it was ever broken.

'That'll be the oil rig. You OK?' Buckley says.

'Just about.' Although if that happens a lot, I'm not going to be.

The patter of his fingertips, like drizzle on a window. 'Readings aren't pretty. You can see how the drilling is causing damage to the cephalopods.'

'No joke.'

But the last trembles of the roar have stilled to silence, so there's nothing to do but pull myself up and keep going.

At my passing, a tiny fish buried in the sand throws up a puff of silver. One tentacle snakes after the meaty taste, returns grudgingly at my command. This is getting stupid. I whip them behind me and start jetting. The squirt of water from my sphincter feels like a wet fart.

My body distorts under the speed, the bulb of my head stretching as if trying to separate from my eyes. My largest heart throbs at my nape, seeming to tow behind a beat late.

Furrows of silt sprint below; above, canopies of coral, the sky fractured into serpents of light. Pressure washes over my skin like headwind, as if I were not so much swimming as floating on heavy air. I've had dreams like this, where, with enough willpower, I can rise over the houses and glide.

When my sphincter starts to ache from the passage of water, I return to my crawl. All the while, I'm looking, eyes puckering and bulging from my head. But still no sign of octopus. The tentacles aren't helping the search; they make a beeline for every crustacean and piece of flotsam we pass. It's got to be bad control on my part ... or a sign of failing plasticity, but it's hard not to think of them as other creatures tethered to my own body.

I start an inner monologue with them, careful not to let it rise to the level of sub-vocalisation and freak Buckley out.

Leave the crab, leave the crab, leave the fucking crab. Run. Run, you useless pieces of spaghetti. I'm doing this for, you know. That is just a pebble, get over it already. Will you drop the goddam crab!

A foul taste prickles over my skin, all three hearts jolt as one. A silhouette sweeps across the sky, the beat of a tail taking bites from the heavens. *Danger.*

The jet bursts from me and I race for cover. Even at a sprint, the foul taste is growing, water turning putrid. Wrong. Wrong. Wrong.

I flatten to the coral, suckers clinging to the foamy taste. A violent shudder passes through me, then stills. Without eyelids there's no choice but to watch the seabed turn black.

I am stone. I am coral. Not a tasty octopus. Coral. Coral.

It stops overhead, plunging me into night. Pressure bulges inside my head, gills paralysed, though my hearts beat so fast they feel like birds lodged inside my head. Waves beat me from the monster's lazy turn, fetid with the taste of death.

Can't die. Not again.

But the light has started to return, death receding into the salted freshness of water. And it's gone.

'That was amazing,' Buckley says.

My suckers release the coral with a shiver.

'Amazing is not the word I would use.'

'I mean your camouflage.'

'Camouflage?' I say.

'You went from brown to the same rusty red as the coral, just like that.'

That explains the prickling sensation I felt upon reaching my hiding place.

'Oh,' I say, not sure what to think of the fact that my skin can sense colours where I can't. Though the ability did just save me from becoming dinner. Perhaps it's not so bad my tentacles have ideas of their own.

'OK to get on? We don't have much time left today,' Buckley says.

'Yeah.' You can't let being hunted get to you too much as a phenomenaut.

But being out in the open no longer feels safe. I run between the outcrops, the raised puffs of sand thickening my passage with the taste of chalk. At every rock, my tentacles fling themselves out in a hug. Letting go is harder. Eventually, I build a routine: taste, listen, look . . . now run, run, run.

As the next outcrop nears, I slow. There, in the fissure – octopus. Its gills flicker, one eye bulging between sensual tentacles and cold tingles over my skin. However many times I come eye to eye with something so other, I am never prepared.

B-movies make it seem so simple – kill them before they kill us. If peaceful, a simple 'take me to your leader' will suffice; after all, most aliens are just blue space ladies beneath the tentacles. But octopuses have no language; no leader to be taken to if they had. And yet the octopus's eyes are studying me as intently as I am it.

It makes me feel inferior as a phenomenaut. My whole job, trying to understand, when how could I? It's like trying to hammer a square mind into a round hole. Translation turns to static in the wires.

The octopus's body has blackened like an ink blotter; its tentacles stiffened into a disc. I'm alarmed to see that mine have echoed it; this must be a threat display. *Loosen*, I think, but nothing happens; if anything my unease is making them turn darker.

'Stop tormenting it,' Buckley says.

'I don't mean to! These tentacles have a mind of their own.'

'Leave it to its territory then. I've marked its position.'

Buckley's right, the first of its tentacles is edging out, even though I am clearly larger and healthier. If I stay any longer it will probably attack. This is its territory – what choice does it have?

As I speed away, my bowels loosen in a thick spurt. I'd bet anything it's ink, this body is such a coward – or rather, *I* am.

My search continues, sluggish, fruitless. After another hour I begin to wonder whether there aren't as many octopuses here as the scientists think. You certainly can't blame them for not choosing to live here – every time the roar returns, my head seems to splinter.

In the distance, a mountain of rock glooms up from grey water. I jet towards it, its mass revealing coral cities of spherical palaces and skyscrapers, swaying with the waves.

Fish work over the coral, transformed into angels as they pass through the breaks of light. One draws near as I land, darting in clear aggression. I herd my tentacles away as they start to reach for it – that beak could hide a nasty bite. It stays in pursuit as I pull my way over the roots, so I stop and regard it with my best eye, trying to remember my earlier threat display. The tingling returns to my skin and the fish speeds away.

My gill hearts feel weak from the exercise, so I crawl into a crack in the rock.

'How much longer until Come Home?'

'We can give it another half hour. I'd bet anything this outcrop turns up another octopus.'

'That was my thought.'

A saline taste alerts me that a tentacle has grabbed a scrap of seaweed. In my distraction, the other tentacles have started to snatch for the scrap too.

I hurl the seaweed from me, wincing as the tentacle bashes against the rock.

'Fuck!'

It's as if these limbs were toddlers, into everything unless I keep an eye on them at all times.

'OK?'

'I'm losing it. I really am.'

Of course I failed the plasticity test. I'm nineteen. It was only a matter of time.

'That's not true,' Buckley says.

'Then why can't I handle this?'

'Because it's an octopus. Two-thirds of the neural matter is outside the brain. You've never handled a Ressy like it.'

All three hearts have lifted into a tidal wave.

'I should be able to,' I say.

'It's an invertebrate, anyone would find it hard.'

'It's not like I'm getting sensory deprivation.'

'That's not the point. It's a biological system that diverged from the type of bodies you're used to 700 million years ago. You're not going to adjust in a matter of hours.'

He's speaking sense, I know he is, yet that can't stop the dread.

'Kit. You're our best phenomenaut, they're not going to lay you off unless there's an inescapable reason.'

'Like a failed plasticity test?'

Now it's his turn to not answer. I pull the tentacles beneath me and stare out into endless ocean.

'What am I going to do?'

'I don't know,' he says.

Uncanny Shift

'We were all very relieved to hear that there's no lasting harm.' Mr Hughes swivels as he talks, the creak of his chair almost pained. 'Very relieved indeed.'

I give a quick nod by way of reply. He's always had the ability to make his bulk appear to take up even more space than it already does and my body has replied, almost subconsciously, by shrinking into my seat. Whenever I delude myself that the Centre is my territory, his presence is enough to correct the error.

'I'm sorry not to have come and said hello properly until now but, as you'll understand in a minute, I have been preoccupied lately.'

Catching my expression, he pauses on a smile but from Mr Hughes this is no reassurance. Seven years as my boss and he's still an unknown entity. Considering that my job is to understand the perspective of other animals, what does it say that every time I try to imagine stepping inside his shoes, I hit a horizon of static? He's just too good at dissembling, Mr Boss Man, smile, handshake, bark.

And yet sometimes I catch a glimmer in those dull eyes, as if he were watching himself through mine, smug at the effect. If I had to give this unease a name, I'd call it Uncanny Valley.

But I can live with that. I can live with the two-faced attitude, glibness, shit-eating, smile, smile, smile; with Niti's check-ups and the lack of privacy; with the corporate lingo, buzz-words, acronyms, 'let's watch the profit margins', *team-building exercises!*; watercooler rumours, stakeholders, HR, marketing. I can live with all of it, if they'll only let me keep jumping.

'So.' He darts forwards, alarmingly fast for such a large man. 'You're looking well. You're feeling well, I take it?'

'Fine.' My throat is almost too dry to speak. 'Thank you.'

'Excellent. Excellent.'

His bluster is more disconcerting than reassuring. The familiar space of his office has taken on a waiting quality, the gleam of chrome and black glass an almost claustrophobic intensity. Buckley sits stiffly in the chair next to me, as if he were a patient awaiting prognosis.

Glancing at his arm, lying on the rest between us, my fingers twitch with an irrational urge to reach out and dig into the firmness of muscle. I press them between my knees instead, not trusting them to wander, octopus-like, and cling. Noticing, Buckley smiles; eyes winced, as though my imagined grip were real.

If I am laid off, if he stops being my neuroengineer, what will we be? The idea is so monumental that processing it is impossible. I'm left instead with a blank, like turf over a fresh grave.

'I suppose we should be thankful that inRessy deaths don't happen more often, this job being what it is,' Mr Hughes is saying. 'Though, of course, that doesn't make them any easier when they do.'

Yet noticing our quiet, his hands come together in an abrasive clap. 'But to business. I've received Niti's latest report and am delighted to say that everything is looking excellent, as ever. However, she is a little concerned that this – incident – may have caused some distress. Her recommendation is that we should err on the side of caution.'

Caution. ShenCorp really does has a euphemism for everything. Dying, being sacked, having your brainwaves mangled to remotely connect with another body, do they really think what you call it makes a difference?

He sucks in a breath. 'I've therefore made the decision to remove you from Research.'

And there it is. Over. No more. But as I crumple, Mr Hughes holds up a hand.

'Don't look so glum. The new job I've lined up for you will be much more to your liking. Research, as you know, relies on long-term projects, which Niti felt could be causing unnecessary—' He clicks his fingers to summon the word.

Why is it only now that my body has chosen to tremble?

'You're saying, I can keep jumping?'

'Of course.' His frown suggests genuine puzzlement. 'Just for a different department.'

'But, I don't know anything about the development side of things.'

'Don't worry. We have no intention of putting you with Tech.'

I open my mouth, then shut it. ShenCorp *doesn't do* anything outside of Research and Tech.

A strange intensity has pulled Buckley to the edge of his seat.

'Of course, you're confused,' Mr Hughes says. 'That's because you don't know what I do. Regardless of your little accident, I've been planning for us to have this conversation for some time. Remind me, North, how long have you been with us?'

'About seven years.'

'Seven.' He shakes his head. 'And all that time without a promotion. Well, let me reassure you that this move is going to put you right where your talents merit, at the heart of Professor Shen's newest phenomenautical venture.'

I look, wide-eyed, to Buckley. His fingertips are practically dancing on the armrest but, catching my eye, he tilts his head at Mr Hughes. *Concentrate*.

Mr Hughes starts swivelling once more, not even trying to hide his smugness – surprise was obviously the reaction he was hoping for.

'Don't worry, you two weren't supposed to know. Though I can't help but notice, Buckley, that you don't seem as shocked as I might have expected.'

Buckley's grin becomes a smirk. I don't think I'd ever get away with that, but Mr Hughes only seems amused. Though he's always had more respect for Buckley; yes, he's my senior, but only by five years or so. I've always suspected it's a man thing.

'Well, I know there has been some gossip amongst the neuro-engineers, but we've tried to keep the project on a need-to-know basis. Believe me when I say that this day has been a long time in the making. So without further ado, let me just say that I am delighted to welcome you on board' – he spreads his hands, relishing the drama – 'the world's very first Consumer Phenomenautism project.'

'Consumer?'

'You heard me.'

'But that's—' I start to say, but out of the corner of my eye, I see Buckley shake his head.

Mr Hughes turns to him.

'This, of course, concerns you too, Maurice. Our longest-lasting neuroengineer and phenomenaut duo. There isn't a pair that I'd more happy to put forward for the job.'

'So we've beaten Sauntertech to the punch?' Buckley asks.

'Wasn't even a competition.'

I feel too sick to join in with their laughter, with relief or shock I don't know. Of course, the idea of Consumer Phenomenautism has been bandied about for years; Sauntertech have been making noises about crowdfunding such a project but they never managed to gather enough backers; for something like this you need serious money. Yet, whilst we've undoubtedly deeper pockets, I'm not convinced that the real hurdles will be different for us.

'So what exactly are we talking about?' I break in. 'Body Tourism?'

'Yes. High-end luxury consciousness projection. Zoological for the present, of course, but – well, who knows where it will take us.'

'Right,' I say. Sure, Phenomenautism is fascinating, mind-blowing, but how do they expect tourists to cope with Sperlman's and Uncanny Shift? Even if they've found a way to diminish the discomfort, how can they get around the fact that Phenomenautism leaves you – what? Exhausted? Confused? No, it's more a sense of . . . slipping, of being stretched . . . like a snake trying to ingest a crocodile.

But Mr Hughes has finally noticed I'm not joining in the celebration. 'North? Is there a problem?'

'No. I was just wondering how, well, tourists are supposed to handle it all.'

But at this he only brightens.

'Of course, this is an important issue, which is exactly where you two come in. You are to be our voices of experience. We aren't going into this blind. The Ressies must be trialled, the experience streamlined. But the board will fill you in on the details. We'd best be moving.'

I put my hands to my knees, uncertain whether to follow as he levers himself from the seat, and watch with bemusement as he stops by the door, where two JumpPallets are set up. Only now do I notice the CP on each. The question seems so ridiculous for a second I struggle to voice it.

'We're jumping?'

'Quickest way to London. Help North, will you?' he says to Buckley. 'There's on-board monitoring but you'll need to calibrate.'

The smugness of his smile belies the extravagance. Buckley looks as astounded as I feel. Though I've never seen a breakdown of the running costs for projection, it has to run to a figure many times that of a train fare.

Mr Hughes sits on the closest pallet and slips on his CP. He's done this before, hasn't he? Of course, adults can jump, we're the only projection company to employ teenage phenomenauts, but, as the competition's profits demonstrate, adult adaption time is terrible.

'What Ressies will we be?' I say.

He just smiles. 'You'll see.'

I hug the CP to my chest. Jumping blind is unheard of.

'But if I'm expected to talk?'

Unless we'll be parrots. I feel myself redden at the thought of sitting in front of a room of suits, cracking peanuts between my beak.

He flaps a hand. 'Why don't you jump up on the pallet and find out.'

At my look, Buckley gives an apologetic shrug. There's no BodySupport laid out so we can't be going for long, but I wish I'd been given a chance to go to the loo beforehand. I'd never be able to live down pissing myself in my boss's office.

I settle onto the pallet and position the cap on my head.

'Quickly. We're short on time.'

I look sideways to see Mr Hughes, jowls spread against the leather of his pallet, the mound of his belly presented upward, not even concerned what this could mean for his dominance. It's then that understanding hits me – he trusts me, I'm not being sacked, this is really happening.

'Just a sec,' Buckley says. I glance up with silent pleading as he fiddles with the in-helmet settings, but for what I don't know. He squeezes my shoulder but there's no time for anything else. The electromagnets clunk as they go live. A light on my CP blinks. Any second now—

———

Noise like rain. Static in darkness, then sounds shape into words.

'Audio, patched in. Testing.'

A sharp note.

'Audio, online. Visuals, connecting.'

The voice is wrong. Too flat. Too dead.

Light flares, revealing a ceiling fitted with a long strip lamp. Why am I lying down? I was in Mr Hughes's office a second ago. I try to sit up but fail to even move.

'Visuals, online. Initial projection, complete.'

Projection? But if this is a jump, where's Buckley? This voice doesn't even sound human.

'Time – three p. m.'

A click separates the words. An AI?

'Location, London.'

London. Yes, I remember now. Mr Hughes, Body Tourism. Last thing I remember is Buckley squeezing my shoulder.

'Buckley? Are you there?' I sub-vocalise.

No reply.

'Buckley?'

His absence has a cold viscosity.

'In an emergency, please psych the exit-potential.'

I roll my eyes, taking in the tight corners of the ceiling, tinged blue in the harsh lighting. A shimmer-like heat distortion ripples across my vision.

'Embodiment – female, human. Patching in proprioceptive signals, in 3 ... 2 ... 1.'

Wrong

In here, out there, this body is *wrong*.

Hair tingles, the edifice of skin drawn taut; beneath, the spasm of muscles. Then sudden awareness of a pounding heart; its beat, huge, inside of me; followed by the splutter of lungs, as if surfacing from drowning. I cough and the uncanniness fades. For Sperlman's, that was nothing.

Before I've even begun to move, I can feel that there's something odd about this Ressy, though it's hard to say exactly what, because the more I think about it, the more normal it seems. With a jolt, I roll my eyes to one side and see a pale arm extending away from me, no fur to speak of.

Yes. The voice said human. A *human Ressy*.

I stare back at the ceiling, not sure what to make of the realisation. No wonder Mr Hughes was acting so strangely. ShenCorp has really gone there. Someone was bound to sooner or later, but still, like Consumer Phenomenautism, I hadn't expected it so soon. Or both at once. What else has ShenCorp been keeping quiet about?

'Protocol, complete. Projection, complete.' The machine's whisper is nothing like Buckley's chatter.

I breathe out and try to settle myself into the rawness of my new presence – though in these moments it can almost feel as if I don't even have a distinct form. Only in my back against the pallet and the movement of air in and out of my lungs is there any sensation at all.

It's as I begin to move that I start to notice the changes – maybe longer legs, heavier chest. The wrongness of Sperlman's has completely vanished, but a different type of disquiet is left in its place – this feels less like becoming something new and more like a distortion of my Original Body.

'Mirror, activating. Please familiarise yourself, with yourself.'

The ceiling flickers on to reveal the image of a slender woman lying across a pallet. She's dressed in a high-collared grey suit with a plunging neckline; pale face crowned by glossy, black hair. I'd forgotten how much hair weighs. The glow of her skin suggests that she is in her early twenties, though of course that's a misleading way of thinking when it comes to Ressies.

I lock eyes with hers, a staring contest I'm destined to lose because she's – well, me. My mind struggles to believe it, but of course it has to be true. Becoming another species is one thing, but this is a human face, imprinted with all the social connotations of personality and history I've been trained to read since birth – now mine. It shows an expression of shock.

But acceptance will come with moving. I start psyching at limbs and the mirror reflects her – my – movements as I fumble across the head; fingering the lifted eyebrows, much thinner than my own; plush lips; an elfin chin. Then further, a sharp collarbone, large breasts, tight ribcage, no belly to speak of. But struck with the feeling that I'm groping someone, I put the hands – my hands – flat back on the pallet. No, for now this is mine, *me*. I poke the belly, marvelling at the lack of fat, and wince as I jab right into bone.

In a funny way it reminds me of the times I'd study myself in front of the mirror when puberty first kicked in. Back then I felt as if my own body was collaborating against me, morphing in front of my eyes. I'd even try to squash everything back into place; ironic, considering a couple of years later the prodding was aimed at emphasising the same curves. Airbrushing seemed so easy, flesh so stubborn. In my lowest moments I wanted to lash out at the doppelgänger in the mirror, who dared to wear my face yet resisted my wishes. But, thanks to Phenomenautism, I don't have to be either of those girls.

An affinity has finally started to grow for the image in the mirror and I think about the nerves responding to touch in my face and hands, how the Relay is, this moment, pinging them to my brain in Bristol.

'North. Are you ready?' A man has appeared by the pallet.

I sit up. 'Yes. Sorry.'

'Excellent. The board is waiting.' His voice has an American twang, though anglicised, as if he's lived here for a long time.

He waits quietly as I swing my feet to the floor. I curse beneath my breath to see that I'm wearing ridiculous high heels, expecting Buckley to laugh in sympathy but, of course, he's not there. My hands tighten around the edge of the JumpPallet.

Perhaps this Ressy is programmed to handle heels. Some kind of inbuilt movement package is standard for most Ressies, no phenomenaut can be expected to intuitively know the 'how to' of flying or swimming, but perhaps they think it's easy adapting to another human.

'So? What do you think?' the man says.

I glance up, double-take at that face: a proud nose; mouth kinked with the hint of a smile. Most of the men who work in Phenomenautism are more comfortable with Bayesian Neurotranslative than bench presses but even obscured by his suit, he's clearly toned. I've only seen men like him in magazines.

'About the Ressy,' he adds at my pause. Though I realise with a strange alarm that he's looking at me appraisingly too. No, someone like that would never be interested in me. Except, of course, this Ressy is far prettier than my Original Body. But surely he knows that he's just attracted to the Ressy.

'Oh. Um, it's – strange,' I say.

One of those shapely eyebrows quirks.

'Strange in that it doesn't feel strange,' I say. 'That it almost feels normal.'

'Ah, yes.' He smiles radiantly. 'This is just an early model, we'll arrange a less "strange" ResExtenda for you soon.'

'How long have ShenCorp been using human Ressies? If you don't mind me asking,' I say.

'Oh, just under a year. All hush hush, of course.'

'Won't people find out?'

'Only once our marketing team has done its work. We're confident that positive public perception can be engineered if they're eased into it.'

'But aren't human Ressies still—' What? Wrong? Creepy? I'm not sure what words to give this prickle of feeling. Though most arguments against *Homo sapiens* Ressies are thinly disguised anthropocentrism, I can't quiet my unease.

'I wouldn't have thought you would be the sort to be troubled, North.'

North. With a sinking feeling I look around and see another JumpPallet, empty, then back at him.

'You're—'

'Mr Hughes, who else?' he says.

Oh god. What on earth was I thinking?

'I can't describe how good it is to be strong again.' His arms bulge against the shirt sleeves as he flexes. Don't do that. Why would he do that?

My glare only seems to amuse him.

'Now you see the potential of the Tourism? It's just zoological for now, like I said, but as soon as the public are adjusted to the idea ... ' He winks.

'Right.' I look away. Being attracted to my boss is more than I can face right now. The image of his ageing, obese Original Body flashes into my mind. It's not fair, not right, that he can slip into another face like that.

'Come on. They're waiting.'

I catch the flash of a grin before he turns, bastard. But I follow, willing my cheeks to cool; this body blushes alarmingly easily. At least it appears I can walk in these heels. In my Original Body I'd be flat on my face by now.

Entering the next room, a dozen pairs of eyes fall on me; businessmen and businesswomen sit at a round table, all young, all well dressed. Everything about the scene, from the sleek white decor and the fresh flowers to the cut of their suits, speaks quietly but forcefully of money.

'Here.' The man – Mr Hughes – gestures to the nearest chair and I perch as he joins the others. The board are seated in a semi-circle up the other end, quiet interest on their faces, though I don't know what they expect to be able to see – I've been this body for less than five minutes, it's hardly to going to bare my soul.

Aware that my face is still warm, I look down at the table. Rainbows pool in the digiglass like oily puddles, sun's whiteness split to reveal colour. A dreamlike sensation ebbs through me . . . as if I'm hovering a centimetre above the seat, or not quite here. Without Buckley to keep an eye on the CP, the signals appear to be slipping a little. I blink a couple of times and the weight of reality returns.

On the opposite side of the table, Mr Hughes has slipped into a chair next to a man I don't recognise. He whispers in his ear, making the other man chuckle. I grip my hands beneath the desk, wondering whether they're joking about me. The rest of the board waits on them; whoever this man is, he's obviously the alpha.

When he turns, the touch of his intense green eyes is almost physical.

'Katherine. Sperlman's wasn't too uncomfortable, I hope?'

'It was fine. Thank you, sir.'

'Good.' He flips an open hand. 'But, please, no need for formalities. Call me Arthur.'

I nod, though really I'm wondering about the absence of a surname. Could he be Professor Shen? The professor leaves the running of the Centre to Mr Hughes, refusing to meet even the most prestigious clients. It's always been clear that the science is Shen's real interest and a new paper appears every year or so, but research requires funding and the smell of money around Body Tourism might have been enough to entice the professor out from the rumoured lab in Switzerland. Or island in the Bahamas, depending on whose speculation you prefer. Admittedly, he looks far too young to have been developing the nascent consciousness projection experiments forty years ago, but it's always hard to tell with the super rich.

'Mr Hughes tells me that you were one of the very first official phenomenauts,' Arthur says.

'I suppose,' I say. Although that doesn't mean much. It was the vanguard of university students like Buckley who took the real risks.

'And the longest-working phenomenaut to date?'

'I guess.'

Arthur glances at Mr Hughes who shakes his head.

'More than guess. To our estimate, North has been projecting for two years longer than anyone else on record.'

'Seven years.' Arthur's eyebrows perk and he leans back with a smile. 'A savant in our midst. I should have worn a better suit this morning.'

His smile includes me in its warmth but I don't like the pattering of laughter. If this really is Shen, it doesn't come as much surprise that he's such a smug git.

'Please do.'

I follow the point of his open palm and I jolt to see a tray has appeared in front of me. On it is a half-moon pastry and tall glass of coffee. At the sight my stomach grumbles and I realise I'm ravenous, the kind of hunger I've only known when a Ressy's been kept on nutrient fluids for a long time. I can feel the heat rising off the pastry, tinged with sweet fruitiness. It's got to just be psychological, but whilst I'm never as hungry as a human as I am in other bodies, it always seems more difficult to ignore. Context, I guess.

'So. We have your CV here.' Arthur pulls a sheet of paper towards him. 'Zoological work. Several papers in *Nature*, I see?'

I nod. The pastry crackles lightly between my teeth, then melts to nothingness on my tongue. No expense has been spared on the food either.

'Good working relationship with your neuroengineer. Excellent plasticity results. Impressive range of Ressy animalia. Extremely impressive. Your specialisation?'

I have to bring up a hand to catch the crumbs from the pastry, swallowing quickly.

'Oh, um, endangered mainly. I've sort of carved out a niche looking at species adaption to the influence of humans. So, animals that thrive in human environments or those that are being driven to extinction. That's why I've worked with such a range; it means that I can be working in almost any phylum from week to week. Well, within reason. Not fungi or anything.'

But I'm babbling.

Arthur raises an eyebrow at Mr Hughes. 'Seven years on endangered. We're wasting her in Research.'

'That was my thought when I recommended her.'

It's hard not to cringe as they turn their teeth back on me. From humans, smiling isn't a threat display. Or so I try to reassure myself.

'Not to be rude,' I say, 'but I like my current role. It's important.'

'Of course it is. And it's because of your exemplary work in that capacity that we're now entrusting you with this important role. *The* most important, one might say.'

'Right.' I search from one face to the next. I have the strangest feeling that our words are piling, useless, on the table between us. 'Sorry, but I'm not even sure quite what this job entails?'

'Of course. We're getting ahead of ourselves. I believe Mr Hughes has filled you in on the basics?'

'Body Tourism? Right?' I find my voice raising in question despite myself. Even now I can't quite believe it.

'That's it! Let's see if we can't flesh out some details. Alison?'

He swings round to face a petite lady. She rises and the room dims, so that I can now see that the table is lit with the soft glow of the Milky Way.

'Body Tourism –' the woman lets the words sink in as she looks to each of us in turn – 'is to be the world's first phenomenautical consumer venture. Eventual markets will include business, transportation and communications, but at present the focus is on private tourism.'

At a curl of her fingers, forms begin to bubble up from the table, the shadowy suggestion of creatures dissolving through each other. A dog, an eagle, a lion. These are true holograms, not SpecSpace illusions. What sort of investors must they have secured for this project?

'As a high-end luxury product, our marketing team is aiming to attract international clientele, especially American. Though due to the US ban on projection, all centres will be UK based at present.

'Later, foreseen advances in technology will allow cheaper packages to be rolled out to the wider public and, with projected improvements in monitoring AI, we hope to introduce home Phenomenautism kits within the next decade.'

A silver horse solidifies from the mist to canter around the table, rendered in perfect detail. One man nods appreciatively.

'The initial ResExtendas will all be animal, but we aim to bring out human models once marketing feels the public are ready. Each body was selected through extended discussions with our focus groups, and they are being produced at the Biolabs in Bristol as we speak. Permanent storage pods will be installed in the field to maintain and heal the ResExtendas between tourists.'

The hologram bursts into points of light and re-gathers into a tiger, fur suffused with a heavenly glow.

'Thank you.' Arthur turns back to me, stroking his jaw. The taste of pastry lingers in my mouth, sickly sweet.

'As I'm sure you understand, before we launch the program we need to quality check the ResExtendas. For the prices we will charge, the product must be excellent, the experience, exceptional,' he says. 'Of course, our customers will know that the trip is not going to be a stroll in the park. We will make a virtue of that fact. The authentic wild experience. But there are areas of projection where comfort and safety can be enhanced. It will be your role, Katherine, to trial each body – to ensure the experience will be of the highest quality.'

He lifts his pastry, tearing the end off with his long fingers, but seems to forget to bring it to his mouth. 'Your responsibilities as consultant will involve testing the whole range of physiological functions associated with each ResExtenda. We will be sending you the full brief after the meeting, but broadly your tasks will include stress-testing of biological functions, infield jumps and lab jumps, testing the reliability of the ResExtenda storage pods.' He's started swirling the end of the pastry; it's almost hypnotic. 'Then, of course, environmental risk factoring, monitoring local prey, social and predatory populations, along with all other factors that need to be considered in the mandatory insurance packages. Not to forget comfort maximisation, appetite profiling—'

My attention slips as he carries on, hazing out on the swirl of his pastry. Put as many fancy words to it as you like, but the job they are describing is to play guinea pig. I glance at Mr Hughes, hoping for some sort of support, but when he looks back I find myself avoiding his eyes, my face heating with the dread that he might have interpreted the look in the wrong way.

Arthur's pastry has finally come to a stop and, as if this were a cue, everyone is looking at me. The napkin tears a little between my hands and, realising that I've been fiddling with it, I drop it quickly back to the plate.

'Don't get me wrong,' I say. 'I'm flattered, really, but Research is all I've ever done. I don't know anything about this.'

'But, Katherine, this is an entirely new branch of Phenomenautism. As of yet there are no consumer phenomenauts. Who would you have take on the job?'

'I don't know. I don't think I'm the best person though.'

'Really? From our position you are excellently qualified. You've remarkable experience with ResExtendas but you're not so old that trialling a range of radically different and new bodies should present a problem. Though the aims of Research may be a little different, through it you've become a wider range of ResExtendas certainly than anyone else at ShenCorp, but quite probably everyone in the industry.' He smiles, finally pops the piece of pastry into his mouth and chews thoughtfully. 'Mr Hughes reassures me that there's no one else he'd rather have on the job.'

That's not the point though. I became a phenomenaut because I love Research – immersing myself in a body, an environment, a pack, until I know every scent, every sound, every taste of my territory as clearly as I do the timbre of Buckley's voice.

'Katherine, this project is going to be game changing. And as the world's most experienced phenomenaut, of course we'd want you on board. In fact –' Arthur glances at Mr Hughes, who nods. 'In fact, we are so excited, that we want you as our poster girl.'

'Poster girl?' My fingers bite into each other beneath the table and I flinch to find the nails are much sharper than those of my Original Body. I keep forgetting that I'm inRessy.

'Yes, poster girl.' Arthur smiles. Despite the unpleasantness of the situation, there's something almost comical about his echoing. 'Nothing too intensive, we know that your heart lies with the projection, but we'd absolutely love to have your face on the advertising.' He sweeps an evocative arm through the air. 'Katherine North, the face of Body Tourism. Just think of it.'

I am, and it's made my decision very easy.

'Thank you, all of you, for considering me. But you know I can't leave Research.'

I don't like the look Arthur shoots at Mr Hughes. When his smile re-gathers, its broadness is almost desperate.

'*Katherine.* As much as we know you love Research, do you really think it's what you need right now? After your recent –' the worms of his lips twist in a way he must think of as beseeching – 'incident, surely dying species are the last type of ResExtenda you need to be working on.'

'But it's my job.' My throat tightens around the words, as if even this Ressy is aware that they're falling on deaf ears.

'Was your job. Believe me, I understand – no – admire your passion. Your passion is why we are so excited to be working with you. And under normal circumstances we wouldn't dream of forcing a change of department but I believe that in your situation the matter is somewhat more complicated. Mr Hughes has advised me that for health reasons, legally, we cannot allow you to continue working in Research.'

'Sorry?' I glare at Mr Hughes. 'Legally?'

A hint of the familiar hardness surfaces in that handsome face, revealing a surprising ugliness, but it's Arthur who pushes the point.

'We have a legal responsibility to keep all our phenomenauts in good health. Please understand that it's only in your best interests that we have had to make the hard decision to prevent you from practising Research Phenomenautism any further. Thankfully the consumer jumps will each last a week at most and should prove far less stressful. I believe that once you've adapted to the change, you will find them very amenable. We're determined not to lose you, Katherine.'

It's too much. Too much in one day. I don't even know what to feel any more. Anger, I suppose, but even that comes at me from a distance. I rub the numbness between my eyes, wondering if they've turned down the physiological inputs.

'But, the seal jump?' I say to Mr Hughes. 'The geomagnetic navigation research? We promised a report by the end of the month. Julie is busy with her bottlenoses right now – so she can't take it.'

'I'm quite aware. You can of course finish your ongoing Research projects. But we can't schedule you in for any new ones – and certainly nothing long-haul.'

'So, it's this or leave?'

'I wouldn't put it in such stark terms. Never lose sight of the fact that this is a promotion. You should be excited. We certainly are.'

It'd be easier to be excited if they'd stop parroting the word.

'Could I at least have time to consider?'

I'm not above feeling pleasure at the frown Arthur gives Mr Hughes.

'Of course,' he says after a beat. 'Though I can promise you that this is not an opportunity you want to overlook. In the meantime, we will send you the literature to familiarise yourself with.'

'Right.' But as I start to stand, Mr Hughes cuts me off.

'You do understand, North, that everything you heard here is confidential. Especially the existence of the human Ressies.'

'Sure. Of course.'

'We cannot risk their existence being leaked before marketing has done its work. Any breach would result in termination of your contract and a legal suit.'

'You can trust me.'

I thought the questioning was revenge for my hesitation to sign up but his look is still locked on mine. 'That includes Mr Maurice.'

'Buckley?' I pause in stepping back from my seat. Buckley's my neuroengineer, he knows me better than myself, to ask me to keep information from him is just—

'You do understand that, North?' There's nothing close to sympathy in that face and, looking at it now, I wonder how I could ever have found it attractive.

'It's of the utmost importance that no word of this gets out before marketing feels the public is ready for it,' he says.

'Right. Yeah. That's . . .' I pull a smile as weak as theirs. 'Sure.'

He sits back, finally satisfied, and I return to the JumpPallet, weak with the choice ahead of me.

13

Come Home

Even now it's hard to piece it all together. Considering the distance they went to trap me – they must have wanted me in the beginning, or at least my kudos – the longest-working phenomenaut ever. What better way to allay tourist worries? Just look at Katherine North. She's been jumping for seven years and she's absolutely fine.

How long had they been planning behind the scenes? Since before the fox jump, certainly, then, the night I died, they were ready.

But it's hard to see it all clearly when the ache of my stomach has spread up my throat. This isn't a superficial habit of food any more but real hunger. My muscles feel light, as if someone has taken a huge spoon and hollowed me out. I walk slowly to be on the safe side, one hand against the wall to steady myself.

At last chancing on some industrial dustbins, I rummage. The smell is putrid, nearly all the foodstuffs have a soft coating of fur. As a fox it might be worth a shot but not in my Original Body; falling sick now isn't a possibility. Still, I pocket some burger buns that the fox might be tempted by. They always were Tomoko's favourite.

The billboards across the road suffuse the street with a flat unreal light. When I was a kid they were everywhere but I suppose the rise of SpecSpace killed the demand. Now real-world adverts mean serious money, a message that someone is determined for everyone to see whether they want to or not.

Currently, it shows the Prime Minister, watching over the street with a benevolent smile. Uplifting but completely vacuous catch-phrases fade in and out of the backdrop. Someone has spray-painted a cock ejaculating into his eye.

Having exhausted the surface layer of this bin, I try the next. Empty drink cans, a shattered old-style TV, carrots turning to liquid in their plastic. I'm about to give up when the yellow of a bread tie catches my eye.

The yeastiness of mould hits me as soon as the bag is open but I sit anyway and tear out the worst bits, working the clumps left through my jaws. Halfway through the bag and I start to feel less giddy, so I pack the rest to cache for later.

I'm standing to leave when I notice the billboard has flickered to the next advert so that the cock now perches atop a familiar logo.

ShenCorp Tourism.

You can be anyone. You can be anything.

Next to it is footage of a bald eagle, swooping to fill the bill-board, but just as it threatens to break through, it's replaced by the maul of a tiger.

Animal Tourism. I wonder how the public are responding to the idea. They certainly wouldn't be happy if they knew what else ShenCorp was up to but how to show them that without proof?

A mouse follows the tiger. I've seen this footage before. What I don't recognise is that of the bald girl standing to one side. Her mouth moves in silent speech; with Specs I'd be able to connect and listen in but instead I can only shiver.

That nose is lifted slightly, as if catching the scent of prey; the snarling smile painted the crimson of fly agaric, coral snake, dart frog.

The bread has slipped from my grip. I kneel to gather the slices back into the bag, wheezing through the lump in my throat.

My reflection sits on the gleaming surface of a puddle like a black hole but when I lift trembling hands to my face, they find the same sharp cheeks and aquiline nose, the same snarling mouth. Because the face on the billboard is mine.

Uncanny Shift

As the last shivers of Sperlman's leave my body, I lie, just enjoying the sensation of not feeling terrible. At times like this, the idea of giving up Phenomenautism is almost a relief.

'OK in there?' Buckley says.

'Think everything is about right,' I say. At least, as much as a Ressy can be this early into a jump. 'But how on earth do they expect tourists to cope with this?'

'Well, I've been reading the manual and—'

'It was a rhetorical question,' I say before he can get carried away.

I wriggle, testing the slack flesh of my new bulk; it's as if I've become obese in a matter of seconds. What would have been called thighs half an hour ago have melded; only the flitter of what were once feet are free to move – hind flippers, probably. I flex what I'm still thinking of as arms and the front flippers flop forwards, claws clacking against the metal floor of the pod. There's a pinprick of pain in my left side where the IV recently retracted but thankfully there doesn't seem to be much sensation in my blubber. Though it's always impossible to fully imagine the reality of a Ressy beforehand, this isn't far off what I imagined it would be like to be a seal.

'Ready?' Buckley says.

'Ready.'

I roll my weight onto my chest and drag my rear towards my belly, then shift back onto my pelvis to heft my front forwards. Even with the protection of blubber, it's alarming how my chin slaps back to the floor.

Level with the door, at last, I press my nose to the window. Outside the vague line of the horizon is visible but not much else; my eyes can't be very good on land, or maybe the plastic is scratched. Transfer pods see a lot of use over their lifetime; chances are I've woken in this same pod before as something else.

'Let's do this.'

The door slides up to reveal a slate sky over the froth of sea and beach. Wind fizzles through my whiskers, cheeks ablaze with the sensation. The spray is sour with seaweed and fishy pungency, plastered over rock's bland metallic.

I shrug my belly over the entrance onto the press of pebbles. They rattle beneath my flippers but after a struggle I manage to wriggle my butt out and the door hisses shut. I shrug the strain from my muscles and snort air into my lungs. Only just out of the pod and I'm tired already.

This early in a jump it's always hard to tell whether I'm doing something wrong or a Ressy genuinely is this inefficient.

I push myself up on my front flippers and look around. Without the window, it's clear that my vision is hazy, but squinting I can make out that the beach is situated in a sheltered bay. The cries of herring gulls ring from the cliff, though they sound more distant than my eyes would suggest, almost as if I were underwater.

A white splodge swoops down, taking on the rough shape of a bird, and pecks at something in the grit with its greenish-grey beak.

Greenish-grey. I look around and note the iron-coloured sea; the sun, a white star in the sky's nauseous grey. My watery eyes blink to no use. Of course seals, like most pinnipeds, are monochromats; they can't even see the blue–yellow spectrum like other mammals.

The wind shoves the fishy scent at me with renewed intensity and I squint along the beach. What I took earlier to be a rock lifts a lazy flipper.

'Bloody genius.'

'Sorry?' Buckley says.

'Mike. The beach already has seals. And I'm male, aren't I?'

This, it turns out, is hard to tell by sensation alone but that's what the manual said.

'Ah. Yeah. Sorry.'

'Shite.'

Trespassing hadn't been something I'd been planning on when I woke this morning. Thankfully it's not breeding season, I don't think, but this could still get nasty.

I lower back into my slump. As far as I can tell the seals mostly seem to be dozing. If I'm lucky, I might be able to slip into the sea without being seen.

Fucking Mike. This is far from the first time he's made a mistake like this. Despite the fact that location scouting and setting up the pods is his only job.

Buckley inhales sharply and I turn to see a slow surge of blubber thrusting itself across the beach. So much for slipping away unseen.

I sneeze at it – *back off*. But it keeps coming.

'Fight or run?' Buckley phrases it as a question but he dislikes conflict as much as I do.

'Let's try a threat display,' I say and push myself up as large as I can. My lips feel rubbery as they peel upwards to bare teeth.

'Fucking Mike.'

The seal growls. I puff my chest out and cough back but it keeps advancing. This close I can see the white scar up its snout. It can't back down, its territory is on the line. And there are few enough wild seals for me to beat one up just for the right to sit on its beach. I twist my weight around and plough towards the sea.

The ground crawls. I'm throwing myself as hard as I can, but I'm still travelling slow enough to weep. Pebbles slide from beneath my flippers, the horizon a sickening bob as I lunge forwards and back. The seal clatters close behind, breath a hiss. The smudge of sea seems as distant as when I set out.

I start to slide as the beach drops into a slope. My belly squashes in on itself, tail thrashing hopelessly, then flesh smacks into me from behind and we both tumble in a tangle of flippers.

Finally skidding to a stop, I flip back on my belly, sky spinning in my head. The seal tries to bite but I worm away. Blubber sings with cold adrenaline.

Sand now, my flippers slough against its grit, broken shells rasping. A wave froths up against my snout and I snort out the brine.

Pain.

My flipper. The seal bit me.

I dive forward, chest buoyed by water – one more push – and slither into the sea.

Darkness. The shiver of water. Free.

There's no splashing behind; territory defended, the male must have given up the chase. The stillness holds me in the infinite space between now and not. Then light blooms.

A submerged beach opens below. Pebbles quaver with the push of water, the glittering sand patterned into neat hillocks. A frenzy of seaweed waves up at me, bubbled air sacs bouncing across my flank. Underwater my vision is almost as good as that in my Original Body.

'How's your flipper?' Buckley says. 'Want me to increase the pain threshold?'

Now he mentions it, I become aware of the sting of salt, but it's not as bad as it could have been – the blubber has cushioned the worst of the bite.

'It's OK,' I say.

The tap of his stylus against teeth reaches me over comms; he's likely to be musing over the pain readings.

'Sure you don't want me to transmute some of it?'

'It's fine,' I say and he doesn't push the point. As a neuroengineer it's important to remember the difference between what your readings tell you and the phenomenaut's experience.

Of course, it's painful, but I don't like him messing with the inputs. Fiddle too much and your sense of reality will dissolve. To reach any understanding of an animal, you have to play by the same rules. Ressies aren't a toy, whatever these Body Tourism people think.

For the second time this jump, I find myself thinking almost wishfully of leaving ShenCorp. As a human, it's easy to forget the pain, hunger and ever-present threat of death.

'Are you sure you're OK?' Buckley says.

'Please don't use that voice.'

'What voice?'

'Like I'm a puppy with cancer.'

He laughs. 'But you have to admit you've been feeling sorry for yourself all week.'

I dip to snap at a crab.

'I'm guessing this bout of despondency has something to do with a certain Tourism project?' Buckley says.

'What gave it away?' I say.

'I might not have mentioned before but the Maurices are known for their telepathy skills.'

'And there I was thinking you were known for your bullshit.'

'Well. That too.'

The snap of crab claws makes my whiskers roil, the movement of water has already set them sparking, so that my snout is now abuzz with pins and needles. Seals can sense vibrations in the water with their whiskers but right now the onslaught is incomprehensible.

'You do know that the Tourism is a promotion?' Buckley says.

'Doesn't mean I want it.'

'Consumer Phenomenautism is going to be huge.'

'Doesn't mean it's right.'

'What's that supposed to mean?'

'Phenomenautism is about understanding other animals, not using them for fun.'

'The two aren't mutually incompatible. People need a wake-up call.'

'You think a tourist would have known how to handle that bull on the beach?'

'No. But it'll all be carefully controlled. This isn't going to be taken lightly.'

I think about the human Ressies and wonder if that's true. But I'm not allowed to tell Buckley about that.

'Let's just get on with the study,' I say.

The shiver of my cheeks is slowly becoming more pronounced. When I turn my head from side to side, it's as if the water varies in excitement. And *there* – my whiskers fizzle, hitting the zenith of a gradient but what that means, I don't know. Understanding a new sense can take hours, sometimes days; in the end all you can do is get on with the work.

I push along the line of agitation. About me, water dances in a lime glow; the disturbed silt a cascade of stars. The tingling of my whiskers grows with every push. Is this sense of a presence ahead just my imagination? It *feels* as if the water remembers the passage of something.

As I slip on, echoes of turbulence start to stand out against the backdrop of waves, growing steadily more frantic, and, at last, a shadow materialises ahead – a fish.

I kick my hind flippers, snaking my body from side to side. Water gabbles, the burden washed from me almost giddying. The bed of seaweed waves me on, a forest reaching up to a bird. How could I have thought I was slow?

The fish is a silvery bullet but I'm gaining fast. Its wake screams up my snout. I rarely make my first catch this early into a jump!

But my snap closes on nothing. The fish has dived into the seaweed. My chest is growing tight so I push back to the radiance of the surface and the cries of seagulls return. I bob with the waves, sucking at salted sky. The beach is a blurry line in the distance; I'm faster than I'd even hoped.

Lungs relaxed, I dive back. A blink and the sea's flame rekindles. The ocean is laid out before me; a whole new world to explore.

Yes, jumping can hurt, yes, it can be miserable, but could I really let this be the last time? Either way, I'm going to live it to the full.

15

Come Home

Seeing a bundle of papers in an alleyway, I tear inside to the sight of chips. My mouth is full of the cold starch before I've even registered what my hands are doing but it's food and every zoological phenomenaut knows that there's nothing like hunger to make a king's feast of scraps. I shut my eyes to savour the sensation of fat between teeth, their weight sinking down my throat into the silence of my innards.

When they're gone, I lick the wrapper, trying to draw out the last precious drops of oil. Beneath the sharpness of vinegar, my fingers taste of soil and rain.

I've been wandering most of the evening and the chips have been the only food I've found, so I let myself sit a while, feeling the satisfaction of something in my gut, though it's hardly enough. Tonight's scavenging doesn't bode well for the future. I'm used to having a stronger nose, not to mention stomach, to rely on.

Yet if I managed to get inside the Centre, there would be food there. Because seeing the billboard has made it clearer than ever that if I don't stop ShenCorp they'll try to claim my identity completely. Though that doesn't help me with how to break in. Nor with what comes after.

I press my face into my knees. Everything feels unreal, as if this were a Ressy with the haptic inputs tuned down. I try to imagine the rest of my life like this, living on the fringes; mind decomposing as words dissolve into the roar of being. It doesn't matter that I've spent seven years as other animals, there was always a human thread to tether me: science, Buckley, purpose. I don't know what it is to live day by day, existing just to exist. For something so vacuous, the future has monstrous weight.

A flicker of light breaks me from my self-pity. On the other side of the road a torch beam slashes into the flesh of the night. It's going too slowly to just be heading somewhere. More like they're looking for something, or *someone*.

I stay very still, though inwardly my thoughts are racing. They're too far away to recognise, there's nothing to link them with ShenCorp – and yet why else are they here so late at night? No. There are lots of other reasons. They could be looking for someone else, a missing pet, anything. They could be a burglar, a murderer. My tongue fumbles along my dry mouth, testing the points of my incisors. Part of me wants them to come closer, to disprove the paranoia of my thoughts, another part wants them to go and not come back.

They're almost level now, though I still can't make out a face. I inch backwards and flatten against the wall. The torch beam wakes a blue bin from the fabric of the night, then stabs towards me. I throw up my hands, blinded, but the torch is already moving on, footsteps following behind.

Perhaps they didn't see me. Or perhaps I wasn't who they were looking for. My knuckles ache from where they grind into the brick.

When the torchlight has disappeared around the corner, I race in the other direction. Whether they were looking for me or not I can't keep wandering around like this – I need a territory, somewhere defendable.

I keep my ears pricked for signs of anyone following, but all I catch is the patter of fox paws: though she's still keeping her distance. Other creatures move through the shadows too: the piercing eyes of house cats and once, in the distance, the solid ghoul of a fleeing badger.

I find the park gates of foreboding black iron, but at least the ostentatious whorls offer plenty of footholds. I land on the other side shaking. Night has sucked the colour from the flamboyance of the flowerbeds, leaving them lifeless. Trees *shussssh*, shivering leaves throwing off embers of streetlight. I race to their cover and drop to my knees to push through the scrub. At the far end, vegetation gives way to a patch of mud and a tall fence that marks the park boundary. Having a solid surface at my back makes me feel more secure; though being cornered is a possibility, I should be able to climb over before anyone human-sized made their way through the brambles. Decent den material as far as these things go.

As a fox I'd think of making a burrow or nestling inside the roots but I'm too large for that now. Instead I claw at the loam until I've shaped a rough hollow. I crawl into it and huddle up to wait for warmth to gather in the crook of my body.

Leaves mutter beneath the creak of branches. The moon peeks between the canopy; a pupilless eye. The park feels a universe away from how it was when I used to visit with Buckley.

————

The last time we were here was in the summer's initial blush before the rains. Warm, *too* warm. My skin was taut, as if the sun were turning it to leather; when I poked a tongue at the back of my hand it tasted of salt. The News was already ordering people not to water their lawns, even though only a month ago they had been churned to mud.

I had finished my frozen shake before we'd even reached the park and was wistfully thinking of getting another but Buckley was sitting right next to me and bound to chide. You can't consume too many calories as a phenomenaut, not when you spend most of your working hours flat out on the JumpPallet.

The park was busy with workers and young parents making the most of the heat. A screaming toddler yoyoed back and forth between the lawn sprinklers and the snatching arms of its mother, delighted equally by the threat of each. Buckley watched with a vacant gaze, one corner of his mouth drawn up in a smile so that the straw, forgotten there, perked to attention. He had been in a weird mood all morning. Only hours ago he was a whirlwind of gesturing, but reaching the park he'd drawn in on himself, like an anemone at low tide.

I reached out to twang his straw and his eyes refocused, wincing to find me through the sun.

'All right?'

He blinked away the question. 'Remember your training?'

'Phenomenautical training? Sure. Why?'

'Dunno. I was thinking about how sure I was you were going to give up.'

'You've said that before.'

'I'm not saying – Of course, I couldn't have been proved more wrong. I didn't know you then, did I? But at the time ... Every Come Home it was like you were having a fit.'

It was my turn to shrug. The training regime had been crazy when I started. Some idiot had the idea of trying to acclimatise phenomenauts to Sperlman's in short, regular bursts. Project the phenomenaut in, pull them quickly back into their Original Body, then back again. Like having your consciousness put through a blender.

'They don't train like that any more for a reason,' I said.

He nodded, agreeing and not.

'*You* weren't trained like that.'

'Well. Not exactly.' He rubbed the back of his neck. 'Still, even if I had been, I don't think it would have driven me to bite my neuro.'

'You're never going to let me forget, are you?'

Not that I really remembered it, those moments have always been hazy. My only memory, more of a feeling – the sensation of his grip, clamping my twitching arms to my sides.

'As your neuroengineer I am bound to complete confidentiality about such embarrassing moments. But that doesn't preclude teasing you mercilessly.'

I swore through my laughter but when I stopped he was still watching, lips parted.

'What?' I said.

'Nothing.'

'You can't not say now.'

Something about his look withered my smile.

'Tell me,' I said.

'It's just … watching you. It always felt like you were running from something.'

'Try Sperlman's on for size.'

'That's not what I mean.' He forced himself to put down the cup he'd been toying with. 'Not running *from projection*. Towards it.'

16

Uncanny Shift

An angel fish nibbles imperceptible flecks from the tank glass. I'm not salivating though, a bit of a surprise so soon after the seal jump. Instead I find myself wanting to experience the cool sensation of glass against my lips too, but Buckley is sitting next to me and would be bound to notice.

I glance at him, only to catch him looking away. Things are still ... awkward between us, our silence like elastic stretched to snapping point. He waited until a day or two after Come Home to make his announcement to let me recover, but the fact that he kept back his decision for so long only makes it worse. I hadn't even considered that he might accept the Phenomenautism job regardless of my choice. I thought we were a team.

It's his job, though I know he can't chuck everything in if I decide to, yet the idea that his voice could live a life separate from mine seems absurd. I roll my head back, so that it hits the fish tank with a dull *thonk*. I wish the children would just hurry up and arrive so we can get on with the tour.

Letting Mr Hughes bully me into Tourism is not something I'm willing to accept but life without Phenomenautism would be unrecognisable. *I* would be unrecognisable.

Blinking, I focus on the remembrance plaque above my head. 'In Memory of Isaac Wallace'. It's one of those things that's been around the Centre so long I'd forgotten it was there. Funny that I could know so little about someone who had projected in this very building only a year before my time. Funny that someone who had been so many things could just – blink out. A final brutal flight, then gone. Is that what makes Buckley so reticent on the subject? I know from the date on the plaque that they must have been undergraduate phenomenauts at the same time, but he's always claimed he never really knew him.

No one really speaks about Isaac, despite his death reverberating through ShenCorp even today. For one, if it hadn't been for Isaac's death, we wouldn't have to face such a litany of counselling and check-ups. And yet, I only know the details from the questionable rumours of other phenomenauts.

'His girlfriend had dumped him,' Susie had whispered to me in the middle of one tutorial.

During another, 'He forgot he was human, not a bird. Jumped right off.'

Another time, 'Mr Hughes pushed.'

'Why?'

'Stole his cream cakes.'

We hadn't been able to explain to Dr Vince what we'd found so hilarious about cellular reproduction and spittle had started to fly.

Sometimes I'd almost forget Susie, it was that long ago. Was her leaving because of poor plasticity or 'family reasons'? I can't even remember now, though it makes little difference; she was just another name that fell out of the bottom of my life, leaving nothing but an imprint in her JumpPallet, obscured as soon as the next body lay there.

'OK?' Buckley says. It must be the fourth time he's asked this morning.

'Yeah,' I say, though we both know that's not true.

At the high-pitched voices, we look up to see a woman waving at the door, a line of children filing up the steps behind her.

Their chatter drops away as they cross the threshold, about fifteen of them altogether, the smallest barely coming up to my chest. I was twelve when I started jumping, and though the blonde girl at the back could easily be fourteen, Shen is pushing for younger recruitment all the time. Though my experience makes up for my decreasing plasticity, for new recruits, it's a matter of the younger the better.

Buckley launches into the introductions, their eyes are wide with awe, though there's not much to see here. Two kids at the back whisper and point at the angel fish. I think I can guess what they're thinking. Mr Hughes does occasionally greet important parties with inhabited Ressies, but they're always a body more impressive than that of a fish.

'So, who knows what Phenomenautism is?'

As Buckley has opened with such a condescending question it's a relief to see every hand raised.

'Anyone want to hazard a guess why we do it?'

The hands plummet, though the teenager at the back runs fingers through her hair in a way that strikes me as knowing.

'Anyone? No? But I bet you've all heard the expression "to walk a mile in another man's shoes"? Well, Phenomenautism is like that. Though it's easy enough for me to have a fairly good idea what it might be like to be one of you, this is only because we're all human and our "shoes" –' he sways as he lifts a foot and bunny ears quotation marks at the same time – 'are similar, so to speak. Yours are just a little smaller.'

This gets a laugh. As much as Buckley complains about these tours, he can't hide his enjoyment.

'Other species have very different bodies and senses to ours. For instance, a bat *sees* the world through sonar. A catfish by smelling chemicals in the water. A platypus can even locate its prey using electricity. As humans don't have these senses, our imagination struggles when we try to fully comprehend what it means to *be* these creatures. To understand we have to wear their "shoes" – their skin. That's where projection comes in.'

He waves them to follow, continuing the spiel as he leads the group towards the cubicles, turning off into Kyle and Julie's.

Julie is laid out on the JumpPallet, mid-projection, so even with the extra space, it's a push getting everyone in. Kyle pokes an elbow in my ribs as I stand in the way of his screens. The visual feed shows a blurred underwater scene. Given Julie's specialism, she's almost certainly some sort of cetacean. If Kyle is to be believed, she's the best speaker of dolphin in the world. Either way, I know for a fact that she's an authority on the European dialects.

Buckley brings out a spare CP cap and crouches to let the children touch it as he points out the components.

'These,' he says, brushing the feathered probes of the lining, 'are the EEG sensors. They can read tiny bursts of brain activity through the skull, so we can monitor non-invasively. It does, however, mean that phenomenauts have to shave their heads to ensure a good contact with the skin.'

I redden at the stares this invites, but Buckley is already calling their attention back to the CP.

'If you look closely, you should be able to see some little coils. These are the TMS, which we use to block the signals coming in from the Original Body – the phenomenaut's human body that is – and replace them with those from the ResExtenda.'

'Wee brats,' Kyle mutters, though his mouth is so hidden by beard that if it weren't exactly the kind of thing expected from Kyle, I might have thought I'd imagined it.

'Why do we have to work in the only industry that recruits from a demographic subsisting entirely on e-numbers and snot?' he says.

'Familiarity with extreme cuisine,' I whisper back. 'It's got to count for something.'

'Right. But tell me, what kind of beasties eat boogers?'

'Most of them actually. Supposedly it boosts the immune system.'

He hums, then changes the note of his voice. 'Yeah, it's Kit. How'd you guess.' At my confused look, he cocks his head at the screens.

'Julie says if any of them starts poking her, slap the little buggers.'

I glance at the prone form on the pallet, momentarily disoriented. She looks different somehow – older – but perhaps that's just seeing her in JumpPyjamas as opposed to her usual shades of pink.

I shake my head. 'Tell her, will do.'

He drawls back into his mic. 'She says, "with pleasure", and I think she means it. Our Kit can put your hair on end at times ... Oh calm yourself, it was just a creative interpretation.'

Finishing with the CP talk, Buckley places it on the desk and turns to the screens.

'If you look for a second at the bottom right, you'll be able to see the visual feed from the Ressy. Our implanted cameras are in the human sensory range, so it's only an approximation of what Julie herself is experiencing, but it allows Kyle here to keep tabs.'

His point swings round to Julie's Original Body. 'So, right now the CP will be picking up her thoughts about where she wants to move and how, and projecting them, very very fast,' – he points back at the screens – 'to the Ressy dolphin out at sea. The relay in the dolphin picks up these signals and makes it move as if it were her own body. The Ressy then sends its sensory signals back, which the CP uses to stimulate her brain and create the experience of being inside the Ressy.'

Their eyes rove back from the screen to her vacant body, still but for the glacial flexing of the pressure relief mattress. She looks vulnerable in her thin JumpPyjamas and the children's curiosity feels like hunger. Despite the fact that Julie's message was just a joke, I find myself wanting to shield her.

But now Buckley is herding everyone out. In the corridor, the group has to slow to let Daisy pass. She's been avoiding me since our confrontation in the common room. Perhaps it's for the best considering her temper. But seeing our group, she puts out an arm.

'You guys on the tour? Only seems like yesterday I was on mine,' she says. 'Want to hear something cool?'

From the caution that's entered Buckley's expression this must be off-piste.

'So I'm currently working on a project in Mauritius, anyone want to guess what I saw there?'

'Mauritius,' the teacher says. 'That's an island in the Indian Ocean?'

'Right.'

The children just look at Daisy, something about her bearing has stifled their chatter.

'No one?' She smiles, a peculiarly grim expression. 'All right, I'll tell you then. Get this, I saw a dodo.'

Buckley stiffens, too busy staring at her to catch my look.

'I thought you were working a spider Ressy?' I say.

'Yeah. And?'

'Spiders have terrible visual acuity.'

'Yeah, *orb spiders*, but I'm working a huntsman, I can see just fine.' From the look she gives me, it's not hard to imagine her as a ten-inch arachnid. 'Besides, I've observed them on two occasions. We're just waiting for a couple more sightings before releasing.'

'Thanks, Daisy' – it's impressive how calmly Buckley waves the tour on – 'but we're working on a pretty tight schedule here.'

She cuts me a smile as I slip pass. 'Look out for the paper, OK. It's going to be huge.'

I bare my teeth and hurry to catch up to Buckley. 'Kay isn't going to let her submit a paper about dodo sightings, surely?' I whisper.

'Let's hope not, for both their careers.'

'You know. I'm starting to wonder is Daisy is a little—' I twirl a finger round my temple.

He shakes his head, but his frown is directed inward.

The children run across the tunnel in a drum of feet. As the teacher shouts after them, I feel a small hand slip into mine and look down into the shy smile of a tiny girl. Iva, her name badge says. Buckley waves his card at the sensor, and the metal doors slide open to fifteen intakes of breath.

The Biolabs. I can glimpse my early awe through Iva's stare. My descriptions have never been able to do the space justice. The closest I've ever come is 'a collision between a laboratory and black magic'. As the class files inside the room, a pair of eyeballs in the nearby tank seems to revolve towards us. Iva's grip tightens on my hand, but they aren't connected to anything, they can't really see.

'Buckley!' A deep voice shatters the silence, almost sacrilegious, and Faarooq strides across the lab. 'How are you doing, my friend?'

'Everyone, this is Faarooq,' Buckley says. 'He's our – the university's – Head technician.'

'Will you look at the lot of you,' Faarooq says, still furiously chewing on his gum. 'Our brave new phenomenauts?'

'We're just taking a tour,' the oldest girl says.

'But you'll be wanting to see the printers, surely? Come come, I'll show you the lab on the way back.'

He claps his hands and shoots forwards, faster than a man of his girth should be able to. Reaching for the door, he opens it with a sweeping bow to invite the giggling children through.

The room itself is largely empty, save for a couple of metal gurneys ready to take the finished Ressies, and the printers that line the sides of the room. The one nearest the door is only the size of a sports bag but the next has the dimensions of a desk, each increasing in size as they go further back, until the printer set into the far wall requires a ladder up the side and could easily hold an elephant.

'Welcome to the printer room,' Faarooq says, obviously enjoying the awed reactions. 'If you want to come over here, we can take a peek.'

He flashes his card at the closest printer and the vacuum unseals with a hiss, but, with his finger hovering over the release button, he hesitates.

'Now, has anyone seen a body-printer before?'

He's answered by a host of shaking heads; I find myself nodding along with the pantomime.

'Well then, you're in for a ride. Though the underlying technology might be the same as your carbon printers at home, these are in an entirely different league. But first things first, does anyone know the number-one rule when looking into a body printer?'

'Listen to teacher?' someone suggests.

'Don't touch?'

'Good, good, but not my thinking. Rule number one is ... hold on to your breakfast.'

He hits the button, the teacher laughing nervously, and the lid creaks back in a flood of light. Necks crane in, childish voices lifting in wonder, only to cut off. I lift a hand against the brightness, then let it slide, to my mouth.

Lying in the wet gel is something that looks a little like the cross-sections found in biology textbooks. It's animal, that much is clear – it has the stubs of what must be limbs and the fleshiness of an organic – but it's only half finished. The red plane of flesh is stippled with creamy blots like pepperoni; the half-finished organs look like ruptured sores. The skull is an empty bowl of bone.

My skin prickles in pointless sympathy, even though there is no one, no hurt, to be sorry for. I never get used to this. Perhaps no one ever really does, though that wouldn't account for Faarooq's grin. The children have fallen silent, the smallest boy bursts into tears.

The teenager shoots him a glare, though I can't help but notice she looks a little peaky herself.

Buckley catches my eye. There's always a crier.

'Come on now.' The teacher puts an arm around the boy's shoulders.

But it's not silly. It's hard to make a rational argument that the process is harmful or wrong, yet every time I look into a printer, alarm bells go off in some primal part of my brain.

'A lion,' one of the older boys says.

Forcing myself to look again, I see that he's right, it does seem to be a big cat, though it's hard to say what species when less than half of it is there.

Faarooq claps the boy on the shoulder. 'Good guess! But what you're looking at here is a tiger.'

I feel Iva's grip tighten on mine and force a smile on to my face. Some of the kids are covering their mouths, eyes wide, enjoying the game, but others have turned an unhealthy tinge.

The teacher catches the sleeve of one girl who grasps comically at her throat. 'Lisa. Everyone breathe normally. There's no need for theatrics.' She looks to Buckley, determined to move the tour back on to serious ground. 'Is that the print head?'

Her finger points to the bar spanning the length of the chest. It's barely moved two centimetres the whole time we've been standing here.

'That's right.'

'And how long does it take to print a complete body?'

Faarooq answers this one, slapping the machine with obvious affection.

'That all depends on the ResExtenda. If you're thinking small, say a mouse, about four hours to half a day. Ah, but if we're being ambitious, like this tiger here, say, it's going to be more like a week. But the technology improves all the time. This printer is mid-line, she's served us two, going on three, years, but she still packs roughly 10,000 CellJets, up to 10 nanometre resolution at a push. Specialised cells or stems with the right growth factor, also cartilage, keratin, or any other bio matter with the right re-programming. Hair, though, we normally leave the Ressy to grow itself. Very tricky to print.'

'And this – grey stuff?' The teacher points out the fine web-like structure that fills the chest cavity.

'Resin scaffolding,' he explains. 'Once it's finished printing we pump it with filtering enzymes and it dissolves.'

Buckley nods at the abdomen area. 'So – this is going to be female, right?'

Following his look, I see what must be the beginnings of a uterus. The fallopian tubes seem intact.

'That's right. This little beauty could give birth if required.'

The class leans in, the disgust of a minute ago forgotten. Are they even old enough to know about the birds and the bees? But now Faarooq is reaching up for the lid.

'Best close her up. Too long an exposure can damage the tissue bonding.'

'Hands!' the teacher reprimands.

'Unless you want them to become part of a tiger,' Faarooq says and the remaining fingers are swiftly tucked into the safety of armpits.

He moves on to the next printer, lifting the lid to reveal another pool of light.

'Now this,' he says, voice softening, 'is something rather special.'

The babble dies out once more as they peer over the edge. Hairless and in cross-section, the body looks alarmingly human. I glance sharply at Faarooq. Surely he wouldn't be so lax on security after Mr Hughes's warning to me?

'That's right, I can see you all thinking it,' Faarooq says. 'What we have here is a gorilla.'

I look closer and see that the arms are too long and muscular, legs too short, but otherwise, it could easily be a squat human. It's weird, I don't normally think of myself as a totality of organs.

There's an urgent tug on my hand, Iva isn't looking too good. I catch Buckley's eye and tilt my head at the exit. He nods.

Back in the main lab I find us some chairs at the side of the room. I wonder if I should say something, but Iva seems content now we're away from the printers. I watch her swing her feet, head craned to stare around the lab.

Exaggerated sounds of disgust come from the printer room, followed by a bout of laughter. Looking back from the door, Iva's eyes catch mine, and, smiling, she points towards a box of raw red, twitching beneath thin electrodes.

'Oh. You want to know what they are?'

She nods.

'Those are muscles. Don't know what species though. Muscle stimulation is pretty important for Phenomenautism, helps keep the phenomenaut's Original Body from wasting away.'

Iva blinks. Despite her muteness, I know she's listening. Thoughts of Tomoko flash to my mind and I swallow back the sadness.

Iva's eyes crease, an echo of my own pain.

'It's OK,' I say. 'I'm just thinking about an old friend.'

She nods, squeezes my hand and returns to the pointing game.

'Ressy brain stem perhaps. Uh, more likely cerebellums, I think. That's the part of the brain that's in charge of motor control – I mean – movement.'

She pulls me over to the tank, and rises up on tiptoe to tap the glass as if the fungal-like masses were oddities in a zoo. After her response to the body printers I'm surprised at how unaffected she is. Though I find brains fascinating in the abstract, actually seeing them makes me a little queasy.

'They're not proper cerebellums, of course,' I explain. 'None of the connectome projects – that's, uh – our mapping skills aren't advanced enough yet to reconstruct exact copies, but they do the job.'

She grins and spins round in search of something else of interest, finally pinpointing a tank holding a tightly packed row of white plates.

I frown. 'Those, those look like baleen. Baleen are what some types of whale use to filter their food from the water.'

Of course, the organ could just be an isolated template for research, but if they were printing a whole whale it would easily be the largest Ressy ever made. How would they even do that? They'd have to repurpose an industrial-grade printer for something that big. There can't be many printers in the world with the size and the resolution. Could it be something to do with the Tourism project? It seems like the kind of bombastic thing they'd be into.

But the pointing finger has already moved on.

'Oh, that's a –' I laugh – 'that's a door.'

The small forehead crinkles.

'OK, I know, what's behind it. Just the room where they store the security-sensitive Ressies. It's not very exciting.'

Her little brow darkens.

'I promise. Buckley showed me once, it was nothing special, no one goes there often.' Though right now it's probably storing the Tourism Ressies and I find myself giving it a curious look too. 'I'd show you but phenomenauts don't have access. Here, this is way more cool.' I walk her over to a microscope screen displaying the crawl of cells up a probe. Her face lifts in trusting expectation.

'Relay integration, I think, where the Ressy picks up the incoming messages from the phenomenaut's brain.'

The small eyes blink. Understanding all the science behind Phenomenautism would take one person a lifetime, but I still feel a little ashamed of not having satisfactory answers.

'Here.' I swivel the turntable so that a new scan appears on the screen. In this dish a maze of green cells spread root-like protrusions. She pulls herself up on the lab stool to get a closer look. At her signal I turn it to the next which shows a cosmopolitan frenzy of dividing neurons.

It still amazes me that consciousness can come from such brute biology, from these tiny individual cells. But perhaps that's the truth of anything: one is nothing, connection is everything.

The tour finishes back in the Centre, all seventeen of us crammed round Mr Hughes's desk as he expresses how much he hopes they enjoyed the tour and that they'll consider applying to the recruitment process. He's even gone to the effort of laying out squash and biscuits, which the children chew on with blank expressions and shuffling feet. He's trying to do the same fun act as Buckley but his efforts are pitiful in comparison. You almost have to feel sorry for him.

When he at last finishes, there's some informal time for questions and Tara and Dillon join us. Si normally takes these Q&As, but he doesn't seem to be here today, leaving the questions to Dillon, even though I'm pretty sure he's younger than some of the children on tour. Tara's hand rests lightly on his shoulder, reminding me more of a mother than a neuroengineer. Seeing me watch, Tara smiles back. Lately, some neuroengineers have almost started to treat me more like one of them than a phenomenaut, though it's probably a matter of age.

'Si jumping today?' I whisper.

She looks surprised. 'You hadn't heard? He left.'

At my surprise she just shrugs – *what did you expect?* My hand feels clammy in Iva's grip.

'Do you know why?'

'Family reasons?' She pushes out her bottom lip, accompanied by another shrug. 'Buckley knew him better than I did.'

I look across the room to Buckley, but he's busy talking to the blonde teenager. How could Si leave without my even having heard? It's not like we were friends but dismissals happen so lightly these days.

My hand is squeezed and I look down into Iva's watchful face and struggle to rearrange my expression.

'So, would you like to be a phenomenaut?'

She dips her head, showing a shy sliver of teeth.

'I think you'd be great,' I say.

I glance back at Buckley, but he's still occupied with the teenage girl. She swivels on a foot in front of him, twisting a strand of her hair round a finger, but he seems too engaged in extrapolating on some nerdy answer to notice.

Did he know about Si? 'Family reasons' is starting to become a bit of a cliché. Knowing Shen's love of doublespeak I've always suspected it's just another euphemism for 'weak plasticity results'. Although some phenomenauts can't handle the stress. How long can I realistically expect to last myself? Sure, I've gone on longer than anyone else but that doesn't mean it won't catch up with me eventually.

I frown, realising the assumption behind this line of thought. Because, of course, I never really intended to leave. Yet the thought only makes me more miserable than ever.

The tug on my arm brings me back to the moment. Iva nods after her leaving classmates. I release her hand and she throws a hug around my waist before hurrying after the others.

I wipe the sticky hand down my trousers and turn to find myself alone with Mr Hughes. He's pulled the tray of biscuits towards him, picking out the ginger snaps.

'Made a friend, North?'

I shrug. 'You're really going for the tours now?'

'Important to get the kids interested early. Exciting projects on the horizon. As you should know.'

'Yeah.' I rub my scalp, it's rough with the beginning of stubble. 'About that . . . I've decided to take the Tourism job.'

'Good,' he mumbles round a biscuit. 'I'll message over your new contract by the end of the day.'

'OK.'

He continues to pick through the biscuits. Shouldn't something more momentous follow my decision? But as I continue to stand waiting, the only reaction I get is a confused look. I pull an awkward grin and make my exit.

My feet clunk down the metal steps with new heaviness. I do love ShenCorp, for all its red tape and faculty of screw-ups. I never really wanted to leave. And yet it's hard to escape the feeling that I never really had a choice.

17

Come Home

Crack

I'm confused when I open my eyes. Sun ripples through a mottle of green but as I squint, I realise that it's canopy, not ocean. That was just a dream – swimming, or perhaps flying.

Crack

Something is under the trees with me. Something close and loud.

Crack

I roll over to see that an oddly proportioned person is beating through the scrub. No, not odd, just a child. It's confusing looking upside down.

The child curls shoulders inward to worm further into the thicket and strikes a trunk steps away from where I lie, apparently oblivious to me. Their weapon is a rotten branch, disintegrating with its fury.

I try to make myself smaller. It's dim in here, my coat is a dark green, but if it comes any closer it'll surely see me. What would happen then? It might just stare or ask a nonchalant question.

Some kids wouldn't realise that there's anything out of the ordinary for a bald girl to be curled up alone in a hedge. But what if it screamed for an adult? If I move now, I'm bound to draw attention.

The child starts to kick the trunk, foot slamming in time with the branch. A huff escapes him with every blow, something between anger and laughter. Perhaps if I stay very still I'll escape notice.

There's movement close to my face – the malleable body of a caterpillar bunching its way up a bramble.

'Tod!' The shout falls limp in the muggy air. 'Tod!'

Tod, for that must be the child's name, sticks his tongue between his lips, focusing hard on not hearing.

'TOD!'

I catch the whites of rolling eyes as he slashes out one more time, then wriggles backwards out of the shrub.

'You're so childish.' A new voice, nasal with pleasure. A sibling?

I listen to their bickering fade across the park, my body shuddering only now the danger is over.

It seems absurd that I should have once been as small as that child, as inchoate. Even the memories of those years feel fabricated. I have an awareness of something, but it feels more myth than memory; a time when it was always summer and people were a hundred feet tall. To place myself alongside that girl, any comparison is fickle. I look in on her through smudged glass. Me and yet not.

It's in this way I remember the weekends my family would go walking, through forests; over hills; along the Levels, so perfectly flat that they seemed to stretch farther than the real world into wild, unbounded time. I remember Dad teaching me silly songs to march to; or showing me how to focus his DSLR, holding it for me as I placed my eye to its window. I remember him chasing me along paths, snapping his arms in the pretence of a crocodile, how, when I was tired, he would hoist me to his shoulders where my hair could brush the sky.

But Mum? The memories of her are more nebulous, not so much a personality as a feeling – the reassurance that should I ever look back she would be there, steady blue eyes above a ready smile. If Dad was the weather that shaped me, Mum was the earth into which my roots spread.

Yet there is one memory in which she has shape.

————

My red wellies churned up white dust, outpacing the clunk of Dad's boots, so fast that any second the horizon must fall within my outstretched hands.

But Dad was calling, we had to slow down, let Mum catch up, she couldn't run like us. *Never rush her, never tug.* She trudged with the weight of worlds. And so we continued like this, sprint then stop, sprint; her sturdy form waxing and waning behind us like the pull of the moon.

Yet when the shout came, it was hers.

Otters!

I raced back, almost stumbling in my excitement, only to arrive and find her feet pointing at a pile of brown mud. Poo?

Otter scat, she explained.

The disappointment was severe. Knowing that there were otters here was not enough. I wanted to stroke their velvet bodies with a look; to feel the touch of the dark eyes that teased from our TV screen. A need close to hunger.

Yet Dad wouldn't even allow that it was the right type of faeces. Blotches broke out in Mum's cheeks as he pressed home that there weren't any more otters left in England, that there are barely any wild otters left anywhere.

The argument ricocheted over my head, Mum not yielding, Dad repeating 'They're dead, poisoned, gone', until I started to cry. Mum wrapped her arms around me, though her eyes remained narrowed on the scat. She didn't care for whatever evidence Dad could lay at her feet, she believed in the otters.

Is that why I remember that day? The senselessness of her thinking? There are never definitive beginnings to such things, but it was a start, and without such markers, where would we be?

I haven't been back to the Levels for years. It's almost always flooded now, that wild horizon swallowed in the reflection of sky.

Perhaps that's why it's so hard to look back? When I open my mind's eye, I find myself submerged in brown, turgid waters.

Uncanny Shift

Suspended. Underwater. This is the feeling storage always leaves me with. The soft breathing of Ressies, as if their consciousness were not absent but lost in dreams. Their forms grey under the washed-out light.

I touch the snake gingerly, not quite trusting those open eyes, but of course it remains still, or as still as the living can be. The skin expands and contracts lightly under my touch.

'You found it then?' Faarooq's shoes squeak across the lino and I hastily remove my hand.

'This is it?' I say. 'I wasn't sure.'

'You sound disappointed?'

'No. No. It's fine, just after all this talk of Tourism's luxury Ressies . . . I don't know what I was expecting, to be honest.' I shrug. 'A rattlesnake was always a strange thing for the focus groups to come up with.'

'You don't look at a rattlesnake the wrong way.'

'Maybe. But that doesn't put off hawks, weasels, king snakes, pigs, badgers—' But as I start to count off on my fingers, I notice his look. 'If it wasn't for the controlled environments, half of the tourists would be eaten alive.'

'Better get on top of it then.' He kicks the brakes off and I get the doors so he can wheel it over to our Centre and into the lift. His forceful whistling curtails any further conversation. If so many people think I'm weird, perhaps I really am.

The doors open on to the humming stacks of the supercomputers. As a 'potentially harmful ResExtenda' the practice jump will have to take place in the enclosure we have down here. Not that I'm planning on biting anyone. It's for my safety too. I'd rather not get stepped on.

The spare set of screens is lined up next to the pallet, a pair of legs poking out from beneath.

'I hear someone ordered snake,' Faarooq shouts out as I help him guide out the trolley. 'Fresh out of fries though, I'm afraid.'

A hand appears from under the screens and waves, followed by Buckley's grinning face, hair sticking up at angles.

'So long as there's dip, I'm happy.'

He appraises the Ressy, eyebrows raised at me, then claps Faarooq on the back.

'All right?'

'Well, thank you. Though your phenomenaut has been giving me a lecture on the merits of hands.'

'She does that. OK if we keep the gurney for now? I think we'll only be a day or two on the physiological tests and then we'll move to the infield Ressy.'

I leave them to it and throw myself into Buckley's chair. He's even brought down his stuffed mascot marmoset, Ursula. Although right now she's sitting on the floor instead of her rightful place, swinging from the top screen. I pick her up and explore the hard gloss of her eyes with my lips, the familiar scratches and dinks magnified to hyperreality by the sensitive expanse of my mouth.

Sometimes when I've picked a spot or scab I like to touch it against my lips and marvel at the huge tangibility of something that was once me, now not. But Buckley has perched on the pallet, that look on his face; he's convinced that I'm going to give myself dysentery one day but if projecting has taught me anything it's that exploring with the mouth is the most natural thing in the world. I brush Ursula off on my hoodie.

'You don't like it, do you?' he says, and nods at the Ressy. With Faarooq gone, there's no need to hide my distaste. I raise my arms – *hands*. Nothing like becoming a snake to help you appreciate the humble state of being *limbed*. He shakes his head and I pick up the chain of paperclips he's got attached to the armrest.

'And don't forget the headaches,' I say.

'Snakes don't have an outer ear. The noise from the supercomputers is hardly going to be a problem when your sense of hearing is worse than a human's.'

'They're still sensitive to vibrations.'

He takes the manual from his pocket.

'"Though snakes don't have 'ears' in the human sense, they are sensitive to minute vibrations of the ground, which they use to help pinpoint prey. These vibrations tend to be experienced as a *pleasant* and *soothing* bubbling against the stomach." There. If the manual says it, it has to be true.'

I poke my tongue back at him and he makes an elaborate show of offering me the manual.

'I'll stick to my SpecSpace one, thanks.'

'Suit yourself. I've got to finish setting up, so why not go get changed?'

I loll my head against the rest.

'Best get it over with?' he coaxes.

I flick a wire thingy at him and he gives the chair a shove.

'Work.'

I wait for it to stop spinning and drag myself to my feet with a groan.

Sticky sweetness. Arid bite. Coffee and lemon. Buzz like baritone bees. Electric?

I lie still as Sperlman's passes, sensing out to find that my flesh has melded into one numbed line. How are tourists meant to withstand this, let alone enjoy it?

'You OK? Give the signal if you want out.'

I presume Buckley is still in the room. His voice is clear over comms, but I can't hear anything through the Ressy's inner ear.

Arid bite. Coffee. Electric bees. Sticky, sharp.

The clamour of foreign senses is painful. Vision kaleidoscopes, points of light gathering then dispersing like starlings. I try to focus, but the sketch of the room warps as if in halo about my head, somehow seeing everything and nothing at once. My stomach is shaken lemonade.

A glow grabs my attention, pulsing with weird energy that heats then cools, heats, cools, my mind absorbed by its presence ... I tear myself away, concentrate on the sensation of cold crystallising in my muscles.

Lemon. Bitter sweet. Stark dust. Concrete.

'Can I have the mirror?' I say.

A second, then a rectangle shimmers into being, frames flickering. Human processing is too slow to see the gaps, but it's not uncommon for Ressy eyes to be affected. I force my attention towards it, but the confusion of colour and contrast eludes sense. A mirror is normally helpful at this stage of a jump, but it's difficult with poor eyesight. In the end I have to piece the scene together consciously. The field of grey – that must be the concrete floor, the blacks just shadows; the brown line – me?

I psych at what twenty minutes ago would have been human limbs. The mirror reflects incoherent twitching. It's frustrating, but I'm running off the Ressy's cerebellum, so it shouldn't take long for everything to come naturally. I experiment, stimulating whatever muscle groups I can. Psyching what used to bend my left leg, my body concertinas. Right leg and it contorts in the opposite direction.

Stark concrete. Arid bite. Sticky, sharp. Long shadows. Bees.

Then everything clicks. I morph, a weird wriggle of tense and relax – wave by wave, dragging forwards. The cold concrete saps my strength.

'Wait till you've warmed up.' Buckley must have noticed the slowness. 'I've got the radiators on.'

I stop and turn to exploring my new body. Without hands I have to make do with nosing but my snout is almost as tactile as fingertips. Flaky scales rub reassuringly to touch, dryness of skin slightly bubbled – a moult must be called for soon, new prints are often designed that way. I keep my gaze locked on to the mirror, rolling my awareness between touching and being touched. The trick of being a phenomenaut is to integrate them into the sense of a whole. This Ressy isn't just an object, but a way of being me.

This snout is mine – I am willing it – the sensation of scales imprints into my mind – I am those scales – the pressure of snout tracing along my length. Flesh *and* me.

Heat steadily seeps through my belly, heartbeat quickening with it. The world seems brighter somehow. And that light. Heating. Cooling. My thoughts slip in time with its pulse . . . not that again. I turn away.

'What's that light?'

'Light? I don't know. Maybe my screens? Anyway, your blood temperature is looking OK now, so maybe start on a couple of laps when you're ready. I got a mouse out of the freezer earlier so you can go straight ahead on the digestion when you feel like it.'

I push off from a clench of tail. Muscles coil to find friction, then relax as others tighten. Dried scales crackle beneath me, shifting as if they were a starched garment against my real skin.

Human. Concrete. Coffee. Arid bite. Sticky, sharp.

About me is an infinite grey plain; horizon a bowl of cracks and ridges, above only endless light. Though I know this is the same room as I was sitting in half an hour ago, it looks more like the surface of another planet.

All the while, my stomach bubbles with sensation – the whole building seems to breathe beneath my touch in peaks and troughs. Once I've learnt to interpret the sense, I should be able to pinpoint anything moving close by.

Sticky, sharp. Concrete. Coffee.

These flares of taste follow the flickers of my tongue; a spit at the air, then back inside to touch the nub on the roof of my mouth. Scents slowly divest themselves as I roll them around my gums.

Sweaty meat. Arid bite. Sticky, sharp.

It always takes a little while to habituate to a strong sense of smell after my Original Body. Compared to the rubbish nose of a human, inRessy it can appear a different sense entirely, like putting on glasses after being short-sighted for years. Not to mention that every scent is a little different for each species and many that are loud in one body won't even register with another. Sometimes, though, I wonder if part of the forgetting comes from not having the language. Without the right words it's hard to retain clarity upon Come Home.

Thud.

My nose has collided with something. Snout throbbing, I slither back, but even when I lift my head there's nothing to be seen. I coil forwards again but the invisible force stays firm.

Buckley struggles to contain his snort. 'Um, Kit, you've hit the side of the enclosure.'

I twist my head, but still sense nothing.

'You're sure?'

'Absolutely.' His laughter only confirms it.

'It's invisible. I mean, completely invisible.'

'From your perspective.'

'Right.' It's disturbing that something so important could be near non-existent to my senses, but then lots of things are to human senses too.

I press forwards again but this time with my flank. Even though it's invisible, I can use it to navigate, and the solidity provides resistance to push off, its straightness reassuring against my contortions.

Human. Concrete. Cleaning fluids. Coffee. Ammonia.

History is written into the floor in a trill of smell. Leather tinged with shoe polish, encapsulated flesh – a trail of footsteps haunting the floor they once trod.

Lemon and cotton sweep – a mop pushed back and forth. Old scents have imprinted upon the world like spoor into soft mud, the past blundering prey. I wonder if this is one reason many animals have a poor memory compared to humans. What's the use in remembering when the world does it for you?

Ammonia. Rich meat. Mouse.

My body shoots forwards with eagerness. This will be the first solid meal it consumes and it knows it. The richness is yearning. I slither into its nebula, scent coagulating with every push, until at last it condenses against my snout.

I nose the blur and find an end of sorts. There's no resemblance to a mouse as I know it in any other body but this has to be it.

Meat. Ammonia, sharp. Arid bite, sticky, sharp.

My mouth suckers around it – without my even meaning to – but the cool mass is already pushing against my jaw. A powerful grip ripples up my snout. Flaps of mouse skin buckle against my gums and its taste explodes against the roof of my mouth.

Raw meat, bloodied sweetness, stark urine.

My jaw yawns wider, wider, *wider*, until I'm nothing but maw.

Reason says it should be disgusting but it's not; my mouth suckles with desire, almost desperate. I can hear the mouse's organs pop inside me, a crack of bones so loud they sound part of my own skull. My eyes bulge as its bulk presses further in.

A kick. My stomach clenches and I arc.

The mouse can't still be alive?

The vibration pummels my belly again, stronger this time. Something large is moving. Close.

I twist, trying to make sense from my eyes, but the world is a clutter of ground and sky. Then I see it. A huge shadow. Darkness turning to heat.

The force hits harder and my skull throbs. Two huge strides and it towers above, a flaming figure that blots out the sky. I've frozen, mouth crammed with mouse.

In my mind, the taste of exhaust fumes and tarmac; my body turning soft beneath a tyre.

147

The flame lurches forwards to napalm. I whip back, rattle spasming.

'Kit?'

'Buckley!'

'What's the matter?'

How can he not see it?

It flares forward again and I writhe back. My head grazes against the floor under the weight of the mouse.

'What's wrong?'

The flaming figure swings around.

'It's chasing me!'

I collide with air.

Shit! Trapped!

I thrash against the invisible barrier. But no use. The monster looms closer in white heat and I beat the resistance with my head. Can't die. Not again.

'Kit! Stop it!'

The giant reaches and I psych the exit.

Black. Warmth. Quiet.

I sit bolt upright. This is the basement. Why am I in the basement?

Then memory crashes over me. I spin around but there's no tower of flame, no monster, nothing but me and—

'Kit.'

Buckley rushes over and I lurch back to the hiss of the air cylinder. We freeze, his face wide with surprise, then I slump.

Stupid. So fucking stupid.

'Kit?' He perches next to me. 'What happened back there?'

I'm too drained by the realisation to answer. How did I not think? Pit vipers get their name from the thermal sensing pits in their snouts. The 'monster' was just heat, heat from a humanoid. From Buckley.

'Are you OK?'

As he puts on a hand on my arm I have to resist the urge to shuffle further down the pallet.

'What is it?'

'I just – something reminded me of the night I died. I freaked out.'

His eyes crease in sympathy but the strip lights render the expression sterile.

'Want to talk about it?'

I shake my head. 'Can we postpone for today?'

'Well.' He searches my face. 'Are you ill?'

'I just need—' I begin but find myself unable to explain. 'Headache,' I finish.

Though he looks far from convinced, he doesn't press. 'OK. If you really want to stop.'

'Thanks.'

On my feet, the floor seems monstrously far away. Buckley reaches out to steady me but I step back.

'You sure you're OK?' he says.

'Yeah. I will be, just need some quiet.'

It's only when I'm back in the changing room that my heartbeat finally slows. I sit on a bench and hug my knees. Nearly everyone started their weekly jump today so I have the place to myself.

What a mistake to make. Especially for a phenomenaut with my experience. Of course, to a real rattlesnake Buckley *is* a monster, all humans are, though that's no excuse. I watch my toes flex against the wooden slats but the shadowy presence continues to flame in my thoughts.

On top of the embankment. A fox. Caught aflame as it steps out of shadow. Eyes, dark coals. The roar of engine. My skull, shattering.

The extractor fan rumbles through the sickening taste of the memory. Because what if a Ressy *could* reveal a truth hidden to Original Body? It happens all the time on a sensory level; I've seen ultra-violet as an insect, the magnetic field as a bird, heard and smelt things I'd never even dream of as a human. But as for a person's character? Is it really possible that a Ressy could flip the coin on someone you know, reveal something raw and ugly beneath? Maybe. But not with Buckley. There's nothing more to be seen.

19

Come Home

I wake to the sky flashing lilac. Thunder follows soon after, a sound like the foundations of heaven grinding loose. The silvered gleam of rain and vegetation writhes against the dark. I've had plenty of time to prepare, the birds have barely sung a note all day, but it's still miserable. And *cold*.

The fox is on her feet, staring out towards the park; I have to squint to see . . . a silhouette, faint against the glow of the streetlight by the entrance. Human. Just standing there, though it must be late evening by now.

Another five minutes and it hasn't moved; perhaps it's just my mind playing tricks in the dark, but then why is the fox so interested too?

I stop chewing the back of my hand and crawl to the edge of the trees, lowering onto my belly to wriggle forwards. My coat is sodden in seconds but I keep pulling myself along the grass, wincing against the rain.

Closer, I can see that it's clearly human – a man, tall, thin, shoulders hunched in on himself. The wind digs fingers into my face, as if the storm itself were trying to drive me back, yet I can't retreat, not before I know. I squirm on until I can glimpse his face.

Water swarms my vision, even as I blink and spit. So perhaps I'm mistaken. Perhaps it's just the dark and rain and madness of these past days – but he looks a lot like Buckley.

Back inside my shelter, I sit against the fence in shock. The fox crouches in the shadows, watching with edgy eyes.

Could it really be him? It seems crazy that he should be here, but then this was the park we used to visit together and of course ShenCorp would put him up to finding me. He was my neuro, he knows me almost as well as I do myself.

My heels sink into the damp earth as I rock back and forth. Should I leave? I'm not even sure it was him. And whoever it was, I wasn't seen. This is my territory now; I don't want to leave.

I run loam through my fingers, struggling to understand how everything came to this. For so long Buckley was my constant, more familiar than my own reflection. Though, of course, there was a time when I didn't know him as Buckley but 'Mr Maurice'. It's hilarious now to think of us referring to each other by surname; that there was a time when our names didn't slip from tongues as if one.

'Mr Maurice' was barely recognisable in the man I came to know; he was withdrawn to the point of sullen, his Canadian accent soft yet grating, like chalk on pavement. He looked like a stick figure brought to life; his mop of hair a hasty scribble; limbs some-how awkward, as if someone had foisted them upon him then walked away and he didn't know how to put them down. Though I didn't appreciate it at the time, he was even younger than I am now, yet to grow fully into his adult body.

He did his job, even I couldn't accuse him of professional negli-gence. I'm quite sure he spent every moment I was projected with his eyes firmly fixed upon his screens, although he never seemed to see me – I was just a lump of flesh to be prepared, the wetware that activated the Ressies. Like the other adults in my life, or what I thought of as adults, his head was absorbed with other thoughts. And so I hated him, like only a pubescent girl can.

Susie couldn't understand it. 'But he's so haaaaandsome,' she would say as we sat on the desks between tutorials, crooning the word in her wonderful Welsh accent, with no irony whatsoever. I thought her crazy. Even though she only had a year on me, and Buckley only four or five on her, that didn't change the fact that he sat firmly on the other side of the divide that lay between us and adulthood.

It took the oriental stork report for things to come to a head. It had been a rearing project, its demands hardly on a par with the scientific papers I'd be responsible for when I was older, but it was one of my first, and it came back red with Buckley's edits; the scrawled comment at the end, 'You obviously don't get birds at all.'

I was furious. He barely even spoke to me and here he was judging. 'You don't get Kit at all', I wanted to spit. I carried the fury around with me for a week, until I had concocted what I considered to be the perfect revenge – I was going to fill his cubicle with birds, though as I had no access to live ones, I made the concession that they would have to be constructed out of paper.

Mum had taught me how to make origami cranes when I was younger and cranes were close enough to storks. So every night I would carry myself off to my room, fold and fold, until I must have had nearly a thousand and all that was left to do was to plant my revenge.

I settled upon a lunch hour and when Buckley left for his haunting spot on the roof, set about carpeting the cubicle. With the last stork placed carefully on the back of his chair, I sat on the JumpPallet and waited for his return.

His first reaction was a muttered 'Woah, shit', then he froze, eyes sweeping the room to find me crouched and pouting. For a couple of seconds he seemed unable to process it. Then he started to laugh.

Fury burned my face but as the laughter continued I found myself confused. This wasn't cruelty but a breathless mirth that ripped apart the mask of his face; it was ridiculous, and infectious.

I laughed until it hurt, only to find Buckley still going. Already, I'd forgotten about revenge and was rewriting the script. Maybe I hadn't done this out of anger but to make him laugh, because I found I enjoyed that. Buckley, I would come to discover, is one of those people you can't help but want to please. I don't know what it is. The way his head tips back in crazed joy? The startled lift of his eyebrows? The sense that he'd somehow never expected to be given such joy in this life, that he'll love you forever just for proving him wrong? Perhaps that's what Susie meant about him being handsome.

When he'd finally sniffed back his laughter, he lifted a foot, then put it back down.

'But where am I going to sit?' he said. And somehow that got us laughing again, until he sank to the floor, stickman limbs folding in ways that no longer looked painful, but touching.

Yet realising he'd sat on one of the cranes, he fell quiet. The silence was terrifying. I tiptoed over and sat next to him.

'Mr Maurice?' I said, though with a new hesitation – already calling him by that name felt wrong.

When he finally looked up, it was with a strange smile. He held out the crane.

'Show me how to make one.'

I shut my eyes and listen to the final moans of the storm. If that was the day that Buckley started noticing me, perhaps it was also the one when I stopped seeing him. Of course, I listened to him, talked with him every day, but did I see him? Really? Or just the friend I wanted him to be? I had to learn the hard way that there's more to him than that.

Uncanny Shift

Even in the white-tiled shower cubicle, the world is startlingly red. Readjusting to a human colour palette after a week of being a snake means that I'm finding instances of the forgotten colours everywhere. Rubbing my eyes doesn't help, though alternating the shower between cold and hot at least makes me feel a little more real.

My arms feel wild as I scrub, almost unattached. My back, however, is a wall of paralysing resistance, though after five days as a snake, these kinds of thoughts are only natural. Even the water disconcerted me until I realised what was missing was the glow of its heat signature. If at the beginning of the week it was a body of a rattlesnake that felt odd, it's now a human body – *my* Original Body. Where Sperlman's Shock is temporary torture, Come Home is insidious, chronic doubt.

Clean at last, I throw on my jeans and hoodie. I want to wriggle from the cubicle but instead I will my stiff joints into movement and walk to the composting bin to stuff in my JumpPyjamas. Step.

Step. Step. Almost mechanical. Swinging the lid shut, I examine my hands, still flushed from the shower. However difficult the return, I've just got to remind myself of the luxury of having limbs.

I've managed to skip ahead of the Friday changing-room rush. One of the showers seems to be running, though I don't know who else has pulled out early. I sniff but it's no use, a curtain has dropped over the past once more, trapping me on the page width of the present.

Passing the mirror, I pause to check how many new spots have appeared during the jump and instead curse to see that my scalp is covered in a new growth of fuzz. If there's one thing about me that doesn't suit Phenomenautism it's how fast my hair grows. I pull out my shaver and tackle the worst of it. I'll need to give it another go before the next jump but I like to feel it's under control.

I'm beating the last flecks off my towel when Julie emerges from the cubicle to join me at the sink. She's dressed in shades of baby pink, a dolphin on the shirt, cut-off leggings and sparkly ballerina pumps. She's only a year younger than me.

'Sorry?' I say at her expectant look. The people who say I'm quiet should meet Julie.

Her face breaks into surprise. 'Can I borrow?'

'Oh right – the shaver? Sure.'

She rubs at the back of her neck as I hand it over. I'd think it was an expression of embarrassment if I hadn't heard on the grapevine that Julie sometimes tries to speak dolphin in her Original Body. The neck could be where the blow-hole seems to remap on Come Home.

I take the brush from the corner and sweep up my cuttings. Yet as she passes my shaver back and turns to go, there's a glint in her eyes that makes me berate myself. It's always a mistake to leap to assumptions about other phenomenauts; though we share our non-normality, that's often where it ends.

I'm returning to our cubicle when Julie comes running back along the corridor. Her face is naked with fear.

'Julie?'

She grabs my arm in answer and pulls me towards the common room at a run.

Through the joining door, I can hear a commotion like two metal stags are squaring off. We creep the last steps.

A glance is enough to take in the devastation. The tables are overturned, like tortoises unable to right themselves. Chairs lie twisted, another in the process of being beaten against the floor. I have to double-check to recognise the aggressor as Daisy; her face is torn open by rage.

Julie looks to me. There's no way Daisy will be calmed by a threat display now but this is my territory, I have to do something.

I step into the room, my heart leaping like a salmon trying to climb my throat. No bared teeth this time, just my shaking arms out-held, palms up. As our eyes meet, the whole universe seems to inhale on the distance between her bloodshot eyes and mine – then she charges.

I dodge and she rushes past, twists back but my shoulder is already ploughing into her, both of us jarred as she slams into the wall. It isn't clear whether the woof of breath is hers or mine but I seize the moment to kick her legs from under her, then, for lack of a better idea, sit on her back.

She claws round for my legs so I hop into a crouch between her shoulder blades and I catch hold of her hair for balance, remembering too late that it's a wig. She rears as I tumble back-wards, but that's when Julie rugby-tackles her.

There's not much Daisy can do with both of us sitting on her. Though she scrabbles at the floor there's no longer any real violence in it, at least not against us – the carpet is still getting a fair beating. Her spitting doesn't need words to be swearing. I pat the baby-smooth dome of her head, uncertain whether this is the right thing to do. Julie gives me a shell-shocked look.

I try for a friendly smile. 'Don't suppose you get into many fist fights as a dolphin.'

She looks away. Did she think the smile was a threat? Cetaceans don't show aggression with their teeth, I don't think.

Just accept it, Kit, you're shit at making friends.

Daisy has stopped struggling or even making any noise now but getting off her seems risky so I'm thankful when Buckley bursts in, followed by more neuroengineers and finally a panting Mr Hughes.

'You can't take risks like that.'

Buckley pauses in his rant to help me right the sofa. I push it back against the wall before facing him.

'It was fine. I'm fine.'

The same can't be said of these chairs. I try levering one against the floor to bend the leg straight but they're going to have to trash most of these; Daisy certainly wasn't pulling any punches. Although she'd stopped struggling by the time the nurse arrived, he still decided to sedate her. I'd be surprised if she comes back to work after this.

Phenomenauts who work with invertebrates are known for being a bit odd; after working long hours on reduced inputs, the complexity of emotional feedback from a human body can send feelings into a headspin. Yet I've never seen anything like today. Today was just crazy.

Buckley takes the chair from me and touches the bruise below my left eye.

'If your Original Body gets damaged you know there's no Come Home from that.'

'It's just a bruise.'

And it's only now that he's mentioned it that I feel it. I'm not even exactly sure how I got it.

Buckley doesn't look convinced but he can't push the point as Kyle has appeared in the doorway.

'Mr Hughes called. He's already tearing into Kay.'

As Daisy's neuro I can see why Mr Hughes would want to talk to Kay, but Kyle's involvement makes little sense. I look to Buckley but he avoids my eyes.

'Well, good luck,' he says.

But Kyle hasn't moved. 'You're not getting it. He's called you up too.'

I perch outside Mr Hughes's office to wait, no way I can go home without knowing what's going on. Though the window in his door is soundproofed, I can see all three neuros straining back from the raw anger of his face.

If possible, my heart is racing faster now than during the fight. At least I could *do* something then. It's not reasonable for Mr Hughes to put Buckley on the spot and expect me not to be a part of it.

It can only be ten minutes before Buckley is waved out, but the toll on his face looks like the work of years. The others aren't so lucky; as he slips out, Mr Hughes's voice snaps through the door like a whip.

I leap up, drawing short of flinging myself upon Buckley, and he almost smiles.

'It's OK. I'm not going to be punished.'

'But, why? What were you doing in there at all?'

His shoulders slump.

'Nothing really. It was Kyle and Kay. Daisy was bullying Julie; you know how defensive Kyle gets. Kay must have been fed up of her too because he persuaded her to play a practical joke. It just got out of hand.'

'I don't understand.'

He sags onto a chair. 'The dodos. You know she's been going on about rediscovering them? Turns out that they were simulations Kay and Kyle introduced into her projection. I don't think they expected her to become so obsessed with the idea. They finally told her this morning. It seemed like she'd taken it calmly enough but then, well, you saw the aftermath.'

'Simulations? But—' The rush of questions leaves me floundering. 'But why did Mr Hughes want to talk to you?'

'I told Kyle how to do it.'

I can feel my own face warm with his shame.

He throws up his hands. 'Just theoretically how one could insert a simulation into the CP. I didn't dream he would actually do it.'

'Simulations, though? You're saying – you can introduce things that aren't real into the projection experience?'

He raises his eyebrows. 'Is it really that surprising? Projection is all about feeding the brain data it didn't get naturally. You know what the VR people have been doing with it.'

'Virtual Reality is one thing but you're talking about mixing false data with real input.'

'It's not easy, but –' he shrugs – 'in a way all projection is kind of a simulation.'

My skin tingles.

'And, the dodos? They were just illusions?'

'Well, made-up data. Programmed well enough and the phenomenaut will just perceive it as real. Difficult, but not impossible. I doubt Kyle and Kay could have pulled it off if Daisy hadn't been inhabiting a spider and there must have been some prompting from Kay for her to perceive it as anything more exotic than a chicken.'

'But if what you're saying is true, what does that mean about ...' But I trail off, the consequences are too overwhelming.

He touches my arm. 'I would never do anything like that to you. You do know that?'

I frown. 'Yeah. No.' I hadn't even considered that possibility. But my processing ability has finally died with a splutter, leaving me with a hollow feeling in the place of thoughts. Buckley has fallen silent too, so we just sit a while, lost in our respective numbness.

Kay and Kyle emerge not long after but as Mr Hughes catches sight of me, his face brightens.

'North, just the person. A moment? No, not you, Maurice, North will be along in a few minutes.'

He falls back into his chair with a sigh, only to stiffen at the sight of my bruise. I don't know why everyone's so upset about it; it's nothing on some of the injuries I've had inRessy.

'It's fine,' I say. 'Just a bit sore.'

'Good, and thank you for handling this morning's – *upset*. I know we hire children but I didn't expect such puerile behaviour from our neuroengineers. But that's not why I called you in. After all the unpleasantness, I thought now would be the moment to share some good news.'

'Good?'

'I mentioned that we would arrange a more suitable human ResExtenda for you, didn't I? Well, now you've got stuck in I'm pleased to say that printing has started on a rather special model.' He smiles as if I should catch the import of this.

'OK?' I say.

His fingers fidget together atop the desk. 'Yes. Well, we've chosen you for the honour of a rather special ResExtenda. To be specific, one modelled on yourself.'

Exhaustion crashes down. 'You're saying, you're printing a copy of me? My Original Body?'

'You seem, hesitant?'

I almost have to laugh at the understatement.

'You didn't even ask.'

'You said that you found the human ResExtenda you were using strange. I said that I'd arrange something more suitable. We wouldn't make the expenditure for just anyone.'

'But you just assumed I wanted it.'

His fingers play an invisible tune upon his chin as he considers me. 'This ResExtenda will be an important aid in shouldering the responsibilities of your new job. Travel required for the promotional work would take you away from the projection tasks, which I was led to believe is where your interest lies. By having a ResExtenda based on yourself, you will not only have a more comfortable projection experience at the meetings but also save time. Think about it objectively and you'll see that it's an extremely sensible move.'

'But how can you just print a copy of someone without their approval? Is that even legal?'

'Admittedly we are setting a precedent here, but in the Tourism contract, you will see a clause detailing that your image could be used and reproduced for purposes of the Tourism.'

It's so horribly messed up that I have to laugh, and it's his turn to twitch.

'Katherine, I can see you're upset and I apologise for that. We honestly thought that you would be flattered. I don't have my own ResExtenda.'

'And it's already being printed?'

'I'm afraid so. But if you really wished . . . I could order it aborted.'

At that the laughter falls from me. I imagine being fed into the decommissioning vat, my face – a face that looks like mine – dissolving into pink slush.

The silence grows between us like a snake dislocating its jaw. I have to be logical. What, at the end of the day, is the problem with inhabiting a body that's a copy of my own? It's more natural than becoming a spider or seal, isn't it?

'It's being handled by our Biolabs if it would help for you to observe the process,' Mr Hughes says eventually. 'I'll let Faarooq know you're coming.'

At Biolabs, the postgraduate on duty won't let me into the printer room with my security clearance. I find myself laughing again, though it comes out more of a snarl. I wish Buckley could be here, but as it's a human Ressy, I can't tell him, or even explain why I left Mr Hughes's office looking like I was about to cry.

The postgraduate fidgets with the pipette she's holding, glances around for support. But before I can do anything else, a hand falls on my shoulder.

'It's almost six, why don't you head home,' I hear Faarooq say. The postgraduate doesn't argue.

Inside the printer room, Faarooq leads me to the door at the far end and out into a smaller lab, empty save for one printer, the shape and size of a coffin. He shuts the door behind us.

'Mr Hughes said you wanted some reassurance about your doppelgänger?' he says, only to stop as he catches my expression. 'Perhaps an unfortunate turn of phrase. The terminology is still, erm, in development.'

He hurries on with a cough. 'We only began the print this morning so there's not much to see.'

I nod and, after a pause, he swipes his card at the printer; the vacuum seal releases with a sigh.

'I'll give you some privacy. I'll be next door if you've any questions.'

'Faarooq?'

He stops.

'How – where did you even get the ... design, to print the copy?'

'It's not a copy, not in any full sense of the word. The internal workings are built from a template, the face and build we modelled from photos. When you project, you will find there are small differences. And of course it has no CNS, nothing higher than a thalamus, all in keeping with the ICPO standards.'

When he leaves, I stand, watching motes of dust drift through the light that breaks through the crack of the lid. The bubbling of coolant coming through the walls is echoed by the gurgle of my guts. I force myself forwards and push up the lid.

The body lies in a pool of light. If body is what it can be called. Archipelagos of tissue have yet to join into one continent. They look like cut fruit on a platter, rims of beige skin encircling the speckled pulp.

The bottom circles must be the beginning of heels, the longer oblongs above the backs of legs. Its buttocks are currently nothing more than two spheres and the strips of arms border empty space. The scalp sits at the apex like the dot of an exclamation mark. As I watch, the print head creeps the length of a toe, eclipsing and splitting the light. Mostly the Ressy looks like globules of gore.

My knuckles are white in their grip on the printer's rim, yet the rest of me is completely calm. I feel as if it were I, not the doppelgänger, floating in the iridescent coffin. After everything, I never expected to feel this – absolutely nothing.

Come Home

Letting them get away with the doppelgänger Ressy was my biggest mistake, though that's easy to say with hindsight. How was I to know at the time that it wasn't just a violation but a stratagem? If I'd just accepted that it was only ever my kudos the Tourism project wanted, then I might have been able to see that this meant they didn't actually need *me*. The billboard was as good a reminder as any of that.

Sleep refuses to come, so I sit in my den working through the remnants of bread. Could it really have been Buckley out there? It's tempting to believe that the figure was a figment of the dark and my imagination but, of course, they must have him out looking for me. And if it were, what then? Am I safer here in the assumption he's crossed this park off, or should I be searching for another den? The decision numbs me.

This bread has become even more fetid in the last few hours, so I throw the rest into the undergrowth where the fox might find it. She isn't back yet, these are prime hunting hours for foxes. I hope she's not in trouble; this territory must belong to another fox. Could that be why she's been following me? Though a lot of young females stick around as beta members of a family, she could be striking out to find her own territory, using me as a bodyguard for her trespassing. The idea is far-fetched, but then so are the alternatives.

If I could hunt too, this would all be a lot easier. I stare mournfully at the undergrowth where I threw the remnants of the bread, but I can't risk making myself ill. This isn't a body that's ever faced the elements. Long hours spent on the JumpPallet filled out its frame even when I was going through growth spurts. On Come Home there was always a moment of surprise at the plushness of fat, shifting with my movements, not something I often experience inRessy. But now, without my even willing it, it's changing.

The continued concert of my existence is bewildering; so much secret inner industry, just to stay alive. All that fevered biology, escaping understanding and awareness – even though it's mine, *me*; so that I seem to stand beyond, left with only the bass line of my heart.

A whisper of leaves alerts me to the fox's return. I roll onto my belly and stare into those deep eyes, my tiny reflection trapped in their fire. With a huff, the fox turns away and curls up for the night.

In a strange way this is almost like being back in Lauren's nature watches I attended as a kid, long before I'd even heard of ShenCorp; though I never got so close to a fox then. The nearest I came were the wet April nights when we'd lift toads from the roads, the small beasts squatting clammily in my hands as if without a care. And, standing there, rain singing against my raincoat, I would swell with love until I felt I was outgrowing my own skin.

Not all the children shared my enthusiasm; one girl couldn't touch a toad without shrieking. But then, for her, foxes were a source of terror too. When I pressed for a reason, her whisper had lisped with the force of emotion.

'They *look* at you,' she said.

———

I was the group's mascot of sorts; Stan and his husband, beer-bellied bears of men, would vie with Lauren for my approval in breathy undertones.

'Lauren's a hard mistress, ain't she?'

'Think she's trying to kill us, making us wait out in the cold like this.'

'I don't think there's any risk of that with that stomach,' Lauren would say, then to me: 'They're like naughty schoolchildren. They could learn a lesson from you.' But her tuts always sounded more like chuckling in the dark.

'She just don't know how to have fun. Not like us, eh, Kit?'

Because, of course, it was Stan that first gave me that name. 'Kit, our own little fox cub.'

Throughout the long waits, he would slip me toffees; he had a whole pocket of them in his weather-beaten mac. In another he kept treats for the friendly Labrador who waited in their car with its ripe pungency of dog. Sometimes he'd mix the pockets up, accidentally on purpose, relying on Mum to stop me before I, accidentally on purpose, put a dog biscuit in my mouth – just to see.

Yet the moment Lauren lifted her hand, everyone would still, our murmurs replaced by the wind's excited pitch. That silence was so intense, my being would seem to stretch, spilling like smoke from my numb flesh and up, up into the dusk sky.

Until *movement*.

A smudged shadow over earth. A visitation from another world.

Please look. I'd mutter beneath my breath. *Please look. Please look.*

And, sometimes, it would. Those eyes like molten silver, nailing me back inside my tingling skin; suddenly conscious of my full bladder and the itch of every muscle to move. A few scant seconds unfolding into infinity . . . over too quickly as the fox would turn and run.

Even when the dark had swallowed it, even after the others had returned to their whispers, I would remain entranced by the space it left behind.

There was no other word for it, just magic.

The night it all started, Lauren accompanied Mum and me back to the road. Mum always had to make her own pace. *Never rush her, never tug.* Her stick snicked a soft rhythm against the turf, her weight rotating on it with white-knuckled grip. Everyone else had forged on ahead, so I ran back and forth between the two groups, relaying the nonsense insults Stan invented for Lauren and her replies of faux outrage.

'Fawning fat-kidneyed gudgeon.'

'Disgraceful little man!'

'Bawdy folly-fallen barnacle.'

'What would his mother say!'

'Bootless dog-hearted coxcomb!'

But eventually Lauren caught my shoulder. 'Could I have a word?'

Her expression was so serious I worried that the insults had gone too far, but looking at me, she laughed.

'I just wanted to talk. Have you heard of something called phenomenautism?'

'Fen-nom-whatsit?'

Mum smiled and placed a hand on my other shoulder, sharing a look with Lauren over my head. They were still colleagues at the university back then; this was obviously something they had discussed in advance.

And so Lauren introduced me to the concept of consciousness projection. By the time she finished, my eyes must have been as large as an owl's.

'You see,' she said, 'Professor Shen is looking to recruit children who are smart and interested in wildlife to help improve our understanding of other species. I immediately thought of you. It would be a paid, fulltime job, so you'd have to leave school, though the company would provide tutorials so you can keep up with your education. My department is planning to commission several studies, so we'd be working together some of the time. Think you'd like that?'

I nodded so hard it left me dizzy. Lauren passed me a slip of paper.

'The contact details are on there. It would be a year or so until you'd start, so you've plenty of time to think.'

We walked the rest of the way in silence, though my head was buzzing.

Distracted by these thoughts, the cry took me by surprise and I jumped to see Mum on the ground, scrabbling to retrieve her stick.

Lauren was already at her side. 'Karen, are you OK?'

As the group surged back towards us, Mum pleaded for calm; she'd just slipped on the mud.

But there was no mud.

'Up you get.'

Lauren pulled on her hand to little effect. Mum begged for time to catch her breath.

But she wasn't out of breath.

'No rush.'

'Would you like some water?'

'Go easy on the vodka next time, eh?'

But she hadn't been drinking.

Stan and his husband slipped an arm under her armpits.

'Ready? 1, and 2, and 3 and—'

They lurched her up like a ragdoll, a hand held against her shoulder as the stick was pressed back into her grip. Her apologies were gasped around laboured breath.

'Don't you worry,' Lauren said. 'Stan's got to work off that six pack he demolished earlier.'

He'd normally come right back at her, but this time he just patted the soft bulge of his midriff. 'That's right, got to keep the old machine ticking over.'

When Mum's eyes finally found mine, the whole group turned with them, almost guiltily.

'Quite a little adventure your mother's had, eh?' Stan said. 'How's about you get her home? That's my girl.'

Back at the car, Mum's hands floundered at the lock, their shaking beyond her control. The keycard dropped to the gutter twice before she finally fumbled it back into her purse and declared that we'd get the bus.

But I didn't like the bus. I wanted to crawl into the safe mustiness of our car. I wanted to be at home.

I didn't like how Mum hobbled up the steps, how a man jumped out of his seat to help her.

I didn't like the stares of the other passengers, or the cruel clarity of the lighting on her grey face.

I didn't like how she kept telling me what a good girl I was.

In my memory, the journey lasts forever and I clench Lauren's note like a talisman.

22

Uncanny Shift

The weekend after the diagnosis, I stood on the patio watching Mum sleep.

She'd taken to napping on the sun lounger in the heat. Wrapped up in dreams, there was a curious vacancy to her features, their gentle curiosity slackened into flesh.

I'd once found a neighbour's cat lying on a verge a little like this; its body lax, the lift of its chest so light that I was uncertain if it was still alive. The last breath hissed from it as I carried it home, the silken wilt of muscles already cooling as I passed it into my neighbour's arms.

Until that moment on the patio I hadn't been afraid. Mum herself had reassured me everything would be fine. To have *it* named was almost a relief. The named can be fought, the named can be defeated. Mum was still Mum, only *it* had stolen inside her, *it* was twisting herself against herself. But standing there, watching, I was no longer so sure.

As if brushed by my thoughts, her eyelids flickered open and she stretched out her arms. I perched next to her and she smoothed my hair. But before I could work up the courage to ask if she was OK, her eyes were already sinking shut once more. The heat was always hard on her, her muscles like an ice cream softening inside its wrapper.

I stayed sitting, playing with the lounger tassels. And that's when her left leg started to spasm. Muscles snarling beneath skin like snakes, such force behind the contractions that the foot leapt off the cushion. A glance at her face made it clear that this wasn't intentional; there was nothing natural about that movement. Although I'd seen her leg twitch before, I'd never seen it do it to this extent.

I wanted to throw myself upon the leg and tackle it, to force it into obedience with my own strength, but even as it had taken on a will of its own, my body resisted mine. I could only watch as she pushed down on the knee with both hands until the juddering slowed and stilled.

We both stared at its stilled form, innocuous, inert – the same as it'd always been – and yet somehow that normality now seemed deceitful. It was my mum – part of her – and yet for a moment it had been in the control of something – *else*.

Hand on my cheek, she gave me the smile that comforted bruised knees and frustrated tears but now it stirred an impossible pain, nowhere and everywhere, finally condensing in heat at the base of my throat.

I looked away, stared at the ceramic parrot hanging on the side of the house until my vision filled with the blotches of primary colours and it seemed irrational that it didn't shatter with the force of my attention.

When I finally turned back, Mum was dozing again. Birds chattered their contentment, the muggy heat holding me like a hug, but the scene had taken on the taste of disaster. Like that time, one balmy July, when the temperature dropped, and from the sky came the fall of silent snow.

Huddled round my knees, I gritted my teeth against a shiver.

That evening, Dad ordered my running shoes on and led us through some stretches. His leg pressed against the wall was shrink-wrapped bone and sinew. Sometimes I'd think Dad would prefer it if he wasn't a body at all but an essence, like the shrivelled sticks of cinnamon and vanilla that he keeps inside his travel case.

And then we ran.

And ran.

By the time we stopped my sides were on fire, my thoughts swerving. It took me a while before I even noticed the view.

Bristol spread below us like an unrolled rug, tower blocks jutting from a jumble of rainbow-coloured doll houses; in the distance the glinting thread of the Suspension Bridge, caught gold beneath the first gauze of sunset.

Dad had his phone out and was busy snapping, always at work, on the lookout for a good picture. I flumped down onto the grass to avoid the lens and dug at the dusty ground with a heel.

When I start as a phenomenaut, I thought, I'll lift over all of this and fly away.

I imagined the rush of wind, the warmth of sun in feathers. But the pain wouldn't allow that thought, so instead I imagined myself a mole, shovel hands hacking the ground to pull myself into the dark damp.

The tower blocks warped through tears and Dad pressed me to his shirt. But I'd barely latched my arms around him when he was already detaching himself, the gentle push of his hand leading us back into a walk, a jog, a run.

Come on, Kit.

Run.

23

Come Home

Danger.

My mind staggers drunkenly around the feeling as I wake. Morning, a blackbird screaming alarm. I open my eyes, the fence a numb backdrop to my straining ears.

Something is padding through the bush. It could be the boy again, or a dog. But no. Whatever it is, sounds too large to be either of those.

At the crack of a twig, the blackbird bursts out of the hedge. In the quiet it leaves behind, I hear the whistle of stifled breath. Human, adult. Part of me wants to keep staring at the fence, to shut my eyes and drift back into sleep, but instead I roll over.

It's not a surprise to see Buckley, somehow it never is. Even after everything, his presence always tingles just beyond my senses. But that doesn't stop the terror.

My hands form fists against the ground but the rest of me has frozen.

'Kit.'

It's that voice that hurts. The voice that formed the backdrop to my every jump.

He offers up empty palms, ventures another step.

'Kit.' The word is soft, but his eyes are sharp with calculation.

There's now as much distance between us as there is between me and the fence. To make a break for it I'll have to be fast and even then I'll be screwed if he grabs my legs.

'There's nothing to be afraid of.'

Another step.

'We just want to help you.'

My lips peel back, sticky against dry gums.

Step.

I hurl myself towards the fence, from behind the crunch of his sprint. Wire bites into my hands and toes, I'm climbing too slow, he'll reach me in a second – time to do something crazy. I stop, leap backwards and my feet slam into him.

I'd been hoping to hit his stomach, to leapfrog as he fell, but by the time I realise I've missed, we're already falling. He grunts as I plough on top of him but then his arms are around me, the pair of us rolling and spitting.

I dig nails into his hands but he won't let go, my chest crushed by his grip. Wings of panic beat against my skull. He's too strong. Speed was the one advantage I had. The fight slips from me and I fall limp.

It's as if this skin has sheared away from me, only my small voice rattling around inside. His gasps rasp over my head and, gradually, the tendons in his arms slacken.

A bolt of orange, the flash of teeth

The fox comes from out of nowhere, worrying at his hand as if it were a rabbit. Buckley cries out in pain. At the back of my mouth, the taste of iron.

I force an arm back into my possession and bring it up *hard* – there's the snick of bone, then I'm free.

It takes me a second to remember to roll off him. I push up on a elbow, wincing at where it jarred from the impact.

Buckley is lying on his back, one hand clutched to his face. A thread of blood traces down his chin. At the fix of his pained eyes, I jump back and stop, crouched.

His speech is too garbled to understand. I look around, not even sure what I'm searching for.

'Buckley?' I whisper.

He mumbles again and this time I understand. 'You broke my nose.'

A hand flies to my own.

His voice is thick with mucus. 'You broke my *bloody* nose.'

I hurt. Buckley hurt. Hurt Buckley. I.

I can't accept the shape of it.

I hurt Buckley.

How can that make any sense?

My lips part, only to find the waiting words absent, and swallow instead.

He gives up on straining to look at me and drops his head back to the ground, blinking exaggeratedly. I should be running away and yet I find myself stuck, clutching my own nose.

'Are you OK?' I say eventually.

That earns me a glower. I broke his nose, of course he's not. A strangled laugh escapes me, only to choke off. I look around, stupefied. Buckley is hurt. Buckley chose ShenCorp over me. He came here to bring me in. I broke his nose. But he's still Buckley. And Buckley is – Buckley is Buckley.

I creep forwards to see his face more clearly but the pain there finds me like a knife and I stumble back – only to find his hand latched on to my ankle.

'Don't,' he says.

I try to pull away but he holds tight.

'*Don't.*' His eyes, wide with desperation.

I jerk my leg and his grip slips. The fox is already perched on top of the fence, snout lifted in urgency.

'No! Kit!'

Buckley staggers to his knees. I put a foot to the wire and clamber up. At the top our eyes meet one more time, a jolt of agony passing between us, but I've already leapt, launched into a sprint. Run, run. Not looking back.

I keep going until the strength goes from my legs and I'm left hugging the wall, waiting for the world to stop its spinning. The coarse brick is cool against the burn of my face.

Buckley found me. Of course he did. How stupid did I have to be to stick around even after seeing him last evening? He knew I felt safe in that park. He knows me as well as I do myself. Better even.

I sink to the pavement. The fox is crouched a step away, eyes still desperate, begging me to keep running, but hiding will only get me caught, I understand that now. They can't let their 'poster girl' loose, not with the things I know. Not when they're still using the doppelgänger Ressy in their billboard adverts. My teeth chatter off each other but stopping them is beyond my control.

Because what's one girl against the whole company? They have money, manpower, credibility, against what? My instincts. It's not enough. But I can't just give myself up.

I dig my fingers into my knees, seeking clarity in the pain. I *need* proof. People couldn't think I'm mad if they saw what I have. If I had the doppelgänger Ressy they'd have to believe.

At the thought my pulse leaps, my body reaching the understanding ahead of the words – because to get the Ressy there's no
avoiding it. I *have* to return to the Centre.

24

Uncanny Shift

The inside of my mouth feels odd. Though my whole body itches with a general uncanny, it's the mouth that bothers me most.

Everyone is elsewhere chasing up tasks for the exhibition's build-up, so I seize the moment to cram a furtive hand into my cheeks. Yet under its touch the interior is even more unfamiliar, my tongue an overgrown slug.

At the rumble of gurney wheels, I snatch the hand out and clutch it with the other as the booth supervisor appears. These fingers seem longer and smoother than those of my Original Body, almost a platonic ideal. Or maybe my fingers really are like that? Despite the idiom, I don't really know the back of my hands at all.

Something about this body is definitely *off*, even if articulating exactly how is beyond me. There was no Sperlman's to speak of on projection, this Ressy is the same size and shape as my Original Body, *it has my face*, and yet there is . . . difference. This doppel-gänger is based on a template so the fine details are bound to be incorrect to a lesser or greater degree. And that's not even mentioning my organs, which, though unseen, form the backdrop to every Ressy experience.

Unless this feeling *is* just imaginary. If I'd been projected into this Ressy without my knowledge, would I even be able to tell? The Sperlman's was alarmingly like waking up.

I wedge my hands between my knees. My clothes feel unnaturally slippy and light against slick skin. This is one difference I am certain of – the lack of hair, *anywhere*, save for the eyebrows and lashes. Visiting the toilet earlier was alarming. They must have deliberately left follicles out of the print. Or at least, I hope so; it's less disturbing than the alternatives.

Mr Hughes has followed the next gurney in; this one carries a tiger, hide twitching, as if shaking off flies. I wipe my hands down my skirt to hide the gleam of saliva.

'All settled in, North?' Mr Hughes says when the supervisors have left, though his wink makes it clear that he's referring to more than the booth. Today's projection is supposed to be an opportunity to acclimatise but I suspect the truth has more to do with his gratification. At the press conference, I'll be standing before some of the most important people in the industry and none of them will even imagine that I'm inRessy.

'Not long now.' Mr Hughes slaps my back hard enough to hurt and strides off to kiss cheeks with a woman from Sauntertech I know for a fact he despises. My pain, my face, so what is it about this body that I can't fully accept?

Poster girl or not, no one has much time for me today. Arthur didn't even recognise me until I willed up the courage to say hello. Even then it took a moment for his bemusement to break into a smile.

'Katherine, isn't it? Pleasure to finally meet.'

Yet even as he pumped my hand, a floor marshal was approaching for his attention and he hurried on. If he really is Shen, I suppose he must have larger things on his mind. Buckley would have been able to confirm; he must have seen the professor lots of times at university in the pre-ShenCorp days but he's back in Bristol. Yet even if he were here, I still might not get an answer; talk of his jumping days is one of the few topics that can make him touchy.

Tired of feeling like a spare part, I slip off our stand and into the bustle of the exhibition hall. Our booth is yet again the most extravagant of all the projection companies. It's not just the fully holographic displays and suede sofas; no less than ten Ressies are laid out on display and another five are already crawling through the crowds. I even saw a parrot flying circuits of the exhibition hall earlier, the banner fluttering from its tail in ShenCorp colours.

To the side of our display, Biolabs is promoting their printing service. Though effectively part of our stand, the people manning it wear Bristol University shirts. It's got to be only a matter of time before Biolabs follows ShenCorp in becoming its own start-up; if Mr Hughes doesn't succeed in buying them out first, that is. He's always sending baskets of fruit and chocolate to the technicians on some pretext or other.

I head into the opposite aisle before I'm seen by them. It's hard not to feel odd about the technicians having seen my doppelgänger vulnerable – naked of clothes *and* consciousness.

The stands here belong to other projection companies. I almost feel embarrassed for them in comparison to ours. Or perhaps I'm embarrassed by our gaucheness. Both?

Lebensweltum and Sauntertech have bothered to do little more than decorate their shell in their company colours. Though Lebensweltum has some footage of their Ankylosaurs they haven't even brought along the inactive Ressy. Yes, there are health and safety issues, but when we've been allowed our tiger, there shouldn't be much problem with a small dinosaur.

The woman at the front shoots a look of disdain at my ShenCorp shirt, though perhaps that's partly because of the white smear creeping over their nameboard, which looks suspiciously like parrot shit.

I leave the flesh projection displays to glance over Nintendo and Sega. They have some cool-looking games but I'm not convinced that consciousness projection will take off for them. It's a hard sell to push an entertainment medium that requires the Original Body to wear nappies or a catheter. Or, rather, 'Sanitech', as our marketing keeps reminding us.

My loop brings me past the mech Ressies of Astro-Phenomenautical, somehow still winning investment from the ex-terrestrial mining industry despite the mind-scrambling signal delays. And I'm back at the start, with nothing left to do but sit on my anxieties in wait for the press conference.

———

It feels as if the blood supply to my face has been cut off. Has something gone wrong with my Ressy? Or is it just the terror? My hands aren't doing much better. If I had to move, I'm not sure I'd be able to.

The pop and flash of cameras is blinding; blurring the audience into a single watchful entity. This is the largest conference hall at the exhibition centre and it's still packed. Mr Hughes must have leaked the announcement for there to be this much interest. But I don't want to think about how many people are watching.

Working infield, when no one looks at me for days, often leaves me feeling ghost-like, but *this* leaves me feeling a stranger to myself. I have to swallow to bring feeling back to the caulk of my mouth.

No doubt this body feels different from my Original now, but not because it's a Ressy.

I slide my eyes sideways to Mr Hughes, his teeth iridescent under the stage lights. His voice comes at me from every direction, I can't quite reach through the tumult to words. He must have made the announcement by now. Or maybe not. The minutes have thickened to treacle, the gravity of attention dilating time.

Instead, I force myself to focus on the animals we've got on display. An eagle is perched on the lectern and the tiger I saw earlier makes rounds of the hall in lazy steps. I know one of them is Julie, though neither is her usual order of animalia. Whoever is the tiger has my envy, easier that than being displayed as a parody of myself.

But at the sound of my name, I jolt. Mr Hughes is looking at me and with him the entire room. We must be on to questions.

Just smile, keep smiling.

My mouth feels as if it must be set in anything but.

As the audience mic squawks into life, I have to squint to find the face it belongs to in the crowd.

'How do you describe being an animal?' Was that the question? Not that humans aren't animals. Even so, how do they possibly expect me to describe? But in my hesitation Mr Hughes has stiffened beside me.

I stutter something, anything, surprised as my voice returns to me in an ocean of sound. It must have been an OK answer because the person sits.

Yet there's no respite. More questions. More answers. Their words ring at me as if from a distance of miles; my mouth batting back of its own volition, no time to think. These lips feel unnaturally large, tripping over themselves in reach for absent answers as I flee from one moment to the next, uncertain of what I'm even saying.

A woman near the front is on her feet. Her posture is that of a heron preparing to strike. The question gets lost in the hum of my ears.

'Sorry. Could you repeat ...'

'The Tourism,' she says. 'Don't you think it's wrong to create living creatures for the purposes of entertainment?'

To my relief, Mr Hughes takes the mic and spiels off his well-practised line about 'the ethics enshrined in ShenCorp's philosophy', how we're 'taking all the necessary steps to ensure the highest stand-ards of integrity'.

But the woman is still standing.

'My question was for Ms North. Do you or don't you think that the Tourism is unethical?'

'Unethical?'

As I blink, I'm suddenly somehow aware of my eyelids, a flicker of blackness between me and the world.

'Well. That depends how you define ...'

Blink.

'Not that I'm saying it's wrong. Not fundamentally ...'

Blink.

The words wrestle against my tongue and I watch from outside myself as one by one they muscle up my throat and plop into the room like blinking, glistening toads.

Walking.

I am walking.

I have been for a while.

The swerve of heavy steps, the career of passing people.

Where to I'm not quite sure, just away – away from the disaster of the press conference, from my own stupidity.

What did I say? I can't even remember. But it was bad. Did I really say that Body Tourism was wrong? The last hour is disjointed.

Snapshots of disembodied questions. Mr Hughes lunging for the mic, grasping it as if he were drowning.

My fingers find their way back to my mouth to explore the blunt landscape of gums. This face feels emptied by all those eyes. How can people remain themselves under such scrutiny?

As my feet swerve, a steadying arm finds me.

'Madam, are you well? Here, sit.' The scrape of metal alerts me to the chair being positioned behind me and I collapse onto it. The voice says something about 'water'.

Face to my knees, there is nothing but the sound of my own breath. I drift.

But now the footsteps return. The smoothness of a glass brushes against my hand. The small kindness almost hurts.

'Better. Yes?'

I nod but stop as it brings a new spate of dizziness. The face is crouched level with mine. A man, not anyone I recognise, tilt to his chin as if he doesn't know what to make of me.

'You want more?' He nods at the glass and I tense as I realise his accent is German. If he's from Lebensweltum . . .

'No, thank you,' I say. Though as he stays crouched, I wonder if maybe I should say yes, just to escape the scrutiny.

'It was, erm – how do I say? – *intense* in there, yes?'

So he was there for the announcement. Did he follow me? I shuffle back in the chair.

'You are not happy?' he says. 'Not happy with what ShenCorp are doing?'

'Who are you?' I say. 'Lebensweltum?'

He chuckles. 'No, no.' He pats his breast pocket and brings out a business card. 'ICPO.'

'International Consciousness—' But my tongue feels too large for my mouth to struggle through the name.

'Projection Organisation, yes.'

I'm not sure that this makes talking to him better or worse than to Lebensweltum. ICPO handles standard compliance, letting the wrong thing slip could be even more disastrous than my screw-up at the press conference. They haven't actually banned human Ressies, but I'm not sure if that's just because they've assumed no one is crazy enough to go there. I break eye contact, suddenly worried he could tell I'm in doppelgänger just by looking, though I know that makes no sense.

But the man is still talking. '– this is a big step. But I come to speak to you because we have heard other – worrying – things about ShenCorp. And we wonder how it is that Tourism's poster girl, Katherine North, who has been with ShenCorp for seven years, is unhappy too?'

I freeze at his expectant look, all too aware of the potential fuck-ups that await. Yes, I'm unhappy, but if Mr Hughes hears I've been speaking to the ICPO I'll be sacked for sure. I have to get rid of him but threat-displaying someone from the ICPO isn't an option either.

Thankfully my panicked stare does the trick. 'I leave you to your space,' he says. 'But if you wish to talk, you call me. Any time.'

And with that, he hands me his card and walks away.

———

It's not until the next day that Mr Hughes finds the time to call me up for 'our little discussion'. The worry kept me awake most of the night, discomforted even in my Original Body. It must show – Mr Hughes takes one look at me and laughs.

'Take a seat, North, it's not all that bad.'

'Sir, I just wanted to say once again that I'm sorry. I didn't—'

'Take a seat.'

My knees buckle.

'The truth is,' he says, 'we owe you an apology.'

'You—'

'Yes, us, North. Let me finish. Public relations is clearly not your specialisation. By asking you to take on the role we've not only distracted you from your important projection work but pushed you outside your comfort zone. We must shoulder some of the responsibility for yesterday's mishap.'

'You're saying I won't have to do any more publicity?'

He inclines his head and I slump with relief. Mr Hughes is not one to easily admit mistakes.

'Of course' – his voice rises – 'as we've already announced you as poster girl, this does leave us in a bit of a quandary. But we believe that we've come up with a solution that will suit all parties.'

I tense again.

The tip of his tongue passes over his lips, a snake tasting the air. 'Now that we have a ResExtenda in your image—'

'No,' I say.

'If you'll let me finish.'

'No.'

I find myself standing.

'North.'

'No.' Why now, of all times, does my body start trembling?

'Sit down.' Warning rumbles behind his voice.

'This is . . . this is wrong.'

For a second it seems as if he might lunge from his seat but instead he releases a long breath.

'I know the idea might seem frightening—'

'Not just that. All of it. You shouldn't be doing this.'

He slips arms behind his head, leans back.

'You're going to have to explain what "all of it" is. This isn't like you.'

I shift on my feet, uncertain in the face of his calmness. All the times I had this argument in my head, it never went like this.

'All of it. I mean, the Tourism, using Ressies for entertainment.'

'I didn't take you as a pro-lifer.'

'That's not my point.' But I flush at my own shout. 'It's not that they're alive, they're not conscious but that still doesn't mean . . . other subjectivities *aren't* a consumer item. Their habitats aren't playgrounds.' I find myself searching his face beseechingly but my words make no impression on it. 'Phenomenautism is meant to be about understanding other perspectives, not *buying* them as some – some – luxury items. They're not . . .' Yet, under his nonchalant look, the words fail me. I glance back at my chair.

'Do sit down, North,' he says and I find myself almost grateful to do so. He waits for me to settle before leaning forward. 'Now am I to understand that you wish to hand in your resignation?'

'No,' I say, though this time all force has bled from the word.

'So, are you saying that you'd prefer to continue handling the marketing work yourself?'

'But—'

'But what?'

I drop my look to where my hands claw in my lap. But it's *me*, I'd been going to say. Yet is it? Really?

'North?'

'No. I don't want to handle the publicity.'

He slips into the pause. 'Let me finish then. You have my assurance that none of this will be carried out without your permission. There will be firm rules in place. We'll run all scripts past you; in fact, we'd ask you to add your own flourishes for authenticity. Only one person, other than yourself, would be approved to project into the ResExtenda and each projection would be signed off by you beforehand. Really, it'd be no different than were you to handle the projection yourself, except that you won't have to deal with the stress and the work will be handled by someone with the necessary experience. A win–win, wouldn't you agree?'

I feel the moment slip away from me.

'You said only one person would be allow to project into it?'

His lips stretch into a smile he must think of as reassuring.

'Why yes. Who better than myself?'

Come Home

It must be past three in the morning at least by the time I work up the courage to set out for our Centre. Even the distant rumble of traffic has given way to stillness. But I keep low and to the shadows anyway. There's stupid and *stupid* with these things – I still can't decide which this is.

Round the last corner and there it is, ShenCorp. Wind mutters through the foliage.

Turn back.

The windows are dark but there must be people inside; a security guard, one or two neuros monitoring studies, the night nurse. From the way Buckley used to talk about the nocturnal shifts it sounds like people tend to stick to their cubicles, so evading them should be possible. At least they shouldn't be expecting me, it's that ridiculous an idea. And yet this is their territory, and you don't mess around on someone else's, not without good reason.

The thought glues my feet to the spot: the plummet of possible futures trapped within a microscope slide of time.

I force myself to think of the day Mr Hughes lay on his pallet and fell still, rising seconds later from the opposite gurney, his face mine. Of how, when I met my eyes, one winked back.

I force myself to remember the filming, how my voice in his mouth sounded girlish and trite. How he placed his hands on my hips and moved my tongue around my mouth. Although I'd grudgingly conceded to the script, the sentiments weren't mine.

I force myself to relive standing, after, by the sinks, grimacing at the mirror, daring the reflection to wrestle from my will. To wink, scream, punch through the glass. Because, ultimately, I've never been sure of my reflection. It's always seemed uncertain. It's always seemed malleable.

Doing this isn't a choice. I *have* to stop them.

Besides, people always leave food around the cubicles and the hunger has become a second animal inside of me. I scurry over the road.

Though I didn't grab my access card during my escape, it'd be foolish to come this far and not try the door. At least the security booth looks empty, although that must mean they're patrolling inside.

Still, I stare at the first step up a long time. In the past I'd never even noticed it but now raising one foot to it seems a monumental effort. By the time I reach the top I feel as if I've sprinted uphill.

Save for the faint glow of the fish tanks, the doors are dark. My neon ghost hangs in their frame, hugging herself as she regards me. I put a hand out to hers and push ... but the door doesn't budge.

My courage snaps and I fly down the steps and around the corner of the building. My whole body is buzzing, sparks in my fingertips.

None of the windows I pass are open, nor the fire escape: that would be too lucky to be true. I wedge my nails under a jamb but am only rewarded with pain.

My hiss escapes in condensation. If only I was a bird or something small, I could fly onto the roof or sneak my way in. Human bodies aren't good for anything.

I make another round of the perimeter, this time giving each window a tug. But every entry point is shut tight. My stomach has contracted to a fist. Stupid or not, smashing a window is the only option.

I head back to the room furthest from the road. The interior is barely visible in the dimness but at least that means there's no one inside. Do this right and maybe I can get out with the doppelgänger before anyone realises.

My foot plants through the window in a burst of glass stars. A moment swallowed by a blink, though the crash replays in my head for a long time afterwards.

Only as the last crystal note falls quiet do I realise that my leg is still raised. I drop it, beat the remnants of glass from the frame with a coat sleeve and crawl inside. As my bare feet land on cubes of broken glass, I can't hold back the whimper.

Nothing is familiar in the dark, but this must be one of the corridors on the opposite side of the building to my cubicle. If I go there first I can find some food before heading up to Mr Hughes's office. Though it's a long shot, the search for my doppelgänger seems best started there.

I have to tread carefully to stop the slap of feet on lino. After being out on the street, it's odd to feel such a smooth surface beneath my soles. Though they offer nothing close to the sensitivity of a rattlesnake belly, I can still feel the subtle vibration of the supercomputers below.

At the creak of a door, I freeze. It comes from the corridor up ahead. The sound of feet follow.

Shit! I cast around, but there's nowhere to run.

A hand clamps around my mouth, pulls me backwards through a doorway. I squirm round, ready to bite, only to stop at that face. Grandma Wolf.

She releases me, touches one finger to her pale lips. Light flares in the corridor but we're crouched to one side of the door. Her eyes are rheumy in the brightness, yet their intensity is cutting. I press my back against the wall, one held breath between us.

The footsteps are almost on us now. My lungs feel punched; if I have to run I'm not sure that I could. But they pass without hesitation, heading straight towards the room where I broke in.

Stupid. Stupid! Of course smashing a window was going to call attention.

The footfalls stop. A voice breaks the quiet.

'Shit.'

Grandma Wolf's face cracks in an obscene smile and she steps into the corridor. My hand reaches after too late, finding only the door shut behind her.

The voice returns muffled. 'Hey! You did this?'

More footsteps. Any second the door must open and—

'Hey!' the man shouts.

The patter of running feet is followed by boots.

'Hey! Stop!'

I stay frozen until the thuds are swallowed by distance, still numb with surprise. Grandma Wolf *saved* me. They won't expect another intruder if they think she broke the window. Yet why would she do that? I alerted her to Mr Hughes when she broke in. But whatever the answer, it will have to wait, there's work to do.

The Centre seems another place entirely at night. White corridors are replaced by shadowy tunnels, thrown in dim red or green from the bulbs above the cubicle doors. Green is safe but I slow at the reds; though the blinds are down, there must be neuros inside.

Passing Julie's, I see the blind is up despite the red. Kyle probably forgot. No sign of him, though. One of the screens shows a watery storage tank and a sleek back. A dolphin no doubt. They normally only ever sleep with half the brain but that's not something you can ask of a phenomenaut. Is it lonely being cut off from your pod like that? Perhaps not, dolphins can be bastards.

The tubes of Body Support glisten under the half-light; bags of fluid almost looking lit from within; one is amber with urine, another saffron from nutrients. Enmeshed in this web Julie barely seems human. The glint of eyes stare sightlessly at the ceiling. I don't like looking.

Inside our cubicle – my old cubicle – I lean against the wall, just breathing.

Ghosts of memories play in the dark. Buckley, long legs propped on the desk, the spark of his eyes as he tossed grapes for me to catch in my mouth or rapt as he studied his screens. Or the two of us just sitting in silence, safe in the knowledge that we'd only have to reach out to touch, though of course we never did. Apart from the day everything fell apart. Apart from the day I saw him for what he really is. But I won't, *I can't*, think about that now.

Torturing myself like this will achieve nothing. I came here in search of food. Buckley's drawer yields a packet of biscuits, my mouth salivating before the sugary fat even reaches my tongue. Drool overspills my lips by the time I'm cramming in the second. Third. Fourth. Fifth.

It's hard to resist demolishing the rest but they go, grudgingly, into a pocket. Always cache if there's the choice.

Back in the corridor, I inch on towards the stairs. Someone is moving about on the floor above, the creak of their steps unnaturally loud, but they don't seem to be coming any closer.

Still, my legs tremble so much I have to cling to the banister. There's almost no light here; with fox eyes this wouldn't be a problem but as it is I'm practically blind.

Back on the flat, I speed up to a hobble. It takes one glance inside Mr Hughes's office to see that the gurney is empty. But what did I expect? He's not stupid enough to leave a Ressy that looks like me out in plain sight. Biolabs then.

Yet as I turn to go, I realise that the room isn't empty. An angular figure crouches on top of the desk, white hair luminous in the moonlight. I'm glad to see that Grandma Wolf evaded the security guard.

I push on the door, only for the thanks to die on my lips. Liquid hisses against the glass desktop, in my nostrils the stench of urine. Her stare holds mine. Territory marking.

My courage breaks and I back out of the room.

Biolabs looks even more sinister than usual in the dark. The twitch of raw muscles in the glass cases draws my eyes in panic. Backlit growths of neural matter look like fantastical mushrooms, seemingly bobbing under their own volition, although I know that they must be pushed by the passage of oxygen through the fluid. Still, I can't stop myself glancing back as I cross the room.

In storage, I shuffle along the aisles of gurneys, breathing through my mouth to dampen the queasy scent of disinfectant and bodily musk. The low breath of Ressies join into an ocean's shush.

Zebra. Gorilla. Wolf. Bat. Fox.

I stop. Lauren's group must have found the funding to print another fox. If I stole it and a CP – could I? But no. It would never work. I'd still have to keep my Original Body ticking over. Still, I pause a while, sinking fingers into the warm fur.

After a full circuit of the room, there's no sign of any human Ressies. That would be expecting too much when they're being kept secret. I try the handle of the secure storage room but no such luck. Even if I had my own card, I wouldn't be able to get in; that's for Bio and neuros only. If I steal one . . . but how am I going to do that?

Tiredness claims me and I slump onto the nearest gurney. It won't hurt to sit. Just for a minute.

The rise and fall of the chest against my back is comforting. I lie down next to it and press my face into the strong-smelling fur. Odd to find what was once mine, warm flesh.

I reach up to the face and gingerly slide back the lids; beneath are bright, auric eyes.

26

Uncanny Shift

The eyes are blank, limbs limp. One ear twitches to shake off a fly but it's just an automatic response. Russell can't have arrived yet.

I back out of the pod and amble about the clearing. Heat blushes through my paws, even in the shade. I'd go in search of water but there's no time to wander off now with this *tourist* on the way. An associate of Mr Hughes, I'm told, influential blogger by trade – hence the invite to beta-testing – but it's hard to imagine how these details tell me much about what he'll be like as a tiger.

A bird shriek tears through the crescendo of leaves. In the distance the whoop of monkeys is shh-ed by the estuary I know to be over a mile away. Though I've only been here a week, I've already come to know and love the forest's rhythm. It's hard to imagine sharing it. But perhaps that's because tigers are solitary creatures.

A shrill note precedes Buckley's return to comms, his absence has been uncomfortably loud.

'Russell's all set up now. Mr Hughes is talking him through some final exercises but we'll be starting the projection soon.'

'OK.' I sit back and give my face a last-minute clean.

'He's under now. With you in three.'

'Remember, Mr York's endorsement is very important. Make sure he has a good time.' This second voice is Mr Hughes. The fact that no one would appreciate their boss's voice inside their head is clearly not something he's considered.

But if star treatment is what is demanded, that's what Russell will get. I even spent most of yesterday catching a boar, left it right outside his pod so he won't have to walk far. Despite keeping it overnight, it still smells great, so long as he doesn't mind the evacu-ated bowels.

'Bringing him round now.'

I poke my head back inside the pod in time to see the body twitch. Waves of contractions push beneath the skin, nothing about the movement natural, but when it stops there is a difference to its stillness – the tenseness of inhabitation.

'Hello, Russell,' Buckley says. 'You're probably disorientated right now but there's nothing to worry about. You've just projected as ShenCorp's very first official tourist. Congratulations!'

It's strange to hear Buckley inside my head but talking to some-one else. I'm not sure I like it.

'If you get too uncomfortable please let us know or, in the case of an emergency, psych the exit-potential Mr Hughes taught you earlier.'

One of the legs jerks.

'Hello, Russell,' Mr Hughes adds. 'You're not uncomfortable, I hope. Acclimatisation will take a while.'

The blunt face clenches, as if fighting the creep of daylight on a pillow.

'Try talking,' Buckley says. 'You remember our sub-vocalisation exercises?'

Static scratches against my skull as Russell must try and fail.

'If it's difficult, don't worry. You've got a lot to adjust to right now. I'm going to start patching in the visuals.' Buckley's voice is followed by the patter of fingers. 'And OK. That seems to have worked. Try opening your eyes.'

Its expression twitches. As I lean in, the nose scrunches under my breath. Then the eyelids open on to deep, saffron orbs. Tiger.

But then the eyes come to rest on mine in a long, searching look. No, not tiger. Human.

'Hi,' I say.

Its expression remains empty but perhaps he hasn't linked my voice with sight. I lick his nose.

'Give the man some space,' Buckley says.

Though that hardly seems fair, I leave the pod.

'Sorry about that, Russell,' Buckley says. 'Phenomenauts have their own way of thinking about things. How are you feeling?'

More static, then—

'Strange.'

My fur prickles at that voice. It's completely empty of tonality – a pre-set. Buckley obviously didn't think it worth creating a simulation voice for such a short projection.

'The feeling will pass with time.'

'You're doing very well,' Mr Hughes says.

'Right. You should have seen me on my first projection. But if you're feeling up for it, I'd like to get the proprioceptive signals plugged in. This might be a little uncomfortable, but it'll pass quickly.'

Sperlman's 'a little uncomfortable', how about that for understatement of the century?

'OK.' If Russell is afraid there's no way of telling from that flattened voice.

'Great. Then in, 3 ... 2 ... 1.'

The writhing is painful to watch. I leave them to it and return to my pacing. Dragging the boar has left it in a gruesome tangle so I nudge the head into a more natural angle and straighten out the legs.

By the time I've finished, Buckley is encouraging Russell to stand. Through the frosted glass of the pod, the Ressy flops like a rag doll in an invisible hand. Presumably trying to exit, he lunges and smashes head-first into the ground, lies crumpled, mouth hissing open and shut like a rusted hinge.

Just watching brings back the memory of clinging to the toilet bowl after my first jump. Even with the reduced inputs, how can they expect this to be *fun*? I settle down for a long wait.

By the time Russell stumbles from the pod, my tongue is stiff from panting. He turns slowly in the light, blinking and slack-jawed, and I pad over to join him. The canopy is dappled in brilliance; the air a humid honey that ebbs with the forest's rhythm. Scent here has a composted zeal, the sweet and sour bloom of death and life.

'Amazing, eh?' Buckley says. 'You're through the worst of it now. Everything gets better from here.'

But Russell has transferred his stare to the boar. I nudge it towards him.

'What is that?'

My pelt tingles under those eyes. With a voice so empty, it's hard to imagine anything sentient behind them.

'A boar,' I say.

'I don't understand.'

'You must be hungry.'

His nostrils flare, the tip of a tongue slipping between his lips, only for his head to jerk away.

'Eating really would be—' I say, but Buckley cuts me off.

'It was a nice idea, Kit, but leave him to it.'

Easy to say when you didn't spend a whole day catching it.

But complaining will only invite trouble with Mr Hughes listening in. I sit and groom, watching Russell lope around the clearing from the corner of an eye. It's a strange sight; short of trying to stand on two legs, he's moving like a human, which I hadn't even imagined was possible as a tiger. The Ressy has an inbuilt cerebellum; all it should take to move is the intention and the Ressy will do the rest. Instead those great paws wrench up, one, at, a, time, as if from thick mud. The trick of jumping is to give in to the body, not dominate it. It must be taking considerable effort, yet Buckley's coaxing is doing little good.

As it's going to be a while until Russell is ready to go anywhere, now would be the time to eat. Letting the boar go to waste is not something I'm willing to do, whatever Russell thinks.

The tail twists off with a few bites and I lick around the rough hair of the rump, then up the belly and bite into the hide. A few tugs later and the flesh rips, intestines sliming out in delicious heat. A sniff reveals nothing fetid so I shove my head inside and tear off a mouthful. The meat is warm, buttery, almost melts down my throat. Hearts are normally the choicest part, but with Russell around that might be a step too far. Instead I gorge myself on the fat around the haunch, filling myself as quickly as I can in case Mr Hughes criticises me for spending too long on lunch.

Chewing the flesh on the other side, I see that Russell has stopped to watch, face contorted. Under that gaze I become aware of the blood matting my face, its sticky heat up my muzzle. Though it's nothing to be embarrassed about, I lick the worst of it clean.

Mr Hughes saves me, though I doubt from pity. 'Good work, Russell. You're adapting excellently. Wouldn't you agree, Buckley?'

'Looking pretty good.'

Despite their conversation, Russell's gaze remains on mine. I hold back a snarl; surely he's not aware of the threat in the gesture. Yet both of us twitch at Mr Hughes's clap.

'Now you've the basics under your belt, what would you like to do with your time as a tiger? You've the whole forest at your disposal.'

Russell doesn't even have to think.

'Hunt.'

'You don't want to eat a boar but you will hunt one?' I don't even try to keep the disdain from my voice.

'North. Russell is the customer.'

I let silence be my answer, display a sliver of teeth.

'My apologies, Russell. A hunt sounds like an excellent idea. North will be able to induct you into the art.'

'It won't be easy though.' And Mr Hughes can't rebuke me for saying that. Young tigers take months to become proficient hunters. I only managed this week by applying tricks picked up in other Ressies. 'It's all down to stealth. We can't keep up speed over long distances.'

Russell nods. His confidence, if that is what it is, is misplaced. Yet something about that guarded look makes me think it might be possible for him to learn.

As part of the Tourism project I've made a survey of the local prey population, so it doesn't take long to pick up a trail. A path of crushed grass in the glade is the first clear sign. The blades are heavy with boar scent.

I shut my nostrils and poke out my tongue – it's a young male, here no more than half an hour ago. Russell watches, his emotion inscrutable.

'Flehmen,' I explain. 'Gives a stronger sense of smell.'

His tail waves and I return to my examination. The scent seems familiar. I've probably smelt it here before. Although there hasn't been the time to memorise the habits of every animal, I've a rough idea with this boar.

It's too far ahead to see, so instead I listen: the grumble of Russell's breath, nibbling of deer, the chatter of birds . . . and there – snuffling in the trees up ahead.

I nod at Russell and slink on. The placement of each paw follows careful examination, even the rustle of grass could give us away. Through these eyes the stalks seem luminous yet greyed, as if the light has bleached colour from the world. Though we're a long way off, we're not the only creatures here with good hearing. If the deer were to be alerted, their stampede would send the boar into flight.

At the drum of hooves, I freeze, but it's just two deer play-fighting. In the absence of wild tigers, the prey here have lost some of their natural caution. The fight could provide the distraction for a kill but with Russell in tow it wouldn't be wise.

I'm preparing to move on when I realise that our quarry has stopped. We're downwind; it has no reason to be suspicious, but perhaps it's just listening to the deer.

'What now?' Russell says. It's hard not to read irritation into that robotic voice.

'The boar's stopped,' I say. 'Listen.'

'Can't hear a thing.' Though with tiger senses, it's more likely that he can hear too much.

'You just need to adapt, senses are always overwhelming at first.'

The sound of hooves returns, our quarry has switched direction, now heading towards the lisp of water.

'What's the hold-up?' Buckley whispers, despite being thousands of miles away.

'It's going round the estuary. An ambush seems our best shot.'

'Sounds good to you, Russell?' Mr Hughes says, but whether or not an ambush is less exciting, it's Russell's only chance of making a catch.

We head into the mangroves. The gnarled trunks push skyward above us; below, their roots stick up from the iron-scented mud like teeth.

I let Russell slip ahead. Now he's distracted his walk is more natural, although something about the poise is still distinctly human. The self-assurance perhaps? Only a human would walk unfamiliar territory with the expectation of safety. Even for tigers that would be foolish.

When he glances back, I look away. His inscrutability is different from that of the creatures I normally cross during my jumps. This quiet is almost guarded.

At the river, I rush in. The muggy water is still blissful against broiled paws, delicious on my stiff tongue. Russell waits on the bank, though if Buckley hadn't turned his inputs down he'd be as parched as I am.

The estuary mutters around us, a soft breeze toying with my whiskers. With eyes shut, I can almost imagine the humidity as sultry breath against my neck.

'How long do you think since another tiger stood here?' I ask Buckley on our private channel.

'None in this part of the Sundarbans for at least a decade.'

As sad as it is, it would be disastrous for tourists to come face to face with the real deal. I glance back at the man-tiger to find him watching again. It's becoming difficult not to read disapproval into that gaze.

'Even if you're not feeling thirsty, it'd be a good idea to have a drink,' I say.

His top lip peels back.

'You'll start feeling terrible in other ways than thirst.'

'It's brown.'

'Not a problem inRessy. See.' I lap another mouthful. The freshness is clagged by clay, but still good. 'You'll find it tasty. We've taste buds tuned to it.'

He shakes his head.

'The man doesn't have to drink if he doesn't want to,' Mr Hughes says.

If anyone in Research left a Ressy in such a state Mr Hughes would give them a bollocking they'd never forget. Though the insurance packages are making more sense to me now. If all tourists are like this, the Ressies won't last a year.

'You're OK with swimming, at least?' I say. 'If we're going to catch that boar we have to go now.'

He pads in, in answer. Mud sucks at my paws then slides away. As my ears submerge, the world is blanketed in water's rumble. The silence is almost scary; in this body it's close to being blindfolded. I wince my eyes above the bite of salt and snort out the waves.

The far bank writhes as we pull ourselves ashore – the scatter of mud skippers. Russell lunges after one and smacks it to a wet squelch. His paw lifts back up to reveal the squashed body plastered to the bank.

'What the fuck?' I say.

Russell flicks it into the water.

Mr Hughes switches over to the private channel. '*North.*'

But how can he be angry at *me*?

'He killed a mudskipper. For no reason.'

'That doesn't excuse swearing.'

'And what excuses random killing?'

The mic crackles under his sigh. 'This isn't Research any more. Your job is to help Russell enjoy himself and frankly you could be trying a lot harder at that.'

Buckley interjects before I can growl. 'Kit, you can have this argument later, but right now Russell's getting ahead of you. If you want to keep him out of more trouble you'd better catch up.'

And he's right. Russell has blundered on, despite having no idea of where the trail is.

'Listen to Maurice, North,' Mr Hughes says. 'I'm going to get more coffee and when I'm back I'll expect a dramatic improvement in your attitude.'

I snarl and bound up the bank. Russell is being so loud there's no point being quiet. Hopefully the boar can hear him too.

Buckley lets his voice soften now Mr Hughes is out of the room. 'Try to relax. It's a dangerous Ressy to get angry in.'

Yes, the unfamiliar physiology of Ressies can interact alarmingly with feelings but right now I've good reason to be angry.

'Want me to talk you through the breathing exercises?' Buckley says.

I suppress the curse that would only prove his point.

'Let's just get this over with,' I say.

But that's when I realise that I'm being watched.

I stop, unsure of the feeling, but with nostrils flared all I can smell is tiger. Then the twitch of ears alerts me to something creeping through the undergrowth ahead, not the sound of it giving it away so much as how the birds mute at its passing.

Whatever this is, is dangerous.

I crouch, my fury turning into terror. Whatever it is, is taking pains not to be heard. But what would stalk a tiger? My surveys picked up nothing like this.

Then I see it.

'Kit?'

A shadow. Eyes of struck flint.

'Tiger,' I say.

'What?' Buckley sounds confused.

'Tiger. There's a tiger.'

'Sorry?'

Can't he see it? Now it's closer, not hearing it is impossible. Its heartbeat is a battle drum.

'Tiger,' I repeat.

'You mean Russell.'

'No. No.'

This isn't Russell's empty presence. This is the real deal.

My tail fuzzes with déjà vu. I find myself thinking of the growl of engine, the fox's eyes the moment before I died. That condensed presence is the same. Yet why would a tiger remind me of a fox?

'Fucking Mike,' I whisper.

But it isn't funny this time, this isn't a scrap with a seal. What am I even doing out here? Pretending. I pale beside the real thing. We have to run, and now.

Which is when I remember Russell.

I glance away in search of him. Yet when I look back the tiger is gone.

A bird chatters overhead, something small hops in the undergrowth, the forest picking up its melody as if it were never broken. But how is that possible? With these ears, I should have heard the tiger leave.

'Kit? Talk to me.'

'There was another tiger. But it vanished! I didn't even hear it go.'

'There've been no sightings reported here in decades,' Buckley says.

'But I saw ...' What did I see? Not much. And no tiger would give up on its territory. No tiger would just leave.

'You were probably looking at Russell.'

'It was nothing like him though.'

'Come on, Kit. You've rarely co-projected. It's easy to get confused.'

'I – don't know.'

'Are you sure it wasn't a deer or something?'

I pass my tongue across my nose. My head feels taxidermied. Because it *doesn't* make any sense.

Could it really have been Russell? It seemed so different.

'It was ...' I began, but how could I explain?

And why did it make me think of the fox?

'You're OK.' Buckley has gone into full soothing mode but I'm too weary to get annoyed. 'It's been a tough day. Until you had that drink you were overheating and dehydrated. You know how easy it is to misinterpret when you're inRessy.'

'I guess ...'

'I'm going to decrease some of your inputs. Let's just ride this out.'

'Don't—'

But I can already feel flesh paring away, the numbness leaving only a tingle of skin.

'Buckley ...'

Another click and the forest tunnels; its orchestra, putting down instruments, exits the concert hall, only a small quartet left behind.

I have to catch myself before I stumble. The ground feels insubstantial.

'How's that?' Buckley's voice echoes inside my skull.

'It's . . .' I start to say, but my thoughts are too thinned to finish.

'What now?' Russell says when I finally catch up.

His empty voice makes me want to giggle but instead I loll my tongue.

Come on, Kit. Be professional.

He stares. And as I peer back, I wonder. From a distance, could I make the mistake?

'The trail,' I say. 'Pick it up. I mean, we've got to. Here somewhere.'

I lead on as best I can, though the ground keeps trying to swoon beneath my steps. The forest is as flat as if this were a film. Without the keenness of smell I'm almost as lost as Russell, but eventually we stumble across a crushed pathway I recognise. Now all that is left is to wait.

I slump into the ferns and slop my head onto Russell's flank, face planting as he pulls back. Lie here instead. Floating.

The ebb of forest trickles through my ears, soothes muscles like silk. The burnt colour of a bee-eater zips overhead, its whetted song jubilant against the forest's muggy lungs. Could almost sleep . . .

The snap stirs me. A twig, underfoot, not far away. Instinct pushes against the wool of my thoughts.

Prey.

Its footfalls trace closer, accompanied by the heavy draw of breath, and the boar steps into the clearing. It's carved of clean angles, blunt face and jutting spine. A young male, but not that young. It will put up a fight.

It gives a damp snort and scrapes at the ground. Small eyes, suspicious.

Russell crouches as if preparing to pounce. From this distance he's bound to miss, but who cares? I let my eyes fall shut.

'Wait,' Buckley says.

The boar grunts and continues towards us.

Despite myself, my back legs are starting to wriggle in readiness, though with reduced inputs they feel more like noodles than the normal coil of the hunt.

The boar lifts its snout. Daggers for eyes.

'Now!' Buckley says.

Russell storms forwards. The boar squeals. Claws flash red and the dream sours.

I blink away cobwebs, watch Russell and the boar roll about in a messy tangle. He's biting clumsily into its flank, paws bludgeoning. The throat is the easiest way to make the kill but it looks like he's trying to beat it to death.

The boar wriggles from under him, starts to run, only to see me and rear back. Russell pins it down again; technique doesn't matter when he's three times its size. Its side is scoured with welts, the earth churned bloody.

It's the snap of a leg breaking that decides it; the boar has no hope for survival now. I push Russell off and bite the boar by the throat. A squeeze is all it takes. The windpipe buckles and it collapses into my embrace, almost peaceful.

My jaw releases and the boar slumps to the ground. The forest is mute in shock.

Russell's glare passes from me to his bloodied paws, face curdling as he wipes them on some ferns. It doesn't do much. Perhaps he thinks to wash them. He steps over the body and walks back towards the river. But I stand a while, blinking at the dark stain spreading from the body. Too late for regrets.

I turn from the corpse and leave.

27

Come Home

The supple body flows across the garden, jolting from stillness to flight, steadily drawing closer. Enough patience and your prey will come to you.

The squirrel stops, rummages, dark eyes darting here and there, then leaps again. A stop–start wave. Quicksilver. Meat.

I lash out, close it in a fist.

Twist the neck. Bite off the head.

The squeaks are harsh in my ears, its belly velvet. Eyes, black panic.

I let go at its bite. No time for regret, the squirrel has already bounded away and it'd be useless to give chase.

Blood bubbles to the surface of the cut; I lick it, savouring the metallic taste across the back of my tongue. Mercy is all very well, but I'm still hungry.

Causing upset when I'm trying to hide wasn't smart. Thankfully there's no sign of life at the windows, though the struggle startled birds from the feeder. Several sit on the fence screaming.

Most humans will just think of it as singing but with Buckley I can't be sure. His bedroom curtains remain shut but I wriggle further back into the scrub, just in case. Fail to steal his card and I've no idea how to break into storage.

Now it's nearly morning, I'm certain this is his house. The scruffiness threw me at first – how can someone who's so anal in our cubicle let his own garden overgrow? But in the light I can see the strings of origami animals in the kitchen window. We used to decorate our cubicle in this way until someone from HR decided that they were a fire hazard.

I wriggle around until I can wedge my head on top of my coat sleeve but sleep isn't easy here. Buckley lives round the corner from the zoo and the air is already disturbed with the trumpet and screech of waking animals.

It's been years since I visited.

———

Mum always loved the zoo. Back amongst the animals, her flame would rekindle in the pink of her cheeks. My mum was almost visible in that face – the old Mum – because she had changed, was changing, so incrementally that I had to look at the photos to see it. It was in the slightly shiny puffiness of her flesh, in the distance of her eyes, twitching about their sockets as if seeking escape. Occasionally her hand would spasm on the joystick of her wheel-chair so that Dad and I had to stay close, ready to steer her away should she veer towards a lake or passer-by. To understand what those days must have been like, extracts a heavy price. For her world was steadily growing crueller; heavier; features feathering at the edges, as if the oneness of the universe were inhaling back in on itself. A Sperlman's for which there is no Come Home.

If I squinted, my memories as a infant were still here; in the penguin tunnel, flitting with the shadows overhead, a memory of Mum pointing as she spun fairy tales from her visit to Antarctica.

Or by the elephant enclosure, shivering with the echo of heat from her stories of traipsing through the bush.

Or in the parrot cage, where her old grin would alight on her mouth, even though she trembled too much for the birds themselves to land.

But every visit the ghosts of these past selves thinned, eclipsed by the growing mass of the woman in the wheelchair.

In the cafeteria, she accidentally ran over a stranger's handbag, only to reverse over it again in the horror of realisation. The handbag's owner bloated like an octopus on the attack, their words harsh ink. We relocated to the other end of the restaurant.

Dad tried to be cheery over the meal, but neither Mum nor I were in the mood. I watched them over the top of my new specs, still not quite believing that this could be our reality. Because they were both changing. Whilst Mum's face thickened, Dad's was turning to ash. White had settled in his hair, like an arctic hare growing in a winter coat after the long summer.

I turned the burger into a flat pat with my fork. The chips sat stodgily in my stomach. Peas kept escaping Mum's spoon across the red Formica and the yogurt missed her mouth, running down her coat like bird shit. In the end, Dad wrestled the spoon from her and she had to gape for his administrations like a baby bird. She, who had always been the hand that fed.

I crammed the rest of my cake down my throat and left them to it.

At the monkey enclosure, a couple were rapping on the glass. They ignored my glare, kept knocking until the nearest monkey looked up; but its eyes were dulled to smooth pebbles and the couple drifted away.

The monkey returned to stirring leaves and I stayed still, making sure not to stare, and, after a while, it swung up to pucker at the glass. Forcing myself not to smile, I watched it reveal a brown lump from its closed fist and swipe the shit across the glass.

I love this monkey more than my mum. This monkey is my best friend. This monkey is my only friend in the whole world.

'Looks like you've made a new friend,' Dad said when he wheeled Mum over.

Mum craned forwards, eyes fretting behind her thick glasses. Earlier we had had to point out a tiger that had stood so close that its watchful breath misted the glass, and we'd laughed, because what else can you do?

'There.'

But at Dad's point, the monkey swung away into the ropes and I stalked off too.

————

I must have fallen asleep because the next thing I know, Buckley is at the window. My body contracts into readiness for a pounce, but there's no opening yet.

He's bent over the sink, washing something, but even from this angle I can see the purple welt across his nose. His shoulders seem to wilt over the heat of water. When he glances out at the squabbling sparrows, I can see grey beneath his eyes. His face looks like a used paint palette. I have to bite the back of my hand against the guilt – even after everything, I hadn't meant to hurt him.

With the last plate placed in the rack, he pushes the crook of his back and sighs. Something about him is different. Perhaps it's just seeing him out of his work clothes, but there is an unfamiliar looseness to his movements as he sets about making breakfast.

He must be distracted because an alarm starts to pulse and he rushes from the window, eventually returning to view to run a pan under the tap. When he opens the top window segment, I smell burnt mushroom.

A hiss escapes me at the possible entrance. Now he just has to step away from the kitchen.

A minute's opening is all I need.

He crosses to the fridge, brings out a pot to sniff, puts it back, wanders out of view, though I can see the door to the next room so he must still be in the kitchen.

Come on. Come on.

At last, he reappears, passes through to the living room, a glimpse of movement up the stairs.

Now.

I'm halfway across the garden before I know it, leaping for the window, my toes digging into the sill. A pigeon bursts from the bird table in a warning clap of wings, but my torso is already through, legs squirming to worm the rest of the way. A larger person would never make it but with one last wriggle my second leg is over and I'm in.

I slip onto the washboard, gulping the room in, almost blinded in the panic of the search – but there – his work jacket. I grapple with the fabric, scrabbling through each pocket three times – nothing.

His trousers. He always keeps his card in his trousers. But I can't see them, they're not likely to be in the kitchen.

Overhead comes the sound of a flush. I scurry to the living room; there's a sofa but hiding behind it would be too risky and behind the curtains is just laughable – the cupboard under the stairs! I wriggle in and draw the door shut behind me. The interior is cramped and the bulk of an old vacuum cleaner wrestles me for space, but as I crouch I'm almost glad for its solidity at my back. Above comes the slow creak of steps.

A few seconds later a shadow crosses the slit of light at the bottom of the door, back towards the kitchen. I could slip out but that seems too risky with him so close. Better to wait until he leaves or goes to sleep. If my calculations are right, it's the weekend, but that's good. I wouldn't be able to steal his card if he takes it to work. At least from the state of the house, it's safe to guess that he's not about to get out the vacuum cleaner any time soon.

I ease my legs into the free space. The carpet is impossibly soft after lying on earth for days. Through the door comes the thin sound of Buckley's whistling and I have to bite my bottom lip at the ache of familiarity. Of fondness.

And I'm suddenly sad, sad and tired. I'd give almost anything to go back to the days before he made his choice.

Or had there always been a distance between us that I'd just refused to see? Isn't that why I always refused his invitations to visit when I could? Because whenever I did, I realised that this was the home of a stranger.

———

The last time I was here, it had been Buckley's birthday, I can't remember which. I must have been fifteen, sixteen? So perhaps his twenty-first. I made excuses to avoid them when I could; letting him down made me feel bad but parties aren't the natural habitat of phenomenauts. Why would anyone willingly gather with strangers in such a tiny territory? Everywhere, humans squaring up over possible mates, dropping threats behind a sharp joke or enacting dominance displays in the cramped space over drinks. All those voices, chatter, yammer, yip; conversation transparent as bird song, 'Fuck off', 'Fuck me', 'Me, me, me, me'.

I had retreated to the kitchen, cramped against the snack table. At least this gave me the opportunity to fill my pockets; though I knew there'd be food at home, it's when pickings are good that you have to cache. A gaunt-faced woman glared to see me tipping the bowl of Bombay Mix into my hood, so I showed her my teeth.

Who were all these people? Some neuros I recognised but there weren't any other phenomenauts. Buckley had vanished long ago, already tipsy when I arrived. Kyle appeared only long enough to dump a bottle in my hand, then was sidling on to flirt with a Bio technician.

The bottle had no label and looked decidedly home-brew. Whatever was in it smelt rancid, like the nameless, fetid things I'd forage as a fox. To a human tongue the taste wasn't any better, but drinking was something to do and safer than risking someone taking my staring as a threat display.

It was half finished when my stomach started to squirm like the desperate animal I felt. The sounds of the party had taken on a distant quality, the unfamiliar faces seemed to press together in an amorphous mass. I needed out.

I stumbled through the clot of people to the stairs, squeezed past a drunk groping couple and on to the dark landing. If I'd ever been to the bathroom up here, I couldn't remember but seeing the light from a half-open door I made towards it.

But it wasn't the bathroom, and it wasn't empty.

The senselessness filtered through my mind like mud. Two figures were entangled on the bed. It was obscene; that those clever fingers that would fold paper into birds and beast, that the hands that would help me with my CP – that they could do . . . that, was absurd. The laughter burst from my lungs but emerged choked.

The couple startled.

'Kit?'

The voice was worst of all. The voice that formed the backdrop to my every jump, turning inside my head until it narrated even my dreams; only to now come from those lips. Those lips that—

I fled.

'Kit!'

At the thunder of steps behind me, I halted, uncertain of what I was even running from. Bombay mix showered onto the couple below as I caught myself on the banister. Buckley drew up above me, his eyes going from the snacks to my face; the pinch of his mouth frozen in the moment before sound. 'Sorry' – is that what he'd meant to say?

Finding myself level with a thicket of chest hair, I stared at my feet.

'Are you OK?' he said.

I nodded, clutching the banister more tightly as the world bounced with the movement of my head.

'You don't look so good.'

I lifted the bottle, sweaty from where I'd forgotten it in my grip.

'Fucking Kyle.' He snatched for it and there was a brief struggle as I held on, even though I didn't want it. He tucked it under his arm.

'We should get you—' he said, but my attention was on the girl at the top of the stairs, her arms crossed for reasons other than modesty.

My temple hammered. Getting away was the only thing that mattered.

'I'm fine.'

'But you're—'

I ducked from his hand. It was invested with something new, something I didn't want to think about.

'Happy birthday,' I said and pushed past the couple back into the crowd. This time he didn't follow.

The evening air was a kiss. Blackbirds lullabied. Each inhale rich with fresh-cut grass.

I didn't make it to the end of the street before throwing up.

———

Back cramp wakes me. I claw the grunge of sleep from my eyes and see that the light has gone from under the door. Complete black.

How long have I been asleep? I'm bursting for a pee. Despite the danger and cramped quarters, the luxury of warmth and carpet means I must have slept through the day. There's no sound of movement inside the house. Perhaps Buckley's out or already asleep.

Back in the kitchen, there's a loaf of bread on the counter. My hands and mouth act of their own accord, tearing, biting, the claggy dough sticking in my throat as slice after slice is crammed into my maw. I have to duck my head under the tap to stop myself choking. By the time the loaf is gone, I feel swollen but it's better than the aching hollowness.

No longer distracted by food, the first thing that strikes me is the mess. Unwashed dishes pile in the sink, or wrestle for space on the work surfaces with piles of books and potted plants. A bag of laundry has collapsed off an upturned bucket, one sock halfway across the floor as if caught in escape. The vertigo is hard to name. Buckley is meant to be the voice in my head. But here he's more than that.

My foot sticks to the floor as I cross the room – a glob of honey? Does he even like honey? Or perhaps I'm the one who doesn't.

Scrabbling through the laundry doesn't reveal his work trousers, though he wouldn't wash them with the card in there anyway. I give up and lift one of the books for a cursory sniff. It smells like old forests, tree corpses touched with sap. Buckley always said that reading is the closest an ex-phenomenaut can get to wearing another skin.

A pile of loose papers sits next to the books: ShenCorp business. I flick through, squinting in the dimness.

Interpersonal conflict and resolution in the bonobo troop.
Using UV urine trails in raptor hunting technique.
Semaphonic communication of the honey bee.

Buckley's edits scrawl up the margins in red ink, leaving a slight indent beneath my finger; cast-off cocoons, the husks of old selves. Yet nothing to foreshadow his betrayal. I place them back on the table.

In the lounge the clutter of books is replaced by origami pieces, lying around the floor and sofas as if hungover from a crazy party. Buckley always used to christen each of my new Ressies by learning how to make it in paper.

I nearly step on one; put it safely on the sofa. A whale.

But it's dangerous to stick around here. I have to find the card and go. If he keeps it in his trousers like I remember, it'll most likely be in his room.

My skin is electrified as I start up the stairs, each groan of the floorboards delivers a hundred volts. It's all I can do not to flee.

On the landing, I examine my options. The nearest door was his bedroom, wasn't it? That's where he was with the girl. I chew the inside of my cheek and push.

It's so dark in here, the lump beneath the duvet could be anyone. I squint and make out the shadow of a chair by the bed, what could be trousers thrown over the back. But even if my feet are game, my hands don't seem to want to let go of the door.

Coward. Coward. Coward.

I sink to my knees and squirm forwards on my belly, bladder fit to burst. Is this stupid? This *is* stupid but there's no stopping now, I just wriggle on, eyes fixed on my quarry.

Whoever knew there was such distance in such a small stretch of carpet? *Just keep going. Keep going.*

One hand brushes against the chair leg and I scrabble up at the trousers. First pocket: nothing.

Come on.

Second pocket. The stiff material of a card. *Got it!*

I clutch it to my chest and, for several dizzying breaths, just lie there.

Buckley's hand dangles over the edge of the bed, almost level with my face. The hand that used to help me with BodySupport, the hand that folded paper animals, the hand I once saw caress. The hand that once…

The fingers are long and blunt, curled almost vulnerably in sleep. Wouldn't it be nice to hold it, for a while? To lie here together in the dark?

The force of the tears is surprising. And infuriating. How can I cry now? He'll hear me. Surely he'll hear me. Yet the thought only makes the tears flow faster.

I press my face into the carpet, cursing in time with the gasps – *stop it, stop it, stop it, you stupid idiot.* Because I'm not sad, but furious. I don't want to sob into the floor but beat it. I want to leap on Buckley's chest and hit him and hit him and hit him and tear the bastard's throat out with my teeth. How could he choose Tourism over me? How could he leave me?

He left me.

My shoulders still, the tears drying as quickly as they came. Because what am I still doing here? I squirm backwards, biting my tongue as one foot hits the wall, but then I'm on the landing, down the stairs, out the window and into the night.

28

Uncanny Shift

Water reverberates, a groan bulged with static. The song is a kaleidoscope of shape and sound, its motif in Euclidean stitches. As I acclimatise, the variations begin to unveil; here a staccato tremble, now angles of shimmering blue. I just wish I could understand.

Julie would, but I never handled enough cetaceans to justify a language course. And if I'm being sent to test this Ressy without even the basics, they'll not do any more for tourists. I've suggested enough similar ideas before to know that Mr Hughes would consider it an unnecessary expense.

The notes fade away, leaving behind grating white noise – the metronome of human sonar and the scratch of engines, the promise of a headache.

I flex my tail and make towards the direction from which the song had come, grey in every direction. The touch of water is lighter than air, as if I'm not swimming or even flying, but suspended within a void. No matter that I'm currently one of the largest animals on the planet, the unbroken infinity leaves me feeling tiny.

When the song returns, another cry joins it. This second voice is louder, deeper, a virile bubble that wells around the first. Two whales. I hadn't expected any at the beginning of the migratory season, but the warming sea has disturbed many patterns. Not to mention the fact that the whales could be hundreds of miles away: but it's reassuring to know that I am not alone in this vacuum.

I face into their voices. The first is lilted with an inquisitive note, the return a happy bounce. My lungs swell with the desire to join them but embarrassment holds me back.

'You have to wonder what they're talking about,' Buckley says. 'Good krill here? How's the family? I guess conversations about the weather are out.'

The ocean has its own types of weather, I think to reply but remain silent. Human conversation pales against such song.

At the compress of my lungs, I kick out and surface. My back gulps the liquid luminescence until my chest balloons, then it's back into the grey, daylight fading to memory.

I find myself in hail, the scatter of trippy 3D – a school of fish. Each tiny dot is crystalline, scales and fins, like sculptures in grains of salt. The blue of their advance turns red in retreat. A real whale wouldn't perceive in this way; the only colour it can sense is green. Routing senses like sonar through the visual cortices often leads to results like this.

The fleck of jellies follows the fish. My sonar gloams through their innards in a spectral echo, tentacles sparkling streamers.

The whale song returns in a scream of blue, condensing with each pulse – it's heading closer. Did it hear me examining the jellies? To pick up my sonar it would have to be nearer than I thought.

Its unearthly rumble carries something like a question in muscular ultramarine, and a reply bursts from me, without my understanding, without my even meaning to. I squeeze my sonar to a stop in horror. Three heartbeats of silence. Then it replies.

I swim towards it, tail churning my passage into a soar. Its response grows and the waves shape into a caressing hand, as grey parts in a sigh of blue. Solidity, where before was nothing.

My sonar fumbles along its sleek flank then inside to gushing innards, the pulsing rose of a heart. I hear my flesh explored in turn, contours traced in its cyan groan.

It found me, I found it. Without even knowing I was looking. I could laugh but instead I hum, a tune I've never heard and yet seem to have always known. It chortles back, voices merging.

We swim for what feels like hours. Bodies barrelling, the stroke of fins, partners to the dance. Its strong flank nudges mine to keep me in line, I'm happy to be shown the steps, to join the rhythm of a shared heartbeat.

All the while the song, *our* song, grows. I shout it, to flesh, to the grey infinity, to the joy of being here, alive.

Something inside me, long dormant, has kindled. And it feels *right*. This is what I was made to do.

A lungful of heaven and we sink back into the harmony. An entwining verse, a snare of melody. Until it's time.

I spin, offering my belly to the sun and its shadow swoops overhead. The hard shape reflects my moan. I startle as it slips within me and pleasure ruptures my entire being.

Then it's over.

The whale surfaces, clucking, but I stay submersed, stunned by the realisation.

Buckley coughs.

'And that – is what we call whale sex.'

———————

Drifting through blackness. Weightlessness into mass. The pink of eyelids, peeling back on to a ceiling of strict angles. Come Home.

I had sex with a whale.

I shut my eyes and try to return to unconsciousness. But I can't.

Buckley is by his desk but he hasn't said anything yet; normally he at least asks if I'm OK. My cheek feels unnaturally hot against the leather of the pallet.

I had sex with a whale.

My first time ever, with a whale.

But what am I going to do? Lie here forever? That won't undo it.

I sit and start to remove BodySupport. The light seems more severe than usual, pricking tears from the corners of my eyes. Buckley hesitates before coming forwards to take the CP, a flush of red beneath his collar. He won't quite look at me.

'I didn't know,' I say.

'I know.'

'I can't even speak whale. How was I supposed to know?'

'I know.' His eyes have come to perch somewhere above my left ear.

'It should have been Julie doing this,' I say.

He breaks from his stillness, as if with considerable effort.

'Here.' He takes two objects from his desk and shoves them in my hands. An unnaturally even rectangle, the blandness of white bordered by neat brown and a green oblong.

'Had to go with apple juice. Oranges are pricey at the moment.' He clears his throat, as if the silence were too dangerous. 'You know, what with the fungal infections.'

'Right,' I say.

A juice carton and sandwich, it's still not quite clear to me how such geometry could be put inside my mouth and digested.

'Your blood sugar could do with the boost,' he says. 'And good to get some fluids.'

I put them aside and hide my head in my hands. The pallet sags as he sits next to me, but he doesn't say anything. I will him to leave me to my oblivion.

He clears his throat. 'You know what they say. What happens on jump, stays on jump.'

'Yeah,' I say but stay huddled. Because other people knowing doesn't bother me. It's my knowing, and there's no escaping that.

29

Uncanny Shift

You can be anything. You can be anyone.

My eyes look back at me from the mirrored surface of the brochure. Or rather, my doppelgänger's eyes. I don't like to meet them; their touch seems dirtied by the knowledge that Hughes has seen through them.

The board make small sounds of pleasure as they flick through their own brochure. It takes me a while to locate Mr Hughes. Although I know what his meeting Ressy looks like, I'm yet to make the automatic connection. He nods to himself as he reads, too absorbed to notice my glare. Arthur is so enthused he's left his seat entirely, an uncharacteristic energy propelling him in pointless circuits.

ShenCorp Projection.

You can be anything. You can be anyone.

The more I read the slogan, the less sense it makes. How is it possible to become anyone whilst remaining yourself? What is it that survives the change?

You can be anything. You can be anyone.

You can be anything. You can be anyone.

You can be anything. You can be anyone.

Re-reading doesn't reveal meaning so much as leach it, until the words are empty marks like insects squashed against the page.

Inside, another pair of eyes looks back, these completely black. The furry features flow with my own bemusement, following my movements exactly. This is serious tech for just a brochure, but ShenCorp is sparing no expense with the marketing.

Romulus the Field Mouse

Small body, Big Experience!

Jump! Climb! Scurry! See the world as you never have before. Experience the incredible expanse hidden beneath human feet.

Features include: – Agility of a gymnast, – Acute senses, – The tail experience!

'Are we sure about the names?' the woman across from me says. 'I would have thought it invites the kind of anthropomorphism towards ResExtendas that we're trying to avoid.'

I can't remember her name. Introductions were made at the start of the meeting, yet there is a fungibility to all these smug, beautiful and young-looking faces. And they all turn out the same shit.

The previous fruits of their genius have included a suggestion to release sedated prey for tourists who struggle with hunting; to construct synthetic environments to replace habitats that might suffer floods or drought; to shrink-wrap each Ressy before projection to give the impression of freshness – as if it were possible for disease or parasites to be transmitted to the tourists' Original Bodies.

In response to the discomfort at defecating and drinking unprocessed water, it was agreed that neuros would simply dampen the feedback of these needs. Yet it's the function not the experience that matters if they want to maintain the Ressies.

'And what would you suggest?' Arthur has advanced round the table to the woman and perches on the arm of the adjoining chair. I can see the struggle it takes her not to retreat in her seat.

'My preference was always for the model numbers.'

'Numbers aren't sexy,' Mr Hughes says.

Arthur crosses his arms, leaning in. 'Exactly. Don't you think?' What hideous school of management book is to blame for this change since our last meeting? Why not just piss on the table and be done with it?

But the woman refuses to be cowed. 'Perhaps not numbers but names aren't better. Not only will they subtract from the wild experience but they imply self. We can't afford to suggest that ResExtendas have anything near personhood.'

'We needn't worry about any of this once the public perception campaign has done its work,' Arthur says. 'Louis?'

'Shouldn't be a problem once we've reframed the issues,' a man across the table replies. 'Though avoiding names isn't necessarily a bad idea.'

The first woman leaps on the support. 'There's also the matter of purchase motivations. You'll remember from page fifty-six of the research document I sent out that we highlight the consumer's desire for self-reinvention. Naming the models is counter-intuitive.'

'Naming the models doesn't prevent the customer from using their own, or indeed any other they wish to use.'

'We should be selling ResExtendas as a blank slate.'

Louis pushes Specs further up his nose. 'My team have identified the impetus towards reinvention as part of a broader dissatisfaction with the disparity between actual and ideal self. For zoological models we offer customers the chance to transcendence through achieving archetypes impossible for the human body.'

And that's where I stop listening.

Next page of the brochure, my eyes change to gold orbs, plumage ruffled by wind. The mountain range below looks like gravel.

Bald Eagle

Sentinel of the Sky

Shake free the shackles of gravity and rule the heavens, Fly, hunt, kill! The authentic wild experience.

Features include:

– Flight, soar above it all! – Amazing vision – colours never before seen by the human eye! – Talons and beak. Be a powerful creature of the wild!

The meeting notes ask whether the copy is dynamic enough for the target audience: for this Ressy, American males between the ages of thirty and fifty.

Next page. Tiger, baring teeth. It's probably intended as a growling shot but it looks more like flehmen. At least the lunging rattlesnake on the next page is demonstrating real aggression, though from my experience it's hard not to interpret it as fear.

I keep skimming through.

With our cutting-edge technology your consciousness will be transferred into your new body quickly, safely and securely . . . The most thrilling . . . All our ResExtendas are ethically grown in our state-of-the-art laboratories . . . Recommended by . . . You can!

Images shimmer as I flick the pages with a thumb. Fast enough and my face merges into the mouse, eagle, tiger, bat, whale. Even faster and it becomes a surreal mess of scales, feathers, fur.

I push back my chair.

'Bathroom,' I tell the questioning eyes.

On the toilet, I study the perfectly smooth legs that look like mine and yet aren't. Did Mr Hughes use the toilet in this body? I don't think I want to know the answer.

The brochure lies in front of me on the floor where I placed it whilst I rucked up my skirt. The emotions it woke are too complex to name. Embarrassment? Anger? Sadness? All I knew was that I had to get out of that room.

You can be anyone.

How can they sell Phenomenautism as image and experience? How can they sell it at all? A Ressy isn't a consumable. Phenomenautism is meant to consume *you*.

I grind the sharp nails of these hands into their palms, almost glad of the pain. This body is mine, for the present.

Exiting the cubicle, I jolt at the women standing there. We freeze as one, fear slowly fading from our faces. As I step up to the bowl of mirrors more clones materialise. I splash water over our cheeks, but those eyes remain wild.

Back in the corridor, a doorway opens further along and a gurney emerges, on it a human Ressy. Its feet are bare, the shoes and jacket hang in a bag from the end. A man in a blue boiler suit steps after it, whistling softly. Even though he can only be in his forties, his is the oldest face I've seen here. The Ressy stares blindly at the ceiling as it passes but the man pauses in his tune to flash a smile.

The door they left by isn't locked. Inside, is a storage room, and row upon row of Ressies. All of them human.

Clamminess pricks out across my face. How many Ressies do they have here? Far more than they'd ever need for meetings. The ICPO would have a meltdown if they knew. One or two human Ressies are one thing but this ...

I shut the door behind me and start down the closest aisle. What is it about empty Ressies that makes them feel like anything but? The sounds of soft breathing remind me of a dormitory or hospital ward. Because they aren't quite silent, not quite still. Eyelids twitch. Chests rise and fall. Occasionally a muscle spasms; the flicker of movement stilling before I can pinpoint the source.

Halfway down the row, I start to notice duplicates, perfect twins, laid side by side. These are back-ups, I guess, but why they need so many, I don't want to know.

By the time I find a familiar face, it's no longer really a surprise. Arthur lies inertly, an almost plasticine quality to the face. At least it explains why his mannerisms were different today; the Ressy model I thought of as him was occupied by a different person – if Arthur ever was anyone at all and not just a glamorised serial number. After spending so much of my life in projection, it's just foolish for me to have assumed that those around me were their Original Bodies. No wonder everyone at the board meetings always looks so young and attractive. If offered the choice, who wouldn't?

My thoughts feel hazy, as if the truth of it isn't quite able to filter through. Only my shivering body seems to have processed the enormity of 'what this means', though it's an emotion far beyond words. So by the time I pass another familiar Ressy, the only thing I feel is tired.

I watch my hand tremble as it makes contact with her face, somehow surprised at the warmth of skin as my other hand slowly traces my own respective features. We might look the same but there's little similarity to the touch. One is me, the other meat.

I drop my hands and watch the subtle movements of its thoughtless living.

'North.'

Although only one person calls me that, I find myself uncertain of the handsome man approaching. He *says* that he's Mr Hughes but how is it possible to know who anyone is any more?

'You didn't mention duplicates,' I say.

He stops, calculation flashing across his features. He doesn't have as strong a mastery of this face as he does with his Original. When his eyes dart back, his tone has softened.

'How else could we offer you a ResExtenda for here as well as that required for the filming in Bristol?'

Calling out his bullshit doesn't even seem worth it. The tiredness has become crushing.

'How many are there?' I say, but as the calculation returns to his expression I shake my head. 'Actually, don't tell me.'

He reaches for my shoulder but is somehow unable to finish the movement. 'We can discuss this back in Bristol but for now we should return to the meeting.'

'Who are you?' My voice sounds as flat as I feel.

'Mr Hughes.'

His surprise isn't enough to convince me. I'm not even sure what proof would be.

'Katherine?'

It's my turn to flinch. I've never known Mr Hughes to call me by my first name.

'Is it the duplicates?' he says. 'We can discuss the matter if you're upset.'

How am I supposed to recognise a lie when that face is so un-familiar? I don't even know if the truth or a lie would be more terrible. Because if he is genuinely worried, then what – who is Mr Hughes? It was so easy to hang his identity on that of a rotund blustering man. Out of that body I don't know him at all.

'Speak to me,' he says.

'Hi. Yes,' I say.

I don't like the concern in his eyes. Mr Hughes isn't kind. I didn't think he was kind.

He pats my shoulder, actually carrying it through this time, if with self-conscious stiffness.

'How about you head on home?' he says. 'We've got the marketing covered.'

Explaining my early return to Buckley isn't easy, not when the human Ressies are still a secret. Yet I can't hide my upset. When he looks at me, I know that he's thinking about the whale sex, thinks I'm still shaken from that, but of course he doesn't mention it. And I'm damned if I will. In its place we're left with an itching silence.

Though I'm grateful for the lift home, it just prolongs the awkwardness. Worst of all, he insists on seeing me inside. It's kindness, I have to remind myself of that.

In the kitchen, I stand back to watch him look around, suddenly uncertain of what to do with my strange configuration of limbs and face. In the end, I settle for hugging myself. The house almost seems doll-like in his presence, our thoughtless arrangements of appliances and knick-knacks seem the friezes of a make-believe family. I can't remember the last time he was in my house.

'Your dad around?' he says.

'He's away at the moment,' I say, distracted as Mum starts muttering in the living room. Thankfully Buckley doesn't seem to have heard. 'Why?'

'Just wanted a quick word.' He shrugs.

I move to block the line of sight to the living room. 'A word?'

'Just to touch base.'

If he told Dad about the whale sex, I'd die. But no, Buckley wouldn't do that, would he? But what 'touching base' actually means I don't find out because Mum's groaning is getting louder.

'Sorry. Sorry. I'm SORRY.'

She can get lost in a word, chase the syllables round until it is worn smooth of meaning; until speech is revealed as barks and howls.

Buckley frowns over my shoulder.

'Is that your mum in there?'

I open my mouth, stranded by a plausible lie. I should never have allowed him in.

But he's already moving round me, into the living room.

'Hello? Mrs North? It's Buckley, a friend of Kit's.'

In front of her wheelchair, he stops. The expressions race each other across his face and, through them, for a second, I meet my mother as a stranger.

It's the smell that hits first. Lavender and talc, a bucolic meadow that fails to quite hide the hint of excrement.

And, of course, no amount of perfume can hide the crackle of breath, nor the inward curl of her body, those clawed arms both foetal and predatory.

'Sorry,' she mumbles. 'Sorry sorry.'

Buckley has commandeered his mouth into a smile, yet his eyes fly about the room as if in search, or perhaps escape. Hers dance about his like a moth around a flame.

'Handsome.' The word drops from her mouth like a stone. Panic purges my mind but Buckley laughs.

'You're not so bad yourself.'

She squeals happily. I give Buckley an apologetic look but he just smiles.

'Handsome,' she says again, that voice dead of all animation.

'Mum.' I grab her sippy cup. 'Here, have a drink.'

She sticks her tongue in the spout so that the juice trickles down her chin.

'Handsome.'

'Please. Mum.'

'Kit's been doing very well at work,' Buckley says. 'You must be very proud.'

'PROUD,' she shouts.

There's an art to it, drawing Mum out, one I don't have. When I sit with her the silence is so deafening I want to scream. The trick is simple enough in theory. To converse you just have to talk in soliloquy, let her interject a gurgled 'goood' or 'baaad'. But I don't want to.

I can't bear to talk to her like everyone else does, to sink my hands into the loose dough of her psyche and mould. I can't bear to leave her with the imprint of my fingers. Because that's all that is left of her now, an infinitely reflecting mirror.

'HANDSOME,' she says again, heaving to breathe around a cough. 'Sorry. I'm sorry. I'm SORRY.'

It's too much. I pull Buckley away, into the kitchen, out of the door into the grey evening.

I have to turn away before Buckley can see my face. The flutter of wings in the hedgerow is followed by a magpie screech.

'I . . . I didn't know it was that bad,' he says.

I can't stop myself trembling at the softness in his voice.

'How long has she—' he starts, but it's a nonsensical question and he can't finish it.

When? How? Who? Do any of them make sense?

There was never one day, or even one year that divided the healthy Mum from the sick – and yet there is a before and after, a Mum and a Mum. Though I'm not even sure I know who the mum before was.

To Dad it's always been simple.

'She helped raise endangered chicks. She lectured at Bristol, then Bath.'

Yes, she was a zoologist, but that's a function, not a person. Who was she?

'She was a mother. She loved nothing more than watching you grow up, still does.'

But who was she for herself? Surely there must have been more to her than giving?

'She liked to read.'

And?

'She didn't have much time for anything else. She was a mother and full-time professor.'

Is there a person amongst the fragments? Squint on a dark night and I can just about glimpse it, how some might see a figure in that constellation – The Mother. See it? Those two stars, that's her hair, there, the curve of a hip. The bright point, a baby at her breast.

But look inside, to the flesh and there is only dark vacuity.

'Kit.' Buckley has come to stand beside me. 'Why don't we ever talk about this?'

His hand closes round mine and I snap away with a hiss. But as his eyes widen, I can't keep up the stare, can't face myself in his reflection.

I speak instead to the paving slabs.

'Please go. I'm sorry. Just go.'

Come Home

Getting inside is easy with Buckley's card; I go right up through the front steps. The normality is almost disconcerting, although in the dark, the light from the fish tank turns the lobby a rippling turquoise, as if underwater.

The silhouette of a guppy bumps up against the glass, as if curious at my shadow creeping through the beyond.

Go back to sleep, guppy.

I keep my eyes fixed on the blank screen at the far end of the room, trying to move too slowly for it to turn on at my presence. And for once I manage it. Unless, of course, it's just been switched off for the night.

The hunger pulls me to our old cubicle first. With any luck Buckley will have replaced the biscuits. Though rifling them regularly would be asking for trouble; tonight will be the last time.

A glance through the window tells me my luck is in. A packet of sandwiches sits on the desk, along with a bottle of soft drink. Almost too lucky. My hand freezes on the handle. There's a body on the pallet.

I press my nose to the glass but the view is lost to the condensation of my gasp. Because it's not a phenomenaut, but Buckley.

I leap back. There's no sign of anyone in the corridor. If this is a trap, he must be relying on my entering.

So he put the missing biscuits and card together? Or maybe he's only guessing at this stage and fell asleep waiting?

With one last mournful look at the sandwiches, I creep back the way I came. No one stops me.

In Biolabs, I swipe Buckley's card over the door. A click of the bolt sliding free and I'm in.

The high-security room is much the same as normal storage: there's the same warm musk of unkempt bodies, the same gentle snorts of unconscious life. Apart from the human Ressies, it's hard to see why many of these are confidential. Why, for instance, is a mouse here? It looks so innocuous, wheezing into BodySupport, swamped by the expanse of its gurney. But such questions are just distractions right now. I head down the aisle, weak with relief at the sight of my doppelgänger.

Its unconscious vulnerability is painful to look at. Even without the need for evidence, I'm glad to get it away from Mr Hughes.

I disentangle the BodySupport, glad that the breathing stays steady. This was never my expertise but surely it should survive a couple of days disconnected, long enough to figure out how to get it to the ICPO. It'll likely pee itself at some point but I've dealt with worse.

Puppy fat gives beneath my hands as I try to get my arms around its waist, its diaphragm flutters against my grip. I'm heavier than I thought, or rather my doppelgänger is; it must have a good couple of pounds on my Original Body now. Carrying this weight down the stairs will be impossible. I kick off the gurney brakes but the squeak of wheels quickly kills that idea.

After several more attempts to lift it, I crouch by the side of the gurney and tug on an arm so that its weight slides onto my back. The head hangs limp next to mine, breath humid against my cheek. I wriggle until both of the arms are around my neck in a flaccid embrace, then grip the gurney and struggle up against the scream of knees.

Within five steps my legs feel crushed. I let the doppelgänger slip down my back, the soft protuberance of its nose squashed against a shoulder blade, and start to drag.

Spots are already gathering behind my eyes by the time I reach the door but giving up is not an option. Just keep placing feet, left, right, left, right, like wading through water. If anyone comes across me like this, there's no way I'll be able to run.

At the top of the stairs, the corridor seems to swoon. I swallow back a bitter taste and lower a foot to the top step. Dragging the doppelgänger behind is bound to cause some damage, but if I couldn't carry it on the flat, there's no way I'll be able to on the stairs.

Second step, a dull thud as its feet hit the first followed by the grind of toenails on the metal lip. My face screws up at the sound. Yes, it's a Ressy but how can a sound like that not result in pain?

Another step. I press an elbow against the banister to help take the weight. My back is slick with sweat where it presses against my coat. I grit teeth in readiness for the bash of its feet against the next step and the arm under mine spasms. It's too much. I stop, snatching at breath.

A reflex. That's all. It's not conscious. Ressies don't feel.

I crane over a shoulder to see dark liquid smeared down the steps. My own toes throb at the sight. Keep this up and its feet will be flayed, or worse. At least it'd be less harmful if it landed on its heels.

I wedge myself against the banister and shift my grip to flip.

One. Two. Three.

It rolls, too fast, my hands slip, grasp at fabric only to hear the terrible sound of ripping, a scrap left in my clutch, it tumbles into the dark.

The sound is the worst. No scrabbling, no yell, just meat down stairs.

A long way down.

I sink to the step. The doppelgänger lies below at the turning in the stair, a jumble of limbs. One arm has fallen across its face as if shielding itself. If it's still breathing I can't see it.

I listen but the silence is treacle, it saps even the memory of sound. My fingers abrade themselves on the metal step edge. Without the pain I feel I'd melt away.

The dark inhales even my own breath until my mind starts to regurgitate ghosts.

Help.

The gurgle of a strangled voice.

Help.

———

Mum's room is next to mine. The walls are thin. Her cries carry.

Help.

In the morning, I listen to the carers bubble nonsense over her as they wash and dress her for the day. In the evening, I listen to Dad's silence in the face of her shouts.

Sorry. I'm sorry. I love you. I love you. I love you.

I listen to his footsteps, angry from the room.

I listen in the night, when all is lost.

Help.

Someone please help.

I listen. And lie stiff between the sheets, wishing I was curled up inside a den or tree roots, beneath floorboards or a sea bed, anywhere but here.

Help.

Her voice is slow and gargled, as if speaking through mud.

Please help.

When I drag myself to her bedside she is always so surprised.

'Kathy! What are you doing here?'

Where is she in the maze-like corridors of her mind? Hard to say. Place is a shifting shadow. A hospital ward is a favourite, but other times she finds herself in a field; an exposed rooftop; the middle of a city, surrounded by empty faces. Sometimes boys sit at the foot of her bed, winking, and she growls to make them leave.

'Kathy, I'm lost.'

'You're at home, Mum. In your bedroom.'

'No, I'm not.'

'Look, see your pink lampshade?'

Her eyes fidget, swifts always on the wing. It's hard to say what she sees.

Her clammy hand crabs around mine. 'I'm scared.'

'It wouldn't be here if we weren't in your room, would it?'

'I don't know,' she says, pauses, faulty neurons throwing sparks. 'I'm not home.'

But what is home when the brain's embers turn to ash? Not geography. Not place.

'What about your bed then?' I say. 'What would it be doing anywhere else?'

'I'm not in bed.'

'You are.'

'I'm not.'

'You are. You're in bed. Look!'

'I'm not.'

'What are you lying on then?'

'I'm not lying, I'm sitting. I can't get up.'

Her body, a contorted lump beneath the duvet.

But what can I say? There aren't the words to breach her prison or dispel the waking nightmare of her life. To reach for her is to sink my hands into tar. I can't pull her out but it can suck me in.

In the end, I always leave her to drown.

Uncanny Shift

Blood presses behind my eyes in a decisive beat. I open them on to a black abyss.

Yet, as I flail, it dawns on me that I'm not falling. Craning my head up, I see angular toes sunk into the wood above.

Bat. I am a bat. Since yesterday lunchtime. Although it's completely dark, Buckley's breath rolls inside my head, so it must be working hours.

The blackness trembles with the flickers of flight. Even with these eyes, I can make out very little, yet my hearing is a different matter. Chatter lifts the air in popping candy, the creak of wings like ship sails; every flick of tongue and shuffle imprinted into the tingling scallop of my ears.

At a scream I find myself in a yawning expanse, barely time to process before it blinks out. Another shout and it returns, ghostly in another's voice. Sonar.

My own tentative pips set the space abuzz and find it a cavernous edifice of beams and boxes. The floor, or rather ceiling, is fuzzy with bats, like mossy growths.

Despite the noise, the female next to me hasn't stirred. Her snout snorts gently, body wrapped tight in the stretch of wings. She's huge.

'Evening.'

I cling to Buckley's voice, thankful for its familiarity.

'No problems in the night?' he says.

'Slept right through.'

'Cool.' His voice is muffled, eating something maybe, although there's no sound of chewing. Perhaps he's just tired; there's no natural way for a human to arrange their sleep alongside crepuscular shifts. Sometimes I suspect he doesn't even bother to go home.

'Buckley?'

'Yeah?'

'Would you keep talking, please? I kind of need . . .' What exactly? Grounding, warmth. But he doesn't require an explanation.

'All right. But it'll have to be the news, my brain is pretty shot right now.'

'Thanks.'

His cough mixes with the rustle of wings, somehow flatter than the noises that enter my ears.

'The Thames Debacle. How much is too much?

'Following Parliament's announcement to pledge yet another four billion towards the already over-budget Barrier improvements, many are starting to ask – at what point is the price too much?

'This was the question on everyone's lips when I visited the protests in Somerset this weekend, where it is estimated over three hundred families have already had to permanently vacate their homes due to last year's flooding, and less than half are yet to receive the promised compensation . . .'

Another commentary piece. They'd only contribute to my stress if all that didn't feel so distant here. I let my focus drift and the words disrobe of meaning, leaving only the melody I know so well.

He pauses, slurps something. Time I got moving.

I focus on my left foot and flex it to release the claws, keeping the other leg stiff as I swing the freed foot sideways to drive my claws into the beam a step along. Now the right. Repeat. The drop beckons in a shiver of upward air.

A shriek and a bat bursts past my head. Its voice is like vertigo. The disembodied space splinters and I have to stop.

'What are they up to?' Buckley asks as a second screams past.

'Your idea is as good as mine.'

Although I prefer the social jumps in theory, infield my ignorance is terrifying. Absorbing the dialogue of a new community can take months and even then there are peculiarities that resist human understanding.

I keep shuffling until my path is blocked by a young male, his mouth opens on to sharp teeth. But there's no point delaying this any longer. I made a short circuit flight yesterday, I can do this.

'OK. I'm going for it,' I say as Buckley reaches a gap between articles.

'All right. Don't worry, you'll be just fine.'

'Right.'

'And if you do fall, remember your terminal velocity is too low for you to actually get hurt.'

'Great, thanks. Helpful.'

'But true.'

Even though I've been jumping for many more years than Buckley, he's still the expert when it comes to flight. Every phenomenaut has their thing.

My wings open in vulnerable sensation. The flesh of my underarms feels as if it's been stretched, on and on, until pinned to my feet. The sensitive skin tingles with the play of air. I swing my arms and pivot as air pushes into their give. Now, I just have to let go, though that's easier said than done.

This body knows how to fly. If I stop worrying the Ressy will handle the technicalities. So just stop thinking. But how am I supposed to do that?

'Want me to talk you through your breathing exercises?' Buckley says.

'No. Just let me . . .'

I wince my feet loose and gravity lurches through me, the floor yells upward—

Shit!

I fling out wings and a sudden force shoves into my armpits; the air thickening into custard skin.

Flying.

Sonar slurs, surroundings blinking faster than I can understand – breeze and bats, a ceiling of growling mouths, the tumult of wings. Too much.

Mouths above open in a hiss – I'm flying too close. A tug of arms and I stumble, air emptying into nothing, the weight of my feet kicking over a sudden drop. Gravity closes me in its fist, but stretching out wings I bounce off the renewed uplift.

'Eeeeeasy,' Buckley says. 'Easy.'

This body knows what to do, I've just got to let it.

To the right, a slant of light breaks into the attic. I psych towards it and my wings billow and stabilise. All I've got to do is not think.

I swoop up to the hole, almost graceful until my crash. Night breeze whispers just ahead. I pick myself up and crawl forwards on fingertips and knees, wings hushing as they drag along the ground. There's something disturbing about the oddity of the movement so soon after flying but a few more steps and I emerge into the lick of sky.

The heavens are grey, smudged with the residue of sun. Behind and below, the building stands in compressed angles but otherwise my cries empty into nothingness. It's terrifying but I'm not going to let myself have yet another freakout this evening.

Get a hold of yourself, Kit.

I limber up, making slow circles with my wings, the strain between my fingers is almost satisfying. The weather is overcast but warm, perfect for hunting.

A snout shoves into my back. I chitter but it keeps on pushing and my feet slip, tumble over the edge.

Grey swallows me and I find myself sliding along the invisible fabric of wind, dizzying infinity all around. At the huge swirl of a leaf, I dodge in a giddy dive. Air chuckles at the easy glee of speed.

The hum of bats in the distance reaches me in jumbled flashes. To my beginner's ears it's chaos, so I angle away. Exhale into the silence.

'What's planned for tonight?'

Buckley gulps back a mouthful of drink. 'Yeah, um, mostly testing the aerodynamics, make sure the handling is OK. Oh, and of course get a hunt in too. The Ressy should handle fasting better than a real bat, but you'll still get weak if you go hungry.'

'Nothing like a tasty bug.'

I'm being sarcastic, but with the right tongue, anything can be delicious. The tourists might take more convincing though.

The world thrums under my sonar. Below is the fuzzy path of a hedgerow, its leaves a gushing stream; far off is a pinched whisper of houses; to my right the mosquito whine of a pylon. Its spit grows at my approach, so I twitch my fingers into a somersault and the world flips back towards the hedge. The space between the two should make a suitable hunting ground, so I start tacking, reaching out with hungry clicks.

After five minutes, I'm rewarded by the mutter of a moth. It condenses into the frill of wings, now the shout of fuzz and antennae; every hair rendered as if to touch. I swirl overhead and it slaps into the skin between my legs. Its struggle is surprisingly strong, so I toss it up and catch it in my mouth. Legs flurry against my chin but I'm already crunching down. The husk bursts in sour goo, clagging my tongue.

'Nice,' Buckley says.

I'm too busy trying not to choke to reply. Despite the juice, it's surprisingly sticky. I mulch it around my mouth and swallow, then swoop back towards the wire, chewing on a fibrous wing.

My next lap is less successful, as is the next. The tennis ball rush of gnats are something to chase but nothing special in terms of taste. Moths flit at the edge of my hearing only to vanish as I get close. Perhaps the first catch was more luck than skill.

At last I close in on the hum of a larger morsel, but as I do, sonar drums my ears – another bat. I snap the meaty fly and swallow it whole. You snooze, you lose.

Yet the other bat is still following. I've already swallowed the fly, it's not getting anything from me now. Even without spitting my sonar towards it, its presence has eerie weight, like a stone in the pith of night. Perhaps I'm trespassing on its hunting ground. Some faux pas are inevitable during social projections.

A twist of wings and I'm off route and into the gush of new sky. Below the sea of grass parts around islands of cows, a flitter of hedge to my right. But still the bat follows.

Speeding up doesn't make its sonar fade. I can almost feel its onslaught against my back.

'We've got a follower,' I say.

'Another bat?'

'Think I've upset it, no idea what I've done wrong though. With the distance I've flown, I can't still be in its territory.'

'Search me. I'll have a look through the literature.'

There's no reason it should want to fight, unless there's something off with this Ressy. It wouldn't be the first time a small mistake in scent turned a group against me. If that's the case then it's no use for Tourism.

The pound of sonar is beginning to make my ears ache, its gaze is almost heat. Something about that look is familiar.

I spin round to paddle on the spot and it hovers in turn. To my weak eyes it's just shadow, and yet it's livid in my ears, each wing-beat wind. Our voices buzz across the divide. Its chatter like laughter.

The attention is unbearable. I flee, its sonar joining mine in a kaleidoscope of double vision. The world shimmers like fever.

'What is it? . . . Kit? You're panicking.'

But I'm too terrified to stop and explain. Hard to even explain to myself. I just have to get away.

I fling my whole being into the swirl of arms, lungs raw, heart slamming, and at last the watchfulness subsides, blinks out.

Yet even as I skim above the reassuring bulk of hedge, my ears crawl with the memory of that stare.

'Talk to me.'

'It's OK. I'm OK,' I say.

'Your pulse rocketed there.'

'Was just a bit scared. But I'm fine now, I managed to lose it.'

'Was it attacking? I couldn't see a thing on visuals.'

'I don't know,' I say. 'It was acting strangely. I had to get away.'

A beetle rushes past but my stomach is too unsettled to think about eating right now. The electricity wire cuts the horizon in an agitated hiss.

A bullet ahead. The trippy arc of wings, mean with intent. My ears ache under the onslaught.

'There!' I cry to Buckley.

'Where?'

'There! That fucking crazy bat!'

'I can't see.'

'Right in front of me.'

'I'm not getting anything.'

His camera feed must be too poor. To my ears it is a struck match.

I shout at it, pour the entire strength of my lungs into making it condense. The beat of its wings holds it in space, both of us frozen. Because I know it. There is no rationality to the knowledge, but I *know* that bat.

My scream reaches for it – only for it to disappear.

Shout after shout empties into the space it leaves behind. But nothing. Gone. The question of where doesn't matter right now, I just want to get away.

I fly back to the house as fast as my wings can carry me and nestle into the huddle of bats.

Could the crazy bat be here too? The collective voices turn the air to static. If I was being watched, I wouldn't be able to tell. Distantly, I'm aware of Buckley's coaxing. We haven't finished tonight's work yet, but nothing could persuade me to go out again now.

My ears are still imprinted with its stare, a look so familiar. Because it's found me before. Once in the muggy undergrowth of a jungle, balmy with tiger's breath; once on a mild English night, dressed in the musk of fox before headlights turned the world black.

But how can a bat remind me of a tiger, a tiger of a fox? It makes no sense.

———

It's raining on Come Home. Despite the return of colour, the world seems grey and wearily 2D.

I don't feel much like Friday-night takeaway, so we go to a cafe instead. Buckley is already scribbling ideas for the report on a napkin but I don't have the headspace. The migraine from Come Home was worse than usual and pinpoints of light flicker at the edge of my vision.

Buckley gives me concerned glances when he thinks I'm not looking. Of course he knows something is up. Although there wasn't any sign of the bat the rest of the week, I haven't been able to provide an answer to my panic that satisfies him.

He's more worried about it than he lets on. Returning from the shower, I saw him going over the readings from the jump, though he exited quickly when he realised I'd slipped in, almost guiltily. I was too tired to call him out when he pretended they were a file Kyle had sent him. Of course, I'd have my doubts if our situations were reversed, yet they're not. I *know* what I experienced.

My spoon leaves crescents in the soft fudge of my cake, poking it is all I have the energy for right now. My arms feel thick, gravity stifling. If only I could just leap into the embrace of air and away, away from this noise, from these crazy thoughts, from everything ... Because they are crazy when I try to rationalise them. How can a bat seem like a tiger? A tiger like a fox? Unless they were the same being? A phenomenaut? But why would a phenomenaut stalk me? The idea is mad.

Or is it? I don't even know what qualifies as mad any more. With this job anything can seem normal looked at in the right way.

Because *that presence*. The barrage of watchful sonar. The golden burn of tiger eyes. The glinting gaze of fox. Their watchfulness feels so familiar.

I think of the difference between Mr Hughes in his Original Body and the man he is during the London meetings. They're so different in behaviour and appearance. At the marketing meeting I barely recognised him. Would staring him hard in the eyes reveal the person within?

The coffee machine hisses at the bar, the clamour of plates and voices pulsing inside my skull. What if Mr Hughes *was* behind the watchers? It would explain the feeling of familiarity. And he's been projecting a lot recently. My being hit by a car meant he could argue to remove me from Research. Could the fox really have been a planned distraction?

But why follow me into the Tourism jumps? Because he doesn't trust me to handle them? There's already so much surveillance inRessy nothing would be achieved by the expense of the extra Ressies. Unless he thought he might have to intervene.

The idea is too unpleasant to digest. I stare numbly at the mess of my cake. This would be poison to most of the bodies I've been in. A large majority wouldn't be able to sense the sugar. Others would experience chemicals my Original Body doesn't even have taste buds for.

Whatever way I look at it, nothing adds up. Could I have just been mistaken about these watchers? At the time I'm so certain but in memory it's easy to doubt. If Phenomenautism has taught me anything, it's that there are countless uncharted crevasses of the mind. Falling into them happens to everyone at times.

I drop the spoon and settle into licking my hands instead.

Buckley swallows his mouthful of coffee. 'Little pro-tip: *Homo sapiens* digests food by ingesting it first. Here, let me demonstrate.'

I know he means me to knock his spoon out of the way but I push the plate towards him instead.

'Take it.'

But he pauses now it's being offered.

'Stomach upset?'

I shrug.

The look he gives me is too concerned to be questioning cake alone. But after a blink, he pulls it towards him and polishes it off in two spoonfuls. And we can finally leave.

The cold outside feels good in my lungs.

Wake up, Kit, back to reality.

All these thoughts of watchers, of being stalked, they just have to be the anxieties of someone who's been jumping too much of late. It's the only thing that makes sense. If only it was so easy to believe.

————

'How many baby bunnies have you killed?'

The moonlight tinted Susie's dark skin silver, her eyes wide and glinting to match.

I paddled my feet out of the bottom of my nightie, fabric stretched tight over the huddle of my knees. Our breath collected in thick droplets upon the glass, the kind of cold that brings your skin alive.

'You promised,' Susie said. But I knew she wouldn't like the truth.

At her mother's she had a big grey buck with floppy ears. When I nuzzled it, its pelt was soft and musky, like the inside of Dad's slippers; nothing like the wild rabbits I hunt.

The only pet I'd had in years was a buff ermine moth pupa, christened Fuzzy. I'd found the caterpillar in the scrub of Mum's once vegetable garden and, after stuffing it silly on dock leaves, kept the cocoon in a jar on the kitchen dresser.

I was crazy about moths, had been ever since Kyle showed me some scans of their metamorphosis and blew my tiny mind. When I was still at primary school we had cut caterpillars and butterflies from crepe paper but the teachers never thought to mention that inside the cocoon the pupa digests its own tissues into a gelatinous soup from which the adult can reconstitute.

'You have to wonder how the buggers can be called the same animal,' Kyle had said.

In honour of the process, I had decided that once Fuzzy had shaken its petticoat wings free from the cocoon I would rename it Wendy.

Yet in the end this was superfluous. Neither Fuzzy nor Wendy was to emerge after Mum crashed her wheelchair into the dresser and the jar shattered into a thousand pieces.

But I was hesitating. Susie cut two sharp lines above her heart with a finger.

'You *promised* to tell the truth.'

'Yeah, well, what counts as a baby?'

'A *baby*. Don't act stupid.'

I frowned. Babies are easier to catch and it's not like I kept a tally.

'One? Two? Ten? One hundred?' she said and I relaxed, glad to be able to truthfully profess to not being completely depraved in her eyes.

'Oh, not a hundred.'

She punched me, hard enough to produce a yelp and I made hurt eyes at her.

Why did we submit ourselves to this cringeworthy game? There were questions we'd both rather were not asked. It was how I'd found out she had a thing for Buckley for one. I had thought she was going to stop being my friend after she told me, but instead we'd only become closer, as if the sharing of a crush was as profound as the mixing of blood.

'Have you ever eaten a rat?' I asked.

She rolled her eyes. 'Not as a dolphin, obvs. But as other mammals, like, yeah. Loads.'

Perhaps, considering our profession, a simple crush really was the most shocking truth.

A lull followed. She watched me from the corner of an eye, chewing on one of the braids of the wig her mum made her wear, even though it was more often in her mouth than on her head. The question had to be a good one. Perhaps too good. I held my breath, to keep the answer in, even though I didn't know what it might be. Eventually the soft lisp of hair between her teeth became too much.

'Ask me already.'

She picked at the hairband with her crooked canines and I pinched the fat of her arm.

'Hey.'

'*Ask me.*'

Her face flushed, voice following like a shot.

'Do you ever feel like you're being watched?'

'Watched?'

'You know, like in Ressy.'

'Well, duh. Buckley watches all the time.'

'Not by Buckley.'

'Who then?'

Her face screwed up and she wedged it between her knees.

'Fine,' I said, 'my turn. Who do you think is watching you?'

'This is a stupid game, let's play something else.'

'You crossed your heart.'

She gave me a squinty eye but she knew the rules. To back out would be unforgivable.

Her whisper was so soft, I missed it the first time.

'What?'

'Just – them.'

The soft words ran a frisson up my nape.

'Them?'

It was too much. I dispelled the fear with a laugh and her face disappeared between her knees.

'*They're watching you,*' I intoned.

'Shut up.'

'*They're watching you, Susie Hammond.*'

'Shut up!'

I pulled my head inside my nightie, holding out arms in zombie leer.

'*Susie Hammond. Suuuusie Hammond.*'

'You're so immature.'

My own face turned hot at that. There was only a year between us; admittedly if we were at school she might not have even acknowledged my existence, but at ShenCorp I was the closest she had to a contemporary. She only ever brought up the age difference when she wasn't getting her way. It was a shitty card to play and she knew it.

I raised my voice in earnest. '*We're watching you, Susie! We see everything you dooooo! Susie, Susieeeeeee.*'

I expected to be hit, or sworn at in her mild-mannered way, 'gumrotter' or 'piddlestick', but instead I heard her scrabble down. When I popped my head free, she'd already picked up her duvet and retreated to the far corner of my room.

'It was just a joke.'

She ignored me, curled up, face to the wall.

'Susie.'

Her body was stiff under the duvet, the bald egg of her head perfectly still.

'Susie?

'Susie, I'm sorry.

'Really sorry.

'Really really sorry.'

Nothing. I retreated to my bed and stared up at the ceiling.

When I woke in the morning, she was gone. At breakfast Dad told me she'd knocked on their door in the night and her mum had come to take her home.

A month later her plasticity results came back unsatisfactory and ShenCorp removed her from active duty. I never saw her again.

32

Uncanny Shift

The hollow sockets stare from bleached bone, teeth a wicked grin. A shiver runs down my back, although it could just be my hide shirking flies. I replace the skull and sprinkle the old leaves back over it, their dried husks crackling beneath the pinch of my trunk.

'What are those?'

It takes me a moment to connect the high-pitched voice with the hulk of the bull elephant standing next to me. Her pre-set has the flatness of Russell's but it's most definitely feminine. I'm not sure what to think of the fact that they've prioritised programming gender vocals when they've not yet bothered with the intonation. At least, I assume Britta is female, we've never met in our Original Bodies.

'A funeral wreath,' I say. 'At least, that's the closest comparison.'

Britta's small eyes regard the bones in silence. Pitch-like ichor weeps through the skin of her cheeks and my own are stiff with the seepage. It's as sticky as tar and smells as bad. Although it's been days since I last touched it, a cake of dust clings to the tip of my trunk where it's still tacky with the stuff; its dark pungency lurks behind each breath.

I've never experienced musth before; as elephant studies tend to focus on social dynamics they mostly use female Ressies to enter the matriarchy. Yet even the Tourism board could see that people won't have the expertise or manners to pass off as part of a herd. Solitary bulls are much more practical but it creates the problem of musth. Though Bios reduced the testosterone levels by nearly half, they've failed to eliminate the cycle of aggression completely.

I swat away the crust of flies that have gathered on my left eye.

'Let's go.'

Where to is less obvious. Mr Hughes recently added the task of formulating activities and tours to my prep for each body but I'm yet to grasp what tourists expect of each 'experience'. As a tiger, it was easy enough to lead a hunt but what is the essence of an elephant? To a human it might seem like one thing but actually *being* an elephant is another. Yes, an elephant is large in comparison to a human but inRessy your body always feels normal-sized, and in this vast landscape it's hard not to feel small. What else? Elephants are known for never forgetting but mental qualities are the tourist's own. At least the trunk is distinctly elephantine, I suppose, though these projections aren't nearly long enough for tourists to get to grips with something so complex. Once Britta gained her feet, she spent half an hour swinging hers around like a propeller. Now it hangs from her face like dead meat, occasionally almost tripping her.

To the elephant, the elephant is just everyday life. And like any other body, its life is eating, sleeping, mating, surviving, but apparently these aren't 'experiences' enough for the Tourism. Or, as Mr Hughes is fond of saying, 'Where's the Wow?'

The beta tourists haven't been keen to engage with the banality of their bodies, as if defecating degrades them, despite carrying it out daily as humans. Misled by buzzwords and marketing, they really seem to believe that there is an 'animal experience' separable from the flesh.

I glance at Britta, pacing alongside me in a creak of dried skin. At least she seems more reasonable than Russell, but her seven tons of elephant feels more of a wall than a window.

The heat isn't helping. Every footstep raises a haze of dust that chalks the inside of my trunk. Grass has all but turned to ash and leaves are small mean things that scratch the inside of my mouth. In my Original Body I would have long since collapsed but even inRessy my skin feels baked and my joints are as stiff as if I were wearing leathers several sizes too small. I'm not exactly light-headed, not in a body this strong, but my steps are clumsier than I'm used to.

Water taunts from just over the horizon. I savour the smell by curling my trunk up to touch the roof of my mouth. The scent of water is easily the one I miss most as a human. Sweet is the only word I can think to give it, though it's not sweet at all. Even Britta's trunk has stirred inquisitively. Though Buckley has muted her thirst and hunger, a trip to the watering hole will be something to do even if she doesn't want to drink. I turn towards the scent, though the shimmering flatness ahead looks no different from our previous course.

Britta makes no comment at the change of direction; it's hard to tell if she's bored, awestruck or just loath to speak. So we walk in silence until dull thunder wakes beneath our feet once more. Britta gives me a quizzical look, at least I assume that's what it means.

I rock onto toes and the vibration clarifies. Maybe six or seven elephants, one small, maybe young. Although seismic sound can travel many miles, to be this loud, they must be close.

'A female herd,' I say. 'Can't tell if it's the same as earlier. Maybe a mile or so off.'

'Can we go to them?'

'Safest not. Bull elephants aren't always welcomed.'

She tosses her head and though it's a distinctive elephant gesture, knowing she's human, it's hard not to read it as disappointment.

'Come on,' I say. 'The waterhole isn't far now.'

The beat of sun is becoming almost physical. I'm glad for the ripening of the air as we draw close. The watering hole unfolds from the shimmer of horizon like a pool of polished metal. The musk of previous visitors lingers in invisible threat, some of them so strong that we must have missed their owners by minutes. I snort the scents: giraffe, some kind of large cat and a menagerie of others unidentifiable in their stampede. Whatever they are, as elephants there isn't much cause for us to worry.

Reaching the pool, I wade in. The earth is hard and slick, only turning to mud near the centre. When I kneel, my skin almost seems to sigh. I suck water up my trunk, the pressure bulging there as if I had a cold, then heft the weight over a shoulder to sneeze over my back. The stifle of my hide loosens almost immediately.

Britta stands on the side, eyeing the muddy water.

'Sure you don't want to come in?' I say but she makes no sign of hearing.

Even with the inputs turned down, the tightness of her skin must be getting uncomfortable. You have to ask, at what point will the tourist experience become one of total numbness.

I siphon the next few trunkfuls into my mouth with greedy gulps. Sun plays across the pool, a cool murmur in my ears. Buckley is talking to Britta. I let his melodic voice wash over me as my eyelids sink under the softness of sleep.

'Kit. Kit.'

I open my eyes to see Britta knuckling the mallet of her skull against a tree. The desiccated trunk is already starting to groan. Keep this up and she'll actually push it over.

I trudge out.

'Hey, Britta. Leave it, OK.'

She keeps shoving.

'You've seen how few trees there are, no need to kill another.'

Her only response is to shove harder. I curl my trunk around a tusk and pull. She roars and I only just manage to stumble from her swipe. Her small eyes are slightly mad. The thick ichor glistens on her cheeks. Bio was clearly not as successful at dampening musth as they thought.

'Easy, OK.' Buckley keeps his voice light. 'Are you feeling angry?'

Her head tosses, mouth opening on a wordless rumble. Whether she's failing to sub-vocalise or has moved beyond speech altogether is not clear.

'It's natural to be feeling angry. Your Ressy is in a natural state of arousal and—'

Britta rushes at me. I try to dodge but the tip of a tusk catches my cheek. I seize her trunk and lean the weight of my body into the shove. A beat starts in my temple.

'Calm down!' Buckley says. 'Everyone, please.'

But I'm not letting some tourist get the better of me. Who does she think she is? I add my tusks to the push and grind my feet against earth. Her face is so close to mine I can count the lashes.

'WILL EVERYONE PLEASE CALM DOWN!'

At Buckley's shout I jerk back.

'Thank you,' he says. 'Kit, don't be pigheaded. Britta, I'm sorry you're frustrated but you have to understand that your feelings are being compounded by the ResExtenda. Sometimes what seems like anger can really just be the unfamiliar sensation of having a stronger heartbeat.'

Rage still hunches in her posture but at least she doesn't charge.

'I'm going to decrease your inputs a little,' he continues. 'You'll feel a little numb but more calm.'

At the patter of fingers, she starts to droop.

'Now, let's go find that female herd,' he says. 'It won't hurt to take a quick look.'

Though I vowed not to let the tourists near, Britta's posture is slack enough to almost be vacant. If we keep our distance, it can hardly hurt.

We follow the earth's thunder until their shapes grow on the horizon. Even at a good hundred metres away, the matriarch lifts her ears uncertainly, no doubt worrying about the safety of the baby between its legs. The baby swings its trunk as if trying to dislodge something stuck to its face.

Under the matriarch's stare I feel almost naked. How can I feel so alien amongst humans, yet irredeemably human at a time like this?

One of the females has to be in heat. The seductive scent is hard to ignore, as is the stiffness between my back legs. I sit to try and quash the arousal but it's just really painful. The matriarch shakes her head, the crack of ears like a gunshot.

Which is when I realise that I'm on my own.

'Britta!'

If she hears she doesn't stop, the scent must have been too much for her. I stumble after, wincing as my penis is bashed between my back legs.

The elephants reel around to block her charge but Britta doesn't even slow. It wouldn't help for me to barge in too, but what else can I do?

'Britta!'

Buckley joins his shout to mine.

The matriarch meets her with a trumpet, only for Britta to blunder past. I rock on my toes, caught between making things worse and doing nothing.

Tusks flash under the baked sun. Elephants roar and stamp. Britta's hide is striped brown with blood but with her inputs turned down she might not even feel it.

'Buckley, get her out of there!'

'But the Ressy—'

If it drops on the spot they might stampede it but it's wounded as it is. I take a step forwards but an elephant at the edge of the tussle tosses her head – back off.

'Stop numbing her pain,' I say.

'If she feels it she might not have the strength to get out of there.'

Britta charges again, reeling almost drunkenly from their tusks, her back legs tangling.

The moment lasts longer than it should. The trajectory of her fall sears into my retinas even as she starts to tip. The calf is trapped behind her by a cluster of legs – the seven tonnes of falling elephant have nowhere else to go.

The smack replays in my ears long after the dust has settled.

The calf stays still when Britta stumbles back up. As the elephants turn on her, she doesn't try to stop them.

———————

I rise through the feathered edges of awareness. Surface into a strange pool of calm.

The anger of minutes ago has flattened. It feels as if my consciousness has been cut and pasted back together like an old film reel.

I sit up and unravel BodySupport. Buckley appears at my side, a hand on my shoulder, but he has no jokes today.

Once I've swallowed the dizziness, he leads me down the corridor to a cubicle where Mr Hughes stands, arms crossed, watching the woman on the pallet.

Britta, for that must be who this woman is, is still in her JumpPyjamas, a blanket over her shoulders. At another time she might be called pretty, but right now she looks haunted, her straw hair faintly greasy. I glare, squashing the flicker of doubt that this body, this person, could be the same as the killer of the elephant. As she looks up, her eyes widen in a moment of similar non-recognition and realisation.

Mr Hughes has to steady her as she pushes herself up.

'It's? Is it—'

I have to look away from the desperation in her eyes.

'The baby is dead,' Buckley says eventually. 'We should be able to retrieve your ResExtenda but we're not yet sure whether it will be usable.'

'I'm not sure what came over me.'

Elephant testosterone. The impulses of an unfamiliar body. But that doesn't mean she had to give in to them. I try to bite down on the building fury.

She rushes to fill my silence. 'You don't know how sorry I am. You have to believe me. I'll pay for damages. I'll pay for all of it.' She dives for her handbag beneath the JumpPallet and extends a wallet towards me. At my look, Mr Hughes nods.

Calm descends, an ocean stilling after the storm. I take the trembling hand in mine and drive my teeth into her thumb.

Flesh parts more easily than I'd imagined it would with human teeth. It takes two whole seconds before she screams.

Then everything descends into chaos. I'm grabbed from behind, lifted. Red bubbles from the wound. Only now do I taste the blood, sitting on my tongue like old pennies. Britta holds the hand out as if it weren't part of herself but something unsavoury, something other. No use denying your body now! I kick my legs and laugh, though it's not all that funny.

Mr Hughes swings around, his mouth ripped open in rage and it hits me – this is his true face. All that glib posturing and smiling only ever hid disdain. He hates me.

And in that moment, I know. Know that he's behind my watchers. The fox, the tiger, the bat; all him.

But Buckley is dragging me from the room, down the corridor, back into our cubicle.

With the door shut, I try to slip free but he won't let go of my forearm.

'Look at me. LOOK AT ME.'

His eyes are too terrible to meet.

'What in god's name were you thinking?'

I can't force the explanation the distance to my tongue. My head is still reeling from the fury in Mr Hughes's face.

The fox: he must have distracted me so I'd be hit. That way they could force me to take the Tourism job. As for the tiger and bat? A change of tactics? When it became clear I wouldn't play ball he must have decided to scare me away instead. After all, who needs the world's longest-serving phenomenaut when you have a Ressy copy?

Buckley lets go of me in disgust, starts to pace. I have to tell him what's going on but it's clear he's not going to listen until he's calmed down.

'How did you think *biting* her would make anything better? Did you even stop to think? If this gets out, the publicity . . .'

As if that's what's important right now. Maybe I should bite him too.

But at my snarl, he swings back. 'And us? Did you ever think what this means for us?'

At his anguish, I almost wish I could take it back, but I can't – that's the whole point. Money can't undo everything.

He sags into his chair, face in his hands. I sweep up my wash bag and race from the cubicle.

By the time I reach the changing room, my whole body is shaking, but it stills at the sight of the darkened blood on my mouth. I pull back lips to find my teeth tinged with pink saliva. No one would mess with that girl in the mirror, so why is everything going so very wrong for me?

I press my hands to the chill glass, trying to reach through to her, to myself.

33

Come Home

How long have I sat here? I'm not sure. Long enough for the dark to unfold into hesitant blue. The twisted limbs of the doppelgänger are almost pearly in the half-light. From this vantage point, it looks as small as a child. After hours of staring, I've yet to see its chest move.

One day, my Original Body will lie like that. Someone will look into a similar face and find it vacant. I feel vacant enough to be dead already.

When I gave myself up to sitting here, I was sure I'd be discovered in minutes. Capture would almost be a relief. Because wouldn't it be nice to rest, to be warm, to sink into oblivion. But if that's how things are going to go, I wish oblivion would hurry up. My lower body has gone completely numb and though my shoulders shiver uncontrollably, even that exertion leaves me exhausted.

The building is so quiet, when I first hear the footsteps, I think I'm imagining them. Yet the noise keeps growing. Panic stirs against my temple in moth wings.

My apathy of earlier disintegrates but, trying to stand, I find my legs leaden. Only a hand flung at the railing saves me from joining the Ressy. In the complete lack of feeling, I have to guide my steps by sight. My foot that collides with the step has the soft resistance of meat.

At the top of the flight the pain of returning sensation begins in shards. Running is impossible. I sink down and try to rub the feeling back.

Yet the footsteps below aren't in any hurry, a thin whistle rises over them, almost bird-like.

Come on. Come on.

My toes are nearly wriggling. If whoever approaches is distracted by the Ressy it might give me time to run.

But as a stooped figure rounds the corner, a croak escapes me. Grandma Wolf.

It's not dead. As my hands cup beneath its armpits, I could cry at the warmth and stickiness of life. Grandma Wolf grunts as she takes the feet and we make our way back up the stairs.

Its hands bash against the steps but it's the least of the damage that it will take away from tonight. I'll kill it if I try to take it any further, that much is clear. Even if it's not bleeding internally, without BodySupport it wouldn't make it as far as ICPO.

My arms are already screaming but Grandma Wolf's expression shows only concentration. At the storage room we back in through the door and deposit the body on the empty pallet.

Plugged back into BodySupport, the Ressy breathes more easily. Still, the face is puffier than it should be, its right side puce and purple. Bio is bound to notice but the upside is it means that they'll look for internal injuries. For, as much as my doppelgängers discomfort me, I don't like the idea of one dying. And

Mr Hughes won't be able to puppet me for a while, at least, not until he ships another of my doppelgängers in.

Free of her load, Grandma Wolf has moved to the window. The sun has already breached the horizon. We'll have to leave soon before the Centre starts to fill up. But then what? I haven't just wasted a whole night but ruined my only plan. I sit heavily on the gurney.

A blackbird lifts its voice, a tremulous laugh at the sun's return, so loud it could be inside the room. I look up, but of course it's just Grandma Wolf, head tipped back, singing as if it were her mother tongue.

After a few rounds, the pace changes, its pitch changing to robin's, excited by the promise of morning. The robin is followed by a creaking tweet of two intertwining notes, now lifting into the whoop of a swift, sliding across the heavens. Hunger and sex, warning and greeting, her song captures it all. When she finishes, the last mournful note peals outwards to unveil the crystal dimensions of air.

'How do you do that?' I whisper.

If she hears, she shows no sign of it. Under the waking light her stooped body has a terrible beauty. I could live a thousand lives and never belong like she does.

'What do I do now?' I say, ashamed of the whine in my voice. 'The doppelgänger was my only plan. I know it was foolish, but what other evidence do I have?'

She turns and I flinch under the intensity of that gaze. My hands are suddenly clammy, her look enough to render me a foreigner to myself.

But her attention has already shifted to the doppelgänger, expression ineffable; and, as if aware of my sudden awkwardness, she takes hold of my hands. Her touch is warm, skin like vellum. She pats me and nods as if to herself, somehow human in an instant.

Only as she walks away do I register that she's slipped something into my grasp: hard plastic – a card.

'Hey,' I call softly after her. But she's already gone. I can hear the sound of traffic outside the window. I need to get out of here myself. But first I move closer to the light and hold up the card.

It's the same design that's issued to all ShenCorp personnel, though the layout is slightly different to any I've seen. That explains the mystery of how she keeps breaking inside the Centre at least.

The photo shows a suited Asian woman in her fifties or sixties, expression set with the haughty assurance of your typical human. So much so that it takes me by surprise to suddenly realise that I'm looking at a younger Grandma Wolf. The rumour that she was a lecturer here was always the most believable.

To the right, where there would usually be an employee number and expiry date, is left blank. The only other information on the card is a name – 'Professor Miu Shen'.

34

Uncanny Shift

I'm not sacked. The fact only sinks in as Mr Hughes stands to show me out. I bit a tourist, yet I'm not sacked.

The last half hour was easily the bollocking of the century, but he smiles as he opens the door. The skin beneath his eyes is as loose and grey as an elephant's. It's hard to hate him faced with such exhaustion but then I remember how he snarled yesterday and shiver.

And yet, I'm not sacked.

I try to make sense of this as I stumble into the corridor. It helps that the company will be bringing a legal case against Britta for wilful destruction of company property, but wouldn't this be the perfect excuse to be rid of me if he really was trying to chase me away? At the top of the stairs, I glance back to see him watching me leave, but as I meet his gaze he turns back inside.

Down the stairs. Thoughts thud about my mind with a heavy footfall. If anything, isn't the fact that I *wasn't* sacked suspicious? There's been no sign of Daisy since her freak-out and attacking a beta-tester is surely worse than trashing chairs. Which means what? That Mr Hughes needs to me stay on staff? Or leave in a certain way? Because it wouldn't reflect well on Body Tourism if its poster girl was sacked. Yes, he has the doppelgängers but even if he could legally use them without my consent, it'd cause no end of trouble if I revealed that I no longer worked at ShenCorp. To have me leave and remain compliant, it'd have to be of free will. So the watchers? Is that his plan? To make me think I'm crazy, so that leaving becomes my own idea?

By the time I reach our cubicle, the thought has sunk sickening roots into my innards. There's no sign of Buckley, but I know where he'll be.

It's cold on the roof, Bristol is lost in a scud of cloud. Buckley stands motionless at the wire, staring out at the encroaching rain.

I sink down on the wall next to him.

'So. I'm not sacked.'

The look he shoots me is incomprehensible. I hunch my shoulders against the wind, eyes watering as I peer out over the mist.

The doubts about Mr Hughes squirm inside me like blowfly maggots. I need to tell Buckley but he's standing so stiffly, even the small gap between us feels like a chasm. Somehow I know that if I were to reach out, his touch would be cold.

'Aren't you happy?' I say.

'I—' He shakes his head.

'You what?'

There's something hard in his expression.

'You're still pissed off at me for biting that tourist, is that it?'

'I've every right to be. And Mr Hughes had every right to sack you.'

I recoil from his words. 'She killed an elephant. She destroyed the Ressy.'

'That's no reason for you to act so unprofessionally.'

'I don't care about what's professional, I care about what's *right*.'

'And what's right is biting a customer, is it?'

'And keeping the customer happy is all you care about? What is it with you and the Tourism?'

He squares his shoulders verging on a threat display. I usually forget how tall he is. 'What is *your* problem with it? It's a good thing. Why can't you get your head around that?'

'You can say Tourism will increase empathy until you're blue in the face but it hasn't, has it? Russell didn't care, Britta didn't, it was all just an experience to them. Kill and trample over everything then go home.'

'Not everyone will be like them.'

I humph.

'Listen to you,' he says. 'You're not twelve any more. This is your *job* and if you can't be professional then maybe you shouldn't—' He catches himself, tosses his head as if to chase the argument away. 'This wasn't how I meant this to go.'

I find myself standing, trying to put distance between us, but he takes my shoulders.

'Kit. Just . . .' It comes out close to a sigh. 'What I'm trying to say, what I *have* to say is, don't you think, maybe, what happened might have been a sign?'

'A sign?'

'That, maybe, it's possibly time.'

I look blankly at him.

'What I'm trying to say is that you've had a good run. An unbelievable run. No one else has been projecting for as long as you have but there comes a point when, for your own good, maybe . . .'

His face is a cold geometry of features that won't quite add up to the man I knew as Buckley.

'I don't understand.' My voice is so weak, the wind threatens to snatch it from me.

He takes my hands in his. Although his lips move, all that comes out is just gibberish. I have to wince against the static of my ears.

'Sorry, I didn't—'

'Kit. I don't know how else to say it. You need to give up jumping.'

'No.' The sound coughs from me, more of a grunt than a word and I have to repeat it, just to find its meaning for myself. 'No.'

He frowns, grip increasing on my hands.

'No,' I say again, smaller this time, a mouse's no, tiny, yet with a force of feeling inside.

'I know it's scary but at least stop a second and think about it. You know I'd never ask if I didn't think it was necessary.'

I wrench my hands from his grip. His tone is almost accusatory.

'You're not yourself, Kit.'

A snort escapes me, of dismay or amusement, I don't know. My job is to *be* other creatures, what self is it that he thinks I've been abandoning?

I can't take this any more. Yet I only make it a couple of steps before I have to lean against the fence to stop the ground from giving beneath me.

Buckley. Mr Hughes. What if they're in it together? Wasn't I just thinking that they're trying to get me to leave of my own volition? Mr Hughes knows I trust Buckley more than anyone. But I never thought that Buckley would choose Tourism over me.

But he did once before, didn't he?

Distantly, I'm aware of him hovering by my shoulder but I can't even bear to look at him. All these years and I thought that to see him was to look in the mirror. It's as if my own reflection has shattered the glass to stab me with a broken shard.

Rain starts to clatter against the concrete, its grey turning dark in seconds. Buckley hunches against the downpour and I can see the bird in him, heron or crow, eyes dark and glinting.

'You know this conversation is as hard for me as it is for you.'

My only response to that is a snarl.

'There comes a point when it's best to stop. For your own good.'

'You *wanted* me to take on the Tourism.'

'I'm not saying . . .' He gives up and looks away, hands tightening to fists at his sides.

I grit my teeth. I *will not* let him see me cry.

'Kit.' His tone is terrible. I clench my eyes against his pain. But I can't help it. He's Buckley. The voice inside my head. As close as a shared heartbeat. I sit and rest my head against the fence and after a second he follows suit.

'Did I ever tell you why I decided to give up?' His voice has an unfocused quality, as if the words weren't addressed to me.

'You said it wasn't for you.'

He laces his fingers through the wire. 'They say it's Sperlman's and Uncanny that are the hardest, but it's Come Home, the loss, that gets you in the end, isn't it?'

My throat is too raw to agree.

'It's – it's harder than anything isn't it? You discover new worlds. Worlds that had been right underneath your nose all your life and yet you'd never even known were there. You find new ways of being you . . . Then you have to say goodbye. Always goodbye.'

But to give up Phenomenautism would be to do so forever. I look away in to the haze of cloud. Even thinking about it isn't bearable. Not jumping, ever again. Being this body, me, for the rest of my life. My chest is tight.

'Even the part-time projection we did for Shen as undergrads,' Buckley is saying. 'I could feel what it was doing to me. It got inside my head. It was –' his hands form fists round the wire – 'I remember, one day after Come Home, back in halls, I was in the shower, just washing the conduction gel out of my hair, and, I don't know. I was watching strands of hair straining to escape down the plughole and I just saw it, that if I continued like I was, nothing good was waiting for me.'

His eyes don't even reach for mine any more, are fixed instead on some inscrutable distance. He feels miles away from me. And I wonder if he really could mean what he said. That he thinks giving up would be for my own good, not for the Tourism's, but just the thought of doing so is like staring into an abyss. A thin wind rushes through my ears making it hard to concentrate on his words.

'At the time I thought it was just me. We were quickly learning that more plastic brains adapted more efficiently. I thought maybe someone younger, someone different, would be able to withstand it. But I'm not sure I believe that any more. No one can live so many other lives without losing – I don't know, something.'

I shut my eyes. Just stop talking. Stop everything. Let the sky consume us. But he won't.

'I get the buzz. I *really* do. All the new ways of seeing the world, all the new ways of seeing yourself ... there's nothing like it. Nothing even comes close. I'm not saying giving it up is going to be easy but ...'

As I swallow, the clarity of sound returns with the pop of sinuses. 'Do you remember that time I was a sparrow?' I croak. 'You took me out into the courtyard, I stuffed myself on the hawthorn berries, then fell asleep on your shoulder. When I woke up, you had made me a nest from your jumper.'

He shuffles closer. Even in the rain, I swear I can feel the warmth radiate through his thin shirt. 'Of course I do. All I've ever tried to do is protect you. I know I haven't always done the best job at that. I know that I fuck up sometimes. That I *really* fucked up when I let you get hit by that car. But it's been – it's been a learning curve for both of us. God, I was barely eighteen when they put me in charge of you. I feel barely older now. But you have to believe me when I say that all I want is for you to be OK.'

I study his frown, find myself imagining what it would feel like to trace my fingers over the knot of muscle. Even though he's coming out with these terrible things, he's still Buckley.

'I never did tell you about Isaac Wallace, did I?' he says, speaking carefully, as if not quite trusting himself.

It's a peace offering, of sorts.

He smiles at my expression, then bites it back. 'Sorry. I did mean to eventually but –' he shrugs – 'I was embarrassed? Afraid? Ashamed?'

'So, you did know him?'

'I suppose.' But at that he laughs. 'Not in the sense people normally mean by the word. He was two years above me on our course, we never really socialised. I wouldn't be able to tell you anything about his family, what food he liked, what he wanted to do after university; none of the things people usually mean when they "know".'

He studies his fingers twisted around the wire, as if suddenly noticing something remarkable about them.

'He was another of the experimental phenomenauts?' I say. 'The same as you?'

'Yes. My Ressy Buddy.' He glances up to confirm I don't know what that means. 'Ressy Buddies; something we did in the early days. I've told you about how undergraduates could get extra credit for taking part in Shen's experiments? It was a big part of my time at university, but we still had our other studies to get on with. So

Shen set up a rota whereby a couple of students would timeshare piloting the same Ressy. Isaac was who I was paired with.'

I lift my head to the drizzle, touched by the strangeness of the idea. Sharing a Ressy. Of course, there's no reason why not – I suppose at points other people must use the same Ressy as I used for the first London meeting, and Mr Hughes uses my doppel-gänger for marketing – but sharing regularly, body after body between the same two people . . . I jolt as Buckley laughs.

'I think it was some kind of joke of the postgrad who was in charge of the rotas,' he says. 'Professor Shen used to call me Young Isaac, apparently I looked like him, even though I never saw it, he had a face like –' he boxes his hands around his own – 'you know, proper rugby-player type, like he'd had a run-in with a wall at some point – and won. But,' he shrugs, 'we were both tall and dark haired, and when you don't know someone that well, sometimes you can't see the differences. *And* Shen had cottoned on to the fact that it annoyed me. She had a wicked sense of humour in those days.'

She. Why had I always assumed the professor was a man? Why is it that no one ever tells us phenomenauts anything? But Buckley hasn't finished.

'Isaac had always been her star pupil so perhaps it was even a compliment. Or just coincidence. We were different years so pair-ing us off made sense, our lectures rarely coincided and our papers had different deadlines, which meant that if one of us wasn't free the other normally was. With that setup I barely even saw him. And yet we shared this—' He spreads his hand in lieu of words.

'You shared Ressies.'

'Right. I'd project and feel my stomach heavy with a meal that he'd eaten, or the ache of scratches I hadn't caused. Just as he'd feel the aftermath of my experiences whilst I was away. It sounds crazy for someone I barely exchanged the time of day with when I passed him in the quad but we were—' He pinches off in exasperation again. Sometimes words are meagre things.

'I get it,' I say.

He nods. 'One time I saw him at the student bar, I think he was hitting on this guy; he must have pushed it too far because the guy slapped him, and I actually felt it, the slap. I mean, not *really*, not like he must have felt it. But it hurt, I actually felt pain. Does that make any sense?' He seems relieved when I nod, hurries on as if pausing could lose me. 'It's fascinating how easily one's sense of, I don't know – self? Being? – can be extended outside of this ... this ...' he picks up one hand with the other.

I lie my head sideways on my knees to watch him, letting the murmur of rain fill the pause. When he speaks again, his voice is soft, as if he isn't quite sure whether he wants me to actually hear.

'The strangest thing was that for the longest time after he died, I'd walk around feeling like I was wearing his face. Sometimes, I still do.'

He drops the hand to the concrete beside him; it looks dejected, lonely.

'I felt projecting do something strange to me. And I think it might have had something to do with what happened to Isaac. If it was to hurt you ...'

The clouds have completely swallowed the city, leaving a cold void like the one inside of me. Is this what Isaac felt when he stood here? If anything could have driven him to it, wouldn't it have been the idea of giving it all up? To calcify into one being? I try to imagine what it must have been like, tipping over the edge, death rushing up to meet him. The closest I can come to it is the memory of plummeting over the roof as a bat.

But Buckley is staring at me.

'It won't,' I say and place my hand over his, so large and solid beneath my touch.

As his eyes lift to mine, my centre of gravity seems to tip.

'Kit.'

His lips cradle my name like a baby bird. Those fathomless eyes flicker over my face leaving a trail of warmth. What really lies behind that look?

'I'm not ready.' My voice has shrunk to a whisper, too; my throat has contracted to the point where I've no choice. 'I can't stop before . . .'

'Before what?'

'Before I understand.' It escapes me as a bark, as if the volume could force my full meaning into the helpless fumbling of sound. 'Before I *see*. Seven years. All those bodies, all those ways of seeing, and I'm still not sure if all I've ever seen and understood is – is just myself.'

When did the distance between our faces vanish? His eyes are so close that those pupils have swollen to pools on a moonless night. My reflection drowns in them, my guts turning within me, sounding the alarm before my thoughts catch up. After the bat jump, when he'd been looking at my recordings, why had he looked so guilty? Why had he lied?

But the heat of his lips is already on mine. His mouth is a strange landscape, scattering all thought. I freeze. Unable to press into him, unable to retreat. In that spiralling moment, I feel I must be outside my body, or trapped inside; only a butterfly heartbeat against this edifice that isn't truly mine.

In my mind's eye I find myself back at that party, watching him and that girl, stunned with the realisation that he was capable of such things. That I didn't know who this man really was.

I draw back and he startles away too. My mouth burns with the memory of his. I can't meet his eyes. Buckley is the voice in my head, the eyes behind my eyes, not *this*. The touch of his hand around mine feels clammy. I wrench it free.

He stands with me, the distance between us already defined in paces. My whole body jangles with sick energy. I open my mouth, but I don't know what to say. It feels as though my lips aren't quite my own any more.

I turn and run.

On the bus back home, I can't rid myself of the memory of his face, so close to mine. Nor the heat of his hand. It's as if his touch has branded me.

Fuck.

I scrub the hand against the fabric of the seat but it only makes the heat grow worse until my whole face is burning with it. Buckley has always been my constant, so predictable he hasn't even had to enter my reckoning, but how well do I really know him? Seven years and he hadn't even mentioned his connection with Isaac. Seven years in which the idea of him wanting to kiss me had been completely ludicrous, and then this . . . What else is hiding behind those eyes?

You need to give up jumping.

Echoes of his words ring through my head, making even less sense now than before.

And why does the memory of finding him looking at my recordings after the bat jump trouble me so much? He had looked so guilty. What if he kissed me on the roof to distract me from stumbling onto something he was hiding? To make me believe he only wants what's best for me? Surely he'd never manipulate me like that . . . and yet, before tonight, I would never have thought he'd ever ask me to leave ShenCorp.

The answer slams into me, as viscerally as if the bus had come to an emergency stop.

The simulations.

The simulations Buckley showed Kyle how to create for Daisy. What if my watchers were not Ressies, but inserted code? The tiger disappeared in a blink. The bat vanished right in front of me. The fox never showed up on Buckley's recordings.

My innards roil but now I've started on this path of thought I can't stop. It would explain the strangeness of their presences, the sense of their not being quite substantial. And simulations would be more affordable than shipping in new Ressies just so Mr Hughes could stalk me. After all, didn't Buckley say that projection was a form of simulation itself? And after the bat jump isn't the only time he's tried to hide recordings from me. What about the day I returned to work after my death as a fox? They hadn't been recognisable as my scan but what if that's because they were showing signs of his manipulation?

My fists are clenched so tightly they're collecting sweat but it's not enough. I put a fist to my mouth. Bite it.

Think about it realistically and who's the only person with direct access to my brain during jumps? Who knows me inside and out, who's watched me every minute of every projection for years? Whose role is to feed me what's essentially false sensory information? It's practically his job description.

But Buckley isn't – Buckley can't—

I grind my teeth deeper into my knuckles.

No. Buckley is just Buckley.

———

Back home, a carer's car sits in the driveway. I can see their silhouette against the curtains of Mum's room as they prepare her for bed.

Leaving my bag on the path, I squeeze my way past the back of the shed and worm under the overhang of the leylandii. The branches whisper, the single note of a blackbird threading through their stream. I hug my knees and hunker down into the patch of earth that has been worn smooth by my visits.

I let my eyes fall shut, only a slit left open to watch the puppet show behind the curtain.

The figures dance and merge, trailing cords from the hoist as a stiff body lifts into the air in paralysed flight.

Uncanny Shift

The forest is frantic with detail. Trees shoot up in green effervescence, each needle a quivering sequin. Glimpses of ground scud between the foliage: a blink of rabbit tail, the flowing back of a deer, hundreds of tiny eyes. Birds toss themselves up in swirls of feathers, flitting from branch to branch as if they could hide from me.

Wind shakes the canopy in a green river. Its sigh merges with the slow heave of Buckley's breath, somehow unbearably loud, when more than ever I want to forget him. Just listening turns the protrusion of my beak tender as if the heat of his kiss could find me even here, in this body. I clack the two parts together and the sensation bursts the memory.

Buckley and I have barely spoken since what happened on the roof. Whether it's out of guilt or embarrassment, I'm not sure I even want to know. But I'm not giving up my job. I haven't projected for seven years through all forms of hell and weirdness to be scared off by watchers that aren't even real.

With a beat I pull myself into the thermal current, flexing my wings to catch the lift. Air purrs beneath feathers, carrying me steadily higher; my fists of feet hang over nothing.

Up here, the tapestry of landscape unfurls beyond what seems possible, each sparkling stitch picked out in clarity. The horizon stretches in a frenzied surround, as if I were focusing on everything at once.

I twist my neck so that one eye is to the ground, the other to heaven; a tempest of colour, adrenaline rush. Alien colours trumpet and splinter, headfuck. Even within my own wings there are a hundred colours I can't name. They don't *have* names; a select few phenomenauts are the only humans to have ever seen them.

Then there are the textures: a tickle of ground; scratch of evergreen; milk water, curling up into the froth of cloud. The intensity threatens to swamp me, as if my feathered body might any second *pop*, leaving me as just a pair of disembodied eyes in an endless horizon. Humans are blind compared to this.

The hot buoy of the thermal sighs into my embrace. The air is a landscape as detailed as that below. Amazing that humans can look up and think the sky empty. Up here the peaks and troughs are unmissable. I ride the upward warmth of wind; its tide pushing me up and up.

As the thermal tapers out, I slide out to soar over the dizzying plain. Stray dots of cloud meander below like sheep, vast lakes shrunk to winks of sun. All of this filling me, becoming me. I stretch my wings and encompass it all.

By the time the heat has settled into the throne of sky, I'm starving. I turn back downwards and plummet. Wind whines through feathers, land rushing to fill my vision. Meadows become forest. That puddle a lake.

Closer I can see that the navy is stitched with glints of silver, sinking to shadows as the fish swim deeper. I pinpoint the brightest and drop. Wings yawn back, claws thrust into the fall, and the fish grows larger, larger, a blink of scales, a beady eye – now! I gape talons, slash – but close on water only just managing to pull myself from the crash.

Buckley's breathing became pinched with my plunge but he makes no comment on the failure. His presence feels opaque. I wish he'd just talk or go away. The thump of my heart has thinned into an uncertain skip – fight or flight, I don't even know.

I scoop arms of heavy air, lazy as treacle. Without a thermal, lifting myself is tough work. Although a bald eagle is bound to be good for American business, had they really been thinking about the experience they should have gone with something lighter. But Mr Hughes wasn't impressed by my suggestion of a pigeon.

I keep rising in a corkscrew until I'm high enough to drop again. And plunge – my stomach pushing upwards, the tingle of outstretched claws – meeting only the resistance of liquid.

The third and fourth tries are a little more successful, although I still miss both times. My muscles are already burning with the upward effort but hopefully it won't take much longer. Hunting is a different art for each Ressy. I just have to get the knack.

Fifth time I'm not expecting anything, when my claws meet flesh. Talons snap automatically, the fish thrashing in my grasp, and I tear myself up with a downward punch of wings and beat over to the bank.

It's dead by the time I land. A trout. My claws are warm inside the bloodied meat, one toe sticky with the goo of a punctured eye. I shift my grip and peck off a chunk, throwing my neck back to work the bulk down my gullet. It doesn't taste of anything but the notes did mention that bald eagles don't have a developed sense of taste. Mind you, perhaps sparing tourists the taste of raw fish isn't a bad thing.

When my stomach is finally bloated to satisfaction, I set to preening. Will tourists know how to do this? Probably not. The storage tanks had better have a function for it or the flight will quickly become impaired.

It's nice to feel my head embraced in a den of feathers. I could go to sleep like this, but I should really finish the perimeter survey. Until I've worked out how to return to Research, I'm going to have to play along with Tourism and Mr Hughes's stupid games.

I sweep the air into a clap and the ground crawls away. Beat, beat, beat. Such hard work, but at last I'm sailing into the still and can start searching for a thermal. If they don't teach these basics to tourists they will flap themselves silly.

Finding the ridge of a lift, my muscles lock into the glide. This thermal is tight, so I corkscrew up the pillar, already searching for the next. Cumulus clouds are a good pointer but the midday sky has emptied to an unblemished blue. I turn my head, neck twisting further than seems possible.

Which is when I see *it*.

A stark shadow, between me and the sun. It could just be another eagle but I'd recognise that intensity anywhere. Another watcher. Familiarity shivers the length of my wings. Though I have little sense of taste, my tongue is ripe with bitterness. Buckley's breath rolls in my ears like distance thunder.

'Tell me you can see this,' I say.

'See what?'

Doubts are all very well when I'm in the safety of my Original Body but here there's not even a question. *I see it*.

The eagle banks around on the thermal. Angled against the sun its wings catch fire. That auric gaze pierces right through me.

No denying it now. The watcher is real. Or rather, the simulations are. Buckley has really sided with Mr Hughes over me. I feel as if the sky has emptied from under me, then replace it with fury.

No more running. No more mind games. I fling myself out of the thermal into a glide. The air slopes beneath me until I catch the draught that will carry me up to it. Its shadow spirals above, waiting.

If it's a real eagle I'm starting a pointless fight but, if so, why doesn't Buckley admit to seeing it? Even his human senses can't miss it this time. I'm not sure whether an attack on a simulation will work but I guess I'm going to find out.

The auburn feathers dance between sun and void, a burnt blackness that grows in my vision.

I tilt my body into an arrow, my beak levelled at its heart. This close the familiarity flares through me in pins and needles.

The sky is a gabble, my body a bullet. Now—

I flip over, talons reaching – only to tear through it with no more resistance than air.

It vanished.

I swoop round and round to no effect. A simulation. It really is. Meaning Buckley . . .

Oh fuck.

'What is it? Your adrenaline levels are through the roof.'

Of course, it's only now that Buckley starts speaking. The voice that has comforted me for years is nothing but a thinly guised sneer.

Air kicks as I exit the thermal by mistake, suddenly aware of the drop beneath me. My heart thrashes like a fish between claws.

Shit. Shit. Shit.

'This isn't looking good,' he says. 'Try to land. We don't want the safety bringing you home when the Ressy is still in the air.'

Because, of course, it's the Ressy he really cares about.

Land swarms below, like writhing grubs. I clip a stray buffet of wind and stumble, nothingness yawning open in miles. But Buckley's right about one thing, I'm in no fit shape to fly right now.

I turn my body into a plummet and the ground land swells up to meet me. There's nothing more I can do now.

36

Come Home

Back in the safety of a nearby hedge, I turn Professor Shen's card between my hands. Under full daylight, I can get a clearer look at the picture: she looks so serious and neat, the sort of person who would insist on proper conduct at all times, but it's her all right.

Grandma Wolf. Professor Shen.

Little wonder she kept breaking in. Little wonder Mr Hughes tried to keep her out of the way. Did he plant rumours about the lab in Switzerland himself? It's one thing for the shareholders to stomach a reclusive CEO, but a crazy one is something else entirely. If crazy is the right word. Sometimes it's Grandma Wolf's lucidity that scares me most.

I drop it into a pocket to hide the questions behind those dark eyes. She must have given it me with something specific in mind. The card of Professor Shen herself must have access to everything in the Centre, so could there be any secret rooms? Suspicious Ressies I don't even know about? No, more likely she's thinking of something on the central server. Stealing data is easier than stealing a Ressy and the server has to have the files on the simulations somewhere.

The fox returns so quietly I miss her entrance, roll over to just find her there.

'Where have you been?' I say but she ignores me, intent on digging a cache.

'Grandma Wolf was Professor Shen,' I say, ashamed of this need to speak.

She squats to pee on top of the cache and I bite a lip. That's not normal fox behaviour. If Grandma Wolf is Professor Shen, why can't my fox be Tomoko? It's the only explanation that makes any sense.

The fox leaves the cache and turns in a circle to find a comfortable position to sleep. I watch for a long time after her breathing slows.

'Buckley wouldn't believe it,' I whisper. 'You know what he thinks happened to you.'

———

Lauren finds us in our cubicle. Perhaps that alone should have warned me; it was the first time she's visited in person. For that matter, I can't remember the last time I'd met her in my Original Body. She seems both larger and smaller than my mental image. Those pre-Phenomenautism nature groups feel part of another life.

She waves away the offer of Buckley's chair, remains standing in the doorway, one hand clutching her neck scarf.

'You OK?' I ask.

'I come bearing bad news, I'm afraid.'

Buckley and I share a look.

'Bad?'

'Yes. I don't know how to say this. I'm very sorry but the little fox cub of yours—'

'Tomoko?'

'Yes. Tomoko.' Her eyes search mine. 'I'm so sorry to be the one to have to tell you this, Kit, but she passed away yesterday.'

I can only blink back in confusion.

'A car?' I say eventually.

'No. No. We don't have the resources to do autopsies on all our foxes but we think she might have ingested a plastic bag.'

'Oh.'

The pair of them stare at me.

Lauren continues carefully. 'Crystal brought the body back to the department, we've got it in a freezer. She thought you might want to bury it.'

'And you're sure it's her? You only chipped the cubs after I had left.'

'We're as sure as we can be. She always was the smallest of the pack.'

'But she put on weight when she was with me.'

She looks to Buckley, uncertain. 'I have a photo, if it would help you to check.'

I lift a hand to accept the SpecSpace packet and find myself looking at an image of a mangy body, lying limp on a pavement, the abandonment too complete for it to be just asleep. I shove the image from my lens.

'Thank you for thinking of me, but that isn't her.'

'We're fairly certain,' Lauren says, if this time a little more hesitant.

'I'd recognise Tomoko. You must have got the chips mixed up.'

Of course, it's sad to think of any of the cubs dead, but you have to be realistic; the life expectancy of all urban foxes is pitifully short.

'Kit. I don't want to be the one to say this but you only ever met her as a fox. To human senses she's going to appear a little differently,' Buckley says.

'I know, OK.' I glare at him but he just returns the look with sadness.

'Well, I'll leave you to it,' Lauren says. 'But if you—'

'Thanks,' I say and return to my report-writing with determination, but Buckley isn't so easily put off. He keeps on giving me worried looks, doesn't even make the hour before coming over to sit next to me.

'Are you sure you wouldn't want to give it a proper burial? Just to put your mind at rest?'

'It's not her.'

The pity in his expression is worse than anything. In the end I leave to work in the common room.

37

Come Home

When it finally turns round to night again, I return to the Centre. Though it makes little sense, I feel safer with Grandma Wolf – Shen's – card. The fact that she keeps returning must mean that Mr Hughes has been unable to wrestle power from her completely.

Though my first instinct is to access the server via my old cubicle, I can't risk running into Buckley, so instead I head up the stairs towards Mr Hughes's office.

Footsteps come down from the stairway above, torchlight throwing the flicker of bars across the walls, and I have to slip back a floor to hide, but the clunk of boots passes without pause and after a minute I can continue on my way.

I'm still shaking as I enter Mr Hughes's office. Snatches of movement follow my own in the dim glass. I perch in Mr Hughes's chair, dwarfed by its size. There's no scent of urine; if Grandma Wolf uses it as a scent marker the cleaners must be used to getting rid of the smell. Not that I need scent to tell me I'm invading territory.

The holographic display blinks to life in a curved bowl of light. The fingers I dip in to open the system sink through the illusion of solidity.

Grandma Wolf's desktop is more ordered than expected, though, on reflection, I wouldn't have guessed that she'd use a computer at all. But then again, what do I really know about her?

A couple of loose files appear to be papers on the neurointerfacing and zoology, all published within the last few months. Despite her eccentricities, Grandma Wolf has clearly been staying abreast of the science. And why wouldn't she? She practically invented the field.

I tap open the server only to sag at the hundreds of folders that populate the list. Unfettered access to the servers is all very well but I've still got to find the evidence of simulations.

I scroll my way down to get a sense of the most promising folder. A lot of them are labelled with strings of numbers that mean nothing to me, although some are more straightforward: 'ResExtenda Reels' presumably contains the footage from the projections, though as these feeds come from the inner Ressy cameras presumably they won't show the simulations. 'Neuroengineer Notes' could be more promising but the really incriminating data has to be in the 'Wave Function Archives'. If only I had the expertise to understand it.

Inside it are more folders, these titled with strings of numbers too. To comply with data protection, no doubt, but this is one time I wish ShenCorp was less discreet.

After a long minute of staring, I realise that as the longest projecting phenomenaut, my folder is likely to be the largest, and when I arrange them by size, there is indeed one that's a couple of hundred terabytes larger than the others.

Yet the smugness doesn't last long. Inside are more folders, and even more inside those. When I finally reach an actual file, the metadata tells me that it covers ninety-six hours of data. Needle in a haystack doesn't even touch on the idea of finding a few minutes of inserted data in a file like this.

I almost have to admire it. It's easy to hide secrets when you produce such a glut of data. Even if I could afford the storage to transfer the whole folder, it'd take hours to upload. I could copy some files at random to my cloud but the easiest way to do this will be to hand ICPO Shen's card. What I need, then, is something smaller that's suspicious enough to persuade them that the investigation is worth their time. Evidence of the human Ressies would be enough to raise a flag.

I wave the server off the screen and watch the desktop animation weave a mumuration of starlings in and out of the screen. Grandma Wolf might be odd but she's also smart. She wouldn't have given me her card unless she knew of some realistic way for me to access the information I need.

I open up her 'My Documents', glad to find that at least these are carefully labelled. From her response to my doppelgänger, it clearly wasn't a surprise. With any luck there should be something here. Although Grandma Wolf has obviously kept everything that's come her way about the company, there's little sign of her input, and the instances of her signature I can find have clearly been copy-and-pasted. ShenCorp must really only be hers in name now.

But a folder has caught my eye.

'Isaac Wallace'

I open it, eyes watering under the hard light of the screen. The first file is a download of an old webpage from the local news, 'Student Jumps to Death'. Yet it's the photo that grabs me, a headshot of a morose male, caught somewhere between teenager and adult. I don't have to read the caption to know this is Isaac. It's easy to see why Shen said that Buckley looked like him. Though his face is brute ore where Buckley's is refined, his gaze cocksure where Buckley's is quizzical; the dark hair, intelligent eyes and whimsical mouth, these they share.

The statement from the police says that they didn't suspect any foul play. Quotes from fellow students mention that Isaac had been acting oddly over the previous months, but mostly they seem shocked. None of them had thought him depressed.

The following document contains snippets from emails. A quick skim reveals that Isaac had given up his place on the university rugby team, barely ate except for seeds, and that his passion for Phenomenautism was verging on the unhealthy. My fingers tingle where they touch the screen as if waking from numbness.

The next file contains more copied emails.

Mr Hughes <CHughes@shencorp.org.uk>
To: Staff Mailing List <AKake@shencorp.org.uk,
    APinbor@shencorp.org.uk . . .>

Dear Staff and Faculty,

It falls upon me to inform you of Professor Shen's sabbatical, starting immediately. She has asked me to apologise for the abrupt nature of her decision at this crucial stage of the company's launch and to convey that this is out of no disrespect or lack of confidence in the company's launch. She would not have made this difficult decision had poor health not made it for her.

As some of you might have gathered in these trying past months, recent stress has led her to the realisation that her interests and aptitudes are more suited to the science behind Phenomenautism than the business side of operations and, as of yesterday, she has moved to her labs in Switzerland.

She hopes to return in a few months, once the company is up and running. Until such a time, she has asked me to oversee the launch of ShenCorp and the company's daily running, so please direct all related issues and enquiries to me.

She asks for your understanding in this matter, which I am sure you will all be forthcoming with. Any messages of condolence or urgent queries can be conveyed through myself.

All best,
Mr Hughes

Dr Kimberley <FKimberley@shencorp.org.uk>
To: Mr Hughes, Staff Mailing List <CHughes@shencorp.org.uk,
    AKake@shencorp.org.uk . . .>

Charlie,

No one is buying this sabbatical talk. Phenomenautism is Miu's baby, she wouldn't leave only months before the launch. Everyone knows she's been on edge since that student suicide. If the rumours are true and she's had a breakdown, I think we've a right to know.

Fran

Mr Hughes <CHughes@shencorp.org.uk>
To: Dr Kimberley, Staff Mailing List <FKimberley@shencorp.org.uk,
   AKake@shencorp.org.uk . . .>

Dear Dr Kimberley et al,

Dr Shen's health is a private matter between her and her family and I ask you to respect that. However, I can reveal that, as of this afternoon, the board has installed me as acting director until such a time as Dr Shen wishes to return.

As for these 'rumours', I had hoped that the world's leading Phenomenautical and Neurocognitive scientists would have better sense than to believe in such supposition. ShenCorp launches in under a month, it's in no one's interest to entertain such falsehoods. You all know the trouble we had securing child work permits after Mr Wallace's unfortunate death. Let's not invite any more unnecessary controversy, please.

Best,
Mr Hughes

Acting Director of ShenCorp

Dr Kimberley <FKimberley@shencorp.org.uk>
To: Mr Hughes, Staff Mailing List <CHughes@shencorp.org.uk,
   AKake@shencorp.org.uk . . .>

Dear *Acting Director of Shencorp,*

Surely after 'Mr Wallace's unfortunate death' we should be questioning whether to employ teenagers. If the kid really did think he could fly then we need to be doing more than just putting up a fence. I know I'm not the only one thinking this.

Fran

Mr Hughes <CHughes@shencorp.org.uk>
To: Dr Kimberley, Staff Mailing List <FKimberley@shencorp.org.uk,
   AKake@shencorp.org.uk . . .>

Dear Dr Kimberley,

Whether or not you're the only person thinking such, emailing the entire staff mailing list is unacceptable. I invite constructive critique by private appointment but please refrain from spamming company inboxes in future.

Mr Hughes

Acting Director of ShenCorp

The exchange stops there. If there's more I'm not sure I'd want to read it. Joking with Susie about Isaac being mad was one thing, but for the staff to have actually thought it a possibility...

I feel sick. And sick with myself that we used to milk the idea for thrills. But back then, he was just a myth, we never thought of him as a real teenager like us.

Was this exchange what Grandma Wolf wanted me to find? I'm not sure it's enough to get the ICPO to investigate. Although the emails don't make Mr Hughes look great, they're effectively hearsay. Yet the creak of footsteps from the floor below is making me nervous. I can't stick around here much longer. If I can just find a reference to human Ressies, the two together will have to be enough.

I return to the main folder and flick through files at random until I find a list of tourist acquisitions that details a new line of human Ressies. Also attached are the copyright agreements of the people they're to be based on. It's not much but as the ICPO is already suspicious, it might give them enough liberty to go digging, and with the professor's access, who knows what they'd find.

I open my cloud and transfer the file, then as an afterthought, add the whole of Grandma Wolf's 'My Documents'. There must be more evidence about the human Ressies there. I can hunt it out when I'm not in a compromised position. I send ICPO an access email, then disconnect and get out as quickly as I can.

Waiting in the dark feels different after everything I've found out, a restless energy drives me in cycles of the park. I have evidence of the human Ressies; all that's left is to get Shen's card to ICPO in the morning and let them hunt out evidence of the simulations. But the victory feels hollow when thoughts of Isaac keep running through my head. The staff really suspected him of mistaking his Original Body for that of a bird.

Yes, there are times when your identity – slips, when it can be hard to let your inRessy abilities go. But jumping off a roof? That's just crazy.

The fox stands in the park entrance, the dismembered leg of something in her mouth, but seeing me she drops it and stares. In her eyes are scorched galaxies. My stomach starts to skip.

Her nostrils flare, examining my scent, but whatever she smells must satisfy her, for she crawls forwards and curls up beside me.

I almost don't dare breathe, scared that any movement will chase her away. But as her muscles relax in sleep, I gently stroke the air above her fur.

38

Uncanny Shift

Dad pauses at my door, coat already on, shoulders weighed down under his rucksack. He'll be leaving now, following where his camera leads.

When he comes back the chin will be lost in a coarse white beard and I'll wonder what this man did with my dad; the dad who taught me silly songs to march to, who chased me along paths in pretence of a crocodile, who hoisted me to his shoulders where my hair could brush the sky. Does he ever look at me and wonder the same?

He raps on the door frame, though he already has my attention. 'All right, I'm off now. Sure you don't want me to bring anything back from Chad?'

'Dad.'

The tone catches him but now he's listening, my voice fails. Because what can I say? Work is trying to get rid of me, to make me think I'm mad; my closest friend in the world has betrayed me for the sake of his job? In my mind, the memory of the eagle

306

simulation replays. It's too much to expect of words. My fingers dig into the mattress, feeling the moment stretch from my grasp like elastic . . . and snap.

He shifts his rucksack higher up his shoulder. 'I've really got to go now if I'm to catch my plane. You can call me when I have signal. Remember it's going to be a couple of hours until the carer arrives, I think it's Caroline tonight, so Mum'll need some lunch. There should be some leftover pasta in the fridge. Don't give her the pie, though, she found it hard to swallow.'

'Right. Bye.'

He lifts a hand and leaves.

I sit in the emptiness he leaves behind, trying to sense outward towards its edges. But they're too far to reach.

I drift about for a while, then go to the living room. Mum is slumped in her recliner by the window, unmoving save for the flitter of her eyes, chasing the flight of birds.

Every day. Every week. Every month. Years slipping by in this quiet light; just watching. What does she even see of them? A flash of colour and shadow? With her eyesight it must be hard to catch anything, but she likes the idea at least.

I can't understand her answer to whether she wants a drink, so I put the sippy cup to her mouth anyway. Her lips pucker round it and then slacken so that a dribble of juice runs down her chin. The full-stops of her pupils fidget about my face, something vacant about them. Almost . . . Ressy-like. I pat her dry with a tea towel and sit.

The photo frame next to her shows a picture of baby me, so old it's static 2D. The almost disembodied grin of a younger, healthier Mum hovers at the edge of the frame, brandishing the chocolate that is the cause of the baby's – my – sticky merriment.

I take the frame down and balance it on the arm of her recliner. We got this for her a couple of years back – her grasp on reality is tenuous enough without introducing Specs – although I doubt she can even see it now.

Next shot is of me and Dad: a couple of years later so it's moving but still not in 3D. Dad holds me steady on top of a donkey as I slaver my face with ice cream. He has dark hair but it's still very much him. This was the trip when I dropped the 99 on his head and cried all the way home. Of course, I don't remember it myself, but Dad has tortured me with the story so many times it's tempting to think that I can. I stare at the pixels of delight on my face. That child will keep on licking until the real me is dust in a grave, and still the ice cream won't be finished.

Now a photo of Mum and Dad, sitting on a wall in front of a garden I don't recognise. This one must be out of order because they look so very young, perhaps at university, as old as I am now – they're wearing clothes that are cringeworthy enough to be from the noughties. I stare into those features, but they don't let me any deeper in.

Next, tenth birthday. Sitting in a paddling pool with friends, kicking up white walls of water. I do remember this day, but it's vague, like the memory of a story told about someone else's life.

An excited twelve-year-old replaces it, braces unashamedly bared, not even conscious of the threat of teeth as she thrusts a piece of paper towards the lens. The day I was accepted into ShenCorp. The choice seemed so simple then.

Next, a close-up of a face that's almost mine. Fifteen? Sixteen? What secret geometry of features is it that holds together Katherine North from one year to the next? The expression flickers from a smile to a glower as I realised a picture was being taken. In the background, Mum sags in her wheelchair, her face is puffy but there's still something of the old Mum there. Her smile looks so very tired.

I put the photo frame back on its shelf. The people in these photos are strangers.

Mum groans and I take her hand. What is it about her skin? I can never quite put it into words – clamminess, softness, like old rubber or a newly dead fish. The grip is weak yet desperate, she clings with the little strength she has.

Outside a young goldfinch has alighted on the feeder; its breast is puffed up, mouth gaped larger than its head. Its parent nuzzles into the feeder, ignoring it.

'Look,' I say.

Her eyes shiver as they try to focus. Perhaps she doesn't see – perhaps I watch alone – but I like the idea at least.

As she begins to doze, her fingers slacken from mine. The muscles of her face droop, dough-like. Her breath smells sweetly of fermentation.

After a long five minutes, I disentangle myself, but at the movement her eyes fly open. Her grip closes on my wrist, as if snatching at a thief.

Even slurred by sleep and illness, the fear in her voice is clear.

'Who are you?' she says.

39

Uncanny Shift

The scent lances my stomach: fishy pungency, rich meat, unfurling on the exhale of sea. A beckoning finger. My paws obey without thought.

Brown hills march in time, undulating about me like beaten clay. I crunch through the scrub, face into coarse wind.

The shout grows to a scream and I break into a run – my body a surge of muscle and boiled breath. Tundra subsides to boulders and the hush of waves.

The scent is mixed with caustic salt and the fetid excretions of sea. I snuffle to try to pinpoint it through the tumult . . . *there*.

What looks like a rock lifts moist eyes. In that shared look, we find our respective selves – it, meat; I, death.

Hunger grapples with bleary thoughts. My hide runs hot and cold. To eat or not to eat.

But the seal is already wriggling round and slipping into the waves. Gone.

The chase sags from my shoulders. A taunt of its scent lingers on the breeze. Even here, even as a polar bear, I can remember the sensation of water over sleek skin. How can what I once was become my food? My guts growl in disappointment. Of course, I knew that seals are the staple polar bear diet, but I hadn't fully faced what it would mean to eat one.

'Why did you stop?' Buckley says. 'You almost had it.'

Why is it only in my silence that he's decided we have to speak? I'm not sure whether he's even gathered how much I know yet, but I won't be hounded from my job by some idiotic simulations.

Heat chokes my fur from the run, so I clamber down to the shore. The lick of water on the pads of my paws brings relief and I wade through the surf until my nose is touched by chill.

'Come on, Kit. You have to talk to me eventually.'

I ignore him. Though, unfortunately, that's not enough to get rid of him. Buckley is my constant watcher, the one who can never disappear, though I wish he would.

Waves murmur up my snout but even submersed, my coat is still warm. I overheat so quickly, I'll never catch the quick prey inland, but with the ice sheets in tatters, I can't hunt at sea. The pod will replenish the Ressy once I've left but this jump promises to be a week of hunger. With my fat reserves, I won't die, but I'm starving in only the way a body fed from a nutrient drip for its whole existence can understand. Who'd pay for an experience like this?

Buckley is still trying to get me to talk when I eventually clamber back to shore; I ignore him and snuffle along the rocks. My paws pass over glass shards, artefacts from another world beaten to opacity by the sea. There's seaweed here somewhere, I can smell the sourness. Although it won't fill my stomach, it will be better than nothing.

As its harsh scent crescendos, I catch sight of the stalk caught between rocks. My paws glance off it, so I tilt my head and bite. The frond lies slick on my tongue with satisfying sharpness. The sea rolls in my ears – a steady inhale, exhale, pulling and pushing the rattle of pebbles.

I gaze out over the water. Somewhere out there is the Centre, my family, life continuing as normal, yet it's hard to really believe. The bleak sky presses down in a curtain of steel. The distance between me and the human world is more than miles.

How many days now without a proper meal? Time passes fast and slow here, like the trickle of ocean beneath melting ice. The knot of my stomach seems to grow with every pulse.

Inland, the patchy tundra loses all definition. What difference is there between one hillock and the next? Few peaks are white and those are moth-eaten with heat. I swelter in my coat, dizzy in a way that deserts of sand have failed to ever make me. Even the air feels tacky, sticky with the incense of flowers, cleansed only by the flares of distant prey. Their meat lights the landscape in a constant yowl; criss-crossing the tundra in streamer-like ghosts. Food is everywhere except the now.

If I close my eyes and inhale I can almost feel their delicious bodies brush against mine. Hare, fox, deer; each dance twisting and merging across the dry valley. But when I chase the trails they grow before me into miles. Gutter out into the flat scent of vegetation.

Then there's the *other* smell – oily fur, thick cloy of flesh. A watchful scent. Always just over the horizon. Always waiting. I almost imagine I can hear the twitch of nostrils, inhaling my presence.

There are so few wild polar bears left, I know it has to be a simulation. In its musk there are echoes of fox and tiger; its quiet stalk reminiscent of the eagle and bat. Now I know the simulations for what they are, the familiar unrealness is an itch. In some wordless inner space, I always knew my watchers didn't really exist.

And still Buckley talks.

'Just one word. Say one word and I'll not bother you the rest of the day.'

Or, 'I get that now isn't the right time to have this conversation but you can't just block me out.'

Occasionally, 'What would it take for you to forgive me?'

I keep marching. What else can I do?

Meat.

The smell is a slap to my sluggish thoughts and I blink to find myself back on the shoreline. The yolk of sun has broken across the cliffs, the spits of bird shit luminous in the dawn.

Meat. Fishy, ripe.

The scent demands. I follow. But at its source are walrus. Dangerous, but that fishy wine leaves me almost drunk.

The small eyes, above distinguished whiskers, follow me cautiously. Up close they are bloated slugs, smug with contentment.

I trace a wide circle. Would it be wrong to attack? Although I've never been a walrus, they're the sort of creature I'm more used to being than hunting.

Buckley makes no comment. I realise now that he's been silent for a while, though his breath still rolls behind my own.

The female walrus apart from the rest of the group is markedly smaller. Young. It'd make her easier prey. I sidle in on flayed nerves. Should I? Could I?

At the surge of flab, I halt. Reared up, the walrus is huge.

Rock shudders as she slaps back to the ground and returns to the huddle with alarming speed. The group slashes the air with their tusks.

I run.

'Kit.'

And now. How long now?

Time makes no sense here. The sun wavers in the sky, unblinking.

'Please.'

My mind feels as empty as my stomach. The watcher's scent is a siren. It must be near.

'I'm worried about you.'

Buckley speaks. Buckley doesn't.

'Kit, please.'

Bursts of words that leave me wincing. Nails down a blackboard. Sudden quiet, just as cutting.

'For goodness' sake, KIT!'

But hunger is the only real.

Understanding starts to brush against my senses. I glimpse truth in colour: the shifting cobalt of ocean, the silver of tundra under twilight.

'Kit.'

I taste it in clouds and the angle of light hitting sea.

'Kit.'

I smell it in rock and breeze; bitter growth and rot.

'Kit.'

The balloon of empty stomach lifts me.

'I can't do this any more.'

Click

I hear it in silence, the small death inside a disconnected intercom.

He left. Even after everything, I didn't truly think that possible.

The universe inhales into a still, black pool.

And, at last, it shows itself.

The simulation is the shadow of a dying sun. White against white in a polar bear skin. Buckley must have left the false data running. Only one question remains, who will eat who?

I pace forwards, teeth bared.

It flickers at the threat, ready to splinter into snow. This close, the sense of familiarity makes my eyes sting. When I try to focus, there is only a blur. I have the strangest sense that it disappears and reappears with my blinking.

My innards vibrate with a growl; it joins with its own as we circle. Time to finish this.

I slash out. Claws meet air and it bursts in flying ice.

I shut my eyes. But I can still smell it. Soured milk, human sweat.

My eyes open on to those of my doppelgänger. Its pupils have dilated to fill the entire sockets.

In my shock, she pounces.

But I'm already rearing, a mountain against her frailty. In those black eyes, terror. My paw smashes down—

Flesh is mud. Bones twigs. Strike after strike. Pulp beneath my toes.

The heat of my stomach boils over, nothing but hunger and the rip of sinew, honeyed blood; my snout thrust into the cavern of the chest, the slick guts down a throat—

A gull cries over the roll of waves, sucking up pebbles, spitting them back. My stomach is an obnoxious bloat.

Blood has thickened where it pooled. The white of my paws is stained brown, scraps of flesh stuck in their fur. Its dark eyes are already flecked with feathers of ice.

But it isn't a polar bear. It isn't my doppelgänger. It's a seal.

———————

Nausea punches me into consciousness and I lie, just listening to the hiss of the nasal cannula.

Come Home. I don't remember making the exit.

'Kit?'

I squint through the stab of a headache at Buckley's face.

'OK there, North?' Mr Hughes says from beside him.

Warmth runs along the catheter tube stuck to my leg.

Two of them. I'm weak from Come Home, in no shape to fight.

Mr Hughes reaches and I lunge back, only to misjudge the movement and smash into the pallet. They step back at the suddenness. At least I've alarmed them.

'Easy,' Buckley says, his voice dripping with false concern. 'You're not well.'

'We're going to take you somewhere safe,' Mr Hughes says.

Safe. As if I'd believe that.

I force myself upright. My arms are pink and thin, these claws soft and trembling, barely strong enough to keep their grip on the pallet edge, let alone put a scratch in hide. The cruelty is enough to make me want to weep. If they come at me I won't have the advantage. It looks like they hadn't calculated on resistance, though; a convincing threat display might just get me out of here. I retrieve my tongue from the mess of sensation that is my face.

'Stay the *fuck* away from me.'

It comes out more of a growl than words but they get the idea.

I have to leave, and quickly. Keeping my gaze locked on theirs, I tear off BodySupport and stand, or rather trip. Buckley darts forwards but I wriggle past him and slam against the wall. The room seems washed out and 2D. They're larger than me, and stronger, but I can outrun them easily if I get a chance. But how to get past them in this small space?

'Kit, calm dow—' Buckley shuts up at my hiss. As I spring at them, they scrabble for the door, Mr Hughes's sweaty hand blocking my exit and I land on my backside as the door slams.

I hurl myself at it.

'Calm down.' Buckley's voice comes muffled through the glass. 'Everything is going to be OK. We're going to help you.'

'Bastards. You crazy bastards!' I yell but this feeble body makes no impact. I bite down hard on the back of my hand, yank at the skin until it hurts.

Come on, Kit. Come on!

The window! I leap for it, snatch only a tantalising gulp of freedom before my shoulders get stuck. God dammit! Nearly any other animal would be flexible enough to do this.

I wriggle back to hear Buckley and Mr Hughes talking, too quiet to make it out through the door. They stop suddenly, followed by the sound of leaving footsteps, though someone's still out there. I crawl beneath the JumpPallet.

Even after everything, I never truly thought that they'd go this far. Buckley was my friend.

What do they mean to do to me? They said I was unwell. Meaning what? They couldn't make me leave by myself so they're going to call me mad instead? Lock me up? Medicate me until I can't even string together an accusation? Then Mr Hughes would be free to do whatever he wanted with my doppelgänger. I taste blood as my chewing breaks the skin of my hand.

I'm not sure how much time passes before the door opens again, but when it does I'm ready. I dive forward, only for a hand to close round my ankle. At least I manage to kick someone before the other is seized.

I spit as they drag me to my feet, squirming and pummelling anything in reach. Mr Hughes flinches as I turn bared teeth on him. Yet none of this changes the fact that there's two of them; both twice my size. In a fair fight I haven't a chance. In a fair fight.

I let my body fall limp, a mouse in the cat's jaws, yet in my guts a growl is growing.

'Come on now, North,' Mr Hughes wheezes. 'We're going to walk to Buckley's car. Nice and calm.'

He glances up the corridor as he speaks. Of course, he doesn't want the other phenomenauts to see. I hiss with laughter. Will they call it 'family reasons' or 'poor plasticity'? All these years I thought I was special when I was just blind. Perhaps I should start screaming, but who would take my word over theirs?

They pull me down the corridor so quickly my feet lose purchase. I leave them dangling. Let the bastards tire themselves out carrying me.

The strange angles of the stairway seem to slide and shift about us, almost as if I am hovering across the ceiling. I catch a glimpse of myself in the glass of the lobby fish tank. A girl in shapeless robes, sticks for limbs. She mouths at me. I'm not sure what.

The outside washes over us in cold light, a glimpse of sun, iron-hot, between the rooftops. Buckley's car is parked in front of the steps. How many trips have we made in it? Now the sight crushes me. My eyes swivel like marbles about my skull. There must be some way out but I'm too panicked to fully process what I'm seeing.

We stop and Buckley lets go to fumble with his keycard. The ringing in my ears has grown to a tsunami, black spots burn through my vision, any second and they'll swallow me.

But, instead, there is you.

Where do you even come from? One moment Mr Hughes is grappling with me, the next shouting in pain, and I see you dangling from his arm – a fox – growling round the mouthful of his bicep. Shock makes a white sheet of thoughts but my body doesn't need them to act. I drive my knee into Mr Hughes's stomach and he releases me with a grunt, then I'm running, running, faster than I've ever run in my life.

Their yells beat against my ears.

I don't dare glance back but when I look down you're flowing alongside me, tiny paws pounding the tarmac; together.

We keep running until my lungs are raw and the only footsteps that follow are echoes of our own.

Come Home

Then you're gone.

The thought jerks me into wakefulness. I cast about the hedge, but there's no flash of tail or twitch of ears. Gone.

I sit listening to your absence, with racing heart. It's still dark, I can't have nodded off for long. You could be out looking for an early breakfast, but the patch of ground where you lay is cold, not even a dent in the soft earth, and I know that this time is for real. I got too close and you're not coming back.

Nothing stirs when I crawl out into the park.

'Tomoko?' I whisper. 'Tomoko!'

I slink around, peeking into bushes and rummaging through flowerbeds. Knowing is one thing, but believing? I can't afford to.

Streetlights throw the night in a muddy tint. Each road seems more lonesome than the next. I don't even know where I'm running to, because where would you go? You don't have a den or a territory, nowhere to hide. A cat runs from me to crouch beneath a car, but no fox.

I let myself sink to the pavement. My body feels like crumpled paper, my head hollow with the word I can no longer escape.

Alone.

_____

I can barely believe it myself as I climb the steps to the Centre once more. Every rational thought screams that this is stupid but what other choice is left to me? If I'm to find Tomoko, I need fox senses, and to be a fox, I need Buckley.

There's been a lot of time for thinking as I wandered through the streets. The clearing cloud revealed pearly moonlight, throwing strange new shadows from my thoughts and, with them, a sense of clarity. But that doesn't stop the doubts.

Yes, Buckley sided with the Tourism project and told me to stop jumping, but after reading the emails about Isaac, I can see that perhaps he really did think jumping was hurting me.

And he could have made the last week a lot harder. For one thing, he approached me in the park on his own; then, when he thought I was breaking in, he waited for me in our cubicle when it would have been much easier for him to alert security.

Of course, that doesn't explain the simulations, or why he hid recordings from me, but there's a chance he really didn't know about them. A CP can always be hacked. I want to believe it so much that it almost makes me suspicious. But it's too late for that. I'm not giving up on Tomoko now.

And, whatever arguments and counter-arguments I can marshal, I know in my gut that this is what I have to do.

Still, I pause on the threshold of our cubicle, the churn of adrenaline too complex to give it a name. As I watch, Buckley rolls over in his sleep, the blanket slipping from his shoulders. He looks so vulnerable curled up, his face darkened by the bruise. I *have* to believe that I can trust him.

I tiptoe to Buckley's chair and perch.

The sandwiches are still on the desk. I devour the first so quickly I barely taste it but it's still the best sandwich I've ever eaten. The second is best cached, so I settle for licking the mayonnaise stuck to the plastic. Only when I've picked the last crumbs with a damp fingertip do I put it aside, pulling my feet up onto the chair to rest my chin on my knees.

The building is silent around us, the only sound his slow draw of breath. I hadn't realised quite how much I missed it. His shut eyelids flutter, as if they were a cocoon to his dreams.

Is this what it was like for Buckley? Monitoring a mute body day by day?

Watching his huddled form, I'm reminded of how I thought he looked a stick figure when we first met. He's filled out since those days, his height balanced by the weight of muscle, but curled up now he still looks like a collapsed puppet.

'I can trust you, can't I?' I whisper.

The shadow of stubble softens the hard line of his jaw, the sight makes my fingers tingle. I think what it'd be like to lie next to him like Tomoko, not touching, just close enough to feel his heat.

A long breath escapes him and my hand clenches round the sandwich packet. His eyes are open.

It's a while until either of us speaks.

'Hi.' His voice is hoarse from sleep, eyes blinking as if he expects me to vanish with the remnants of dreams.

'Hi,' I say.

He sits, posture stiff, as if frightened to startle me. I can see the effort it takes him to smile as he nods at the sandwich packet.

'Feeling more human?'

I smile despite myself. He lets out a low laugh, but stops at my expression.

'Kit?'

My voice is clammed in my throat with the mass of the sandwich. I have to grind my nails into my leg to get it out.

'Did you know?'

'Know what?'

'The simulations. The human Ressies. Everything.'

He looks at me, hard, though I only read concern in his expression, not guilt. He thinks I'm mad. But that's good. That's great! Because that means he can't have known.

I turn on his computer and open my cloud. He comes to stand next to me cautiously.

'Here,' I say, bringing up the file I found that mentions the human Ressies. 'This one doesn't say much but I know there must be more on here.'

He's gone very still. 'Human Ressies? But how long—' He shakes his head and scrolls down the document. 'Where did you even get this?'

'Grandma Wolf, she gave me her card. I know about her being Shen.'

Now he does look a little guilty. 'Sorry. It didn't seem my place to tell people. And I did mean to tell you about Isaac earlier. It's just hard to revisit those days.'

'I saw the files on Isaac too.' I poke the backward button and go searching for his folder but Buckley stops me with a touch to the hand, selects another folder instead. The colour has drained from his face.

I read out its name. 'NBD? That means something to you?'

'Neo-Body Dysmorphia.'

'Neo – what?'

'Just, something neuros talk about from time to time. But I didn't know people were taking it seriously.' He trails off, intent on the files. They appear to be a database of phenomenaut profiles. The snapshots flash by like echoes of people I've met in dreams. All ex-phenomenauts. Most of them left so long ago, I'd almost forgotten them.

At a familiar grin, I make Buckley stop. Broad nose and dancing eyes, afro bound up in two fat bunches. We share a look – Susie.

She looks wrong to my mind somehow; as if her photo should have grown up with me, the image of her in my head flickering between child and adult.

I pull her file to the fore. Most of the page is lists of the various studies and papers she was involved in, so it's only as we reach the bottom that there's anything new.

Psychological appraisal:
Susie's plasticity results prove malleable in the mid-range. Psychological examination, including the DIP-2X and Mansell Profiling, suggests healthy self-directed, other-directed and world-directed attitudes as well as stable maturation in line with what would be expected of a non-phenomenaut of her age.

However, careful medical examination revealed multiple lacerations on her abdomen. The scarring suggests that she has been practising self-harm for at least a year. Susie denies feeling distress but after some encouragement explained that she believed cutting was essential to maintaining a fixed sense of body image. Immediate dismissal advised.

Self-harm.
The words cut, my hands halfway to my own stomach before I realise. Susie? Self-harm? I know I was only a child, absorbed with

my own problems, but could I really have missed that? I thought we told each other everything.

She was cutting herself, and I did nothing.

But Buckley is already moving on to other profiles, hands a flurry. Now we know where to look, the passages leap out as if written in neon.

'Severe Anxiety'

'Body Dysmorphic'

'Unspecified Eating Disorder'

I can't seem to stop reading.

'Paranoia, including voices'

'Language Impairment'

'Delusions of Persecution'

'Cotard Delusion'

'Depression'

'Attempted suicide'

It's too much. I lean over Buckley to skip to the end of the list. The name at the bottom is one I recognise: 'Simon Cadwell' – Si. No Daisy, though; they must have dismissed her on grounds of destruction of company property.

Psychological appraisal:
Simon's plasticity results prove malleable in the upper-range. Psychological examination, including the DIP-2X, Mansell Profiling and IAT Scores, suggests that while Simon shows healthy other-directed and world-directed attitudes, his self-directed attitudes suggest the beginnings of erosion to self-concept. His language development displays some retardation compared to non-phenomenauts of his age. His cognitive and emotional maturation over the last three sessions appears to be deteriorating. Although none of these issues is significant enough

to raise red flags on its own, as a cluster of symptoms, it is our suggestion that dismissal be considered.

I sag into the chair. All these ex-colleagues and the only reasons I was ever given for their dismissal were 'poor plasticity' or 'family reasons'.

Buckley presses on, driven by mad energy. Below the database is another selection of emails.

Dr Pitt <LPitt@gmail.org.uk>
To: Mr Hughes <CHughes@shencorp.org.uk>
Cc: Board Mailing List <APattern@shencorp.org.uk,
    APinbor@shencorp.org.uk . . .>

Mr Hughes,

Though I grant correlation isn't necessarily causation, and that the hypothesis is hard to refute when the circumstances make a control group difficult, the effect is nonetheless strong enough for me to consider it professionally negligent of me to deny a significant relationship. We have to treat the time spent projecting as a real factor on the psychological disturbance of phenomenauts.

Of course, there are always outliers and anomalies, but this doesn't change the fact that the large majority of your phenomenauts fit the curve and until you figure out exactly what, or which, variables account for this girl's robustness, you need to turn your energies to damage control.

I will be out of the country until Friday but call my secretary and she can arrange a time for us to discuss possible routes for proceeding from here.

Dr Pitt

Dr Pitt <LPitt@gmail.org.uk>

To: Mr Hughes <CHughes@shencorp.org.uk>

Cc: Board Mailing List <APattern@shencorp.org.uk,
    APinbor@shencorp.org.uk . . .>

Mr Hughes,

I can see that my careful explanations are wasted on you, so let me phrase this in plain English: your current projection practices are making phenomenauts unwell.

Though I understand the plasticity of children is conducive to Phenomenautism, it is clear that it is also increasing the risk of psychotic episodes. I have made tentative enquires with colleagues and they confirm that the age at which individuals start consolidating their identity align with the typical age range from which you source your phenomenauts. These years are an extremely vulnerable time in any teenager's life, let alone those experiencing the stressors involved in projection.

Need I also mention that none of the other phenomenautical companies, with their adult staff, have reported anything like the mental disturbances rife amongst your employees?

I can't extrapolate with any certainty without running more studies but it would be my guess that the huge variation in forms of disturbance is merely a reflection of different personalities. It seems that projection is acting as a stressor, rather than a specific pathology, and that symptoms appear along the extant fault lines of a phenomenaut's psyche.

As these problems are clearly related to the amount of time spent projecting, it would be my recommendation to decrease the time each individual spends out of their Original Body and move all your phenomenauts to a part-time schedule.

How about I clear some time for us to video-conference on Thursday?

Dr Pitt

Dr Pitt <LPitt@gmail.org.uk>
To: Mr Hughes <CHughes@shencorp.org.uk>
Cc: Board Mailing List <APattern@shencorp.org.uk,
    APinbor@shencorp.org.uk . . .>

I'm going to pretend I didn't notice any insinuation that may, or may not, have
been intended in that email.

It's no concern of mine how you handle the data but I want no part of it.
Do not contact me again.

Dr Pitt

My thoughts clunk about my head, like coloured blocks in the
hands of a toddler, refusing to fit the holes made for them.

All my colleagues, Phenomenautism did this to them? I remember
Daisy's bloodshot eyes when she charged me in the common room, how
Si used to carry a stuffed toy around with him at fourteen, the constant
change-over of phenomenauts. I've worked at ShenCorp for so long
such things became my normal, but that doesn't mean they were healthy.

This must have been what Grandma Wolf really wanted me to
find, not just about Isaac. ShenCorp has been hiding so much more
than the human Ressies and doppelgängers. And I sent these files
to ICPO. There's no way ShenCorp can survive this. Grandma
Wolf must have known it would end this way eventually, despite
the company being her life's work.

'Tell me you didn't know,' I say to Buckley. 'Promise me.'

He looks shell-shocked enough to not need to answer, but he tries anyway.

'I didn't – I hoped that my doubts were just—'

But at that his eyes go wide and he returns to the folder, pounds a string of numbers into the search bar, looks horrified when it returns with a file.

'Buckley?' I say, but he doesn't answer.

Because inside is a picture of me.

Phenomenaut: Ms Katherine North

Time with Shen: Seven years

Psychological appraisal:

Katherine's plasticity results prove malleable in the lower-range, though this is expected with her advanced age. Psychological examination, including the DIP-2X, Mansell Profiling and IAT Scores, suggests that Katherine shows self-directed, other-directed and world-directed attitudes all within the acceptable range.

Whilst Katherine possesses what might be called an eccentric personality and her sexual maturation shows some retardation, including amenorrhoea, she displays no outward signs of psychological disturbance.

Considering the uniqueness of her case we recommend special attention is given to both maintaining and understanding her stability, especially in regard to the fact that her performance vastly outpaces what would be expected considering that her plasticity is now in the lower-range for this company.

I release the breath I hadn't been aware of holding.

'See. I'm fine.'

But Buckley is already clicking on an attachment at the bottom of the file. I stand and clutch his arm as we read.

Dr Punjab <NPunjab@shencorp.org.uk>
To: Mr Hughes <CHughes@shencorp.org.uk>
Cc: Tourism Team Mailing List <APattern@shencorp.org.uk,
    APinbor@shencorp.org.uk . . .>

Charles,

I know you never listen to me on this matter, but after Ms North's session with me today, it is my professional recommendation that we exhibit extreme caution in this case. I know Ms North's appearance of stability has made her progress of particular interest to you and the board, but the more time I spend with her, the more I have come to believe that she has been deliberately hiding certain symptoms from me. This is not only reflective of an inclination towards paranoia, but suggests she is using Phenomenautism as an unhealthy coping strategy.

As you know, Katherine has difficult home issues, and Phenomenautism provides a convenient mechanism for dissociating herself from aspects of her life that she struggles to process. Have you considered the possibility that she is not the phenomenautical savant you believe but a troubled girl clinging to what she thinks of as home?

Whilst I admit there is currently little negative impact upon her job performance, it is my fear that continuing to project will have severe repercussions for her wellbeing. I don't need to remind you that she has just experienced a severe incident of ERT and that all but one phenomenaut has in the past either chosen, or was encouraged, to withdraw from projection within three months of their respective accidents.

It is therefore my recommendation that Ms North is encouraged to take an extended period of ill leave, if not a permanent dismissal on grounds of health.

Yours,
Niti

Mr Hughes <CHughes@shencorp.org.uk>
To: Dr Punjab <NPunjab@shencorp.org.uk>
Cc: Tourism Team Mailing List <APattern@shencorp.org.uk,
    APinbor@shencorp.org.uk . . .>

Dear Dr Punjab,

Thank you for your email concerning Miss North. As ever, I value the insight you
bring to this company and have the uttermost respect for your comments on this
matter. However, you do not seem cogent of what a valuable asset Miss North is.
Not even Sauntertech can boast a phenomenaut who has been projecting for
seven years. To discard her would be beyond foolish. I would therefore
appreciate an answer to my initial question.

Kind Regards,
Mr Hughes (CEO)

Dr Punjab <NPunjab@shencorp.org.uk>
To: Mr Hughes <CHughes@shencorp.org.uk>
Cc: Tourism Team Mailing List <APattern@shencorp.org.uk,
APinbor@shencorp.org.uk . . .>

Charlie,

I wish I could say your response was a surprise. I am, of course, aware of what
an asset Ms North is to ShenCorp, yet as her therapist it is my responsibility to
seek the best for her health as well as the company's.

Though Katherine appears stable for the present, I fear that this may only hide
larger problems down the line. I admit that I have no concrete evidence at this
stage but it is, nevertheless, my professional opinion.

Her neuroengineer, Mr Maurice, might be able to provide us with a more conclusive picture. I've tried making subtle inquiries but at present he's being evasive. As you know they have a very close working partnership and I worry that he may be covering for her. However, were you to press him on the matter, I believe that he would be able to provide us with a more conclusive picture.

Niti

Mr Hughes <CHughes@shencorp.org.uk>
To: Dr Punjab <NPunjab@shencorp.org.uk>
Cc: Tourism Team Mailing List <APattern@shencorp.org.uk,
    APinbor@shencorp.org.uk . . .>

Niti,

Rest assured, your concerns have been noted. Nevertheless, you continue to ignore my question: *Is Miss North capable of projecting for the new project I described, or not?*

Dr Punjab <NPunjab@shencorp.org.uk>
To: Mr Hughes <CHughes@shencorp.org.uk>
Cc: Tourism Team Mailing List <APattern@shencorp.org.uk,
    APinbor@shencorp.org.uk . . .>

Yes.

I turn away from the screen.

I know I should be feeling something right now, I'm aware of that, but the numbness is overwhelming. No anger. No fear. Just . . . emptiness.

Could it really be true that Phenomenautism has made me unstable too? That Buckley never saw my watchers because they didn't exist outside of my head?

Because they were just . . .

Me?

Dimly, I'm aware of Buckley steering me to sit. He crouches on the floor next to me, although words seem beyond him too.

All those times I'd stumbled upon him looking over my recordings – he must have been looking for sign of trouble after Niti had sowed doubts.

'You covered for me?' I say.

'I'm sorry,' he whispers. 'I didn't believe that things had got so bad. I didn't want to believe.'

I watch my hands lie listless on their backs, too numb and still to really be mine. And at the shiver of doubt, I will the fingers to curl, glad to find they respond.

And if the watchers disappeared because they were never real, then that would mean my fox . . .

'Help me,' I say.

Buckley takes my hands.

'I'm here.'

'We have to find her,' I say.

'Her? Grandma Wolf?'

'No. The fox.'

Mad. I can see it in his face. He thinks I'm mad.

'Tomoko?' he says.

'Maybe. Yes. I don't know. You said you'd help me.'

'And I will. I will.' His eyes flit about my face, as if looking for a handhold on which to catch me. 'The fox you saw at the accident?'

'No. I don't think.' If they are the same, does it matter? 'My friend.'

His lips move, but he doesn't seem to know what to ask.

'The fox that bit you,' I say. 'When you found me in the park.'

I can't meet that frown, look instead at my toes, grimy and bruised against the leather.

His voice comes out a whisper. 'Oh, Kit. But you bit me.'

As I shake my head, he draws up a sleeve, holds out the arm.

'See?'

A purple circle sits just below the elbow, greening at the edges.

'If a fox had bitten me it would have at least punctured the skin.'

I keep shaking my head, as if movement will prevent the idea from gaining traction.

'No,' I say at the arm. 'No.' But what power do words have to change flesh? 'I can't leave her alone.'

'Kit, I'm not sure that—'

'*I know.*' I bite my lip so hard I can taste blood. 'Don't make me say it. But I have to *try.*'

He rolls the sleeve down, eyes cast down, but when he lifts them again, his voice is resolute.

'Then tell me what do.'

It's strange to fall back to our old procedure. I'm glad I'm already sitting when Buckley brings over BodySupport.

'OK?' he asks.

'Just a bit sick.'

'You're sure about this?'

I take the wires off him in reply but when Buckley reaches out for my coat, I hug it to my chest. After all this time, to remove it would leave me too vulnerable. Still, I have to unzip it to attach the catheter. The stink surprises even me.

Buckley hovers. 'Nothing infected?'

I show him the smooth skin around the cap. The relief on his face is palpable. All this time and I hadn't even thought about that.

This shouldn't be a long jump so we leave the nutrients aside, though Buckley seems tempted after how much weight I've lost. I lie back and look across at the fox Ressy on the gurney. With Buckley's help there was no problem bringing it over from Bio.

'Wait,' I say when he returns with the CP and I pick up the Ressy. It's so light, barely larger than a house cat. Buckley looks doubtful as I lie back with it on my chest, but what harm is there in ignoring another piece of protocol at this point?

The CP nodes scratch against my scalp, struggling to work through the fuzz that's grown whilst I've been away. Buckley mutters over it, fiddling with the settings.

'You know, I'd completely forgotten you're a ginger nut.'

I smile and for a second it's as if nothing has changed.

At last satisfied, Buckley retreats to his screens. 'Just going to check that the connection's OK.'

I hug the fox, rest my chin against its wet nose. The fur is soft beneath my fingers. But it's not Tomoko. I look to the black square of the window and wonder where she is now.

Buckley swivels his thumb up and down, stopping on the upright at my nod. I stare up at the ceiling and shiver with déjà vu.

Here the click of Buckley's fingers over switches. Here the clunk of the electromagnets going live. Here the jangling excitement of skin.

Any second now. Any second. Any

Come Home

To be weightless again.

The lightness is eviscerating. Freer than flight. I teeter on the edge of a perfect void. And wonder, is this what I've always yearned for? To be nothing, and yet not.

But this is nonsense. Nonsense. I can feel the threads of thought unspool from my grasp, much longer and I will unravel completely. Because what am I without a body? Just echoes.

But then there is his voice, emerging from the void as if he's been here all along, waiting.

'Kit.' To hear him is like the warmth of sun in winter. 'All OK? I'm about to patch you in.'

At the patter of fingertips, sensation flourishes. I am reborn.

Even Sperlman's is a kind of blessing: in pain is clarity and recognition, a self long forgotten. The remembrance sweet enough to choke—

This is what it is to be myself. *This* me. Not that. But this. How else can I say it? Me. And not. I, fox. I'd laugh if I could.

Smell is the loudest. A firecracker so bright it blinds. But, gradually, it subsides into definition. This and that, distinct scents, *just themselves*, until names step forward to claim them: sweat and mud, the smell of human beneath almost imperceptible.

Her face – my face – lies ahead of me, barely recognisable. A huge landscape of flesh, the slightly parted mouth a fault line. Her colouring is pasty yellow, though that's likely just because foxes can't perceive red.

I lick a streak of mud from her cheek and find the oils of the skin sour. But where is this taste? In there, or out here? Neither?

My back is crushed by her arms. I rise and fall with the movement of her chest. I have to scrabble at her shoulders to pull myself loose.

'Wait! Let me.'

Buckley's voice comes from everywhere, inside and without at once, so it's only as the pressure lifts that I realise he's beside the pallet, unpeeling her grip.

I jump to the floor. His feet are almost beast-like, the large toes curl within frayed socks.

'I'll open the window,' he says and the feet bound skyward, one then the other, ground shuddering as they land. With the creak comes fresh air and the intoxicating jumble of its smellscape.

I peer up the length of his legs, to the pale face far above. When those lips move, the voice is birthed inside my head.

'Be careful.'

Outside is car fumes and dog shit; the sticky grit of spent bubblegum, chemical mint mixed with the leather memory of past feet.

Electricity cackles overhead. An ocean sigh of foliage hides the skitter and crawl of small creatures. Someone, somewhere, is shouting.

The world is singing. It never truly stopped, I just lost the ears.

I patter along the pavement, sinking into every sensation. The delicious fetor of a black bag; the ripeness of a puddle, its taste in tarmac tang. The thrum of a fly dives from my paw and vanishes into sound.

Smelling the old scent of a dog fox, I sprint over the rubber reek of road, to the perfume of cut grass. Urine is flaked up a stem – a mouse, here not so long ago. But of Tomoko? Nothing.

She's not out by the nearest industrial dustbins I find, though the rot set my stomach grumbling from down the street. Nor is she in the quiet back gardens. I vault fence after fence, only pausing long enough to sniff.

She's not even by the rabbit hutch, though their scent must be a temptation for every fox within a mile. I press my nose against the cruel wire and listen to their quivering. Tomoko was still learning to hunt when we were last foxes together, but she must be adept by now.

I leave the hot smell of their blood and pace the pavement with its flat-lined concrete.

The moon is opened from its wink into a watchful eye. I return its stare, chill tickling through my fur. My empty stomach pulses in time with my heart.

A woodlouse clambers up from a fissure in the paving slab, its antennae flex thoughtfully. As I study it, my fur starts to prickle and I flatten myself to the ground.

Because, of course, she's been watching all this time. Her musk is so overwhelming I don't understand how I missed it.

She steps from the hedge, coat mottled with the brown of a cub. Her ears are perked, head tilted, a question that reaches right to the heart of things, yet I never know the answer.

There's a wicked glint in her eyes. A meaningful blink and she runs.

Tarmac flashes by in a slick river, paws so fast I'm almost taking flight.

I was a bird once. Flew over cities, saw the secret patterns of land.

Our steps ring sharp between the houses, the night alive and shouting.

I was an elephant once, earth alive with sound.

We dodge under monolithic cars, their smog of petrol.

I was a whale once. One note in the ocean's song.

Tomoko twists through darkness and street light, more fire than flesh.

I was a tiger once. Forest burning bright.

The strain of lungs. Pain and pleasure.

I was a spider once. Impulse. Desire.

Racing through the dark, together.

Everything I've been, everything I could be. Even if it's hurting me, can I really give all that up?

Tomoko dives through a hedge and I follow. Her fleet shadow melds in and out of the night. But at last she stops and I rush to meet her.

I was a fox once.

I can hardly see through the ache of my eyes, but that doesn't matter – she's here. I find her ear and chew, listening to her pant slow into contentment, join the mutter of the wind. Her ear has the texture of felt, paper, air.

I was human—

Once.

I keep chewing even when there's nothing left, I don't want to stop, can't stop, to do so would be to admit . . .

But eventually my jaw slows of its own accord. Her scent still lingers, one last breath, exhaled into the dark. Then gone.

Silence. It crushes my lungs and tears into the softest parts of me. Because that's all that's left now – me.

I hide my muzzle beneath my paws, my heart huge inside my chest. Why can't it just be still? Why can't I disappear too?

Static builds at the edges of my hearing. I'm ready to let it take me, but the voice won't stop.

'Come back, Kit. Come home.'

'Can't.'

'Of course you can.'

'Not strong enough.'

'Nonsense. You're the strongest person I know.'

My paws are numb, but, somehow, they manage to support my weight. One step, then another. With each, I think this body will give beneath me – but it doesn't.

The world hangs beyond, almost wraith-like, a memory before I've even left.

This is it.

But his voice pulls me onward, a thread reeling me home.

The light from our window is a beacon. I jump up and look back one last time. But what am I hoping to see? A glimpse can't compensate for never again.

Buckley's feet push themselves round as I land, mournful grey creatures, whiskers of thread along the seams.

I leap onto his knees and he startles but after a second the muscles beneath my paws relax. There's a bedrock of bone beneath the give of flesh and I settle against his stomach. His large hands glide across my back.

I breathe in his balmy nebula, the smell of home, and let my thoughts unwind into the dark.

A smell wakes me. Melted tallow, stark cologne, the hint of leather. Human.

A white dome towers above, rising with the rasp of labouring lungs. I look up the mountain of belly to the pinched eyes. Mr Hughes.

The ground shifts beneath me and I tumble to the floor. Buckley is gabbling, Mr Hughes shouting, so loud it's just noise.

I think to flee but Mr Hughes is blocking the doorway. I hide beneath the desk, breathing in dust and stale biscuit crumbs.

As Buckley's legs move away, I whimper, but no one is interested in me right now. He's placed himself between my Original Body and Mr Hughes.

I'm down here, I want to shout. *This is me.*

The polished points of Mr Hughes's shoes turn towards me and I bristle. But he's not coming for me – he's going to shut down the projection.

I leap. Flesh gives beneath my teeth. The dryness of cloth moistens with the taste of iron. Then fingers bite into my neck and I'm flying. The wall slams into me.

Pain. Mosquito whine.

I blink.

Get up, Kit. Get up!

I waver from the floor. There's yelling, the clatter of fingers on keys. I edge a paw forwards but pain snatches it from beneath me.

Come on!

I'm struggling upright again, when the feeling starts to drain; my inner sky clouding over.

Don't leave me. Please, don't leave.

But I can't hear my whimper. Sound has already receded. My ears pop as if dropped into a vast chamber.

The paw before me lies obstinate to my will.

Move! Please ...

But there's nothing I can do. So I just peer at it with fondness. I'm glad it was me, if only for a while.

I see the collapse more than feel it. The room seems to shudder as my jaw bounces off the floor. Then sensation leaves me completely.

Come Home

I wake to dark and warmth.

My head lies on something soft – a cushion. My body is wrapped in the cocoon of a duvet. Buckley's living room. We came back here after Mr Hughes found us. From the darkness, I must have slept through the day.

I lie perfectly still, feeling my way out into the silence.

So. What now?

The weight of the question threatens to suffocate me. Who am I if not a phenomenaut? A beached jellyfish, dribbling out into sand.

But perhaps I can't rely on other forms any more? Perhaps I have to let all that go or follow Isaac into oblivion. I do see that now. Perhaps the trick is to make my own shape. Build it up. Slowly.

Yet it's too much to think about in the moment.

For now, I wriggle free of the duvet and flop onto the carpet. Even after a proper meal and sleep, I feel disorientated and weak, my limbs like those of a newborn deer. But, on a count of three, I find my feet and stand, staring into the dimness for a while, thinking of nothing much.

My hands scratch at my arms mindlessly, scales of mud flicking off beneath nails, and it's only as I watch them that I realise I itch all over. For the first time in over a week I feel dirty.

My wash bag has been dumped in the middle of the room, along with the other personal belongings we had to remove from our cubicle, so I snatch it up and go in search of the bathroom.

Inside, I recoil at the flick of the switch. Light blooms blotchily across my retinas, the room impossibly white, all right angles and uniform space – like stepping inside an equation.

My fingers are grudging on the coat zip – it's been my hide against the world for so long. But the itching is becoming unbearable. I tug and the coat sloughs to the floor. The lightness is giddy.

Into the shower. Fumble with the controls. The shock of water leaves me gasping. Its heat merges with the warmth of tears.

As my JumpPyjamas turn heavy, I try to pull the shirt over my head, but with the weight of water it rips instead. It's been decomposing all this time, another week and it probably would have disintegrated completely. I peel a swathe from my belly, fabric crumbling to balls of lint between my fingers. The flesh beneath is puffy and soft, like new scales.

I grab handful after handful until I stand naked amid a pile of sodden shreds. My heartbeat is a flutter against the cage of ribs, stomach pushing into my torso as I lift my face to the water. With eyes shut, it's impossible to tell if this is falling or flying.

Clean clothing is a forgotten luxury. It's bizarre to feel the fabric shift against my skin as I move. My old clothes, sticky with dirt and sweat, had almost become a part of me.

I dance for a while, or rather hop, spin, feeling the crisp glide of cotton, and pull my jumper over my face to breathe in the scent of lemon. But, blinded, I bash my thigh into the sink.

My face watches from the mirror. This is you now. Maybe even forever. There are other Phenomenautical companies. There are healthier ways of jumping. But if I can't learn how to be this, this face, this me, then it's all for nothing.

This is you, Kit.

This is me.

A pale smudge, uncertain features; even with the fuzz of new hair-growth, there is something egg-like to its smoothness. Though I suppose time will change it too. The years will suck the pulp from its flesh, sediment experience into skin, but acceptance, even of this, must come with time.

I sigh and pick up a comb from the cabinet beside the loo. Strands of dark hair cling to it and I pick them free, wondering at these fragile artefacts that were once part of my friend. There are other random items here: a biro, plastic-feathered by teeth; a piece of quartz dimly throwing light; a shell, still smelling faintly of sea. I study each in turn, brushing them against my lips to feel their secret expanse. Buckley's. Somehow the knowledge alone is enough to make me want to secrete them away in my cheeks but I sneak a couple into my pockets instead.

But in his doorway, my confidence wavers. Who are we now if not phenomenaut and neuroengineer? I lost him his job. Not that he wants it after seeing Grandma Wolf's files. But still.

His strong arm clenches the sheets to him as he curls in on himself, in sleep at once more closed and open than when awake. Rain splutters against the pane in fat drops. I crawl onto the mattress, resting on my haunches to watch.

The quartz in my pocket is rough against the fidget of my fingers as my other hand explores the kink of his nose, still discoloured by the bruising.

I do know him. I do.

His eyes open and widen as they take me in. There's something desperate hidden there, as if he were a hermit crab and I a shell. It scares me, so I hop off the bed and walk to the window, toy with the plastic toggle of the blinds. He rises in a murmur of sheets, his presence tingling up my back even from across the room. The rumble of wind echoes my insides.

'Come with me,' I say.

Buckley crouches with me as I place the burger outside our old den. It's greasy and misshapen, we could only find a kebab van open at this hour, but I'm sure that Tomoko wouldn't have minded.

At my nod, Buckley digs the grave marker into the ground. He made it out of a chip fork and a pickle. Though Buckley never met Tomoko, he has other losses to mourn. We both do.

Rain drums against the shed roof as we crouch, regarding our work. It echoes the flood inside me and I suddenly find myself too tired to keep the sorrow in. It rips through me, more than tears, shuddering in every muscle, turning my chest and throat to heat. I press my face to the wet grass and let the force pull through me. Until, gradually, my breathing begins to ease.

Buckley squeezes my shoulder and I look up to see that a light has come on in one of the nearby houses. We slip back over the fence.

There's a strange quiet inside the storm; everything holding itself within. What would I hear if I had the ears? The creep of mice?

Muslin wing beats of owl? With the right senses I'd perceive everything. But I don't.

And perhaps that's good. The thought aches through my sadness in a strange kind of joy. Because perhaps life is about boundaries? Breaking them, building them back up, guarding against the yawn of infinity?

We pause at the Suspension Bridge. Below, the swollen river rumbles in slick ink, bursts against rock in pearly froth. And as I watch, static dances behind my eyes, as if the thought alone could pull me over.

Everything is so fragile, so ephemeral. Seven years. Seven years of projecting, and what have I really understood? What have I really changed? Species are still being wiped out. The world is still being abused. And Mum...

But I did my best, isn't that all anyone can ask?

I turn to see Buckley watching, huddled deep inside his waterproof, misery drawn tight in his expression, but his gaze slips mine, almost guiltily. I let my eyes rove over the feathers of hair sticking out from under his hood, over the new kink of his nose, that gentle mouth.

He is a kind, handsome man. Susie and Mum were right. He's so handsome it hurts. How could I have missed it all these years?

'I see you,' I say.

His eyes twitch, but he pretends not to hear. I throw my voice against the wind.

'I see you.'

Again, no response, yet as my hand settles on top of his, his whole body jolts. His look is questioning, certain this must be a mistake. But it's not.

I curl my fingers around his and the storm retreats to a sigh, our entire universe encompassed by the movement of eyes about each other's faces. I push up on my toes.

The kiss is like Sperlman's. A sensation so startling that it seems this mouth can't be mine, can't be me. Heat radiates through his lips into mine, right to the tingling tips of my fingers embedded in his hair.

When we pull apart, my tongue still burns with the memory of his taste. He opens his arms and I press into his chest. His breath is warm against my ear.

'I see you too.'

We carry a bubble of warmth around us as we walk back to his house in the breaking light. The wind sings as it flies into the gorge. My face aches from the strain of laughing and crying.

I tense to see something move on the other side of the fence but Buckley squeezes my hand; he can see it too.

Its profile is almost wolf-like as it steps out from the shadows. Although no bigger than a house cat, it isn't afraid of us at all.

My flesh thrills beneath that look, my amusement emerging as mist in the cold air. I could never have truly understood. I could never truly become. But sometimes, the trying is enough.

Its tail waves its uncertainty, ears twitching as they pinpoint something beyond us, but whatever it hears is lost to me.

As it runs towards the gorge I strain forwards, but Buckley's hand is firm around mine. I can't follow, not this time. I press my cheek to the fence and watch it catch fire beneath the streetlight, one last second aflame, before it fades into silence.

DISCLAIMER

I'm not a zoologist – let's get that out of the way. Despite a lifelong interest in, and affection for, other species, I find taxonomy taxing. Latin names are, well, Latin to me. And I'm more likely to be found stuffing ducks with bread than staring at them through binoculars.

Still, I have researched this novel to the best of my ability. I devoured books and documentaries. I pestered naturalist friends and family with unanswerable questions. I looked into paper after paper on the senses of other species, on the physiology of the eye or on suggestive behaviour – such as how scientists have *watched* tigers seemingly *seeing* a distinction between red and green buckets, but only in a certain percentage of *observations*, which the scientists *perceived* as meaning . . . I honestly don't know. And, eventually, I came to the conclusion that the pursuit of the particulars could blind me; that really my eye should be on the fundamental fleshiness of the living, breathing, feeling, 221.2kg beast in front of me. (And, yes, I did just look up the average weight of a tiger.)

For all the good that science achieves, it's important not to lose sight of the fact that it's a discourse of the third person; its aim, the seizing and solidifying of the other. Science permits only one Truth, one Reality. But what if there are other valid ways of knowing? What if the world is not one, but multitude, with as many ways of being as there are beings? What if literature were the opportunity to glimpse such refractions, thrown by the world as though from a diamond?

For to walk a mile in someone's shoes is not just to take on an element of their embodied experience but to take part in their journey. Such skin-walking is the magic of fiction, which invites the reader not only to slip into the lived experience of other people but also to share, for a while, the cares and joys of their narrative journeying. My work here is therefore perhaps closer to that of a seamstress than a scientist; this novel, a fantastical wardrobe of skins.

So, while I make no claims for the factual accuracy of this novel, I hope instead that it might inspire you to a different way of questioning, sensing and feeling, of which Kit's story is only the beginning. For we are all immersed alongside our brethren of tooth and claw in a world that is more spectacular, wonderful and uncanny than one creature alone could ever perceive.

ACKNOWLEDGEMENTS

Would I have started had I known?

A certain amount of naivety can carry a person a long way. After all, isn't a book just letters? Letters and gaps? That isn't so hard, surely?

This, I think, is a little like saying a person is just neurons. The reduction misses the essential bodiliness of the thing, it misses its interactions – it misses the possibility of sense.

For all the paradoxes it entails, a person is not just herself – she is made up of others. And the person as author is no different. Though the burden of a story is ours to carry alone, we would not be ourselves without those who surround us. The following thanks are therefore for the people who have, in their own unique way, made me – the author – possible.

To my writing group – friends who have been there for me in the most forbearing fashion, from the very first word, to the first word again, and again, and again (I lose count of the rewrites) . . . to that seemingly impossible last. Your love and belief were essential not only to the fruition of this novel but also for my flourishing as a person. Tanya Atapattu, Victoria Finlay, Susan Jordan, Sophie

McGovern, Peter Reason, Jane Shemilt and Mimi Thebo, you have been more than a writing group, you are my writing family.

To my editor, Helen Garnons-Williams, for your editorial brilliance and loveliness, and for trusting my nose when it called me to hare off down muddy, thicketed paths.

To my agent, Will Francis, and others at Janklow & Nesbit UK, for your hard work and belief at times when this novel could have easily been abandoned on a cold mountainside.

To my second editor, Alexa von Hirschberg, for spiritedly taking up the torch where Helen left off. To Imogen Denny, for taking up the baton where Alexa left. To Oliver Holden-Rea, for your feedback, enthusiasm and introduction to the creative potential of whiteboards. To Philippa Cotton and Myfanwy Nolan for their publicity and marketing magic. To David Mann, Mari Roberts, Ben Turner, Elizabeth Woabank and all the other Bloomsbury staff working behind the scenes. Although I don't know all your names, know that your work was, and is, much appreciated.

Thanks to my aunt, Georgine Lawrence, and father, Matthew Geen, for providing a roof over my head and food in my stomach at the most difficult periods of this novel's creation. Your generosity allowed me the privilege to dream.

To my brother and true friend, Sam Geen, for your chatter and support throughout the long, lonely days. Your mad humour kept me sane.

To Hadiza El-Rufai, Kesia Lupo, Vanessa Vaughan and Phoebe Wood-Wheelhouse, writer friends who offered valuable critique and encouragement at various stages of the book's emergence.

Thanks to my MA Philosophy tutor, Havi Carel, for introducing me to Phenomenology, and for the inspiration of your book, *Illness: The Art of Living*.

To my MA Creative Writing tutor, Richard Kerridge, and other lecturers Paul Evans and Samantha Harvey, for advice during the novel's first baby steps. Thanks also to my fellow students on the Creative Writing MA, for your critique and support.

To Steve Gill for the neuroscience tips. To my grandpa, 'Boo' Lawrence, for bequeathing me the funds needed to study Creative Writing. To all the other family members, friends, teachers, associates, and jolts of insight in the guise of strangers – too numerous or elusive to name – that mixed into that heady blend called creativity.

Last, but far from least, thank you to my mother, Jo Geen. It is impossible to acknowledge everything you gave me, so instead I shall confine myself to thanking you for believing that this day could come, over a decade before anyone else even took my writing seriously. My only regret is that you could not be here to see your belief vindicated. I love you.

A NOTE ON THE TYPE

The text of this book is set in Bembo, which was first used in 1495 by the Venetian printer Aldus Manutius for Cardinal Bembo's *De Aetna*. The original types were cut for Manutius by Francesco Griffo. Bembo was one of the types used by Claude Garamond (1480–1561) as a model for his Romain de l'Université, and so it was a forerunner of what became the standard European type for the following two centuries. Its modern form follows the original types and was designed for Monotype in 1929.